MIGHT & WISDOM

A BURNINGSOUL NOVEL

MIGHT & WISDOM
A BURNINGSOUL NOVEL

REGINA WATTS

PAINTED BLIND
PUBLISHING
LITERARY ALCHEMY

PAINTED BLIND
PUBLISHING
LITERARY ALCHEMY

Burningsoul Saga Book III: Might & Wisdom
© 2022 Regina Watts
ISBN: 978-1-957469-00-3

Text: Regina Watts
Typesetting: M. F. Sullivan
Cover Painting: Vanette Kosman

http://www.hrhdegenetrix.com
http://www.paintedblindpublishing.com
publicity@paintedblindpublishing.com

With great thanks to John Deathridge,
whose translation of The Ring Cycle
enriched my understanding
of the story I was writing.

1

PIRATES!

THE BATTLE SWAN rocked. We were about to be boarded.

Though I'd like to say I launched right into action, in truth I perceived the danger only after delay. Only after I realized the boy I'd found spying on my luggage compartment rendezvous with Branwen was not a boy at all. The interloper was, in fact, a woman—and one known to me.

Elishta-bet Highwind: my dearest friend since childhood, and the last person I would have expected to find aboard the ship with us.

"Rorke?"

Branwen's voice, stern despite her waifish elf's frame,

snapped me from my shock and into action. I released my grip of the voyeur's arm, but not before sternly looking into Elishta's captivated hazel eyes. Behind us, Branwen hurriedly dressed.

"Stay with me. Let's discuss this later."

Nodding, her eyes ringed with fright, Elishta asked me, "What's going to happen?"

"What's going to happen is they're going to board us—probably are, even as we speak—and Branwen and the rest of my friends and I are all going to fend them off, by Weltyr's grace."

My Master led me back into Elishta-bet's life, in fact, to put an end to her forced marriage with the captain of my former Order. Such measures were designed to normalize the magical talent out of her one way or another, and as another blast rocked the *Swan*, I found myself all the gladder to know that Zweiding never had the opportunity to doom her so.

Finding her cloak and boyish clothes to be pitifully poor protection, I asked, "Can I count on you to fight alongside us?"

The flush chased the freckles from her cheeks. As I made quick work of throwing on the clothes Branwen pushed into my hands, Elishta said, "I'll do my best."

Somewhere, many compartments away from ours, someone screamed. I clenched my teeth and buckled my belt, then strode for the door while the women assembled behind me.

"Then may Weltyr make your best sufficient to carry us through to safety...and mine, too."

Pressing a finger to my lips, I cracked open the baggage compartment door. In the dim corridor between the compartment and the coach seating, a few stewardesses whispered in frantic conference.

The only thing for it was to move quickly.

Lunging from the door, I clapped a hand over the mouth of one while her conversational partner jumped. I pressed my finger to my lips to urge them to the same silence I had already requested of my companions, and their frightened eyes flickered to the black sun tattooed upon my neck. The stewardess I did not subdue, her mouth poised to emit a scream, closed her lips and looked at me sternly. I recognized her by her red hair and brilliant blue eyes—it was she who took Exigence from my hands when we boarded the *Swan* and were forced to relinquish our weapons.

"I mean no harm—I mean to solve our pirate problem."

When both women's bodies relaxed, I lifted my hand and hoped they would hear my whisper over the explosions of gun and cannon fire echoing from another deck of the ship.

"The checked weapons," I asked the redheaded stewardess, my tone calm but serious. "Where are they? We need to get to them before our new friends do."

"Checked weapons are in a storage compartment below the forecastle. They're under guard, but—"

"But it will take more than one or two guards to protect a cache of weapons from a bunch of greedy pirates."

Before I'd had time to take a breath for my next sentence, a nearer explosion signaled the bursting inward of the door on the other side of our compartment.

"I'm going to have to hope I can get there first," I

said with a shake of my head, slipping past the women and drawing open the door while Branwen urged them both to hide.

In coach, Valeria and my other durrow friends were doing much the same. Stances wide, Indra and Odile stood in the aisle and exchanged glances with one another. The high priestess of the durrow, Valeria, Materna of Roserpine, already had magic settling on her lips and weaving through her hair.

But, remarkably, my lovers didn't catch my eye near so much as the pirates striding through the smoking door with dwarvish firearms in-hand.

Each brigand, a woman more beautiful and wild than the last.

"Ladies and gentlemen," called the shortest of the three, her arrogant gaze skipping over my friends, "please remain in your seats! We have some business to get to, and the more of you cooperate, the faster we'll get to it. Got it?"

"Do yourself a favor and turn around," said Odile, her features arranged in a hard, defiant mask. "There's nothing for you here—we'll make sure of that."

The slender, dark-haired pirate examined Odile with a curt laugh for her empty fists. "And how do you propose to do that with no weapons? Look at you three! "Adventurers," eh?"

"I'd stake my life on it," said the third one, a blonde with her hair piled high and a few curls escaping from beneath her hat. Folding her arms beneath her straining bustier, she said with a sneer, "And foolhardy ones, at that. Don't be so silly, girl! Stand aside."

"I'm at least six times your age," Odile estimated,

rolling her shoulders and barely glancing over them when I arrived at Valeria's side. Her lips still at quiet work, she did not acknowledge me save for a kind of current that lit up the air between us—an electricity of nearness that fired both our bloods and inspired me to the passionate love that made me natural for the role of her protector in the Nightlands.

While the pirates laughed at Odile, one of them raised a gun. That protective instinct sprang into action for all of my companions—for every one of Weltyr's carefully crafted lives, like the souls aboard the *Swan* who brooked no such fate as this.

I shoved past the durrow to stand between them and the pirates. If I had been surprised to find these outlaws to be women, up close I was all the more surprised to find them such intensely attractive women. Perhaps it was only that their eyes, lined with kohl and twinkling with the levity of their heinous lifestyles, brought to mind the witch. Gundrygia.

And the baby she had declared herself to be carrying.

Unwilling to let the wenches do harm to the women I counted as my friends, but likewise unable to sacrifice myself to their escape when a wild woman had my progeny under her complete control, I stared defiantly at the most aggressive of the trio—that dark-haired, willowy pirate in the center—and demanded, "You would fire upon unarmed women?"

"They look like they could hold their own in a fight, so why not?"

"I had always heard there was honor among thieves," I assured the three of them, my affect grim as my tone, "but I suppose that's one of those wives' tales."

"More like old husband's tales," said the one with the gun, looking me up and down before striding toward me muzzle-first. Soon the warm metal of the gun pressed against my tunic; I stared unfailingly into the woman's face, the best of her many fine qualities made unbearably ugly to me by our circumstances.

"You must be some kind of knight," she declared.

"You mean you don't recognize the sun of Weltyr?"

Her blank eyes looked into and through mine. "That some sort of cult? I don't go in for that. But we've been known to take men aboard from time to time." She examined my face with suddenly somewhat heavily lidded eyes. "Perhaps you might sit down like a good boy and have a good time with us—"

Valeria's soft chanting rose to a pitch, and the long-building spell flew from her lips with a force equivalent to the amount of time it required to prepare. The words, I swear, rippled from her lips and over my shoulder. The air shimmered, as one sees on a hot day upon the Skythorn streets.

And that final word, upon slipping into the ear of the woman pressing ever closer to me, had a frightful effect.

The pirate's eyes widened with her gasp of terror, her pupils shrinking to dots in seconds. Though first she stumbled back only from me, when given sufficient distance her eyes fell next upon the women behind me; then, upon the passengers cowering in their seats.

Then, with visible panic, she whipped around and consulted the two companions who had burst into coach with her.

Seeing them, she cried out and raised her pistol

rapidly toward the taller of her companions. "What hell-dimension did that bitch cast me in to?"

"What have you done," hissed the short one, making a move to point her gun at Valeria.

This was, naturally, the wrong decision to make. The wench would have been better served by assisting her companion in detaining their friend, who had been maddened by Valeria's chthonic magic and forced to see all aboard the airship as Weltyr only knew what heinous abominations. Instead, by attempting to avenge the spell upon its sacred caster, she provoked Indra, Odile, and myself into springing at her in unison.

With three assailants rushing her, the pirate lost any idea of where to aim her pistol. It discharged into the ceiling, firing into an upper deck and acting as the starting gun for a cringe, a scream, a flight that rippled through the crowd and caused the mass evacuation of all those who could. Coach emptied out through both its doors, people flowing around the fighters and back through the corridor to baggage.

By the time the dust had begun to settle, I had gotten the one of the lasses in a firm grapple. She thrashed against me, of course, but Indra and Odile worked together to easily divest her of her weapon. The ensorcelled one, meanwhile, had managed to get into something of a shoot-out with her companion. Vacated seats acted as poor cover while they exchanged missed rounds amid the stench of gunpowder.

"Drop the guns," Branwen cried, her green eyes bright with a spell of their own. "We don't want to hurt you, but we will."

Seeing her companion already in our grasp, the

pirate lass on the defense gritted her teeth but lowered her weapon.

The ensorcelled one, madly fighting invisible monsters too horrible for comprehension, took her chance and managed to fulfill the promise of her aim.

I cried out at the sight, weak when it came to seeing even an evil woman wounded in such a way. Though I jerked toward her to help her, I told myself I owed these pirates nothing.

Vines upon the printed wallpaper of the coach car sprang out from their flat rendering and, beneath our druid's command, real-ized themselves well enough to grasp the cursing, thrashing, wily wench who had not yet realized—would not realize for some time—what she had actually shot. As they took hold of her, my companions rushed to claim the guns.

While the one in my arms cried out for her shot friend, the one who had been shot groaned and clutched at her bleeding shoulder.

Jaw tense, I called, "Indra," and pushed my captive into her arms when the durrow responded to my call. When Odile came to help her keep the woman detained, I knelt at the edge of the struggling woman's row. Passengers continued rushing back and forth behind us, desperate to escape the pirates but trapped in the air along with all the rest of those aboard the ship.

"What's your name," I asked the woman, blithely moving the hand she struggled to press to the wound. Blood pulsed out of the dark little hole with every heartbeat; I thought of my own wound, the grave injury from which Indra and Odile rescued me not so very long ago. Such mortal wounds were beyond the limit of those miraculous healing acts my Master permitted to flow through my hands…but a bullet hole, so small in spite of its hateful nature?

"Dinah," hissed the woman in answer to me, her reluctant eyes rapidly flickering down to the uncovered wound.

"Well, Dinah"—I fit my hand firmly over the wound and frowned as she cried aloud—" I suggest you look away, and breathe out."

She looked away, all right, but she didn't manage to get a full breath against the pain. Instead of breathing out, she released a scream while I laid on hands.

There are those who would reduce Weltyr's domains to those of the mind and soul only, claiming the physical world is a separate force from the Godhead. These secularists are not wrong to call him the root of consciousness, which is the popular estimate, but the truth is the Master embodies far more than that. His body is the very material ground: his will is flesh, itself.

And so, much as the simple animation of the hand of the spirit-thief Al-listux was within my then somewhat limited range of battle prayers, (how simple those days of journeying with Branwen, Grimalkin—ah, Hildolfr!— seem to me now, and even seemed to me then aboard the *Swan*), the matter of reversing the small metal slug's damage was one of faith.

Dinah's scream faltered, rose, faltered again. The bullet, extruded by the knitting hole, soon pressed up into my hand and rested between us as the internal damage was undone. Then, the external.

Soon, her screaming—almost unnoticeable, in truth, among all the other screams and chaos, the flight of passengers, the sulphur of gun smoke—faded to a few sharp gasps of discomfort. As I lifted my hand away, catching the bloody bullet before it fell to the floor, my prayer ended to a punctuation of profanity.

"Cor," remarked the wench, her expression one of genuine wonder while she first studied, then rapidly felt her own perfect shoulder. "How'd you do that?"

"I didn't." I dropped the bullet into her hand. "Our Master, Weltyr, healed your wound."

"Convert later," Branwen demanded with a roll of her impatient eyes. "We've got to go!"

While I hauled Dinah her to her feet, Indra nodded to the third gun. It sat in the aisle, waiting to be used.

"Someone should take that. Don't you think, Odile?"

"You want it, Rorke?"

At Odile's question—and, seeing that they used their guns primarily as devices to attain cooperation from prisoners whose strength was a match for their own—I shook my head and gestured to the woman whose healed arm I gripped.

"I have no training in such weapons, I'm afraid. Branwen?"

The elf wrinkled her nose sharply at the mere idea, patting the demi-real vines as they slithered back into the wallpaper. "No way! I'm not using a dwarvish weapon."

"Someday, Branwen, we're going to have to talk about your racism," I told her, ignoring the way she balked and glancing but briefly at Valeria.

I was just about to consent to giving the weapon a try when, her expression more driven than ever I had seen it, Elishta-bet stepped forward.

"I'll take it," she said, stooping to grab the pistol.

10

I nodded, meeting her eye in approval. The color in her face! It had been quite a long time since I had seen my friend regularly, it was true…but it embarrasses me now that I somehow missed in her the signals that were so obvious when exhibited by the other women around me.

"Let's go," I said, dragging Dinah along after Indra and Odile took the point with their prisoners—one of which struggled a great deal more than the other. Odile often had to strain and clench her teeth against the maddened woman. She glanced over her shoulder at Valeria, begging to know, "Why, madame, did you have to *so* derange her?"

"In the spirit of our dear Rorke, I shall give all the credit to Our Lady, Roserpine."

Though I chuckled wryly at Valeria's good humor, mine soon vanished.

Devastation had been thoroughly wreaked in the rest of the airship. While we had held down our car, those ahead of us had been, evidently, defenseless. The door hung loose upon its hinges: when it was kicked aside, the scene was one of crying children and women, humiliated (and one or two bruised) men, and a number of pirates who were making their ways aisle by aisle to rob whatever valuables passengers had worn with them on their journey.

Each and every one of them, as were the three we had detained, proved to be gorgeous women…but none were half so gorgeous as that sneering captain at the back of the car in the direction of her officers.

To call her hair 'black' was to call the richest velvet 'black,' or the void of space 'black,' or the heart of a murderer 'black.' Black was not enough to describe the luster of her locks, which tumbled along with one shock of a white streak from beneath a long hat concealing one eye. Her bosom heaved from the white ruffles lining her leather bodice, and the plundered military coat whose tails trailed in her wake appeared to be the colors of no regiment I had ever seen.

And Odile, bless her, dispelled the wonder by raising her gun.

"Tell your girls to drop the valuables and get back on the ship where they came from," she shouted, aiming straight-on at the captain.

Attention grabbed, the brooding woman's head whipped toward us. Her lip curled in absolute derision to be addressed by one of her intended victims.

With a quick hand, the captain drew her rifle from the long holster along an even longer leg and raised it toward my friends. "It'll take more than words ta match with—"

Odile did not hesitate. The durrow fired rapidly, her aim so precise that I was left to marvel at her apparent familiarity with the weapon class. There was so much I still did not know about them as people, and I was awed by Odile's confidence.

I say that because I want you to understand, my friend—there was absolutely no way she missed the captain. Its rounds could have gone nowhere but into the woman at whom it was very competently aimed.

Yet the air was cut with the triple whizz-strike of round after round flying through the empty air and embedding into wood.

Unmoved save for a small, cruel smile, the captain stepped aside.

Three smoking bullet holes were spread across the already largely broken door to the observation cabin.

"As I was saying," the captain resumed, turning upon us and leveling her rifle with the universal ease of muscle memory, "it'll take more than words to match with us…and more than bullets, too. Heed my advice and give up now."

Her head lifted. The veil of dark hair fell away, uncovering her face.

No eye lay beneath. She had only a black pit with a single red pinpoint; an evil ember, glowing in the back of what very well might have been an exposed skull.

"If yehs command my attention too much," she warned with a cruel laugh, "y'er liable ta become the short-term guests of *The Flying Rhinemaid*."

2

THE BOARDING PARTY

THOUGH THE NAME struck a bell in my memory, I did not connect the pirate ship's moniker to anything distinct until Elishta-bet gasped.

"It can't be!" My friend's cry drew the focus of a few dangerous-loo' ing women who had been overseeing the robbers. "The *Rhinemaid* is a legend!"

"Would that it were...you lot would be avin' a far more peaceful voyage!"

While the rest of the crew laughed, the evidently undead captain gestured with her rifle and continued darkly, "But *you* fools is lookin' at entirely too much peace, if yehs see my meaning…release my crew and return their arms."

After grimly regarding the woman before us, I told Odile, "We'd ought to do as she says."

"Are you kidding?"

"I'm very serious." The captain who now studied me, and I returned her stare without a flinch. "My Master's higher teachings include ways of overcoming many kinds of foul undead—aberrations borne of Oppenhir's pale hand, or by other methods—and the means of identifying them. None are so dangerous as a dirge."

"Been a few seasons since I've heard that one," remarked the captain, the red light in her skull glowing just a little brighter. "Maybe not since the last time we found our way to Ramshead, eh, ladies?"

Grimly, with a glance into Dinah's eyes, I released my captive and waited for my friends to do the same. As the pirates hurried to collect their dropped arms, Dinah glanced briefly at me from the edge of her dark hair. Then, adjusting the bandana tied over her head, she darted into the most open section of the aisle with the wild, erratic motions of an animal.

"Be careful, Captain," she cried while Odile maintained her hold of her struggling captive. "Two of em's used magic against us—but him, though, the man—"

Dinah faltered, then went on to say with a glance at her shoes, "He healed my bullet wound, Captain."

"That so?"

The captain lowered her gun, stepping toward us

and saying with careful consideration of the tattoo upon my neck, "A paladin, arentcha? I seen a fewa yer sort before. I admit, though…not a one lived up ta's title."

"Perhaps, if I had no assistance, neither would I."

"And 'umble! That's very charming. Well, paladin, if y'er as strong as you are good-looking and foolishly noble, you might be of some use to us. You! Release Priscilla, damn you!"

Although Dinah began a protest, Odile cruelly shrugged. "If you want."

The grinning durrow released the maddened woman whose thrashing, kicking and futile biting had never stopped. Gasping to find herself free, Priscilla looked around until her eye landed on the gun at her feet.

She snatched it up and pointed it at the first thing she saw: the captain, whose good eye narrowed.

Priscilla was too slow.

The rifle shot cracked through the car to a symphony of screams—of parents throwing their hands over their children's eyes in a reflex that was inevitably too late. While a few of the younger ones, already crying, wept all the harder to see the deranged pirate drop to the floor, the captain bared her teeth and unloaded an additional round into the ceiling of the cabin.

"Now everybody *calm down*," the captain commanded, sounding a little bored. "You five, stay here. Keep emptyin' pockets. Don't even bother with the next car. You know where I want yehs after y'er done here…"

"Aye aye, Captain!"

"And you two"—she pointed at Dinah and her remaining friend, both of whom looked pale with shock—"let's accompany our volunteers to their first

17

task."

The ship lurched so sharply I swore I heard its structure groan. Valeria cried out and fell upon me. While Elishta-bet caught herself against a seat's edge, the captain's hateful eye landed heavily on us.

"Are we changing course," I asked with an urgent look through the red curtains of the nearest window.

"Don't you worry your pretty head about the details," said the captain gruffly, turning with her rifle lowered but clearly ready. "Jes do what Captain says, and yehs might get to live."

With Dinah and her companion shepherding us from behind, my friends and I were marched through the airship and, ironically, to what had been my intended destination since the fatal alarm had rung through the ship.

My heartbeat hastened at the thought of what awaited me there.

Twice now, I had consented to release my weapon for sake of peacekeeping. There would be no third time. The lesson had been harshly delivered but, at long last, learned. Exigence never should have been relinquished on my boarding of the ship, and I eagerly awaited laying hands upon it by one contrivance or another.

Of course...what was I going to do about those guns?

There was a lot to think about, and my train of thought was interrupted by Odile's hiss.

"Way to go, warrior-priest. Now what are we going to do? We're captive."

"No talking," barked the captain, who pushed open a door into the broadest corridor I had yet seen aboard the ship. On either side, stairwells crowded with cowering passengers led the way up and down. Turning around to train her rifle on us as a group, ignoring the screaming citizens who cringed away from the whole ordeal as was only safe and rational, the captain nodded to her crew.

"Catalonia said it was downstairs. Dinah, check."

Though she slipped through my group without much complaint, as soon as she met with the cluster of passengers upon the landing, her expression sharpened. "Move," bellowed Dinah, clearing the way with the wave of a gun.

Once she had disappeared around the landing, a handful of seconds passed before the call came. "Clear, Captain!"

"After you," said the captain, jerking her head.

A set of stairs, a short corridor and one broken door lock later, my companions and I stood along with our captors to survey the weapons check compartment.

"Gorgeous," said the captain with a dark laugh. "Never gets old…now, what's the matter!"

"Priscilla didn't deserve that," insisted the second wench.

Though the captain looked shocked to be so addressed, she seemed poised to listen when Dinah spoke up. "Yes, Captain—she was sickened by some sorta magic from these elves."

"And you're next," said Odile with a hard look at Dinah.

"Careful," the captain and I intoned at once. After a glance, she generously permitted me to continue. "Let's try to cooperate and see where it gets us."

"Maybe y'er not so stupid after all…listen ta the

paladin, ladies, and get ta work."

The airship gave another lurch. Valeria merely touched my back to stabilize herself this time, saying with her hand upon me, "What are we to do here?"

"Y'er ta take all the booty from this room, and you'll put it aboard the—"

From the darkness, something peeled itself with a warrior's cry.

The captain whirled around and fired. To my amazement, the short figure dodged the round and plunged into the light of the corridor axe-first.

I was so shocked that Branwen recognized him before I did.

"Grimalkin!"

"Drop the guns, ya cowardly bunch of brigands!"

"Grimalkin," I cried before he struck her, "stand down!"

But, amid his battle-cry and all his bravado, my former adventuring companion did not listen. The axe sliced right through the pirate captain, whizzing through flesh and bone as though both were but dreams. Grimalkin, wide-eyed, followed the swing of his axe all the way through her incorporeal body.

"Dunnun's gold," he barked as he pushed himself back up with a groan—then froze when he heard the click of the captain's rifle.

The dwarf glanced up at me with his teeth grit. "Don't suppose her bullets go through you, do they?"

Not long after, Grimalkin stood as another prisoner in our midst while we decided who was to carry what and which teams might be best. The pirates lit the lamps in the room and, her eye greedily aglow, the captain made her deliberate way around the shelves of tagged weapons.

"There's a small fortune here, ladies...enough to keep us satisfied a few weeks, at least!"

While Dinah and the her friend, put at ease by the sight of treasure, laughed and sorted through swords, spears, armor and shields, I took a close study of my own.

Most of the weapons, I suspected, were for those travelers who had dreams of protecting themselves from brigands just such as these; whose travels were bound to continue outside of their destination port and across a countryside rife with not just dangerous wildlife, but sometimes beings as strange or stranger still than the gimlets and oozes and misshapen of the Nightlands. A few were cheap arms that perhaps belonged to the crew for emergency use of their own.

And from among these dull, neglected armaments belonging to amateur adventurers, the gem-encrusted gold of Exigence's sacred hilt sprang like the full moon from a dark sky.

"Would you look at that! Oh, now—"

I began to demand the captain stop, for her fingers extended toward its grip—but, as it does from time to time, Weltyr's voice in my heart urged me to silence. Those who have felt such a voice understand what I mean when I say it is a call stronger than mere intuitive sense—and I am glad, always, that I listen to it.

Then, I was especially glad. I stopped myself from arguing with words, weak words, and instead let her pick up the sacred sword transmuted from the veiled Scepter of Weltyr.

I let her try, anyway.

"What the—"

The captain's arm jerked strangely. Exigence remained where it lay, unmoved as an ill-trained dog that ignored the tugging of its leash.

Frowning, the undead woman glanced up to find us all watching her.

Jaw set, she tried again.

The sword remained upon its shelf.

Now, the captain applied both hands to the task. She grunted, pulling at the handle, saying, "This some sorta decoy, or—"

"Here, Captain, let me try."

Dinah hurried over and, when the captain had stepped aside, pulled the handle to the same useless if comic effect.

"Cor! Come on, you—"

"See, idiot, it's not *me*. It's the blasted sword! Like it's fused."

"Let me," said the other wench, rushing up to make a last attempt while Dinah trained her gun on us.

I must admit I quite enjoyed the show. Exchanging mirthful glances, my lovely companions repressed their giggles to avoid antagonizing our captors.

The mystery of it! Was this because they were undead? I thought it had to be—as, of course, the redheaded stewardess who had taken Exigence and promised to see to its care had been perfectly capable of carrying it.

Yet, that theory soon proved incorrect. Grimalkin, his ego uncontrollable even in a time like this, (when he, just defeated, ought to have shown a little humility), stepped up. "Let a man try, ladies! That doesn't look so heavy..."

"Besta luck ta yeh," said the captain, stepping back with her crew members to join us as audience to a comedy of errors.

With a casual crack of his knuckles, Grimalkin stuck a foot in the lowest shelf and boosted himself up to get some leverage on Exigence, which sat upon the third level. Smiling smugly beneath his reddish beard, the dwarf tugged on the grip.

His expression changed and, clearing his throat, he looked at the blade as though accusatory of its defiance. Not very long after he was tugging with both hands, grimacing, bending his head repeatedly to see if the weapon had been somehow fused to the shelf.

"Bloody—buggering—come on—"

The captain and her crew laughed, and so did we—until the sharpness of a one-eyed look struck us silent. Striding forward again, the captain caught the dwarf by the back of his armor and threw him down to the floor.

"Back ta work, the lota yehs. What are we ta do about this blasted thing? Can't just leave it here, not looking so pretty."

"Perhaps"—Valeria's bold voice drew the captain's look—"its owner could move it for you."

I smiled humbly. "No, not its owner. Only its caretaker."

That sharp red pinpoint swiveled a few degrees toward me.

"Pick it up," said the captain with a jerk of her head toward the sword.

Moving slowly, so as to draw no fire from the three guns pointed at me, I stepped toward the shelf. The shining blade called to my hand. I thought again of

23

that ethereal connection, that mysterious vibration, that quivered between my body and Valeria's.

"Don't get smart," said the captain, her eye fixed upon me, her finger ready for the slightest ill movement.

Looking back at her, I extended my hand to find the sword's pommel.

With nothing more than a firm grip, I lifted the blade from its shelf.

"How in all Oppenhir's hells," Grimalkin began, but the captain looked sharply at him.

"Back at it, unless yeh'd like ta find yerself in one of 'em."

While my staring friends busied themselves with the tasks they had abandoned, the captain said, "Looks like you'll be carryin' that, then…and much else, besides. Suppose if I want it smelted down I'll have ta keep you around, eh?"

She laughed; I didn't.

Seeing my face, the captain's expression darkened.

"Speed it up," she said, briskly clapping her hands. "I expect ta be sailin' by sunrise."

3

IMPRISONED

ALLOW ME TO save you the tedious details of our slave labor for the crew of the *Rhinemaid*. Suffice it to say, the brunt of the task fell upon Grimalkin and myself. The very instant the crew turned away to see to the control of the crowd, the only woman who showed the least inclination toward doing anything was Elishta-bet.

"This brings back memories," said Odile at one point, watching my face redden with strain beneath a particularly hefty crate of plundered armor pieces.

Rest assured, I let her scowling face meet my smiling one when she and Indra later bore a chest of the booty stolen from passengers.

This may be surprising to you, knowing as you do my firm belief in the value of honor as a guiding compass in a man's life, but I did not feel urgency in the matter of returning the stolen goods to their owners. The truth is that piracy is a widespread phenomenon, as much as might be disease, or the presence of various creatures that, if Gundrygia is to be believed, are unnatural in origin save for their inspirations. There was also an ancient saying recited by priests of the Citadel: "Submit to the Emperor that which is his."

In other words, these tangible goods were little more than trinkets beside my holy quest. I pitied those who had been robbed, because it was of no small amount and quite a few of those aboard the *Swan* were clearly in migration to begin a new life. For a few ships of thought I did wonder if there might be some way to return the goods or fight the pirates, but the crew was sizable and skilled, and I was not certain that we would be able to defeat the captain without costing another life. One of ours, this time.

So, weighing life and goods, I leaned upon my Master's advice and did as I had done in the Nightlands. I submitted to adversity, tolerated the cruelty of other sentient beings, and waited for an opportunity.

At long last, the storage rooms of the *Swan* were emptied and the galley contained barely enough food to provide each passenger a meal while they returned to Skythorn. My friends and I had made constant passage between the two airships, harbored in an empty field where a great number of the passengers had arranged to console and comfort one another. Above, we moved between ships so often that I discerned quite a few things about each. For instance, renovated after its tenure in warfare, the *Swan* was a somehow stern vessel; utilitarian. Its deck of dark steel and darker wood designed to recall its past as much as to appeal to those wealthier passengers whose cabin permitted direct access to the upper deck. It was so spic and span it may as well have been new: showing, so far as I could see, not a one of its many years.

The *Rhinemaid*, on the other hand!

To put it kindly, the ship possessed a 'lived-in' quality that surprised me. I have always heard that women are the more fastidious of the sexes, but the ragged old frigate was cluttered with the evidence of living and work (a barrel of tar had been left out; the mop was simply tragic; I am not sure I saw an escaperaft at any point). Even the figurehead, the lovely Rhinemaid, had been chipped by the cruel hand of time.

But once my companions and I assembled, unarmed but for Exigence, before the plank to the *Rhinemaid*, by far the most shocking sign of the ship's true nature came when the women who sailed it went aboard cheering and singing. One by one, as each crewmember's boots came to rest upon the deck of the *Rhinemaid*, their bodies shimmered like the semi-translucent wings of certain butterflies. Laughing, relaxing, they turned their faces to smile at one another.

And, as they did, they withered and rotted.

Were the pirate lasses of the *Rhinemaid* still lovely? Certainly, in part. Those parts of broken statues remaining in ancient temples long destroyed by old iterations of the Order, they are also beautiful—and all the more alarming against a missing portion of marble skull, or a few snapped fingers, or a jaw conquered by vandals long before the Order ever arrived.

So, too, were the crewmembers of the Rhinemaid, who went rifling through their ill-gained prizes with skeletal fingers and missing eyes. I and my friends—Grimalkin in particular—exchanged looks of horror while the captain and our two chaperones assembled before us.

"Good work. Not much complainin', neither…I like that. You know—"

Having looked from woman to woman amid our party, the captain evidently—and, one might argue, correctly—decided that Valeria was the one who counted as a kind of leader. At the very least, it was Valeria whose eyes the captain met.

"At every ship we stop, we look for new shipmates—and we lost one today. Any'a yehs fine ladies care ta come aboard the *Rhinemaid* as one of her crew?"

"We are surely flattered by the invitation," said Valeria while I, taking my opportunity to move without drawing much attention, unstrapped Exigence from my side and lay its blade carefully upon the deck of the *Swan*. (At least it was a polished deck, I told myself.) "However," she continued without hesitation, "my friends and I have committed to the completion of several important tasks—and one of those is helping Rorke here."

"That so? Too bad for you!" Laughing, her rifle against her shoulder tapping as if to indicate its readiness, the captain said, "Per'aps you'd oughter reconsider my invitation if y'er keen ta help yer paladin friend…he and his sword're comin' aboard until we can figure out how ta smelt the gold from that blasted hilt."

To Branwen and Elishta-bet's simultaneous gasp, (and the durrow's exchange of a set of dry looks with one another, both unsurprised and unimpressed), the captain set her rifle's sights on me.

"I don't recall tellin' yeh to put that down, boy."

"Shoot me, and you'll never find another soul capable of picking it up."

The captain, her expression bleak, said nothing in response. Her gun, however, lowered enough degrees to give me hope.

"Then we'll hack off the boards'a the ship and find a plains-king ta pull it, if we must. You and that damn thing are comin' with us, one way or another."

"If I might—"

The materna of the dark elves stepped forward, her chin raised high and her bearing, despite her borrowed peasant dress, quite evidently of regal stock.

"Perhaps we could arrange something, woman to woman."

"How's that?"

Perfectly collected beneath the focus of the captain's pinpoint consciousness, Valeria smiled. "I only mean to say that you must be the sort of woman who—*understands* certain things." She glanced at Grimalkin and me, and then at the captain, as though to indicate something of significance. "You wouldn't have a crew made up of women, were that not the case."

"Oh, aye...I understand a few things in this world."

"Then I suspect you would appreciate knowing we hail from a mighty civilization not so dissimilar from your arrangement here...all our men are collected from outside our borders and subject to our will. Burningsoul here is an example—my slave."

Grimalkin shot an appalled look up at me before

bursting into laughter. I ignored him, though I did offer him the quick, thin smile of an educated man for one who knows nothing. Valeria ignored him as well, going on while the pirates' curious looks turned toward me. "Perhaps, in exchange for the great service of shepherding us to our destination, we might arrange some duty for him aboard the ship."

Stroking her jaw as though in lieu of a beard, the captain appeared to turn her mind inward. "The dwarf? Your slave, too?"

Before Grimalkin's open mouth could form a sound, I leapt to answer, "Yes," and stifled my grin at his noise of rage.

Satisfied enough by my response, the captain nodded and gestured toward the plank between the ships. Her two crewmates went on ahead. As Dinah's skin grew bluish grey and her eyes were shadowed with death, the captain's red pinpoint focused in on me.

"Then, all aboard the *Rhinemaid*. Come along as our treasured guests, ladies...I'm sure, if we can work out an agreement, you'll find yer ways to yer destination eventually."

With a studied glance at the other women of our group, Valeria drew her hemline a few inches higher and took the first step upon the plank.

One at a time, we boarded the pirate ship. I waited to pick Exigence up until Grimalkin had crossed with an annoyed look my way. Before him, Odile asked of the captain in passing, "Any chance we'll get *our* possessions back? You know...the ones we loaded in your ship with you?"

A twinkle in her remaining eye, the captain said,

30

"I'm afraid everythin' aboard this ship is *my* property, ladies...let's consider it partial payment fer yer voyage until I've had a chance ta hash it out with yer mistress."

Satisfied Grimalkin was on the other side, I bent to pick up Exigence and found the captain's uncomfortable gaze once more upon me when I rose.

"And you," she said, contemplating not the sword but my face. "I get the feeling I'd oughter have a talk with you, too."

About what, I could only shudder to guess. With the sword once more strapped to my side, I crossed to the unclean deck of the *Rhinemaid.* There with my party, I turned just in time to find the captain striding in my wake.

As her boot hit the deck, her features rippled in a transmutation that was, in all ways, the opposite of that which overtook members of the crew. Much as I once recoiled, now I marveled to see her flesh fuse over her open socket and split apart to reveal an eye as beautiful as its twin; and the slight sneer that was produced, I now realized, by a missing portion of lip, completely disappeared. The captain still had the slightly roughened look worn by so many at the brothel where I found Grimalkin, her expression hard and her eyes sharp with mistrust, but there was no question that a gentler heart beating in her breast would have made her breathtaking to behold.

"Let's get in the air, ladies!"

"Aye, aye, Captain!"

"Well, guests...come along with me. I'll give yehs the *grand tour* of our cozy little home." Then, seeing Grimalkin and I were about to step with the rest of the

31

group, the captain produced a nasty little laugh. She waved Dinah over.

"Not the two'a *yous*. The *women* are guests. You lot are slaves, arentcha? Then it'd be inhospitable'a me not ta treat yehs as such."

"What a genius *you* are, Paladin," Grimalkin muttered as Dinah led us down to the brig. "Not only are we hostage to pirates because of you, but we're *prisoners*."

"Do you want your axe back?"

Looking dryly up at me, the dwarf stroked his beard, muttered under his breath, and hastened his pace to keep up with Dinah.

Though there is no way for me to know firsthand exactly what occurred on the deck of the ghost ship, I got a fair idea while sitting with Grimalkin in the dim brig. The revelry was audible through the structure of the ship, and every time a cask of treasures or a bundle of swords was spilled across the battered deck, the cries of delight arose like gales of wind. After an hour or two had passed, the storming of feet hither and thither took on the rhythm of dancing. I detected the distant notes of a violin.

Grimalkin did not deign to return my vain efforts at conversation with more than a grunt. Not until Dinah returned with a metal plate of hardtack and jerky—along with, graciously, a bunch of grapes taken from the *Swan*.

"Thank you," I told her, noting a patch of gray skin through the hole in her tunic. "How's your shoulder?"

"Good as new, but it woulda been that way anyways once I's back aboard."

"Priscilla's mind, too?"

Dinah's sunken eyes dropped to the food she'd given us. "Yeah," she said softly, turning to hurry away.

"Will you tell me—"

With a little noise of frustration, Dinah stopped and at the very least let me speak to an audience that might engage in conversation. My tone measured, I asked her, "How long has this ship been in the air?"

"Millenia," was all she said, disappearing through the hatch.

"*That's it?*"

Grimalkin's withering tone was almost startling after several hours of stony silence.

"What's "it," my friend?"

""Friend," sure... You get a chance to ask a question, and you ask how long the blasted ship has been in operation?"

"One has to build rapport with one's captors," I told him, taking a small cluster of grapes and a few bits of jerky before sliding the rest of the plate over to him. This merited a look of gratitude along with his next smarmy comment.

"'Build rapport,' oh, aye. Is *that* what you did when we left you alone in the Nightlands?"

Regarding him coldly, I assured him, "I survived. *Without* you—without anyone who came there with me."

Snorting, Grimalkin swallowed his mouthful of scarfed food and said, "Spose that's true enough...but you could have saved yourself a little *dignity* while doing it. Really, Rorke—a *slave*? To *women*—elf-women, no less!"

Barking out a laugh, shaking his head, Grimalkin said to himself, "I can't think of a thing more embarrassing than to be a woman's slave. Might as well just let her clip your balls and put you in a collar—or maybe she did?"

"I'll make no comment on my concerns for the depravity of your imagination, friend," I told him, taking a few more grapes for his crass imagery. "Though I have no doubt my experience would have differed vastly if I had been selected by some other durrow—sold at market or traded off as Odile and Indra were probably planning to. Valeria was, is, a sort of queen there."

Popping the last few bites of fruit into his mouth before going on to the hardtack, the dwarf said in a tone not entirely unintrigued, "That so?"

"Yes, and a connection to their goddess. I fear I have lured her away from quite a few vital social responsibilities of hers...at any rate, being her 'slave' was the furthest thing from the sorts of experiences the word conjures."

"Oh yeah?"

"Yes, indeed." With a glance toward the shut hatch at the top of the short ladder into the brig, I leaned toward him with my voice lowered. "Let's just say, there are those trials that Weltyr forces us to endure by the stick, and those other routes along which he lures us with carrots."

"Hm. Hmhmhm." Chuckling as he stroked his beard, the dwarf permitted himself his first genuine smile of the night. "Well, I suppose nothing in this life is *all* bad...still, now that you're aboveground again, you ought not to let her call you such things. You don't want her getting strange ideas."

I didn't have the heart to tell him that some of Valeria's strangest ideas had proven to be her best ones... why make a blind man miserable by describing all those wonders he couldn't experience?

Besides: I had ample confidence in Valeria. I

likewise had much faith in Elishta-bet, although I felt that counting on her for some subterfuge during this time was misplaced. In ways of traveling, battling, and the gathering of intel, she was just not as seasoned as any of the other women; and by all rights, given their elfin heritage, she never would be.

But it was the other elves who gave me pause. Upstairs, as the fiddling grew fierce and feet stomped the deck in a liquor-fueled celebration, the pirates endeavored to seduce my women to their cause. Of this, I had no doubt, and they would have been fools to shirk the attempt.

And I also had the sense that their chances of success did not sit at zero.

Valeria was attached to me, I believed, because of what she sensed was divine command, and I felt the same divine fire coursing through me with our every look. Indra and Odile, on the other hand, appeared to be loyal first to one another; then, to Valeria; and then, perhaps in a small way, to me. Then there was fair Branwen, who, despite her sweet demeanor, had already once been seduced against my cause.

But was it not my Master's will that twisted hers?

A shudder wracked me there in the dank cell, although it was as stifling and hot as the rank belly of a beast.

All along, I had been a fool. All along, I had believed that evil deeds were contrary to Weltyr's will.

Instead, with a thought of Gundrygia and the child growing within her, I knew they were a mere step in that sacred will's enactment.

The hours passed and the fiddling reduced to

something more restful than outrageous. Somehow, owing perhaps to his small size, Grimalkin managed to fold his arms over his chest, tuck himself against the wall, and fall asleep on his cold wooden bench. I rested as much as I dared, my hands folded between my knees, my vision giving in to sleep snatched in brief spates of nodding until, against expectation, the hatch of the brig's dark cellar blinded us with familiar lantern light.

"What ho, prisoners! The Captain'd have a word wit'che. Not you," barked Dinah, waving a bony hand as Grimalkin sat up. "You, Paladin."

I did not correct her; I merely stood before the door as she brought the padlock key, my chin jutting toward the lantern in her other, more complete hand. "Beware, Dinah; you hold a sacred relic."

"If it were all that sacred it'd do me a favor and free me from this curse."

"You'd rather be dead than the slave on a pirate ship, you mean?"

"Slave! Hah. The only slaves aboard are you, I hear." Grimalkin cleared his throat obnoxiously while Dinah snapped open the lock. "I'm free as any man; I only wish I might remain free and undying when I left the ship. Now—"

Dropping the padlock, her motions quick, the jailer drew a pistol from her holster and thrust its muzzle against my jaw.

"—don't make any trouble fer me and I'll tell yer mistress you was a good boy."

Grimalkin gave up resistance and laughed. I shot him a dirty look and, when the pirate commanded me to replace the padlock, I confess I did so with some relish.

The decks of the *Rhinemaid* were far less wild with activity than they had been on our arrival. With festivities ended and everything in its place, the pirates had resumed their usual duties and fallen into the rhythm of sleepless work. They sang with the music while tending to the ship's needs, those unoccupied by the usual tasks instead responsible for throwing overboard empty liquor bottles or picked-over remnants of the banquet stolen from the *Battle Swan*.

Amid all this, I caught a glimpse of Indra and Odile speaking to one of the cleaners. It was always hard to tell from the faintness of their milky pupils against their light lavender eyes, but I swore as we passed that each one glanced toward me while maintaining the chatter.

Indra shifted her welding goggles upon her head, frowning at the black sky. "We'll need to go below deck soon."

"Ain't needta worry about that," insisted the pirate begrudgingly entertaining them as she mopped. "Captain races the dawn."

"Surely this ship can't be *that* fast."

At Odile's protest, the pirate produced a mocking laugh. Indra responded uncertainly.

"It *is* a ghost ship, Odile…what about that time Rorke disappeared, and—"

My gut clenched in concern while I was pulled out of earshot and set before the captain's door. While my captor knocked, I grew disturbed.

The ship raced the dawn?

Then we were headed the wrong way.

Gundrygia, our baby—they were somewhere north of Rhineland, with Gundrygia's father. I had no doubt he must have been a mighty sorcerer to produce such a dangerous daughter; I also had no doubt that he, like his daughter, was glad to psychologically extort me into this or that fatal mistake.

For instance, assuming the father as evil as the daughter, (or more), was the command that she abscond with my child not, in and of itself, an evil threat?

By the time I had let that thought double my dedication to the task of rectifying our course, I stood in the chambers of the *Rhinemaid's* captain.

And there, upon one of the faded couches, reclined Valeria.

THE CAPTAIN'S QUARTERS

TO CALL ME surprised to find the high priestess of Roserpine enjoying a goblet of wine in the captain's quarters is, perhaps, a mischaracterization. I had expected her to wiggle her way into the captain's trust, much as I could have wooed any wicked peer's trust if he and I had aught in common. However, I ought to have seen on the deck the apparent respect the captain had for Valeria, and counted on it serving us well.

"There he is!" Laughing gaily, her hair tumbling down to frame the dark swell of her bosom from the confines of her country dress with white curtains, Valeria extended a hand to gesture me forward. "Come kiss your mistress, slave."

I flicked but a glance at the watching captain, who, by the starry window, now regarded us without a hat, without deformity. With only queer anticipation and haughty regard for me or us or the situation. Troubled by how striking she was to me, I turned my gaze back toward Valeria and obligingly knelt at her side.

"Let Weltyr's commandment of myself to thy side be the sweetest bond of slavery, the sweetest reminder of my eternal servitude to him, that he ever devised."

While I kissed her offered hand and she laughed in some surprise at a performance nonetheless containing traces of my heartfelt love, Valeria exchanged a look with the captain.

"Maybe he's docile, after all...go on, Dinah." With a wave of her slender hand and the tightly muscled arm attached, the captain perched upon the edge of her desk and took a swig from her gilded cup. "Listen outside for signs'a trouble."

"Aye aye, Captain."

With a disappointed look, the undead wench made herself scarce. I thought to remind myself only after the door was closed that the captain of the *Rhinemaid* just as undead as her crew, although she did not appear as such anymore.

"I don't know that I'd call him *docile*," said Valeria with a knowing twinkle and a stroke of her hand through hair I wished I'd had time to have cut in Skythorn. "In the name of protecting me, I've seen him fight most viciously."

"No needta feel insecure, love," said the captain with a laugh at the messages between Valeria's words. "Though I don't reckon he could do much ta me bare-handed if I wasta decide the mood had changed."

Valeria smiled thinly back at the captain.

"I suppose," she said, "that would be true."

"Here I had the impression that you ladies would get along," I suggested between them.

Snorting, the captain looked at Valeria from beneath an arched brow.

"Let yer slave speak outta turn, do yeh?"

"If I wanted to be served by a beast that never speaks, I would own a dog. We are getting along quite famously, darling, as it happens."

Her hand slid over my tunic and, though her face was dark, it glowed with what I took for intoxication. "In fact, I may have cut us a deal."

"Not so fast, now."

Leaning forward with one arm braced across her knee, the captain regarded me carefully and said, "Yer mistress here has told some mighty wild tales about yer acquaintance, and I'm wonderin' here if you might could match them without her hints. Turn around."

I did, aware of the gun on her hip and the need to play at obedience until the moment was right. Valeria moved her feet and gestured I should sit upon the sofa with her; when I did, she slid those sandalless arches into my lap in anticipation of my caress. I took her delicate extremities in my hands one at a time without thinking, asking only of the captain, "What is it you would care to know?"

"How is it a man becomes a durrow's slave?"

"By luck," I jested, earning a slight nudge of Valeria's foot into my gut. "No—by Weltyr's will alone did the durrow women Indra and Odile rescue me from what would have been certain death. In exchange, I went peacefully to the heart of the Nightlands, which was as I had vowed; thereafter, I committed myself to the service of lovely Valeria…"

On I went, expressing as little as possible of the true reasons for my journey. I left out the Scepter that had become Exigence, and Hildolfr was omitted from my telling altogether. Instead, I maintained focus on our pursuit of Valeria's Ring; on the rescue of Branwen and the duel for Elishta-bet; and, because I saw the captain's interest in the subject, on my struggle with the witch, diabolical Gundrygia.

"I think I know the very witch you mean," she said with genuine intrigue, her forgotten goblet hanging from the tips of her fingers. "But she disappeared years ago—millennia. I seen'r come and go the way I seen so much else."

"Then you must be a truly ancient being, and in possession of profound knowledge."

"I know a thing'r'two," she said, remembering to have a little wine while muttering, "like how t'avoid succumbin' ta men's petty flattery."

"You will have to forgive Rorke for his love of beautiful women," Valeria said with a teasing chuckle, sitting up to slide away her feet and instead press herself against me. "He is as weak to them as the buck to the arrow."

"That I am." I sighed in unfeigned sorrow and shook my head, once again in the pale arms of Gundrygia amid the flowers. "It's what has gotten me into the most trouble during this long journey of mine. Now, the witch is with child by my doing; and Weltyr's will is that I must pursue her to where she waits north of Rhineland. Would you tell me, Captain—is there no possibility of our traveling there as soon as possible? I've heard it said your ship races the dawn—then you must be able to bring us there within twenty-four hours of now. Far sooner."

"Aye, far, far sooner, you're right. In fact, Burnin'soul, that'd be just what yer mistress an' I were discussin' before you were brought to join the conversation."

My interest was renewed. Striving not to look too hopeful, I said only, "Oh?"

"Seems like yer stories are on the level—and, if we're ta do any damned thing with that sword, we need ta bring yehs ta Rhineland, anyway. Never seen a thing like it," she added, shaking her head. "Any rate...I'd be willin' ta let you all go peacefully at Rhineland—even get you folk there in a timely fashion. But the sword's ta be sold there, and—"

"No."

Valeria stiffened against me while the captain scoffed. "No?"

"That sword is a symbol of my service to Weltyr. I can no more give it to you and live than I could shear this tattoo from my neck to be hung on your wall."

"Let us exchange something else," Valeria posited. While one hand raised to caress my cheek, the other slipped something hard into my palm. Her misdirection worked: the captain let her go on. "You would not ask me to exchange my ring to you for this favor, Captain."

"If I saw its sparkle aboard my ship, Madame, I

couldn't promise we'd have the same friendship we're developin' now." The captain's gold-lust twinkled in her smiling eyes, and she drained her cup empty before setting it upon her desk.

Valeria went on calmly while I, pretending to caress her waist, felt the weight and shape of the object she had passed me. "Then Burningsoul's sword is as good to you as my absent ring; for, without his hand, it will remain forever on your shelf. Collecting dust, doing you no good, bringing no money. Only ill fortune, for having severed the will of a god." A small dagger: some plundered letter-opener she had managed to secret upon her person.

Her expression darkening, the captain looked hard at Valeria. "I've received plenty'a divine punishment in my day, rest assured…before the first durrow was blinded by the sun, I was flyin' *the Rhinemaid* fer my nine hundredth year."

"Your crew do not seem to feel that service to the Rhinemaid is a punishment, except that they cannot leave the ship forever. Is the same true of you?"

The captain laughed at my question, as though it were spoken by an ignorant child. "I'm the very reason they can't leave the ship without dyin' in the dawn! The reason they're free, too, from the world beneath us and everythin' it makes us suffer. I was cursed, see…sold my soul to the Devil ta live forever."

Gundrygia, tempting me to come with her to defeat her father and learn some secret for bodily immortality. I nodded in compassion for the captain, admitting, "Such offers are hard to resist."

"Oh, aye, livin' ferever is fine if you look like an elf! But the second I step from my ship, well—you saw me."

"A vile curse. Is there really no way to blunt this gift's cruel edge?"

"I asked a soothsayer once…you know what she told me?"

I waited. The captain laughed in the silence, shaking her head.

"True love's kiss," was her answer.

"The ecstasy of love liberates us from all evil and brings us to the gods," I agreed, glancing over at Valeria. "Perhaps love is not the ends of freeing you, but the means. I would not mock it so, Captain."

Her laughter had faded; she regarded me sternly, saying after a time of contemplation, "No. I suppose I ought not'ta. What I mock is the cruelty of it. What man in his right mind would see me off my ship and come aboard for the love of me? Who'll see my diseased lips, my open skull, and say ta themselves, 'There she is—Venus, the goddess of love'rself!'"

She had a point. I did not envy her, especially since her heart was so wicked that I could not imagine any man would be inclined to see beyond appearance. Sighing in similar pity, Valeria set the cup into my hand and pressed its remaining contents to my lips. I drank up, trailing the fingers of my other hand down her back and into my lap to hide the dagger in the pocket of my tunic. The wine was too sweet, but welcome given all we'd been through in the past twenty-four hours or so. "Well, it is true that a fine female companion as your crew permits is nothing to be scorned," Valeria went on, watching my profile. "But a man like Rorke is truly invaluable to have at one's disposal. What if, Captain—"

The captain focused her distant gaze back in on the conversation, studying Valeria with open ears.

"—rather than worrying about my slave's scant possessions, you deal with me? My Nightlands overflow with riches you might ransom once I have reclaimed the ring and returned to my kingdom; as Materna, my word is good as my bond."

"That ain't much good ta me right now, is it?"

"Hence the second portion of my offering. I thought that perhaps, as a gesture of goodwill, I might provide you with access to this fine man."

While I lowered the empty cup, Valeria's bold hand slid down into my lap to grip the member that was, I admit, already somewhat strained under the tone of conversation and my lady's close proximity. I exhaled in contentment with her boldness, turning to brush my lips over the ridge of her sweeping ear as she fondled me as a pretense for ensuring I'd hidden the knife.

"My slave is *very* well-endowed," she emphasized, steadily returning the captain's lustful gaze. "When given a certain Nightlands herb, I have seen him satisfy an entire cadre of women; without it, he is still capable of pleasing three or four at a time without incident. Two would be no trouble to him."

The captain's blazing eye swept over me. The idea of setting hands upon the undead woman was heinous, but I knew why Valeria offered what she did. Up close, I could plunge the dagger into the demon's skull. I hoped that, as her crew had been prone to injury when in human guise off the ship, she would be in a similar state aboard it.

If not, we would be in for a difficult battle until I set hand on Exigence.

"Yeh think he's pleasin' enough ta be worth that sword, do yeh?"

"The unsellable sword that's no good to you, or me, or anyone else aboard this ship but Rorke? Oh…"

I had taken to kissing Valeria's throat through the tumbling shade of her hair. Goosebumps rose along her dark flesh while she moaned. As my kisses lowered toward the exquisite breasts that swelled from her gown with each gasping breath, she twisted in her my lap and draped her arms around my neck.

"Rest assured, Captain…Rorke's company will prove more than sufficient fare for our peaceful transit to the Rhineland."

"Well…reckon we did get quite a haul from the *Battle Swan*." Rubbing her jaw in thought, the captain regarded us together. "And he's obedient, is he?"

"No man exists that was so eager to please a woman, yet so manly in the doing of it—nor so powerful in being humbled. The first among Rorke's many virtues is his tongue. As fine a speaker as he is, surely you can tell it has many other applications.

"He requires little instruction, oh, Captain, rest assured. Ask Indra and Odile out there, or Branwen, for that matter; they can all attest to his understanding of feminine anatomy. Not to mention the benefits these acts of service have on *his* anatomy, which, in my estimate, is more eager to please than even its master."

The musky scent of her flesh was like a balm to my stressed mind. These last seconds of peace with her body in my arms—I absorbed them as well as I could, certain that we were about to be fighting for our lives. It was safe to say I had grown very fond of my traveling companions—or, in the case of Branwen, succeeded in overlooking her previous disloyalty—but none of them had such an intense, soul-bonded charisma to me as had Valeria. Even in that time and space, I had the acute sense she felt the same.

Yet her culture would not yet let her understand it as I did. To me, the love I felt for her was like the first swallows I took of durrow wine upon rising from certain death. Indeed, what was it but an extrapolation of that first, sacred sip? I had no trouble understanding with my foreign eyes why she, of all the fine women of the Nightlands, was held in such esteem. She was dignified until those moments she was not, making those moments she was not so hot with fire that even the most sincerely celibate priest of Weltyr would have broken beneath the back of temptation. She was removed until those moments when she became dynamic, her first weeks aboveground spent in intense observation of Urd's surface ways until her hibernation yielded to this parlay with our captor.

And she was likewise alternately tender and distant to me, or so I perceived. Perhaps it was only because she always had, running in her mind's background murmur, the single word that had made Grimalkin balk and advise me caution. "Slave."

And Valeria may have been dressing of late in the borrowed robes of our surface friend, but her heart and her ways were still those of the Nightlands. Of the durrow people.

"My hot stud," she extolled with erotic tones, looking into my face even as she spoke to the captain, "is so loyal, he would even thrill to watched me pleased by another of his ilk."

I took to her meaning only after a few seconds

through all the haze of her body fit so completely against mine. Slaves, I thought she meant at first. "Aye, I recall being quite fond of the baths in the Nightlands. What fine women attended you there!"

"You ought to have seen the men…perhaps, when you've brought me back to the Nightlands, I'll free you and buy us each a few slaves of our own. Then you'll see them, all right…"

So went the benefit of the doubt.

With Grimalkin's warning still fresh in my ears, I forgot our play-acting just a little bit. What was said in jest had grains of truth, after all. Despite myself, I looked at her somewhat sternly.

"You do know, Madame"—I caught her face in my hands, the sensuality of her gasp stirring my loins even as I slid her lightly from my lap—"that what was spoken in the passion of the Nightlands' bedchamber is nothing but a word game to entertain the passion of a powerful lover."

Valeria lost her expression of talkative bliss. "What do you mean by that?"

"I just mean to be sure you understand," I told her, my fingers trailing through her long white locks and down her dark shoulder. "That I love you, Valeria. My passion has grown too great to ever tolerate the thought of you in the arms of another man."

Lips parted in shock, Valeria searched my face and found only well-meant earnestness. "And I'm to see you gallivant about with whatever woman't pleases you to seduce?"

"I would have you think them your lovers, too," I assured her.

The passion that she had within her contributed to an equal fury. Her teeth bared, her eyes aflame, Valeria said, "So long as they meet your qualifications? I prefer to be served by men."

"And you have a man in your service now. Forever."

Even as I said the word, it rose from my lips and into my ears as a lover's lie made to soften the truth.

It would not be forever. Not for her. For her, our love would be the smallest window in an unfurling mansion of life. Then—knowing her fairly little, except that we were both in the service of our gods, and I loved her—I anticipated that, when the window was closed, she would mourn for a time and move on to another who could fulfill some pantomime of my former role.

Now, I suspect she feels differently, though I wish in some ways it were not so. I do not like the idea of, as some ancient kings, entombing my brides along with me.

Then, though, in the final hours of my boyhood, I might have liked it. It would have been reassuring. However, I knew it quite unrealistic. Like surface elves, durrow could live two thousand years or more…assuming they managed to survive the devilish dealings of their peers, of course.

All I asked, therefore, was for her loyalty in that one window. For her to gaze only through my panes while she stood at me. For her hands to open me and me alone, knowing that she would have plenty of time to appreciate the rest of the mansion in its time.

And I do think she understood what I was asking. But still, the voice in her heart whispered, "Slave," and it was written as clearly on her tongue as it was on the palm she drew back to strike me.

"I have a *slave* in my service, who would do—"

Her words punctuated in a gasp as I stopped altogether and caught her striking wrist.

"In the Nightlands, within the hive of your city, you had a slave. Where you are now, no man is a slave to anyone but Weltyr."

The captain watched our argument with mirth. I slowly rose, hyper-aware of the dagger hidden within my tunic.

Valeria's eyes blazed. "What is the meaning of this?"

"There is play and there is plan, and I want to be clear between the two while I still can."

She bared her teeth, poised to say more, but the captain cruelly laughed.

"Hell! This is more innerestin' than the sex. I was waitin' until you both were well int'it in fronta me before blowin' his head off in fronta yeh, but you two are mighty amusin'."

My body stiffened, the posture of my legs spreading to narrowly put me between the captain and Valeria. Her fury turned upon the captain, my admonished love half-raised from the sofa with one fist clenched at the waist of her gown. "Is that so?"

"Come on, "Princess." You think a roll in the hay with your gigolo there'd make me inclined to give yehs free passage in exchange fer nothin' more than an IOU? Hell! If I can't make him move the bloody sword, I'll kill him and let the thing stay on my shelf. A pretty trophy. Ah-ah."

Valeria's lips had begun to quiver with Nightlands words barely audible to me; the captain, however, saw the movement or heard the utterances or, perhaps even more likely, felt the developing atmosphere of some magical attack. Before I had the dagger fully drawn, she'd unholstered her pistol.

"Let's not be avin' nonea them witchy words now, love…and put down that toothpick, Burnin'soul, y'er embarrassin' yerself. I think I'll add you and yer friends into the brig. See how yehs like the close quarters. Maybe yer 'slave' here will wise up once he's seen a few'a yehs thrown overboard just as soon as we're well ahead of the sun again."

Though I had shifted more directly between Valeria and the gun, my brain wildly swept the room for a weapon other than the relinquished dagger. I came up with little more than a pair of rapiers making up part of some seal on the wall. Nothing that could stand against a gun; and nothing I could reach before she fired.

Luckily for me, those friends I had doubted proved the most trustworthy of all.

"Hey!"

Dinah's sharp call from outside the door interrupted us. The subsequent noise was muffled by the sounds of a scuffle and a series of thumps. Someone elsewhere on the deck cried out.

Looking witheringly our way, the captain kept her gun trained on us until she'd thrown open the door.

Whatever she saw, she boggled at it before hurrying out with an immediate spate of gunfire.

"Now's our chance, Madame. Hurry—"

Sniffing delicately, Valeria dropped her feigned drunkenness while I took down a rapier to test its edge. "'Madame' again, is it?"

"Perhaps I chose an indiscreet time to make my feelings clear, Madame, but I love you—deeply."

She did not reply. I tested the other blade, nicking my thumb as I assured her above the sound of wild gunfire, of cries and shouts, "Better to speak my thoughts at the wrong early time than the wrong late time."

"But some times are more ill-chosen than others," she retorted, sighing with exasperation for me. "But—I suppose we'll discuss it later."

"I'm glad to hear you're open to the dialogue."

I turned the sharper of the two swords around and offered her the weapon by its handle. She looked down at it, then looked up at me in the queerest of ways. With marked impatience—and yet, somehow, that impatience was almost wry. The impatience of love, I supposed.

Taking the sword, she nodded her head to the door and said, "Lead the way."

I intended to; but, upon cracking open the door and taking a look at the chaos outside, I had some second thoughts.

5

CHAOS

The Flying Rhinemaid was a madhouse, with Dinah's prone body left slumped beside the door to the captain's quarters. Pirates shouted orders at each other between curses for the targets who evaded their gunfire or, in some cases, magically repelled it. Through the fog of war, my eyes leaping from skirmish to skirmish, I discerned those very souls whose fealty I'd doubted above Valeria's. Odile, across the deck, grappled the same pirate with whom she'd earlier conversed; in the distance, a few crouched behind barrels while exchanging Branwen's magical volley for their bullets—one of which whizzed close enough to splinter the doorframe beside my head. Indra was closer to me, fending off a few crew members with her own filched blunderbuss. But I was most of all amazed to see Elishta-bet, who I had supposed too untested for battle. She had shielded herself with some bright blue bell jar of energy in the name of leading the captain away from her cabin.

"I think you should stay here until I come back for you, Madame," I said with a meaningful glance at the splintered crater in the door frame. "Can you move the sofa across the door?"

"I think I can."

"Then do, and prepare some spell to fend off attackers. Stay under cover until I return for you, if you can."

"Very well. Rorke—"

I had been just about to step out and now paused.

"Be careful."

Her words upon my heart like the sigil of the Bright God on my neck, I joined the fray and took to helping Indra. One of her opponents had gotten close enough to make use of a dagger, but before she could strike, I was there to beat the wench back. With a happy cry, Indra glanced my way for but a second before pointing to one of the hatches leading below. I remembered it from first loading the very vault I now planned to rob.

"There, Rorke—hurry, find Exigence!"

Patting her on the back of the shoulder, I followed Indra's advice and ducked gunfire all the way to the hatch. One or two crewmembers made a cursory effort to halt my progress; most, however, were either wise to my battle prowess, or too occupied by my companions. It was not long before I had made it to the port side of the deck. On the other side of that hatch, I descended into the belly of the ship before the captain's glance of my receding back amounted to action.

Below deck, much as I would have preferred to fetch Exigence outright, I instead felt I was held prisoner to the virtuous, godly deed; and I say 'held prisoner' only because the act of freeing Grimalkin was one my petty, mortal heart loathed to perform. Still, after fending off a couple of pirates who realized their daggers were no match for my skill with even a somewhat dull rapier, I did not think twice about bursting into the brig and smashing the old, rusted lock to bits with a few bashes from the sword's handle.

"Rorke," Grimalkin shouted all the while, "what in Dunnun's gray beard is goin' on up there?"

"My friends evidently decided to make a move before we got too far off-course. Come on." Throwing open the cell door, I ushered Grimalkin out into the ship's belly. "Let's liberate our weapons and join the fray! The women need help, and Valeria is alone in the captain's cabin."

"An innerestin' bit'a information. Thank you, Burnin'soul."

The captain's mocking brogue echoed down the corridor. She stood before her vault of treasures, a pistol in her hand and a short sword taken from some crewmember, fighting or fallen, hanging naked at her hip.

She wasted no time setting the gun's sights on me.

Grimalkin, crying out, shoved me back into the brig before I could respond.

Together, on the other side of the door, we crouched

in wait for another shot. Instead, the Captain's mockery echoed again.

"Hidin' from a woman, Burnin'soul! That's where the paladin's vainglory gets a man, I reckon…coddled by the crowd but unfit for proper battle."

"You act without honor, Captain. Nothing could be 'proper' about a battle you fight this way."

"How's that?"

"I have no gun; the fight is unmatched. Face me down with that sword and we can see who's the better warrior."

The scoffing captain sounded on the verge of condemning my suggestion until Grimalkin loudly advised, "She knows she can't…even an undead woman's no match for a man in battle!"

"So, it's a swordfight y'er wantin'," she asked in a tone of sharp distaste. "Very well…"

The sound of a weapon's weight afflicting its holster coaxed me into peering around the door. To make good her swap, the captain drew her sword in the same smooth motion with which she'd put away her gun.

I stepped out into the hall, nodding for unarmed Grimalkin to remain where he was for now.

The corridor into which I stepped was narrow, as I had already found in the fast-moving chaos of my effort to free Grimalkin. Now faced with the prospect of a swordfight with the Captain, I thought as fast as my circumstances allowed.

I meant what I said. When a man or woman has no scruples, no dignity or virtue of which to speak, one's own attachment to virtue becomes hampering if too strictly adhered to. Some virtues are, of course, immutable, and mankind's oaths are themselves maintained by Weltyr's stern eye.

But others, such as the prospect of fair fighting, or of laying down arms against women—these were virtues that varied with the time and the place and level of desperation.

Faced, therefore, by the spectral captain with a gun still on her hip, I jutted my chin in that holstered weapon's direction.

"The pistol, Captain. Set it down so I'll know you won't go back on your commitment to a fair fight."

She snorted.

"And let you pick it up, Paladin?"

"If you think me a paladin, then you should know it is beneath me."

Eyeing me for a time, then producing a thoughtful click of her upper lip against her teeth, the captain walked backward with the sword still between us. The leather of the gun's holster shifted beneath its weight while, the pearl handle balanced on the edge of her palm, my opponent drew it from its place and set it slowly on the floor. She kicked it behind her, her unblinking gaze fixed on mine.

"Very good."

My posture relaxed only a second. Only until the wicked woman darted down the hall, her uncanny nature indicated aboard the ship by nothing but preternatural speed—and, as I found when her sword met mine, her strength.

"You're strong for a woman," I exclaimed in some surprise, forcing her back with a rush and a poorly contorted slice toward her side. The rapier, I was finding, was not the ideal weapon for these halls; the short sword the captain had appropriated was far more useful. Unfortunately for me, my armor was locked away along with Exigence, and Grimalkin's axe, and any device else that was natural to myself or my companions. With her speed and strength, I endured her sword's sharp cut along my waist. The hole she made in the tunic was as clean as the tear in my flesh.

"You're strong for a mortal," she replied when, parrying her next blow, I managed to force her back another few steps before finding the posture to hold ground. Teeth grit, she ducked beneath the weight of my sword and used the butt of her own to strike the wind from me. Then, while I was doubled, the banshee uttered a cruel laugh and made to punch me square in the face.

Though I gasped for breath, I lunged at her and slammed her back down into the hard wooden floor of the ship.

While the surprised Captain raised her sword and had her hand caught, Grimalkin took his chance.

Though it is obvious dwarves are short in stature, I assure you, it makes no difference in their weight; at least, it did not seem to in Grimalkin's case. My fellow captive bolted from the brig and leapt heavily upon my back, using me as a springboard by which he might reach the captain's gun at the far end of the hall.

"Treacherous bastard," she hissed before smashing her skull up toward my nose. Praise Weltyr, her forehead was delicate and my nose did not break, although I did stumble back amid a panoply of colors in a sudden, buzzing darkness that ached my sinus cavities. I grimaced, a hand laying only briefly upon the injury before I realized she was up and in pursuit of Grimalkin.

She was fast; but, driven by desperation, the dwarf and I were faster. I reached her, my sword's swing forcing her to turn and meet the blow or else take one of her own. Next came the click of the gun and the fury in her eyes as Grimalkin brandished the pistol.

"I thought you said it was beneath you, Paladin."

I nodded over her shoulder, saying, "Grimalkin *is* beneath me."

"That a height joke, Burningsoul?"

"Certainly not...I would not jest over what a man cannot control."

But sometimes it was good to have friends who were beneath one. They could engage in all the behaviors one could not, and this was a prime example. With a noise of mild derision for my criticism of his character, Grimalkin used the captain's attention to nod toward the corner of the hall.

"Let's make this easy, Captain. You give us back our weapons and drop us off somewheres, and we'll figure out all the rest."

"Oh, aye, I'd gladly drop yehs off this very minute what with the surly ocean crashin' on beneath us." While my mouth opened in incredulity to believe the *Rhinemaid* could fly so quickly, I reconciled that it would have to if it wished to outpace the dawn at all times. Still, my stomach lurched. We were so far off-course that much farther and we would find the way back as far as the way forward.

"Then give us our weapons now," Grimalkin demanded on, "and we'll all make damn sure your crew sees us through to land."

"Without harming anyone, of course," I clarified.

61

"If you can subdue my crew," she rejoined, easing her sword's posture. Her eye narrowed with her cold regard for my face before, shaking her head, the captain stepped back toward Grimalkin.

"Let's go…I'd jes as soon be done with yehs after all this trouble."

I did not believe her for a second, but glimpsed a hole in an otherwise foreboding wall. Grimalkin left the weapon trained on her as she passed him, and he almost shot it when she lunged to spook him; then, laughing meanly, she went on to the lightly gilded door at the corridor's end.

"You fools…no matter how tough a man is, he still scares like a rabbit."

The captain's hand landed upon the door of her treasure trove. I marveled as the handle's brass glowed purplish-silver in the light.

"There's no key?"

"I am the ship," answered the captain. "The ship is me. We're bonded at the soul; there's rooms here she'll open fer none but me. Enjoy yerselves."

The door swung open beneath her hand and my heart swelled with hope. Grimalkin made a noise of relief but remained lingering in the doorway with a wary glance at the magical entrance.

"You go on ahead in there, Burningsoul…I'd better wait here and make sure the door doesn't close."

The rapier still in my hand, the captain leaning back against the wall, I hurried into the treasure room without a second thought.

Seeing the hoard with new eyes, having once been so busy in the transportation of pilfered goods into it,

I was somewhat staggered by its contents. How many airships' worth of goods lay in these shelves? I did not care to think on it overly long: particularly not as my eye landed first upon the Lantern of Hamsunt, dim upon its shelf; then, upon Exigence, right where I had left it.

The treasure room was a fair bit wider than the hall, though still relatively close quarters. When Grimalkin cried out upon the darting off of the captain, who stole her moment when we were both occupied with admiring the contents of the room, I glanced back to see her receding form and shook my head at my friend.

"Forget her. Her time to regroup is ours, too. Where is your axe?"

Teeth grit beneath his beard, Grimalkin scanned the shelves before gesturing toward one a few rows above Exigence. "That's it," he said as, noting my armor, I stopped off to reclaim my breastplate. "I'd know that edge anywhere…how are we going to get out of here, though?"

"As I said…if we must, we'll hold the whole crew hostage."

"There's bloody twenty of them!"

"More, I think."

"You can't seriously believe we'll overpower them."

"This sort of attitude is exactly why you thought I'd never make it out of the Nightlands."

The centerpiece of my armor strapped on, I fetched my friend's axe and slid it across the floor to him. He exclaimed to heft it to the light, the captain's gun forgotten in his belt.

It was as I set hand upon Exigence that the shot rang out. I thought Grimalkin's stolen weapon had been accidentally discharged. Instead, he swore and ducked into the treasure room, swinging his axe down to jam the door. Much as he predicted, it made as though to shut; but the dwarvish steel was too strong, and the hinge bounced open again.

The captain, flanked by the same pirates I had fought off below deck, rounded the corner and fired another shot. I ducked behind the edge of the doorway, grimacing to have just avoided death, and scanned the room for an additional weapon.

Instead, my eye fell once again upon the lantern.

In all the time we traveled through the Nightlands by its light, we encountered none of Gundrygia's false creations—save for misshapen beings, the spider durrow that were her male contribution to the female species. These beings, I assumed, were excluded from the lantern's effects because they were conscious, reasoning creatures... but I was also not sure that was the relevant distinction.

As the captain called, "Lay down yer arms; come out peacefully or we'll make yer deaths even more violent than they're already destined ta be," I darted into the bowels of the treasury.

Grimalkin called after me, and rightly so. I knew I was edging into the sights of their guns, and for a gamble, at that ...but I had to take the chance.

It paid off.

The Lantern of Hamsunt is a strange device: one that, I noticed from the start, was not of the same design as other lanterns. Though at first I had assumed its fire was summoned by the wisp-producing durrow, I quickly divined that the lantern's light was not made by any perceptible flame. Instead, with a twist of the small switch at the base of the device, light glowed from its glass without definable source. It could be turned up or down, and the higher it was turned, the larger was its area of effect.

While the Captain and her crewmembers pressed themselves to the other side of the doorway, I kept the lantern's light low and shielded by my body.

Only as the devious wench burst in, her new gun fixed on me, did I turn my body and twist high the glow of the light.

6

THE LANTERN OF HAMSUNT

THE SCREAM OF the captain as the glow fell upon her face still plays in my mind: it was a noise so visceral it seemed as though it possessed the power to tear asunder reality. I half-lowered the lantern in an instinctive reaction—but, when the cruel woman gripped her face with both hands, I brandished it until she was forced back from the treasury.

"Back, you unnatural thing! Retreat from the light of the gods."

"I can't bloody *see*," she screamed, falling blindly back beyond the threshold of the treasure. "What *is* that damned light—"

"The Lantern of Hamsunt," I responded, swinging Exigence before me as I pursued her from the room. "And this is Weltyr's sword."

The vast arc of the great, grinning blade swept wide before me—straight into the neck of a pirate waiting on the other side of the door. Stunned as she'd been by the appearance of the light, the undead wench did not even realize she was being beheaded, or so I took from the features that further decayed on the instant of their severance from her body. Indeed, 'decay' is not sufficient. It seemed she dissolved before my very eyes, her rotten flesh withering from the bone of a skull that burst into dust seconds after. By the time Exigence's swing had reached completion, the pirate was little more than a pile of ash at my feet.

Emboldened, I turned back to the captain. With a cry of fury for her fallen shipmate, one hand still covering most of her face and her every perception of the world stolen in glimpses through her fingers, she raised her gun to fire wildly.

She telegraphed everything. Shot after shot was easily dodged until I struck out with the blade and smashed the pistol from her hand.

"Agree to genuine parlay and I'll turn the light down."

"After what you've done here, I'd rather fight ta the death with yehs." Behind her hand, the captain's lips contorted into a mocking smile.

She laughed.

"What's so funny, Captain? Do you suppose I would hesitate?"

"No...it's only that you're a fool who can't listen."

With little more than a brisk glance over my shoulder for the remaining pirate, who had retreated into the treasury and now found herself in a sword-on-axe fight with Grimalkin, I brandished Exigence meaningfully at the captain.

"Speak, or I will force you to."

"I *am* the ship," the captain repeated in defiance, lowering her hands from her face and glaring at me through eyes so narrowly slit I would have been amazed to know she could see at all. "When I die, so does she."

My heart sank. I lowered the blade but slightly while she laughed on.

"If yeh'd like ta crash inta the sea, be my guest. You'd only be doin' me a favor, anyway."

Despite her mockery, her voice was weak, and the breaths she took to speak were tattered as her undisguised, undead lungs. Indeed, the holy light showed her for exactly as I had seen her aboard the *Swan*, and in fact somewhat worse. She stumbled away, falling into the wall of the ship.

The *Rhinemaid* listed hard to port, scattering us about like pollen on the wind.

Cries broke through the battle abovedeck. Even as I was slammed into a wall of my own and just barely managed to stop the door from closing in on Grimalkin, my ears strained to detect the individual voices. Who had screamed at the rattle of the ship—Branwen? Indra, Elishta-bet?

Pray, not Valeria?

"The light," bellowed the captain, her eye socket covered along with her milky, rotten orb. "The blasted light! Put it away, Paladin! I can't endure it longer."

"Then agree—"

My demands were cut short by another lurch of the ship, this one synchronized to the captain's ill-fated effort to scramble around the corner. She tripped instead, and the narrow hallway was not narrow enough for her to catch herself on a wall.

Instead, as she cried out with the sound of an old finger bone snapping in the grave, the ship thrashed forward, descended in altitude, and bucked as wildly as ever has any ship in sky or sea or stars.

And amid all of this, having reached me from the bowels of the treasury, Grimalkin made it to the door in time to be hurled into my unready back.

Grimalkin! At the time, as the lantern flew from my hand and even once the moment had passed, I had nothing but curses for him. Now I see how, even in this oafishness, he was but a tool for those forces contriving each step of my life.

My body responded with a clench of horror as I have felt only one or two times in my long life since. While my mind recorded in slow detail every glint of the spiraling lantern—every shadow that rotated along my face, swept away, returned on the other side of these great swaths of radiant glory—I stretched out my arm and grasped at thin air. Exigence, heavy in my other hand, provided no assistance in the task. Down, down it fell. With both hands, one full and one empty, I lurched for it.

The shattering of the glass hastened my panic, and I still to this day am not certain if the lantern broke open against Weltyr's blade...though, of course, my heart knows the truth, and I will leave it at that.

It did not matter whether the lantern shattered

against Exigence or the ship's hard floor. All I knew was that the flames burst from their container in an explosion that brought me back, with a frightful flash, to the fireball of the spirit-thief, Al-listux. I threw my arm before my face, my body braced both against the rocking of the ship and in protection of the friend who was less armored than I.

But though I could shield him from shattering glass and raging fire, there was no protection from the mad laughter that emanated from the flames.

<At last…Rorke Burningsoul.>

The captain's high, miserable scream echoed from around the corner. I lowered my arms. The flames leapt and licked, slithering up the walls like uncanny snakes and spreading along the wooden floor in a swiftly growing barrier I hastened to help Grimalkin overleap. The dwarf darted around the corner before I did, but stopped short with a curse on his lips.

Before us, the captain's body was wreathed in flame.

I stepped forward to pull her from the blaze, but Grimalkin stopped me with a hand on my forearm. Quickly, I realized why. The flames were not only around her, but leaping up from her flesh as though burning from within her.

<She is damned. Let her die.>

The fire-voice again. I whirled about with Exigence brandished, but once again saw no man. Even so, I addressed the hateful speaker.

"Though she may be abominable in her nature and her crimes, her death means the death of this ship. We will all die."

<I will not die,> the voice said from within the

laughing flames. I swear I briefly glimpsed a face among them while it carried on, although by the time I looked back to confirm it the fire had once more changed its shape. <I will live for as long as Urd spins through the stars. I will not die…and I could save you, and whomever you would wish.>

The story of the captain flashed through my mind. "I do not deal with demons," I told the spirit tersely, eliciting another laugh.

<I am no *demon*, Rorke Burningsoul…I am a god.>

"I know no god but Weltyr," I told him. "You"—I dared name the entity without formal introduction—"Hamsunt, whatever you are—you will always be beholden to the All-Father. A slave to his will."

<Fool! How ignorant you are to the ways of the gods. The only slave here is you.>

Fire had begun to spread along the ceiling, and above the captain's screaming I realized the crew screamed with her. Grimalkin, seeing the urgency, called to me, "Rorke, hurry!"

I glanced back at him, then once more into the fires I addressed.

For a flickering second, there stood among them the dark figure of a burning man.

That quickly, the image was gone.

I turned on my heel and darted up the stairs to the upper deck.

What had been a chaotic battle had grown to bear the hallmarks of a horrific tragedy. While Branwen called my name, I stood agog: and not at the flames, which had by some occult means already spread across the ship. Instead, I my heart gave a wrench for the crew.

Each pirate I saw thrashed about on the deck, screaming and clawing at their burning faces not unlike the captain.

"Are you all right?"

Branwen's hand upon my shoulder drew me back to earth. I nodded, my grip tightening on the handle of Exigence.

"I'm fine. Where is—Valeria."

As I spoke, my eye had followed the flames with a kind of absent but profound absorption of their power. It felt much as it does when one observes a tremendous mountain or vast gulch with wonder that becomes more concentrated, more acute, as one looks on and on. The glory of nature, overwhelming, absorbed only over time. In this case, that acute focus narrowed to a wall of flame that lapped from the door of the captain's quarters.

"Valeria!"

I grew deaf to all else as I charged across the deck, though I did look rapidly around. Indra and Odile were busy, I was touched to say, helping Elishta-bet evacuate some platform from which she had been throwing her magic. This, unfortunately, meant they were not helping their mistress, who screamed from the burning cabin.

"Valeria," I called through flames I hardly felt while bashing the door.

"Rorke? Oh, Rorke, praise be to Roserpine—"

"Stand back."

Branwen's command brought me to attention. I stepped away. The druid swung her arm with a few mystifying words. From the atmosphere through which we flew, a great column of water swirled down to smash the door.

The fire did not abate.

"Rorke—"

"Don't panic, Valeria," I told her, speaking also to myself. "We'll have you out, just wait."

Branwen's eyes were wild. "What fire is this?"

<God-fire.>

The voice was accompanied by the parting of the flames before us, their curtain-like opening revealing the hot knob of the door for my hand. I cursed as I twisted it, my flesh searing hot against the brass; the open door revealed rows of flames that did not show the least sign of reducing.

But I did see, once again flickering and flashing within their edges, the smoldered spirit of their vicious body.

<You are in peril,> mocked the voice as I vaulted the remains of the couch Valeria had moved to block the door, <and where is Weltyr? Nowhere to be seen.>

A bookshelf, its volumes alight, careened toward me with the ship's most recent thrash. I barely rolled out of its way, further grimacing to see it had been pushed out of place by a collapsed roof-beam. The cabin was wallpapered in fire, and among it all, Valeria crouched with her hands over her head and profound terror on her face.

<What will he do to help you? Nothing.>

More flames threatened to collapse more boards—including one above Valeria. I called out, leaping forward and sweeping her into my arms just in time. The ceiling collapsed down through the floor, a great hole burning ever-wider now cut into the ship. The very angle that once permitted the captain's cabin a fine view of the sky now proved deadly.

<But I am here before you now, Burningsoul. I can make all this stop in an instant. I can save you—if you would only swear your loyalty to me.>

"Rorke!"

All my other friends had crowded the doorway, with Odile looking poised to pursue us inside. I called out to them, shaking my head as I shouted, "Don't!"

Drawing Valeria to her feet, I asked, "Can you walk?"

"Yes—"

"Then flee."

I paused only to land a brisk, heavy kiss upon her anguished mouth, then pushed her toward the doorway.

As Indra and Odile stepped aside to let Grimalkin apart hack the burning couch, a new row of flames sprang up to bar Valeria's escape.

<Well? What do you say?>

Exigence high before me, I wheeled to face the dark spirit of the flames. More accustomed to its form, I followed its flickers in and out while I waited for it to manifest close enough to fight.

"There is but one true god," I repeated, striking at the entity with the mighty sword.

Even that sacred blade swept straight through.

<You seem pretty sure about that...sort of a shame.>

Beneath us, the floor cracked and groaned. The terrible whining continued up the wall of the captain's quarters, and I realized the sound signified more of the ship's structure falling away from the floor, the wall, the ceiling.

The hole grew, a full corner of the captain's quarters opened to the distant sea beneath us.

Valeria screamed. Another terrible cracking split the air.

This time, she fell along with the board giving way under her feet.

Her name rose from my lips in a frantic cry.

Forgetting all else, I sheathed Exigence and leaped to help her.

By some miracle of elvish reflexes, she had grabbed hold the splintering end of a floorboard. The flames made their steady approach.

"Hold on," I told her, bending to catch her wrist. "Pull up—"

She obeyed, teeth bared, her strain evident in the tone of her gasp. I watched her elbows bend, waiting for the ideal moment to slide my hand beneath her arm.

A second after that she cried out, losing her grip on the board. Instead, Valeria grabbed hold of my forearm with both hands. This clutch shifted to my neck when she could afford the risk; I dragged her up with the strength of my legs.

Then came more flames, and more splintering wood. I cursed, clutching Valeria around the waist.

The floor gave way beneath us.

The screams of our friends rose above the flames.

<Should have let me help you,> chided Hamsunt, his tone insincere as it had been from the start. <Oh, well…I'm just glad to have a chance to stretch my legs.>

"Rorke!"

Someone's cry from above fell as an empty sound. In those seconds, I had no name. I was not even a man. I was the pure drive to survive to the next moment, and to ensure the woman with her arms around my neck would survive with me. I was the strain of my arm as I struggled to pull us both up one-handed.

I was the panic, the disgrace, as this last board creaked out the notes of its baleful splitting.

"Rorke, hold on—"

Some force greater than any human's grip wrapped around my wrist. I looked up, struggling to make sense of it. A purple cuff of energy kept me suspended even as the board fell away, and I followed its tether to the wild-eyed woman who controlled it: Elishta-bet.

"That's it," she said, her words a gasp as, her glowing hands before her, she shortened the length of the tether by will alone. "That's it—almost there."

<Neat trick.>

Elishta-bet cried out as the spirit flickered into being beside her, its towering form no less perceptible for its proximity.

<Want to see one of mine?>

Now it was at her other side.

Now, it was behind her.

<Boo,> it said, giving Elishta-bet a sharp push forward into the abyss.

She screamed. She toppled over.

And we fell with her.

VORSPIEL

SOMEPLACE FAR AWAY, in a room wreathed with darkness, the odious shared mind of the spirit-thieves wriggled and hummed.

His life-force has been severed.

"Nonsense."

I feel it.

The old man ignored the creature whose telepathic communications arose from the trap door in the center of his lab. The creature awaited a response.

Receiving nothing, it probed.

Does it not please you to think things might be different?

"Nothing of the cradle pleases the man. Urd is but a long-outgrown cradle to me, Entity."

A vent opened in the side of the entity, the bubbles of its exhalation releasing in a cluster to pop at the surface in a great carbuncle of watery cysts.

What will you do with your life if he is dead?

"Consider dying, myself. This hateful cycle will be over with."

"There is no ending it, Father. You know that…and you know you're too afraid of death."

The old man observed the witch who called him "Father," though she did not return his look. Her gaze remained fixed through an old looking glass amid the multitudinous components of the laboratory. She looked beyond the glass; beyond her body and the tower and Rhineland. Perhaps even beyond Urd.

No. Certainly beyond Urd.

"The ring is unbreakable," she intoned, her body slowly swaying back and forth as though an unheard melody increased its volume to her. "There are four diamonds mounted upon its surface, and lo! I see they can be absented altogether to leave the band the same… but the band! The perfect circle, I see it."

One hand stretched above her head as she moved, her gaze lifting to slowly follow it. Her fingers splaying, she caressed that naked hand with the other. Then, clutching it, laughing, she pressed both to her heart and twirled like a girl.

"It will never be destroyed. You will never succeed in freeing yourself, Father. The Wotsung is not dead."

He is dead, insisted the Entity. *I can no longer account for his consciousness on Urd.*

The witch's laughter stopped. She jutted her head and upper body toward the sealed pool with a hiss and an animal baring of her teeth, her movements more those of a snake than the black wolfskins that were her only coverings.

"But elsewhere, Invader?"

The Entity did not reply. Her nostrils flared as she straightened up, hands on her hips.

"As I thought…there are mysteries which your kind can never solve. You would rather see them destroyed because you cannot understand—but, fool! They are mightier than you. The *truth* is mightier than you."

With a dark look that still maintained something of a wry humor, the old man asked, "And you know all the truth, do you, Gundrygia?"

"As do you," she said, her hands pressing to her face and sliding away from her eyes. "As do you, Father. There are those eyes that see only the veil, and there are those eyes that pierce it. And whose eyes could I be said to have, if not yours?"

Her head tipped back. The wild woman laughed at her own joke. The old man threw a beaker at her feet, its harsh shatter ending her levity. She leaped back with a hiss, a hateful stare.

"Leave me," said the old man, yearning for his casket. "Let me have time to rest…let me have a few minutes to pretend Rorke Burningsoul is already dead."

8

WEIA! WAGA!

I AWOKE FROM the dream, which I knew was not a dream, to a surreal lurch, an urgent splash, and the sudden awareness that I had never been so cold in my entire life.

The ship, the fire.

Valeria—Elishta-bet.

I sat up, or tried, and instead lost all orientation. There was no ground upon which I might sit up: water swelled beneath me, providing but slight resistance and causing me to thrash in a panic.

The sea! By Weltyr, we had been over the sea.

And now, we were in it.

Praises be to the One-Eyed God, Skythorn was a city on the cusp of the sea, and it had not been uncommon that our teachers would bring us by the shore to splash about. By no means was I any great expert in swimming, but I could get around well enough that I did not feel the need to remove the breastplate...for now.

How far was the shore? Where were we, precisely, when we fell into the sea? How long was it until dawn reached us, and could we freeze to death in the meantime?

Were the women already dead?

Elishta-bet was the one I noticed first, her white face reflected more obviously amid the dark waves and crests of sea foam. This was ideal, because she had been on many of those shore excursions with me, and I knew her to be a far stronger swimmer than I. I wrapped my arms around her and, hearing her breath, I touched her face and shifted her shoulders until she came to with a small groan.

"Be careful," I advised her. "Be very careful, Elishta-bet, and start swimming."

"Wha—what?"

In her, I saw an emulation of my own awakening; a gasp of shock, a sudden wildness of the eyes, the clumsy jerk of the legs followed by belated kicking. Soon her arms were in motion; then, finding herself held, she pressed close to me with a frightened cry.

"Where are we? What's happened?"

"Hamsunt knocked you from the ship—and us, too. We'll be all right. We just have to find—"

A sudden splashing—and a series of startled cries—alerted us to Valeria's location not far from ours.

"Wh—Rorke? Help—"

The urgency of her cry and sharp, sudden gasp launched me into motion. Releasing Elishta-bet, I kicked through the dark to the sound of splashing and soon enough discovered long tendrils of white hair as they disappeared beneath a surging wave. I held my breath and ducked beneath, regretting my decision to not remove the breastplate when I caught Valeria's struggling hands and pulled her up in the water as I had not managed on the ship.

Soon enough, despite my encumbrances, we broke the surface together. Valeria gasped, retched, turned away to vomit a mouthful of seawater. I stroked her back, my arms around her, my relief profound. Elishta-bet splashed to our side, her expression amid the waves still terrified.

"Are you both all right?"

"Of course not," snapped Valeria, clinging to me like a frightened child. "We're going to die!"

"We're not going to die," I assured her calmly—calmly as I could, anyway. "We can find our way to land somehow."

"You can't even see in the dark well enough to realize there's no land around," she rejoined.

"The stars can steer us," Elishta-bet advised while I nodded.

"Yes, Madame, she's right. See there?"

Perhaps surprised—and somewhat mollified—by my formal address, Valeria followed my pointed finger toward the glittering sky.

As many stars as there had been in the countryside, there were infinitely more, it would seem, upon the darkened sea. The richness of their tapestry was beyond comparison to anything, save for the glory of Valeria's beauty. Interspersed among those that I knew were entire constellations that I swore to be invisible from land. Colors had deepened the complexity of night so that the darkness took on purples and blues; even tints of red, I swore.

They were miraculous, these sights. But of them all, the North Star was my focus.

"We can let the position of that star help us navigate; others, too. That there, that's Siroid—ah, and that's a planet."

A mist of slow confusion settled on my head. My brow furrowed while I scanned the sky.

Valeria, tuned to my body language in this moment of crisis, asked, "What's the matter?"

"I just can't find the moon," I told her as Elishta-bet cried out with a splash.

"Something touched me," was her bone-chilling gasp. "Rorke—"

"Help Valeria stay afloat," I advised her, certain the pampered priestess was not nearly as strong a swimmer as the sorceress. Once freed, my hand rested upon the sacred pommel of Exigence.

"And you, Madame—pray for me."

I removed the sword, its blade breaking the water to shine in the night. Then, with a great breath, I descended beneath the waves.

The saltwater stung my eyes fiercely and made opening them a tall order, as did the cold. Yet, I had little choice. Against the pain, I squinted as much as I could stand to while experimenting with the sword's resistance in the water. My swing was abated, but I could still stab with its tip like a spear.

But the motion forced some breath from my lungs, and I was forced to resurface for a gasp.

"Did you see it?"

"Not yet," I told them, only about to go under when Elishta-bet again cried out—then, Valeria.

"Rorke," cried Valeria, half a second before disappearing beneath the waves.

I did not realize she had been pulled under until, immediately after, Elishta-bet vanished just the same way.

Their names rose from my lips in a shout: oaths uttered but briefly before, taking another sharp breath, I dove beneath the waves.

The darkness was unending. I saw only the barest, briefest glimpse of something that might have been Valeria's long white hair trailing into the water. Then, it was gone.

I swam after it, the point of the sword before me cutting the water as long as I aimed it straight-on. The resistance was lessened, and my hope was heartened.

And then, a shape in my periphery distinguished itself. A darker shadow amid the cold ocean's void.

I wheeled in the water, Exigence before me. A shape like a tentacle whipped toward me from the body of the creature in the dark.

Like it was Hildolfr's spear, I stabbed Exigence at my attacker.

The mighty sword glanced off, unharmed but unharming.

Taken aback, I had few other options but to ready myself for another experimental stab as the being jetted closer.

But when its woman's face emerged from the dark, my hand faltered with surprise.

The smile that unfurled across her mouth was knowing and merry. She touched my cheek with a hand that swept through the water as mine might through air; with the same uncanny movement, she turned to stroke tenderly the length of Exigence's blade.

Then, with no indication of her intentions, the siren clutched the wrist that held the blade and dragged me to the ocean's depths.

Animal panic overwhelmed my thinking mind. I struggled against her grip but found it harder than Exigence. My legs moved to kick at hers, but I soon found she had none. Only a tremendous fish's tail that spiraled on behind us, seemingly without end.

I had no recourse. My lungs burned. My body ached with cold.

Sure I was about to die, I yielded to the urge to take a breath when I could no longer command my body's will.

Water filled my lungs with my gasp.

I'm sure of it—I felt it.

Yet, I did not drown.

My respiration continued, effortless.

Shocked, I looked at the siren who propelled us ever-farther.

She smiled at me, unspeaking. Though there was nothing malicious in her face, I found that I was frightened of her, and felt certain it was wise to be.

The fathoms down which she dragged me must have been beyond reckoning. Indeed, I had never known the ocean to be so deep, although I had been expected to memorize numbers and facts pertaining to it at one point in my schooling. Numbers simply do not provide an accurate portrayal of something's experience, however: and the experience of that long descent was one that seemed without ending until, abruptly, it was.

Something glowed in the darkness. The object was like a great, sunken crown, distorted for reasons that were not apparent to me until we grew nearer. This vast palace was sealed in some kind of bubble, I quickly realized. At the very least, the water domed up and around it, leaving the structure's crystalline surface dry as a cave.

When we broke the surface, I received another unnerving lurch. I had expected to fall down the great height, either atop or before the structure. Instead, it seemed at some point in our transit gravity itself had undergone a shift. While I flinched and gasped at the surface, I realized that the spires I had believed to touch the tip of the bubble were not spires at all. Rather, they were spiraling staircases reminiscent of great conch shells, steps carved clearly between the curved walls of the narrow shaft up. Despite having just breathed underwater without need for that queer root as had gardened the nameless man-beholder in the Nightlands, I was still eager to get ashore. I'm not embarrassed to say I threw myself upon the bottom step with relief.

While I did, the sea-maid's gay laughter chimed from behind me.

"Don't be so frightened, we will not harm you! We've brought you here to ask favors of you."

"Weia! Waga! I got here fastest."

Another maiden cried out from the distance while Valeria, already kneeling upon a platform with Elishta-bet, called my name. I cried out in relief to see them while the maiden who had guided me called, "Wagalaweia! Is it just you, Riviera?"

With a splash, the third of their number grabbed my guide and made her squeal with laughter. "I'm here too, Oceania."

"Lacryma, oh, you surprised me!"

"Heiala wala," sang the one named Lacryma, swimming around her sister. "You're always slow, but lugging this one? I guess I don't blame you. What have you told him already about our holy treasures?"

"All things in their time," Oceania told her disappointed sister. "But these are land-creatures. They cannot listen to what we'll tell them unless on their feet. Go, friend! Climb to meet your companions. We will join you in a short time."

I had many questions, but the two singing and chattering women-creatures swam off toward the column that, inverted, seemed to be a support structure rather than the tower it had first seemed to my eye. And, I confess—I was as eager to meet with my companions as they were with theirs. That muted any confusion.

When I pulled myself upon the platform and rose to my feet, I was surprised to find myself, my clothing, my armor, even Exigence all totally dry. Not a drop of water fell from my hair, but I spent little time marveling. I simply hurried up the stairs, taking the higher sets two at a time when the process began to feel too long.

And, at the great hall into which the staircase opened, I discovered my friends had hurried up theirs with the same anticipation.

"Rorke!"

Valeria and Elishta-bet appeared from their staircase, which was one of eight arranged around the sandstone room. I rushed around this strange foyer's central pool and took both women in my arms, kissing Valeria and then nearly doing the same to Elishta-bet. Her eyes showed surprise, hope, fright all in a heartbeat, and I stopped myself with an embarrassed laugh. She laughed, too, and rested her head against my shoulder while we more innocently embraced.

"Journeying with you is stranger all the time," Valeria told me, laughing in a tone far softer than the one of her recent panic. "Oh, Rorke…"

"Let's not relax too much yet," I advised her. "We have no notion of their intent. It's unwise to trust anything they tell us unless we are given verifiable proof."

Just as I finished speaking, the water in the central pool rippled and rumbled with the emergence of bodies. The women-creatures offered no reflexive gasps as did we land-dwellers. They merely shined us with those merry smiles while drawing the human portions of their bodies from the water. Clearly at home, they reclined amid the shell- and gem-dotted lounges carved from the sandstone around their pool.

As women, they were very becoming, each face prettier and each body more artfully decorated than the last. However, their forms unnerved me more than even the wajita with which Al-listux had attempted to bribe me in the Nightlands. Their lovely skin had about it a certain cold pallor that reminded one of sepulchers and tombstones; and amid the hair of Oceania I realized there thrashed the tentacles of a great squid, writhing through her mossy locks from somewhere beneath the proud miter with which she was crowned.

"We thank you for saving us," I began, addressing Oceania. "If not for you and your sisters, my friends and I would have met certain death."

The maidens looked at each other and laughed, Oceania nudging dark-haired Lacryma. Pushing deep blue locks from her shining eyes, Riviera said, "You land creatures are all the same! You rely too much on your legs."

"And we, on water." Oceania's tone was one of gentle chiding. I had the sense that she was the eldest of the three. "That is why it is best when land and water come together, sister, and serve one another's interests. It's how we were made, after all."

My ears perked. "And what is your heritage, fair maidens?"

They laughed in unison at my honorific, with Riviera answering, "Our heritage is all around! Our mother, in the palace's heart. We are the Deep-Children, making our home in our father's dark breast."

By that time in my life, I was already well-educated on a great number of myths and legends said to be precursors to the revelations of Weltyr and his Order. Among them, I knew of some creatures that were not unlike these. They brought to mind the figurehead of the *Rhinemaid*, though these watery demigoddesses were a far cry from the delicate mermaid adorning the bow of the ghost ship.

I knew they, like the Deep that was their father, were full up with darkness. Although I respected their decision to save us and then ask for our favors rather than extorting us by doing it the other way round, I still sensed with some urgency that we needed to depart as soon as was possible.

Not just for our own sakes, either. Branwen, Indra, Odile—what had become of them upon that doomed airship?

"What ho, noble Deep-Children! I am Rorke Burningsoul, and these are my companions: Her Holiness, the Materna of Roserpine, Valeria of El'ryh; and my dear friend, Elishta-bet Highwind of Skythorn. We appreciate your—"

But the maidens had stopped listening to me. On my completion of Valeria's titles, they trilled another strange melody. Lacryma, whose delicate features indicated her youth, slipped back into the water of the vast pool to surge for us with a laugh.

"We know you, Burningsoul, and better do we know Mother's attendant."

Valeria made a strangled noise, her body jolting. I glanced back at her to find she had stepped forward once, then recoiled in a great, all-consuming tremor.

"What do you mean?"

"She speaks of your prayers when she is fast asleep; you are her witness. She knows you are here."

"Don't frighten our guest, Lacryma."

"Can you three really be the daughters of Roserpine?"

Valeria's hushed tone, I should say, was not yet frightened—only befuddled, perhaps somewhat outraged. Oceania smiled on, answering her question.

"Three of them, O Pillar of the Night. Mother has many daughters: most, by sly misuse of love's strange magics."

The younger sisters hissed; Oceania's tentacles gave a little tremble. While two longer tendrils came to rest over her shoulders as did her hair, she went on.

"We once were her only children, and spent our days happy and free! In celebration, we lived; in joy, we played; in good faith, we guarded the sacred gold given to us by our father."

I and my companions shared a glance. "What gold was this?"

"Deepgold! Heaven's gold—how gaily we basked and played in its shine!"

Riviera clasped her hands to her heart. "How supple and bright our waters grew when the morning light first kissed its cheeks!"

"Merry gold," lamented Lacryma, her face a pale lily at the water's surface. "Grieved gold! That sacred pendulum, waking and sleeping again—stolen from our ecstasy, by guile misused and abused!"

"Perhaps I could help you find this gold again," I allotted, still carefully regarding the maidens. "But I may need your help in return...if it is not too late. Where you found us, were there others?"

"Only Burningsoul, the Materna, and Elishta-bet."

What did that mean? Were the others dead somewhere? With my mind transfixed by images of exploding airships and drowning elf-women, I forced myself to find another solution.

"Then perhaps, once I have done this for you, you could take us back to where you found us before you take us to land. We can look for our friends, and—"

"They will not be there," said sly Oceania. "But

we will gladly bring you back to land when the gold is again in our grasp."

Though I wished to argue, there was already no time. Currents would be sweeping away all manner of refuse from the crashed ship, bodies included. I owed it to my friends to work to save them as I had once saved myself.

And Weltyr would not have sent these saviors if they worked contrary to his will; therefore, I felt obliged to trust them.

"Who is it, then, who stole this precious gold from you and your mother?"

Lacryma shot up from the water, swimming at the surface by little more than the occasional thrash of her unseen tail. "A duplicitous wanderer; a man with no care for woman's worth, but only for gold! Only for power!"

"A father unseen," complained Riviera, "whose violent heirs shall play the central part in the destruction of the world if our gold is not returned."

"A half-blind old man," said Oceania with a sudden falling away of all her mirth. Indeed, her expression grew hard as she pondered on, "A master who is but a slave to himself, and whose fate was sealed along with fair Urd's when he took our happiness from us."

The sinking sensation in the pit of my gut was no longer just for the wellbeing of my friends.

At last, I pieced together what they were telling me.

I stepped back from the pool and set a hand upon the glittering gold of Exigence's pommel.

"You can't mean—"

"Deepgold! Deepgold!"

Tears in her eyes, lurching into motion as though no

longer able to resist the embrace of an old lover, Lacryma threw herself to the edge of the pool and made a grab for the hilt of the sword. Riviera slipped into the brine and held her back by the arms; though she, like her younger sister, sang with her eyes fixed on the gold.

"Look, sisters! See how it shines…bright as its name!"

"Its merry smile is all the memories of youth," agreed Oceania, as transfixed by the gold of Weltyr's sword as were the others.

"Heiajaheia! Heiajaheia! Wallalalala leiajahai! Deepgold, Deepgold!"

As they sang in harmony, I was startled by the emanation of light at my side. Elishta-bet gasped to see the sword shine to the very pommel. My insult mingled into dread.

"Stolen from us, broken in many pieces, used to ransom the house of a god!"

"You lie," I told them, straining to keep the derision from my tone—or to keep that derision from sounding like hope.

"Yet it glows to speak the truth! Our gold was wrested from our palace, from Mother's sacred bed! We fought him back but were too weak to battle with the daughters she had borne him in the night: the Selectrices, fighting at his command, held us back while he stole the holy treasure from our grotto!"

"Why would Weltyr commit such an offense against the goddess Roserpine?"

Valeria's question was one of many I found myself developing, but woman's universal heartbreak overflowed from it as she spoke on. "I had heard it said he vowed her half his heart; that she awaited his visits in the darkness of the underworld to which he descended with the passage of each aeon."

"Myth and mummery, he is a liar! He has not seen her since his cruel theft. He wrested from her knowledge, children, the Deepgold itself, and left us in the dark to pine for its return."

"Why would Weltyr need your gold to pay for anything?" I took another step back as Lacryma once more stretched an arm to caress the sword. "My Master is rich beyond measure."

"The ransom he paid could not have been delivered in base metals, Urd's pitiful gold! But we see you do not believe us...you may ask our mother, if you prefer."

Oceania extended a long arm toward a black corridor that had loomed on the edge of my vision but not been worth my attention until now. My friends and I stared into its abominable depths, each of us, no doubt, feeling similar reticence.

Ignoring that internal warning, I stepped toward the dark.

"Rorke—"

Valeria's stern utterance drew my attention.

At last, true fear filled her face.

"If—"

She stopped herself from completing her thought. The rich colors of her visage took on a somewhat ashen hue, and her head bowed so sharply I worried she was bound to faint. I leapt forward and caught her in my arms, but she remained standing in my embrace.

Slowly at first, then with great haste, her head shook.

"I can't," she whispered, her voice strained with fright. "I can't—Rorke, I can't."

"I understand," I told her gently, my own heart overflowing with memories of my last meeting with Hildolfr. The knowledge; the ignorance; the fear. I pressed my cheek to the top of her head, rocking her slightly in my arms. "You don't have to, Valeria."

"But—I feel so weak! I feel like a fool."

While Valeria uttered a sob, Elishta-bet put a hand on the back of her shoulder.

"If Roserpine is sacred to you," said Elishta-bet, who, like me, was tolerant of other gods and viewed them all as lesser distillations of Weltyr, "then you must be very intimidated by the idea of facing her."

"But don't you see? Don't you understand?"

When the Materna's face raised, it was more contorted with horror and grief than I knew she could feel. How she had wept when I had been forced to kill her snake! That, in retrospect, was a fraction of this.

"Don't you know what it means," she went on, her whisper wet with hysterical terror, "if I walk into that room and do—truly do, with my waking eyes—see my Lady?"

Elishta-bet and I looked at one another; Elishta-bet, in a manner somewhat less comprehending.

"Never mind," whispered Valeria. "Never mind. Only—oh! Rorke. Be careful what you ask of her."

The durrow's hands passed before her eyes. They remained there only a second. When they lifted away, her expression had regained its usual mask of control.

"You will need to ask some things. If she is Roserpine, truly Roserpine, then her knowledge exceeds the limits of mankind's imagination. All time, space, source and destiny are her purview. Assure yourself that she is as she says, but do not test the greater depths of her understanding. There are some things men are not meant to know."

I remembered Gundrygia, whispering in my ear strange secrets I could not evoke since leaving her grove. Even so, they tickled the edge of my brain whenever I reminisced about the experience.

"I will be careful," I swore to Valeria, bending to kiss her cheek and patting Elishta's shoulder as I straightened. "You two wait here…and call out to me if you need something."

The women cast a glance at the singing Deep-Children. The maidens sang on, still transfixed by the gold hilt.

My hand resting on the pommel as though for comfort, I took my first steps into the dark.

9

ROSERPINE, NIGHT-MOTHER

WERE IT NOT for the light of Exigence growing around me with the darkness, I am not certain I would have had the courage to face a goddess alone. However, with the sword's favorable reminder, I was also reminded of one solemn fact: that there is no god but the All-Father, whatever man would name Him.

Thus bolstered, I walked into the thick darkness of the corridor without fear, and I kept my eyes fixed on the path before me. Never did I waver to look behind me and see if my cohorts had disappeared along with the

Deep-Children. Only once did I pause: only to remove Exigence and hold it before me, blade-down, more brightly illuminate the gypsum walls leading me into the belly of Urd.

By this device I could see what was around me, but nothing of what lay ahead or behind me. My discomfort was profound, but I accepted the constraint and kept a loose measure of the width of the walls. If they did begin to narrow, I would consider turning around.

Instead, they remained perfect and even until, with my final step, they disappeared into a greater darkness.

My nostrils flared. It would be a lie to say my grip did not tighten on Exigence.

Yet, into that near-endless darkness, I took my first step.

<My slumber has been disturbed.>

As had Hamsunt's, the voice echoed like bubbles through water, emanating strangely from their source at the heart of the darkness. Boldly forth I stepped, Exigence still before me.

"It was not I who disturbed your slumber, Madame," I began, intending to point out that her daughters had sent me in to her. She did not require my explanation.

<No, young Wotsung; it was not you.>

The mysterious word rang in my blood. My ears and heart tuned toward the voice with more curiosity.

Valeria's warning replayed gently in my mind.

"So you must know, then, why your daughters have sent you to me."

<I have many daughters.>

As I found my way forward, Exigence's glow drew from relief a webbing so great it resembled something more akin to fisherman's nets. I lowered the sword somewhat, wondering if it was wise to look upon the speaker.

<You may look upon me, if you wish. All that was, I am; all that will be, I will become.>

I stopped where I was. Without a single spare movement, I made a slow genuflection while sliding Exigence back into its sheath.

"Your handmaiden, Valeria, has come here with me. She has assured me many times that you speak to her in dreams."

<Your thought is my dream; your dreams are my thoughts. All hear my speech. Few listen. Fewer still understand what they hear.>

"And Valeria seems to understand, if you would forgive the presumption."

<My handmaidens understand what my eldest three daughters would permit them to understand.>

Truly, that darkness was some unnatural enchantment. However long I knelt, never did my eyes adjust to see beyond the webbing. For that, I was grateful.

"Then permit me to understand what I do not, Madame. If answering my questions might yield a result favorable to you and your entourage, would you confirm some things me?"

<Woe to your innocence!>

The mournful response frightened me as the darkness had not. Valeria's sacred spirit went on, her voice as melodious as that of her daughters—yet utterly bereft of joy.

<You shall grieve this meeting for all your days, Rorke Burningsoul.>

"I do not wish to know those facts of nature that Man must not contemplate," I told her, my palms sweating, my tone gentle.

<Nonetheless, you will. Ask on, Wanderer. I will speak the truth as you would hear it.>

My heart told me to satisfy myself with her mere existence. To find another means by which to verify the tales of the Deepgold.

I wish I had.

"Is it true that this sword's hilt is of gold stolen from your kingdom's depths?"

<Dark is my home, but darker still is my heart! Blackened by the deeds of men—as the gold, taken from its home, is no longer permitted its pure, playful innocence. Wandering the world that thrills it, it is false and accursed.>

I strained to understand the meaning of all this. "Yet, if this is true, it wanders the world in Weltyr's service! Is this sword not the product of the mighty All-Father, whom, I have heard it said, you love?"

<Wise as I am, the god-ruler broke even me. I bore him a litter, the youngest of which brightens his eye as the gold once brightened this dark place. She and her sisters do his bidding, selecting from the slain to glorify his army. She is dauntless, and wise, too. Why not ask her the truths of these matters, if you fear to approach me?>

"I do not know her," I answered the goddess with great caution, easing to my feet and forcing myself toward the voice again.

<You know her already. She will not be among your three brides, but instead be the bride of the best of your sons.>

Three brides? Sons, plural.

My mind was not as quick as my mouth.

"There are sons in my future!"

<Three heirs will divide your house when your time has come.>

A strange thrill shot through me; curiosity, doubt, fear all flooded in fast after. I found myself struggling against thoughts of my death. There was no point in fearing it. I could only hope, as all men did, that I would be granted escape by the good hands of Weltyr's Selectrices.

"Never mind that, please," I said, the webbing ever clearer with my approach of the goddess. Resisting the urge to flatter myself with more prophecy, I instead asked, "The gold—why did my master take it from you?"

<In exchange for his home, the god-ruler wagered the worth of a woman. It was by her will that he came to his solution, yet her will but worked in service of his own.>

A dark silhouette had distinguished itself at the heart of the webbing. I paused again.

"There is no will that may work contrary to Weltyr's," I agreed.

<None,> the goddess countered, <but his own.>

While I puzzled over this, the spirit went on.

<Now the gold, spoiled by the All-Father's perfidious designs, rests in the hands of the builder of the Valor Hall: all save for those pieces whose instruction was delivered to the god in the pit of my love-ache.>

"What pieces are these?"

<Two such objects have been passed through the hands of mankinds,> was her surprising answer. <The

Ring—which he, out of guilt, awarded to the first of my handmaidens after seducing her with those same sultry magics he worked upon me—was a trinket of my own design, a gift in exchange for his love. By its making, I taught him the secrets of working the Deepgold, and beneath my tutelage he crafted the Sword, waking and sleeping forever. It was the prize awarded to one of his many sons; so many aeons before your birth, Wotsung, that his name would mean nothing to you now.>

"And the Lantern?"

<It was no work of mine.>

Surprising. "Yet, I have heard a fourth relic moves about Urd. Is the Casket not among their number?"

<The Casket's power came not from the gold, but from a dark force without the boundaries Urd.>

"The spirit-thieves."

<Their lead is powerful, but not at all like the gold. It never was innocent; the gold, though adulterated, cries to be made pure again.>

My jaw tightened. I rested a hand upon the pommel of Exigence.

"Yet it works in the service of Weltyr," I protested. "Is it not his will that I should have this blade? He gave it to me! Should it not work in his service until he releases it back to the Deep?"

<Pay heed! Pay heed! Pay heed, Burningsoul!>

Another surge of fear shot up my spine. I paid heed.

<Avoid the gold! Shun its luster, Wotsung! Return to Skythorn, forget this task, be gone from this curse!>

"What curse could this be?"

<Your trophy will destine the world to annihilation. A dark twilight dawns for the gods.>

"Yet it is this twilight my master beats back with the light of Exigence."

<Your master would stop a rolling wheel. You, Wotsung, are the same as the All-Father in which you place your hopes. That very sword you cherish as a sign of his holy favor will, years hence, bring about the ruin of your house. It will be the sign by which you will know death draws near.>

My mouth grew dry. I glanced down at the glowing hilt with less relish than ever before.

"How could that be?"

<None may lift Weltyr's sacred blade but the one permitted to wield it. A day will come when another's mortal hands will lift the sword. Mark this scene, Wanderer; for when it unfolds before you, your end shall be nigh.>

Cold chills shot from the back of my head to the base of my spine. Did she lie? Had not the woman on the *Rhinemaid* checked the weapon for me? Did that mean my death was nigh? Unless, of course, that woman had been immortal...unlikely. As unlikely as Roserpine lying, I sensed.

At once, I struggled to somehow forget the knowledge I had just absorbed; yet, this effort to forget only served to drive it deeper. I knew at once that I would always remember this ill-delivered information, but that I would have no proof of its truth until, as she promised, I beheld the hefting of the blade by another verifiable mortal.

"If the gold is cursed as you say," I told her carefully, my mouth dry, "is there truly no way to break this foul cycle? Can a rolling wheel *not* be stopped, O Sacred Seeress?"

To my fright, the shape of the goddess lurched forward in the darkness. Her webbing flexed, and the humanoid body at its center was launched until, enfolded in black webbings and waves of blacker hair, the goddess of the durrow dangled with her face perhaps three inches from mine.

Her beauty was impossible, irresistible, and absolutely terrifying to me. Her flesh was blacker than any durrow's; blacker than the darkness around, as though it were not a tone but instead a perceptible absence of being. Even her eyes, her teeth, her tongue beyond her lips were black, yet I detected all their shapes by the shimmer Exigence cast upon them, and I felt sure that Weltyr's love for her had not been entirely an act.

<There is but one way to alter fate, Wotsung,> Roserpine told me, her mouth moving with a voice that still seemed to echo from everywhere at once. <One way to stop the wheel. Defy the will of Weltyr and do that which he cannot: return the entire sum of the gold to me.>

My jaw tightened.

"I will return all that I can return to you and your daughters," I assured her. "But the ring, is it not valuable to your handmaidens? And this sword—I must keep it until—"

<I have warned you,> the goddess advised, receding into the darkness once again. <You know enough, yet you would know more. Ponder my truths, Wotsung! Spend your days in disquiet. All that is will end; all the gold will be returned to the Deep, whether Weltyr wills it, or not.>

The goddess fell silent.

My body thrummed with information I wished to forget.

Head lowering, I turned around and stepped, I thought, toward the tunnel that would lead me from the darkness.

"Rorke!"

Only to realize I was already upon its other side.

Valeria, rushing to me, hesitated several steps away even as Elishta-bet hurried on to my embrace. My head swam. I looked between the two of them, my mind flashing with wonder. Three wives! Three sons.

And a sword that would one day prophesize my demise.

"Are you all right? What was it like, Rorke? Did you speak with her?"

Lips numb, I nodded in late response to Valeria's eager questions.

"Yes," I said. "And she offered no tangible proof of her identity...but, having spoken with her, I do not think her to be a liar."

"The truth is self-evident," Valeria agreed, closing the distance between us with a hand that lightly touched my cheek. "Oh! Rorke—Rorke."

"Now you believe us," sang out the maidens, Oceania's voice rising above the young ones, "we have not deceived you! Bring us the gold and we'll take you to land. Help us retrieve what was stolen and renew our home with the Deepgold's bright mirth!"

"I will," I told them, nodding. "But—the friends who were aboard that ship with us. I'm worried about them."

"When we bring you to land, you'll be able to save them! Our powers are great, and though we abide in the water, we may come to the edge of any land."

"Then where is the Valor Hall's architect, the holder of the gold?"

"We will bring you to him," Lacryma swore, eagerly smiling. "But first, Burningsoul, give us a token of your good will!"

I knew what they were about to suggest a few seconds before Riviera offered it. Wearing the same patient smile as her sisters, she nodded.

"Leave us the sword," urged the middle daughter. "Permit us this scrap of Deepgold to play with in our lonely home! Then we will know you won't be tempted to withhold the price of our transport."

I could not even feign a laugh. Looking at them once at a time before settling on Oceania, I said, "But I will require Exigence if I am to wrest the gold from the clutches of its current owner, I am sure."

"A gallant warrior like you? You could use any sword to great effect! We might find you one here in the Deep; or perhaps the keeper of the gold, great smith that he is, has already crafted many such swords upon the island where he dwells alone! Pray, give us our pretty friend now—this small recompense for a far greater wound."

"But," I argued on, my tone still polite, "there are other pieces yet to be retrieved. The gold of the lantern that broke aboard the ship, for instance; and then there is the gold of Valeria's ring. Why give this small piece of it early, when we will need to search for other scraps on land?"

"Then why give the greater portion to us before

the end of time," mocked the Deep-Children, their expressions hardening against me. "That is what you will say when at last the gold is in your hands. Were it not for Mother's warnings to him, Weltyr never would have paid his debt with it! Its call is too powerful."

"Yet your mother warned me just the same, and I am but a slave to Weltyr's will. Rest assured, my word is my bond. I do not take oaths lightly: and I swear to you, O Daughters of the Deep, that I will return your gold when my task is completed. When my child is secure, in accordance to Weltyr's will."

My friends jolted against me when the Deep-Children hissed.

"Weakling," they cried, "fool! Madman! The gold has already corrupted you: wait and see. You, Wotsung, like all the rest, will fall to its curse! This world will perish! Give us the sword!"

Lacryma launched from the pool in a cold reminder of the lengths of the sirens' tails. I leapt back, pushing the women behind my body while drawing Exigence from its sheath. Only as I struck out against the swing of one clawed hand did I remember my ill-fated blow against Oceania in the waters from which she rescued me; Exigence glanced off, and their song took a furious note.

"The gold's memory of our love for it will not allow it to do us harm! Give it back, return the gold to us!"

"Let's go," I advised my friends, glancing to the nearest staircase and urging them in its direction. Much like her sister, Riviera coiled up from the water and launched herself at me. I grimaced, thrown back against the wall by her strike, but used my new proximity to hurry down the stairs after the women.

"What will we do," cried Elishta-bet, looking over her shoulder when I caught up with them. "How can we swim all that way to the surface?"

"In the Nightlands, we used a strange root to breathe underwater," advised Valeria. "Perhaps, if we look, the same stuff might grow somewhere near?"

It was a fine wish, but I felt it dubious at best. The vast bubble in which the palace dwelled had no land that I could see; no ocean floor, or anything of the sort. There was only the dark abyss, the waves held back by divine will alone.

And, when we emerged upon the platform at the base of the stairs, the Deep-Children had already hastened down into the waters. They rushed our platform, their forms gliding effortlessly through the resistance of the waves.

"Stand back," I advised both.

Valeria looked at me urgently. "You can't fight them if that sword does nothing against them, Rorke."

"Then I'll die trying," I responded, beginning a prayer to Weltyr as, her face contorted and her blue lips peeled back to reveal fangs, Oceania bolted up from the water to loom over me at a height of eleven feet or more.

Knowing it futile, I raised Exigence.

"Hojotoho! Hojotoho!"

The hissing of the Deep-Children turned away from us and toward the water walls arching up toward the palace.

My grip of the sword relaxed out of confusion.

Where had I once heard just such a battle cry?

Lacryma, taking advantage of my lull, sprang up from the waves to grab hold of the blade. The women behind me cried out.

Through the watery abyss held beyond the palace, dark figures burst free.

It was several seconds before my mind could reconcile what my eyes knew they saw.

From the baleful waters, warriors drove mighty horses across the open air as easily as anyone might urge their steeds down a road. Each beast of burden thrashed and neighed, their hooves kicking a fast beat as they thundered down into the fray. The fighters raised their spears with armored hands, calling between one another in voices merry for bloodlust.

"Hojotoho! Heiaha! Heiaha!"

The lead horse, a mighty black stallion, leapt gracefully through the Deep-Children as its rider speared Oceania through the shoulder. The maiden roared in pain and fury, clutching at the wound when the tip was jerked out to allow her blood's mingling with the water. Forgetting my sword, Lacryma rushed down into the waves and emerged again to defend her sister. Soon, she was defending herself from one of the two warriors who kept them at bay.

"Burningsoul!"

I was certain I knew that voice. I looked once over my shoulder, expecting someone on the stairs.

Then the cry came again, and I marked it was from the helmet of the warrior whose towering black horse reared to a stop at the edge of our platform.

"Hurry, Wotsung," cried this glorious rider, one hand extending. "Come with us now, before they regroup!"

My jaw hung open while my eyes searched through the grille of the warrior's gilded helmet.

Each of these riders, I understood then, was a woman.

And much as Valeria had known the truth when she found herself in the house of Roserpine, I at last understood what was happening to me.

Or, more aptly—what had already happened to all three of us when we fell from the burning wreckage of the *Rhinemaid*.

Tears filled my eyes.

I took her offered hand.

10

THE RIDE OF THE SELECTRICES

"RORKE!"

The cries of Elishta-bet and Valeria rose together, but the Selectrix was already pulling me upon the back of the horse.

"My friends," I began, silenced by the brilliant white smile that flashed through the visor.

"My sisters will take them! Come, Burningsoul, hurry!"

Riviera, her mouth a heinous length and her fangs dripping with algae, swept up from the water with me as her aim. Faster than any man I had ever seen, the Selectrix spun her body and spear to meet her opponent's hateful mandibles. Holding back the maiden's fangs with the staff of the weapon, the warrior-goddess boldly laughed, "Ha, ha, ha, ha!" and pushed her opponent back down into the waters in a show of effortless strength.

"Grimmgerde," she cried then, gesturing toward her weapon toward my friends, "here with your steed!"

"Hojotoho!"

While the next Selectrix reared her horse away from the battle and drove it toward us, the one who had saved me looked over her shoulder as much as her armor allowed. "Hold fast to me, Burningsoul. Don't let go for a second! Heiaha!"

"Rorke," cried Valeria above the wild neighing of horses, the screams and hisses and curses of the Deep-Children, the victorious calls of the Selectrices in communication through the fray, "where are you going?"

"Trust them completely," I called out to her in return.

With a great stamp of its hooves, my rider's horse galloped off across the open air and headfirst into those waters I had to remind myself led not down but up, up to the place from which the Deep-Children had kidnapped us.

My arms tightened around the Selectrix as we endured that lurching down-up sensation of coming into the abyss. I had not been ready for the impact of the water and was no more ready for the moment we submerged beneath the waves. Despite myself, I cried out and again took on a mouthful of enchanted fluid against which I coughed and sputtered.

My rider rested one consoling hand upon mine even

as her fighting arm fended off the corkscrew approach of one last Deep-Child. Bubbles streamed from Lacryma's roaring mouth as she leapt for Exigence, her clawed hands stretching for the gold of its exquisite hilt. That mouth soon contorted in a scream; the Selectrix's spear-tip had plunged through her hand and out again so quickly that I saw the maiden's face through the purple hole as our horse rushed past.

The urge to breathe irresistible, I settled into the uncomfortable pattern of inhaling the water that, each breath, forced its eager way into my lungs. By now, of course, I understood it was not truly water, and indeed I still wonder if it were not a substance closer to those waters that secure and feed the infant growing in its mother's womb. Then, I wondered a great many things, having been more chastened by the Selectrices' appearance than I had been by my conversation with Roserpine.

And I had been *truly* chastened by that.

In the dark of the abyss, the higher we rose, the more the light of Exigence's hilt faded off. I glanced down at this sacred relic, delivered to me at a time of utmost need, and found myself regretting it had ever come into my care.

My rider lifted her hand from mine and took up the reins of her horse, urging it up all the faster through the dark. As it had through the air, the beast rode unencumbered; faster than the Deep-Children swam was the speed of the Selectrix's horse. I held as tightly to her as she had advised, amazed by her stature as I was by the beast's wild gallop. A tall woman, to be certain, though I would not tell how tall until she was off her horse.

Until we reached the Valor Hall.

All the emotion that had been momentarily defeated by our urgent flight now returned with acute pain. Did the Deep-Children's wish matter now that we were on a path from which no man had returned? Did what I want matter?

Had it ever?

A grim shadow passed over me. With our rising through the murky waters concealing Roserpine's palace, I felt myself changed. Indeed, I should say that this leg of my journey was the period of the greatest shift inside myself.

Most of us experience Oppenhir's presence not at all at once, but piecemeal through our lives. Each time, his appearance—his closeness to us—becomes more acute. More pressing. Salvation from it by the grace of Weltyr is more than any man could ever dare ask, and all he *can* ask, in truth. This, this coming to the Valor Hall, was always my best possible fate.

But need it come so soon? Need it come in a way that meant my quest ended in failure? Must it have left me with so many questions unanswered? So much of the life I had hoped to experience, unlived?

Yet—there was some consolation. Not all that had been told to me by Roserpine was disturbing to my senses. There was the promise of a future in her words. Three brides, she promised me. I cleaved to this knowledge, and to that far blacker foreshadowing that the goddess had also delivered.

I have said more than once during this narrative that I have a general respect for all gods as components of Weltyr's higher will and consciousness, but I am not sure that was entirely true before my meeting with her. Not before this knowledge, as sharp as Exigence's blade, was set in my hand. There was no doubt that, as she had doomed me to, I would spend the rest of my life in the disquiet of waiting for this sign…and I have.

But she had told me in this that there would *be* a life there. There would be.

And so, I held to this knowledge as fast as I held to the Selectrix's waist, never easing; not even as we at last broke from the surface of the water and rode onward, up into the stars.

"How are you back there, brave friend!"

"Less brave than I am humbled," I answered her merry call, tempted to relieve my grip on her and instead tightening it as a response. "Thank you for rescuing us."

"It is our greatest pleasure! Nor is daily my sisters and I deliver other women—we will have a wonderful time at the feast tonight, wait and see!"

"Of that, I have no doubt…your sisters will be close behind us?"

"As close as Grane here will let them be! Ha, ha, ha, ha, ha." Her bold laugh was echoed by the horse's whinny while she patted its neck and ruffled its great mane. "None of the other horses can catch him in a race. Father gave him especially to me, the beast's holy pedigree being of his own great steed. My horse obeys none but the descendants of my father!"

"And your father is truly—"

"Of course! The Master of the Valor Hall. But you have already met him, Wotsung! That is more benefit than most heroes have to their name on the day they are taken to our home."

Tears brimmed from my eyes. I fought them back, chiding myself for boyish nonsense, my throat clearing. "I suppose that is true," I permitted, clearing my throat one more time. "Ahem—excuse me—"

"It is natural to feel the passage of fear through the body on seeing the Father in his home," said the Selectrix, gently patting my arm once again. "But it is easier with time."

"Time, yes...what I need more of. What of you, Selectrix? You have told me your horse's name, but not yours."

"My name is older than your tongue! Call me Brynhildr, friend."

"It is a pleasure to meet you," I told her, my eye at last drawn away from my sorrow, from the gilding of the armor straight before my face, and instead to the gradual development of vibrant colors from the starry sky into which we rode. "The comfort you provide is immeasurably valuable."

"That's the idea...but don't be so glum, Burningsoul! Think of these wonders so few even among the dead may behold! Look there!"

I had been looking down, at the fast-retreating abyss and its curve around whatever shadow of Urd into which my friends and I had plunged. With the Selectrix's call, I raised my head and caught the racing of a fantastic star across the sky. This glittering comet twinkled off into the distance, and as my eyes tracked it, I found the space around us all the more wonderful than that. Distant suns twinkled and shimmered, glowing like lamps outside of the atmosphere from which the impossibly fast stallion burst like it had from the ocean's surly waves. The firmament was a tapestry of vivid colors, strange gases swirling in shapes like clouds and foreign planets brilliant as diamonds all around us.

The last time I looked behind me, the black void of Urd's dead face was nearly invisible in that cold region of space.

I looked again at my rider, eager to remark on the wonder of it all to Brynhildr; but it was then that I realized the colors around us undertook a gradual shift. The vibrant reddish-pinks of the nebulae through which we sped brightened to a rich orange. As I watched, they grew brighter, still, until they resembled the vivid light of Exigence's golden hilt.

Against all reason, the remarkable horse seemed to go faster. With its increased pace, the colors hastened their transformation. I looked around in wonder, captivated by the melding of yellow into green in a great crevice of color that opened before us, high and low. This slit in the cosmos was not, I somehow perceived, a tunnel through which you or I might walk; rather, it were as though the colors themselves propelled us through a new dimension, or heralded, at least, our passage in it. The green fast faded into blue, and now into deep, mystical indigo, and merry violet, and now again that brilliant pink-red that signaled the repeating of the pattern.

On it went. My mouth hung open, my eyes fixed on the source from which all the colors streamed out around us with increasing intensity. I could not look away, and when I did manage to do so for even half a second, I could discern only that the stars had disappeared—replaced by the ever-faster flashing colors of a kind of hyper-space.

My mind swam with a euphoria, a gravity, as I had never known. A feeling of absolute submission and my miniscule nature beside the will of God came over me not as something to be feared, but as something soothing. A mighty vindication.

Brynhildr was right. This was not what all men were permitted to experience. This was my reward for my loyalty to Weltyr's will: the source of my salvation, no matter the complexities of my master's relationship to the Deepgold.

The cycling colors flashed by so quickly that they became impossible to discern from one another. Pass by pass, I began to take them in all as one: their vibrance merged to the clearest, most radiant white light ever beheld. Brynhildr cried out in girlish delight along with the neighing of her horse, which leapt forward into the crystalline heart of this brilliant radiance.

And through it we passed, alighting upon the landing docks before the Valor Hall.

That strange bridge through which we had ridden had been wonderful to behold, but nothing has or will ever fill me with the awe as did that mighty home of my Master. It swirled in the heart of a queerly vibrant space, a diamond displayed upon an ever-changing tapestry in infinite patterns of color and light. The diamond was likewise veiled in a panoply of other, smaller gems that glittered in one another's presence, each face reflected in its neighbors'. I marveled all around this net while the Selectrix urged her horse to stop, patting it affectionately before offering my forearm a similar gesture.

"You can relax now, friend! Let's stretch our legs while we wait for the others."

I obeyed, releasing her with only faint reluctance before sliding down from the back of her powerful steed. The horse, untroubled with or without my weight, waited patiently for its mistress to leap down and remove its bridle; then, at her slap of its hindquarters and her high call of command, the beast rushed off the platform to ride into what passed for a prismatic sky.

"That is truly a remarkable horse," I offered, speechless otherwise.

Laughing, Brynhildr removed her helmet and shook her wild mane of red curls free around her pauldrons.

Somehow, her beauty surprised me. I should not say that exactly; I was sure she would be beautiful, of course. But, as I have related, there are different kinds of beauty. I would have expected the Selectrices to have a hard, almost maternal beauty to them. A sternness, perhaps.

This could not have been further from the truth. Though in stature she was indeed my height, (perhaps even an inch or so taller, I could never be quite sure), her face had the glow of pure, girlish innocence. Her smile affected her every feature, her mouth and eyes curling along with the winsome furrows of sharp dimples. She was so gay that, rather than finding her very comely looks appealing as I would usually be disposed, I felt a strange flash of almost paternal desire to protect her.

And this, then, passed into a flashing simultaneity of thought. Had Roserpine not informed me that one of her daughters by Weltyr—a Selectrix—would be bride to some son of mine? Had it not been promised to me I had already met her?

And had I not already met Brynhildr—not once, but twice?

"I know you now!" Excitement bubbling from my voice such that she threw back her head to laugh at me, I continued eagerly, "You were the woman who helped me at the brothel! Not only that—you were on the ship. The stewardess! No wonder you managed to take Exigence from me when we checked our weapons!"

"Aye, friend, and fain would I have helped you in that battle 'gainst the pirate captain if Father had permitted it! Alas, it was not his will."

"And what is in his will today?"

Though she smiled sadly, I swore the twinkle did not depart her innocent eyes.

"His will today," she declared with the gentleness of a mother, "is that Rorke Burningsoul, Valeria of El'ryh, and Elishta-bet Highwind should be Selected from the fallen and brought to the Valor Hall."

My throat tightened. I nodded, knowing that no amount of pleading with this good-hearted goddess would do me the least good. She was already nobly empathetic toward my condition. In her workings, as I in mine, she was but another cog in the greater dwarvish clock that was Weltyr's universe.

There was but one with whom I might plead my case. One whose will might open the sealed doors looming over me and let me out again into the life from which I had been plucked.

"You are much too pensive, Wotsung!" I came out of my brief stupor (my eye had been caught by the warping, flashing colors around us, and the effect upon a man already in deep thought was truly mesmerizing) to find Brynhildr landing against my shoulder a punch that might have bruised me on Urd. I winced, laughing along

124

with the woman who exclaimed, "Could it be you don't trust that your friends are coming here?"

"No," I said quickly, then adding with more thought, "though I confess, I am eagerly awaiting their arrival."

"Then wait no more." The smiling goddess gestured toward the slit of bright white light that had burst us into the colorful heart of existence. "Look! Here they fly. Almost as fast as me today!"

I squinted through the chaos of the colors, through the brightness of the light. Sure as she had said, a pair of pinpoint blotches distinguished themselves from the glow. My hopes lifted until I realized two more grew out of the void. It occurred to me that a great many heroes were selected each day.

Brynhildr, excited, called out with her hands cupped round her mouth, "Hojotoho! Hojotoho! Heiaha! Helmwige, lead here!"

"Hojotoho," came the Selectrix Helmwige's merry response. "Hojotoho!"

Those pinpoints grew in size and form at a rapid rate. Soon they resembled two warrior riders, their charges a pair of men who were unfamiliar to me in all but their utterly dazed expressions. That, I could understand quite well, and I regarded them with sympathy as the Selectrices drove their horses down upon the Valor Hall's shining stones and rode them in wide circles across the vast pathway.

"Rest your steed apart from Ortlinde's," urged Brynhildr, laughing, holding her sides as the racing horses shared a look, tangled legs, and reared up against one another before their riders were off. "They fight dead men's battles!"

"Sintolt and Wittig have always been at odds," responded blonde Helmwige, laughing along as she maneuvered her horse away from silver-haired Ortlinde's. "Heiaha! Heiaha! Don't break the peace here, horse, be calm!"

"Hojotoho," Brynhildr called on, directing her oncoming sisters, "Hojotoho! Siegrune, what kept you?"

"Some men just won't die," replied a gay voice as a horse thundered past us.

When I whipped my head and body toward the sound, I was astonished. Above and below and before us, all arcing out of the light-bridge to the Valor Hall, Selectrices bore their charges joyfully into eternity. They swarmed like a cloud of wasps, all swooping down and assembling themselves at Brynhildr's direction. When the peace of a few seconds came upon us and she had heartbeats to smile at her arriving sisters, I asked her above the chorus of calls, "Which of your sisters are bringing my friends?"

"Grimmgerde," she sang, indicating the last pair that tore from the light and charged forth to the Hall, "and Whiterose! They ride neck-and-neck!"

"Hojotoho," cried the Selectrices who had all dismounted and now stood either freeing their horses or consoling their heroes, "Hojotoho! Heiaha! Heiaha!"

They waved in merry welcome, teasing their slower sisters, calling taunts and blowing kisses. To my great relief, I recognized the figures of Valeria and Elishta-bet clinging to their backs.

It is worth saying for those scholars of mystical matters studying this work for clues to their life's great mystery that, when the Selectrices rode their horses out of the void and to the Valor Hall, it appeared to me almost more a change in size than a change in depth. In some ways it seemed they grew up out of that white void, and then all at once galloped upon the cobblestones with my friends on their saddles.

Changed as we all were, it was miraculous we recognized each other.

Valeria's face, I saw when her rider's horse stopped, was covered in the shine of tears, her teeth gritting against the strength of emotion as though against a great weight she struggled to raise. Elishta-bet, normally so rosy-complexioned, clung to her aptly named Selectrix with the palest, most shaken countenance I have ever seen her bear. It were as though something inside of her had disappeared, or retreated somewhere very deep, and I realized as her Selectrix helped her dismount that she wildly shook.

Never had I been so affected by the grief of a woman, let alone two women. I saw in their reactions more open and honest reflections of the shellshocked men around us, many of whom turned wary eyes, then somewhat envious eyes upon me as Valeria fled into my arms. Elishta, with the uncanny steps of a somnambulist, followed silently behind.

"Rorke," wept Valeria, "Rorke, my dreams. My prophecies—"

The man with the sun on his neck, who would show her the stars.

Stirred, frightened, the lids of my eyes flashing with the inky features of Roserpine, I held Valeria to my heart. "I only wish it didn't have to be this way."

While I looked up to Elishta-bet, the two warriors

127

who had died fighting one another appeared to each be regarding our moment of reunion. I ignored them. My pale friend stood before us, her lips parted in wonder and fear.

"Is this real?"

"It is real, Elishta."

"But, oh—Rorke—Rorke, it can't be real—"

"It will be all right," I told her. Brynhildr swept away from us to give us privacy to speak, meeting instead with her sisters in the growing swarm at the center of the landing platform. "I swear, Elishta. We will pass through this and out the right side of it, and we will do it together."

"But—"

"You have to believe, Elishta-bet," I told her firmly. "Do you believe we can do it?"

"I—I don't know. I don't know!"

Her lips trembled. Her eyes watered. I extended an arm to her and she covered her face in her hands, leaning into my embrace along with Valeria.

"None of us are ready to be here," I told them both. "And the eternal celebration of the Valor Hall would do no service to us if we were forever grieving the lives we left behind. Therefore, Elishta, Valeria, hold onto this—this yearning to return to what we had. It will be that yearning that will let us go out from this sacred place again."

A pair of sobs drew my attention. The warriors, Sintolt and Wittig, were locked in an embrace, weeping into one another's pauldrons, at last aware of what each had cost the other. I looked away, my throat tight as I regarded the women in my arms.

Weltyr willing, by the end of this it would be revealed that I had cost my friends nothing at all.

11

RORKE, THE WOTSUNG

I REMAIN TO this day uncertain as to the precise number of Selectrices that assembled in the circular heart of the landing docks, their song rising to a joyous height as they greeted one another with slaps upon the shoulders, jostling, jeers. Brynhildr seemed particularly loved among them and joined their ranks to a mighty cheer.

All assembled, they raised their weapons in a great steeple. Though the armaments glowed brilliantly together, I have not the least doubt that the eyes of everyone were, like mine, drawn to the miraculous unfolding of the structure before us. The glittering veil across the Valor Hall's façade drew itself apart. The wall behind it unfolded like a beggar's paper rose in the hands of a child. My friends and I marveled, layer upon layer of the structure twisting away and transforming in shape until a rising portcullis at last distinguished itself.

And beyond it, a great hall that shamed the very term.

Its floor was inlaid with the material that pearl mimics in Urd's oceans; the gold inlaying it gleamed with such loveliness I might have suspected it Deepgold had not the Deepgold paid its cost; its vaulted ceiling stretched on an incredible length, high above our heads and lit by the wild licking of torches. A vast crowd flanked either side of a pathway carpeted by a substance so fine it could only have been embroidered by the daughters of Roserpine, and the faces of these courtiers were so many in number that I could not distinguish among them a single one before my eye was taken in by the next. Each, I understood, was a Selected hero; and, banging swords and shields, they greeted us with merry bellows and ancient songs of war.

I saw all of this second: only after my eye had fallen upon the pair of thrones that arose on the other side of the unfolding room. Of the two that sat upon them, I knew the one by sight alone. He had called himself Hildolfr on Urd, guiding my companions and myself into the Nightlands in the guise of a wise old man. Now, though still my senior, hints of brown crowned his skull, and the eyepatch that concealed his missing eye appeared to be a great leaf ornamented with flashes of silver. I wondered if it were from that same sacred tree from which he snapped his spear as time began; I wondered much, infinitely much.

My heart throbbed in wonder at the gleaming Court of Weltyr into which, happily calling out for us, the Selectrices marched. Heroes filtered in after and among them, often finding their rescuer and cleaving to her side; but, in our case, Brynhildr dashed into the Hall without the least trace of noble comportment, laughing like a child, her sabatons brightly clanking across the floor even before the twisting of the structure fully assembled it beneath her.

Seeing her, Weltyr smiled and rose from his throne with an arm extended. Brynhildr threw herself into his embrace, kissing his cheek and offering hers for his own fierce smack of affection. When they drew apart, he beamed down at her with fatherly pride such that I envied to have never known such a thing myself. All the father in my life had been this god before me now; who had, in journeying in disguise by my side, acted the part of mentor to his oblivious child.

"Welcome, heroes, to the Valor Hall," announced the god as, row by row, the Selectrices lesser than Brynhildr knelt before the throne.

The heroes followed suit. Valeria, having composed herself, genuflected along with them, but poor Elishta-bet nearly collapsed to her knees. I stooped quickly to catch her, then helped her weakly kneel while I lowered to her side.

"Though my heart is gladdened to behold the many fine heroes joining my Hall today, I know some of you must be chagrined. After all—is it not shameful, where you believe you are from, to make another man a victor with one's death?"

Released from her father's grasp, Brynhildr pranced down the steps from the throne to kneel at the head of her sisters, her fist earnestly upon her heart. Weltyr studied each man with great caution, speaking to each all at once.

"Shame is a measure of the world, and this Hall is not of the world. To die in battle is to die gloriously, fearlessly, as I have always intended for you. To die in battle is to make yourself offering to a greater cause—the ultimate cause. When the world ends, where will you be?"

"Fighting by your side," was the universal answer of the heroes forming that great sea on either side of us. "For the glory of Weltyr and the world!"

"You may stand," he told us, waving us to our feet. "And do not sorrow for the lives you left behind. There are limitless rewards awaiting you here! Fantastic hunts, tremendous feasts, glorious battles, your cup overflowing with wine poured by my beautiful daughters—whatever a man could ask, let his heart find it in the Valor Hall."

Uneasy to do so in the presence of the Greatest, the heroes around us slowly eased to their feet. I alone did so with confidence, permitting Valeria to help Elishta rise in my stead.

Weltyr's eye, cold blue as a wolf's, fixed upon me.

"Let him that died in service to me remain behind; I would address him alone."

My chin inclined. I swore he nearly smiled, then turned away.

"The rest of you, shocked as you are, permit the Selectrices to show you to your chambers, and take all the time you need—then, ready yourself to make merry! Tonight, we're to have a great banquet in your honor."

With the newcomers around us still dazed, the heroes filling the hall roared a wish for our joy; one or two who had been awaiting their friends called with glad hearts from the crowd, waving as they dispersed in anticipation of later reunions. The Selectrices filtered among the heroes they had brought that day, speaking with kind words and exuberant gestures that promised the glory of their new home.

Brynhildr, to my surprise, sprang lithely up to us with her red hair flowing more wildly than her horse's mane.

"What ho, Burningsoul! I'll show your friends to their rooms so I may direct you to them later. Come, heroic sisters-in-arms! Rest before the celebration—you are no doubt weary with your journey."

Valeria looked at me. "Will Rorke be safe?"

"Of course! The All-Father wishes only to speak with him in privacy."

"I don't mean from him," my mistress said with a grim nod toward the thrones.

Because it was, indeed, "thrones," plural.

I must admit that I was so captivated by Weltyr's presence in his own house that I hardly more than glanced at Anroa before Valeria's gesture. When she was pointed out, I could not look away.

It seemed every woman I was to meet on this journey was more lovely than the last. The bride of Weltyr sat with a stern expression, her flashing green eyes sweeping briefly across the exiting heroes, then upon her husband's back—then, inspiring a bolt of fear, upon me. Yet there was no doubt that her cold expression bore appreciating, and that the thunder in her face and eye might have made any mortal man briefly contemplate a few very stupid things. Branwen was her worshipper among our number, yet I confess she reminded me of Valeria in her carriage and affect; at the very least, I had the sense that either one could have struck me with a frigid little hand and yielded the same thrill.

Anroa's lip curled. I remembered I was staring.

I cleared my throat and glanced back at Valeria and Brynhildr, both of whom supported Elishta-bet with either a hand or an entire arm. Brynhildr showed her perfect teeth in a girlish guffaw of laughter, her head shaking with good-humored impatience.

"No one in the Hall is safe when Father's wife is in the mood to storm! I'd stay and watch the skirmish, but I prefer watching men make war—it's sport that's for me! Let Burningsoul weather the storm on his own."

"I'll find you soon," I promised my friends, waving in consolation as they were guided away. "Don't worry… if I survived Roserpine, I will survive this."

Of course, as they disappeared into the reducing crowd, I realized I had not survived my interaction with Roserpine. Indeed, I had not even been alive for it. I was not alive now.

Was I?

I certainly felt alive as the hall emptied around us. My heart even drummed in my ears. Patient, Weltyr waited with his eye fixed on me until all but a few still-drifting souls had left us alone. Anroa likewise waited, unblinking as a cat even when her husband abruptly bade, "You may approach, Rorke Burningsoul; be as friend to us, as we were on our journey to the Nightlands."

"Would that it were so simple! When we traveled to the Nightlands, I thought you were but a man."

"Are not all men but the vessels by which my will unfolds? At any rate, I *am* a man—and divine. Come stand before us! Greet us as you would."

Brynhildr's carefree sprint up to her father's arm renewed itself in the center of my mind. Though more reserved in my approach, I let her inspire me to do as few men dared: I approached the All-Father with my empty hand extended, and it was the device by which he pulled me to his embrace.

A new wave of tears threatened my reserve, my vision of his breastplate wavering as he drew me in to land a familiar pat upon the back of my shoulder. To be greeted by the Father! To already know the Father as a friend. Never had a friendly touch been such comfort to me. Never had I received a smile of such pride, such value, as I perceived upon Weltyr's face when I drew away.

Perhaps I would be better off calling him as he appeared to me—as Hildolfr, the man with whom I travelled. To persist in the naming of his being with that sacred label would only cause the ink of my manuscript to run with tears, and convince my death to come even sooner than its due for the sheer weight of the emotion upon my heart. I felt the same way then, and I endeavored to see him more as a terrestrial friend than as that great commander of life.

I am grateful to say that he made the task easy, saying as he released me, "Few men have the honor of saying they have died in my service; and fewer still die with my eye fixed upon them."

"You saw?"

"Aye, and your dedication to rescuing those souls to whose protection I committed you is most commendable. Not all show such valor in the fray, my friend."

As glad as I was to be called such by him, my heart burned with fury in agreement with his words. "No— some fight with dishonor, using deplorable tricks to turn the tide of battle. If you watched the battle's unfolding, then you saw it was a god who brought about my end."

My master's face tightened. His smile remained, but to a smaller extent.

"Indeed, I did. It was wily Hamsunt that cast you to your doom, along with the others."

"And now not only am I dead, but the world is sure to be in peril. The infant you charged me to protect is threatened. Is this in line with your will?"

Anroa's voice was as stern as her visage; as crystal clear as the ringing of a glass bell through the empty great hall.

"Infants are imperiled every day. Every day, fathers die and leave behind their families. You are not special, Rorke Burningsoul."

"He is," corrected Hildolfr, returning to his throne with a brisk glance at his wife. "Though one might have thought, sacred domesticity being your due, you would have more compassion for our loyal servant's aims."

"Aye—sacred domesticity, that pact which you routinely violate, is my sphere; the law is yours. I would remind you that both a lesser spheres than that which belongs to Oppenhir."

"And what is Oppenhir before my Selectrices?"

"Yes, Roserpine's whelps." At Hildolfr's slightly sharper, far more displeased look, Anroa turned her eyes askance and offered a light sniff. "Still, you taught them to respect and honor me as your wife."

"And I expect you to respect and honor those that are counted among my children."

"The Selectrices, I can honor, for if nothing else they come of godly stock." Her features tighter than ever, as though I were an insect dwelling beneath even the full attention of her disgust, Anroa slid her gaze over me and back to her husband. "I can pay no honor to the Wotsungs, the mongrels borne by that she-wolf with whom you shamed me."

"The love I show to mortals elevates them beyond mere humanity," Hildolfr corrected his wife, poised to go on until I took a gamble and interrupted the bickering of gods.

"Please—"

His eye whipped toward me. Although he was not pleased to be interrupted, he did let me go on, and I did not hesitate.

"I have heard that term many times now, and yet I still do not understand what it is. What is a Wotsung?"

My master's posture relaxed in his seat as his lips did into his smile. "A Wotsung! That is a title to be worn with the greatest pride. The man that bears it is destined to heroism: power, victory, self-knowledge in excess of any other's. Those that carry the Wotsung blood are descendants of my line—and you, Rorke Burningsoul, are but the latest among them."

I was staggered. My eyes widened to take Hildolfr in with greater clarity as I rested my hand above my heart.

"A Wotsung is—you mean—"

"The blood of a god runs in your veins, my young friend! No man on Urd could compare; not in might, and not in my love."

A dizziness overcame me such that I was forced to kneel again. My mind whipped back through time, striving to catch any trace of an early memory that had not been already well-examined.

There was nothing of the sort. My earliest memories were already of the orphanage being run by the Temple. They were of prayers, of incense, of sunlight through colored glass. After a certain point, there was not even color. Only the black wall of pre-memory, of questions and heartache, that confronted all men when they reckoned birth or death. I had always wondered—had craved on long nights to know the mother or father who had delivered me into the arms of the Temple rather than see to my care.

I had always wondered, and still did not know them or who they were. But this, this title that riled my blood and sent my heart racing, was so much more than that. It encompassed and eclipsed them, the parents who had delivered me into my master's service. Now they, like everyone else, were but instruments.

And their designer sat before me, contemplating my shock.

"If I am you descendant, All-Father, then how is it I might be killed at all?"

"For you are but mortal, Burningsoul. Born to mortal life, even with divine blood in your veins. Were it not for my fair wife's sacred fruits, we would be as liable to fall in battle as is your kind."

"And Hamsunt?"

"Hamsunt is a fire that cannot be tamed; only beaten back for a time, to spring up again elsewhere."

"No wonder you condemned him to his sorry fate in that lantern."

I had only thought aloud, but my master and his wife

looked at me queerly. Not understanding the meaning of their expressions and worried they felt I over-pressed the issue of my death, I instead took the chance for an important segue.

"But that reminds me, Master—the Deepgold."

Nostrils flaring with his exhalation, Hildolfr settled back into the embrace of his throne. Anroa threw him a dark, almost hateful look as he said, "As soon as my ravens reported your fall, I sent the Selectrices in hopes the Deep-Children would not find you...evidently, my hopes were misplaced."

"Is it true? Did you take the gold? Is this sword"—I set a hand upon its pommel—"and the lantern and much else stolen from the darkened depths of the Night-Mother's home?"

"I had no other choice."

Somehow, this admission deflated me. I had not expected him to confess the accusation to be truth in any degree—or, if he did, I expected an explanation that somehow mitigated the inglorious nature of the crime.

"But why? How is it a god such as yourself could commit a dishonorable act—stealing the gold of the very woman you bedded!"

"I confess, I did not expect to be so taken with her." Folding his hands earnestly in his lap, Hildolfr listed toward me and explained with not just patience, but a kind of tender consideration for my simple mortal nature, "But love of Roserpine was never my aim in descending to those blackened depths. It was the gold's call all along. Who had previously secured it to their name meant little to me."

"And your plan did not change? Your heart did not soften when you found your love for her?"

"His love for me was greater," Anroa rejoined. "As was his love for himself."

"When the Valor Hall was built, I was but young and reckless—not unlike you, Rorke Burningsoul." Allowing himself a slight smile, Hildolfr sat back again. "We were full of hopes for a future that seemed too far away to be of any trouble to us. It was accordingly that I bargained with Dunnun, whose mighty hammer crafted the Hall in which you stand: that is, I bargained as the man who thinks not of the debt to be repaid, but only the prize to be gained."

Still bitter after so many ages, Anroa fumed. "Fool! You promised him a sacred fruit tree—yet who among gods or men can tend them? None but me."

"I did not expect him to be so insistent...nor to try and take you from me against my will."

"But in accordance with your own laws," she reminded him, nodding at his spear.

"Yes," said Hildolfr with a wistful, almost regretful look at that same weapon resting in the crook of his elbow. "Those laws carved into this holy relic to bind mankind and Urd also bind me. I made a contract and could not break it—so, instead, I bargained. Hamsunt, hearing our quarrel, first told me then of the Deepgold's wonders. I ought to have known better than to accept his advice on the matter...but nothing else could have been done."

This explanation eased me somewhat, lacking in the needless guile that Roserpine and her children seemed to think the truth contained.

"So you used the gold to rescue Anroa from a life of enslavement."

"A life of enslavement," she reminded, "nearly

brought on by my husband's poor impulses. The future means nothing to you! It is only your amorous present, chasing this skirt or the other, that has ever concerned you."

Never having had parents of my own, I had, I am very glad to say, never endured the discomfort of being present for an argument between titans. Brynhildr had not spoken in jest—this really was a storm. I, a mere fishing boat, felt beaten between tides while Hildolfr went on.

"Yet who among all women sits by my side in this place? Who, wife, is counted among my Court? For whom have I cursed my own head, bringing up the gold from the depths and using it to pay your ransom?"

"Not all of it."

The goddess's sharp eyes fixed on me for a few contemplative seconds. When she went on, her tone was dangerously calm.

"You mock holy matrimony, whose protection concerns me greatly. This Wotsung is proof enough of it—and now I see in your heart the temptation to skirt the very laws that grant us our sacred spheres! You would do what cannot be done, and deliver this man back out of the Valor Hall...this mortal man, who is as much a slave to us as any other, whatever sword you gifted him. Is the will of your eternal wife to be worth less than that of your servant?"

Hildolfr's eye blazed with fury, his expression taut with a displeasure I seldom saw on the mild but good-natured man's face.

"Has this loyal man's will no value to you, Anroa?"

"And who engendered this will within him?" With

the derisive gesture of a long hand and her teeth bared in obvious fury, Anroa observed, "You yourself are the maker of all his quarrels and cravings—of his very life, and the weapon with which he defended it! They are *your* ambitions which fill him, Husband. Your will that rules him, just as it rules the Selectrices. The Wotsung is dead by that will. You must accept its consequences."

"Even if," I dared intrude, "Hamsunt roams free?"

With a sharp look at me, as if only just remembering I was a being capable of thought and speech, the goddess rose. Her husband rose with her out of courtesy, making no move to follow.

"What Hamsunt does is no concern of ours; he has been free since before the world began, and, being of purer stock than you, may come and go as't pleases him."

Head high, shoulders back within the rich dark fabrics of her gown, Anroa told her husband without looking at him, "Your oath, All-Father—that you will not profane your own station, nor your wife's will, by assisting the Wotsung with your favors."

"My oath," said Hildolfr with a grim study of my face. No doubt, he read my sinking heart upon it.

Anroa made no response; she simply took her gown in her hands and, lifting the hem enough to step, made her way from the great hall.

She paused only when, to their mutual surprise, Brynhildr stepped around the corner and nearly straight into her.

"Your General is there, soldier," said Anroa, waiting for the Selectrix to step aside and give her room, "as is your charge. See to the Wotsung's comfort, now…he will be as restless as his progenitor."

While Anroa strode on into the corridor, Brynhildr watched her go and slipped into the hall with us. "I fear the battle did not end well, for Anroa to seem so tranquil at its finish…"

Hildolfr lowered himself slowly into his seat while I was struck by two things about the Selectrix. One, having changed out of her armor and into a simple muslin gown with red flames embroidered around her bust, her wrists, and the hem swirling at her feet, she was infinitely more comely than she had been when smiling fresh from her helmet; and two, most remarkably—we were of the same stock.

A Wotsung! The term held so much more than explanation. It held a future: the possibility of striving against the impossible.

How many generations removed were we from one another? I could not fathom it, only to suppose that the Selectrices were some distant great-aunts of mine. This thought swelled others, warm comforts long-delayed to the boy I had once been.

All along, I'd had a family. Better still, a family separated by not near as much as I thought. I had spent all these years assuming I had been separated by those of my bloodline by impassable leagues, by journeys I would never manage to undertake; instead, the veil of eternity was all that had held my family from me. Where once my loneliness had sometimes felt some sort of trial— even a punishment—now I understood that the forces at work were inherently divine in more ways than just my master's will. The childhood experience of a mother and father, they were not and had never been for me.

But, still, I wondered. What of those two? Who

were they, and why had they done with me as they had? I daresay the wondering became more acute in that instant than it had been in even the darkest nights of my boyhood.

At her father's throne, Brynhildr knelt with that same familiar air and clasped Hildolfr's hand. He stirred enough from grim thoughts to look at her, then at me while she asked, "What transpired on the field tonight, Father? How despondent you look!"

"I have been tangled in a web of my own weaving," said Hildolfr, his words slow and pained. "No man is less free than I."

"You frighten me, Father—tell me, please, what is the matter?"

He focused once again on her, lingering upon her earnest gaze for an uncountable time. When he moved, it was only to fondly stroke her hair back from her shining face.

"Do I weaken my will by speech?"

"Who am I, Father, if not your will? Who are we both, we servants to your glory?"

"Yes," said the god, now more to himself than to us. "Yes, Daughter—in speaking to you, I speak only to myself. And you, Wotsung, are a loyal instrument just the same. Yet...how might I create a truly free man? How can a man accomplish what the gods are forbidden to do?"

I did not know how anyone could answer that question, but wise Brynhildr asked on, "What could possibly be forbidden you, O Mightiest?"

"Those same contracts that once gave me power now make me a slave. I am helpless to rectify those accursed deeds that, in the guile of youth, I treacherously performed in the service of ultimate power. Ages hence, I took sacred gold from the house of a goddess and her children—that very same goddess who bore me you, Brynhildr. Most favored among all my children."

She glowed with her smile, leaning her cheek against his hand as he went on with great solemnity, "It was delivered up to Dunnun, the great craftsman who devised the Valor Hall…and yet, the curse it holds for having left its home is great enough to bring about the ending of the world. The deaths of gods."

"But how could that be? For this very reason we bring heroes to fight in your name!"

"Indeed, for this reason. For the prophesied end that will enact a curse upon all mankind if the tainted gold is not returned. Loose in the world, whoever wields it could bring against Urd all number of unnatural armies hateful to my sight: empty of consciousness, but full of the hunger for life."

"Spirit-thieves," I asked, earning a deepening of the god's grim expression.

"By many names and forms, the forces of evil are called…and with them, comes the ending of our reign."

I stepped forward, a hand on my heart. "How could such a thing be possible?"

"Such is the enormity of the Deepgold's curse. It must be returned, and yet I am as powerless to accomplish the deed as I am to send a dead man to the task in my stead."

"But how could you be powerless?" Her eyes aglow with delight, Brynhildr said eagerly, "Fly to Dunnun's home and take the spear to him! He'll yield the gold in an instant."

"But he with whom I entered contract is just the man against which I'm powerless. I know precisely the island upon which he dwells with his hoard, yet to set foot upon it with intent of wresting his prize from him would sap from me all the royal rights that this same staff"—he gestured the spear in his elbow—"grants me by the runes carved in its wood. My strength would be annihilated; the curse would be enacted irrevocably."

Brynhildr's brow furrowed, the expression of worry unnatural on her face. "Then what could possibly be done to abate it?"

"I have devised a scheme of such cunning that not even Hamsunt himself could have concocted it," answered the All-Father, his tone low and secretive but bold with purpose. "A man might do what a god cannot, taking those actions which I must shun and which I have never told him to take. Such a hero would be a man so free that one might think us at profound odds! Yet how could I create a man who acts in opposition to my will? Where is there a man who, liberated, makes himself closest to me by defiance? What man, in doing what he wants, does what I want but cannot? Alas!"

Hildolfr's hand raised to his face, shielding his eye with the heftiness of his sigh.

"In all my creations," he said, his tone warped by emotion, "I see nothing but myself. I am alone: there is no way out for the gods. All I make are slaves. The free man must create himself, and with that same accursed Deepgold that confines me could even free himself from death if he so willed it."

Never before had I experienced the feeling of such incalculable conflict. I craved to be that free man: the commissioner of those deeds that my master, bound by his own laws, could not afford to enact. And yet—I *would* be at odds with him.

My eye was caught by the spear in his elbow. Strife, breaking in my hands.

To whom do you owe your fealty?

"But what of the Wotsung," Brynhildr went on, gesturing toward me with great passion. "Surely his deeds are his own, if any man's could be considered such."

"Yet I am helpless to protect him against those same laws! Here he stands before us, unable to leave the Valor Hall until the final battle." Hildolfr shook his head, disgusted as he said, "How simply Anroa bested me; how chained I am. But, I must accede to her will. I cannot help you, Rorke Burningsoul. That which is dead must stay dead."

"I have heard it said that even death itself may be bested," I told him and Brynhildr both. "Surely, if the Selectrices's mounts may ride into the Valor Hall, they ride out again just as well."

"And yet they, too, are subject to my will, and never before have I commanded that they should take out of the Valor Hall what they brought in." The enthusiastic hope that had momentarily brightened Brynhildr's features slipped away again. Her father went on, "Even you, Brynhildr, are a slave to me—an impulse of my thought. What sorrow!"

Pushing his daughter back, Hildolfr rose to his feet and took the spear in his hand. He regarded it with contempt, speaking no longer to us, but to it. To something, perhaps, within himself.

"What useless vanity, this hateful life! What burden,

this godly grandeur that does me no good but leaves me bound instead to those fates I find most detestable! I must sacrifice that which I love, yielding to my wife's harsh will which itself bends only to these stifling laws. I must accept that I cannot create a man who is free. Instead, I watch placidly as the world marches onward to annihilation. How I long to disown this empty work! How I crave one thing: Destruction! Liberation! There is no such thing as freedom for a god. There is only isolation, the high mountain-spire that constrains all motion but descent. You are dead now, Wotsung."

Turning away to stride after his wife in a baleful cloud, Hildolfr called, "We must all accept our fates."

Brynhildr took a step after him before stopping in her tracks, her shoulders slumping beneath her wild hair. I bit back my bitter disappointment, the walls closing in around me—almost literally, I discovered when I realized the vast portcullis to the Valor Hall had sealed itself shut again.

Perhaps I was wrong. Perhaps it was an act of insane, even dangerous arrogance to believe that I, whatever my blood, was worthy of going out from death once I experienced it. I swore to Elishta-bet and Valeria that the will to leave this place would alone ensure our escape, but for a few seconds I wondered if I should have said such a thing. Had I raised their hopes only to see them more violently dashed?

"I have never seen Father in such a way," said Brynhildr in soft concern, studying the empty doorway through which the gods had departed. "How heavily this matter weighs on his mind! How much you must mean to him, Burningsoul."

"All this time, he has helped me so much—I never understood why. Not before today. How could I dare ask him for more than those gifts he has already given me, my very life and bodily form counted so explicitly among them?"

"Yet it would seem to me he would give you still more, or permit you attain for yourself that which he could not give you—were it not, of course, that you found yourself here."

The Selectrix glanced down at her sandals. When she looked up at me, I swore her face flashed with determination before settling into hospitable kindness.

"But, my father is right. I must see to your comfort here in the Hall. Come along, Wotsung—the feast is nigh, and you must be eager to see your friends. Let's see…where should we start?"

12

REUNITED

I HAVE HEARD it said the Valor Hall is infinite in its dimensions, and surely it must be to accommodate as many heroes as have been and will be Selected in Urd's lifetime. Yet there was an obvious paradox, as it was possible to move between points as though it were a mere finite structure nested within the laws of space and time.

This seemed to be partially due to the perpetually unfolding nature of the structure. Occasionally, when rounding a corner by Brynhildr's side, I would just glimpse the stones of the corridor far ahead of us twisting into shapes suitable for pedestrians. Stairs assembled themselves brick by brick, or collapsed down into a ramp that might open to any number of potential directions.

Yet, without hesitation, Brynhildr knew the way. I marveled at her, her confidence, and could not imagine ever coming to know an infinite space as well as she.

"Tell me, noble Selectrix: How does one come to navigate a structure such as this?"

"The Hall itself is privy to the contents of men's wills, great and small. It will bring them where they are meant to be; where they are called in their best interest, as your friends now call to you."

I looked significantly at the profile of her smiling face. That smile faded as I asked, "Then does the Hall not know the greater calling in my breast? That my friends call me not just for companionship, but to be saved?"

Though her expression had grown more reserved, she wore this solemnity in a spirit far gentler than I had seen from her parents or stepmother. "Yes," she confessed softly, "the Hall feels that, as well. Yet, being but machine of Dunnun's crafting, it is bound by the same laws that hold my father. It cannot set you free."

The free man must create himself.

With Hildolfr's lament still ringing through me, I noted, "Were our shared master not bound by these constrictions, it seems his will would differ in a great many ways."

"His will is constant, in spite of his restrictions."

"I observed that, as well." To our right, we passed the wide-flung doors of a sprawling banquet hall. The kitchen on the other side emanated scents and sounds that made me realize how famished I was; then, recalling my nursery tales, I wondered if it was wise to eat or drink anything I was to be offered. "But what of the Deepgold's curse? Can it be abated?"

The Selectrix's teeth sank into her underlip, her gaze distant as we passed the banquet hall altogether.

"I fear its power," she confessed. "Never in all my days has my father looked so afraid—so despairing."

"Then is it not the duty of loyal servants to ease their master's despair?"

"Would that it were such a simple matter…but there are penalties to be paid when the law is bucked."

"Yet I have no contract with Dunnun," I pointed out, adding with a light touch of Exigence's pommel, "and I wield a sword granted me by our Father's will. A sword of that same cursed Deepgold, no less. Surely, if any man is meant to relieve the gods of this curse, it is I."

"Perhaps, Burningsoul…but, know this."

Brynhildr stopped in the hall, staring grimly into my eye. The shining blue of hers was so startling beneath her red waves of hair that my heart froze.

"The sullied gold, corrupted by its theft, is not a thing easily resisted by mankinds. There is no metal as valuable in all existence. Not even in the walls of the Valor Hall. If you were to find yourself on Dunnun's island—which could be found only by flying Grane far north of the forest on the other side of Anroa's gardens— and you succeeded in defeating a god, would you have the strength to throw away that substance which makes gods blush in envy? That poison for which my father pines still, even knowing its deadliness?"

I realized what she had told me and committed it to memory while casually saying, "Perhaps, then, you might fly your fabled horse to Dunnun and take him in battle. I have no question a Selectrix is a match for any deity—especially one that has not enjoyed Anroa's sacred fruits since his isolation."

"Yet I, too, am bound, Burningsoul. Those laws that bind my father and this house also bind me. Dunnun has broken no contract. I have no recourse by which to challenge him."

"But—are you not your father's will? Are you not loyal to him and his will, above any laws that restrain him?"

The warrior-goddess looked at me in some surprise, her lips parting.

"Rorke?"

Elishta-bet's voice from the end of the corridor drew my attention away. As Brynhildr turned her conflicted face away, my friend dashed toward us and threw herself, still trembling, into my arms.

"Very good," said Brynhildr, that smile once again settled upon her lips. "You have found one another! The Hall always knows, you see…poor Elishta-bet, how she shakes! Perhaps a walk in the gardens would do well for her condition."

"Is it worth asking where they are?"

Laughing at my jest, Brynhildr punched me merrily in the back of the shoulder. I clenched my teeth to avoid losing my smile at the explosion of pain. "Ha, ha, ha, ha! When it's time for you to enjoy them, they'll find you! I'll see you at the feast later, friend."

With a gentler pat of Elishta's arm, the Selectrix turned back the way she'd come and hurried off with her face toward her sandals.

Had I succeeded in deepening the doubts that obviously plagued her? Why had she told me the location of Dunnun's island in such clear terms?

If I stole a sacred horse and did my master's will, would I be punished or rewarded?

Infinite questions rotated through my mind while Elishta, at last releasing me from her embrace, begged to know, "What did you and Weltyr discuss?"

"The better question is "What did Weltyr and his wife discuss,"" I jibbed, lightly smiling. "Where is Valeria housed? Perhaps I could tell you both at the same time."

A strange look came across my dear friend's pretty features. Averting her eyes, Elishta-bet asked, "You are—fond of her, aren't you."

"I love Valeria dearly. Her presence in my life is a gift from Weltyr, himself."

Nodding slightly, Elishta examined her own hands; then, after producing a wet little gasp, she exclaimed, "Oh, this trembling won't stop!"

"Poor doe! Come along." My hand fit to the small of her back, warm through the layers of her traveling clothes, and she started like a wild animal. "I think perhaps, rather than a walk, it would be better if you sat down awhile...where did the Selectrix house you?"

In the matter of a minute, I had guided my overwrought friend to her new—hopefully, temporary—chambers. When I realized Brynhildr had departed before showing me to my own, I was given brief pause. Then it occurred to me that, if Valeria was in fact destined to be my wife, her chamber may well have been the same as mine. Even Elishta's seemed large enough to comfortably stay two people, with a sprawling bed, a vast window that

155

overlooked the impossible gardens I had heard so much about, and a pleasant sitting area beneath this exquisite view. Overcome by the rolling waves of green orchards and curated flowers, I helped my friend into the longue and sat at its foot.

"I just can't believe it," she lamented, one hand upon her eyes. "Dead! Why did I ever think I could leave Skythorn?"

"Better to die adventuring than sitting at home, in my estimate."

"That's very easy for you to say, Rorke. You've always been so brave." From somewhere discreet on her person, she had acquired a kerchief with which she blotted her eyes. Now she wrung it in her hands with a tearful gasp. "I thought that maybe I could be brave like you always are—that I could get away from Zweiding. Now I think I was meant to stay with him, and bear all the—"

"Don't say such things about yourself!"

She looked at me, as stricken as I was surprised.

"No one deserves to be bound to such a hateful man as that. When I bested him in the duel, he showed me a side of himself I will never be able to forget."

Elishta's eyes widened. She sat up in her seat, pushing herself up with one splayed hand while the other clutched the kerchief to her breast.

"You bested him?"

It occurred to me just then how much had happened in the past twenty-four hours, (if hours could be said to mean anything in the Hall), and how truly overwhelmed poor Elishta must have felt. She had not even been there to see the duel, having been in the process of cutting off her hair, disguising herself as a boy, and stowing away in the *Battle Swan*. To her, the journey had been one of almost immediate disaster and death. After all this trouble and bad news, I did not fault her surprise that a sliver of good news could still come to her heart.

Though it only ached her all the more in the moment, her demeanor collapsing into inconsolable sobs.

"I didn't have to leave at all," she said amid her weeping, only when prompted. "I didn't have to do any of this. Oh! I cut my hair, all my beautiful hair…"

"You are still perfectly beautiful, Elishta. Hair can grow back."

Her head slowly shook, her hands balling into fists against her eyes.

"It can't, Rorke. It never will again. Not *really*."

Nostrils flaring, I rested a hand on the one she let drop into her lap. She gripped me with desperation, her eyes rolling against the onslaught of grief.

I knew what she felt. Half of me was wracked with sorrow in every silence between spoken words. My throat tightened at odd moments, and my mind seemed to crave an endless investigation of the memories that led to the arrival of the Selectrices. Inside myself I was engaged in a quest to remember that exact moment that "it" happened, knowing the task to be futile.

I could only pray my external quest would not be so destined for failure.

"I think there may be a way, Elishta. I told you before, hold onto your hope—and I mean it still."

"How can you? Rorke!"

Through her tears, my friend laughed at me and shook her head. Her hand tightened in mine.

"You've always been so optimistic," she went on, her

lips quivering with repressed tears as she forced herself to speak. "I've never met anyone who meets with failure and moves on as gracefully as you do."

"What else is there to do but move on?"

"Surely some failures must be insurmountable."

Despite myself, I smiled. "I am afraid to say, Elishta, that you and I feel very differently on this matter. Even in this, our situation at-hand—there may be a way for us to flee this place, although I am not yet sure of the precise means."

Although her look remained skeptical, she composed herself with a little sniff and a few thoughtful daubs of her handkerchief against her eye.

"What means are these?"

"The sacred gold of the Deep-Children and their chthonic mother. It dwells in Dunnun's hoard, far on the other side of the forest that ends Anroa's gardens in ocean."

Her eyes widened. "But isn't he a god?"

"There is no god but Weltyr," I told her, choosing for now to keep my information on my heritage to myself. "The rest of his court may be powerful, but they are as his reflections in a shattered mirror."

Exhaling, Elishta seemed to settle into a greater calm. "I suppose that's true."

"No matter how great Dunnun's powers are, they are stunted. He lacks Anroa's sacred fruit that, eaten daily, immortalizes the divine courtiers in battle. Between that advantage, and this holy relic"—I set hand upon the sword at my hip—"granted to me as a miraculous sign just before the duel to free you, I am sure to be the one to liberate the gold...and Weltyr said himself that the Deepgold could be used to free a man from death."

"But, Rorke—if you're to liberate the gold and return it to the Deep-Children, how will you use it to save us?"

"That is where I am unclear," I confessed softly. "Perhaps Weltyr meant its delivery would buy our freedom. That we would be permitted to pass out of the Valor Hall and back to our home as a reward. Perhaps the act will soften Anroa's hard heart, and she will allow our master to rescind the vow he took to keep us in the Hall."

Elishta gasped sadly. "Oh, Rorke, did he really vow such a thing?"

"He did," I said warily, "and he is the master of contracts, vows—all honorable doings. Yet I see now that his heart is more complex than that. He is not a blindly-going piece of engineering, nor the engineer. He is the operator at the heart of the machine, drawn to its center because it exists and seeing to its existence by his operation. Each exists because of the other, and nothing has ever been different...but it seems, if the Deepgold is not returned to its owners, something may happen to imbalance that coexistence. To destroy—everything."

My friend grew all the paler. "What will happen?"

I shook my head. "Don't worry about that, Elishta. I tell you this only to console you in your fright—and to show you that, whatever it does or does not earn us, returning the Deepgold is something that *must* be done. Weltyr, bound by his contract, cannot do it."

"I see."

Her lips pursed. Studying our hands together, Elishta sat in the silence with me for a long time, and

I did not press her for her thoughts because I was still processing all these things, myself.

What was right? What was right to do? Was it better to enact my master's will, or to defer to those laws that bound him and all lesser beings—myself included?

When Elishta drew me from my thoughts with the soft utterance of my name, I was surprised to find some color had returned to her face. Her pupils grew on contact with mine and, that blush deepening, she looked quickly away from me.

"Rorke, I—I have a strange question."

"What's that?"

"You don't have to answer, if you don't want to, but...well...I thought—that is, in the *Battle Swan*..."

By now the very tips of her nose and ears had grown bright red. I cleared my throat, one particular memory leaping to the forefront of my mind. "Yes?"

"I thought that I saw you with that druid...that Branwen woman. But it's Valeria whom you love? I'm confused."

"So am I," I admitted with a laugh, mulling over Roserpine's prophecy again. Three brides...but which women in my life, if any, would be among that number? As things were shaping up now, I had found myself assuming the number to be concurrent when in fact it could have been successive; other, future women I had not yet met. This seemed unlikely, but I could not imagine, from among my companions, which three would be so dear to me above the rest. Valeria, yes—I craved more than anything to woo Valeria away from her ring, her culture, even her goddess if required, and I confess the desire to do so became more intense as the days of our journey went on.

But which women among the rest fit so well within my heart? Indra, Odile, Branwen?

A singing, thrashing, moaning wild woman flashed before my eyes.

Surely Gundrygia could not be made a bride... could she?

"Valeria and I became very important to one another in the Nightlands," I explained to Elishta-bet as politely as I could, shaking off the haunting vision. "Her power there permitted her the keeping of multitudinous slaves as it pleased her, but she believes her prophetic dreams indicate I am significant to her."

"Is that what she meant about the stars..."

I nodded, going on. "But durrow women have a very different culture than yours and mine, Elishta. It prioritizes sensuality above all things, I would say... and in some ways, we are still sorting our relationship out. Mutual love between men and women is not their custom; nor is exclusivity in pleasurable doings."

"Oh, my."

"Yes, it was all quite surprising when I was there, I assure you..."

"But what of marriage?"

"They have none that I know of."

Elishta looked baffled—then, in a way of foxy fascination, quite intrigued. "But...what of their men?"

"They have none. Durrow bring forth women only, their male equivalent being unnatural creatures created by a witch now flown far from here."

"What a strange thing to say!"

"It is true—I know her well." Unable to help myself, I sighed. My gaze fixed out the window, far across the gardens, seeking for the forest on the horizon but unable to see any sign of it. "She is exquisite. A mesmerizing being, Elishta, and I am but a man. I yielded to her charms and now—now, she has absconded with my unborn child, or so she claims."

My friend's jaw dropped. "Rorke Burningsoul!"

"One never can tell when such a thing is fated to occur...but that was why we went aboard the *Battle Swan*, you see. We are intent on tracking her down, either before or after we find a certain lost ring for Valeria—but, obviously, there are some other priorities first."

"What will you do when you find her? The witch?"

"Nothing good comes of thinking too far ahead, I find, Elishta...but, when I find her, I hope I will manage to subdue her without doing harm."

Shaking her head, then glancing out the window with a soft laugh of incredulity, Elishta pulled her blue cloak tight while worrying her thumb along its edge.

"What a strange life you lead, Rorke...I wish my adventuring had been half so intriguing. Although, if intrigue came to me, I'm afraid I wouldn't know how to greet it."

"You have always been shy, Elishta, but it's true that the life I lead is not for everyone. Neither is having so many lovers! Trust me when I say it's a matter of stamina."

With the freest laugh I had heard from her in years and a light slap on my chest, Elishta sat up to protest, "Stop, you braggart...you're just a handsome flirt with good luck."

"Handsome, I'll take...but a flirt!"

"Yes," she went on, laughing. "A flirt! Why—"

Half a second of hesitation while her eyes darted toward the window.

"—before I was sent off to the nunnery, I must have watched you banter with every woman but me!"

Elishta-bet!

Now her strange glances at me on my return to the Temple made greater sense—and so did this conversation. There was longing in her face, in her voice, whenever she spoke to me of private matters.

Somehow, I had not seen it. Not because she was not beautiful to me, but because our friendship extended back so far that the development of our love seemed very innocent. And, though we were adults, and though this was a different kind of love, it still held innocent resonance. I had not seen it, but now I could, and I am not sure I have ever felt a bigger idiot.

I squeezed her hand, waiting for her reluctant eye to catch mine again.

"If you wanted me to flirt with you, Elishta, you could have just asked."

Blanched all the more by this new surprise, Elishta-bet uttered the trill of another nervous laugh and shook her head. "No, I—I wouldn't *want* you to flirt with me, of course! It would be embarrassing."

"Why is that?"

"Because I don't know how to flirt back! And, anyway...to what end?"

She was truly among the most endearing of women. I permitted myself a chuckle, not wanting to truly laugh, lest she be insulted. "You seem to be doing just fine at it now," I assured her, patting the back of her hand. "And as far as the end, well—whatever end pleases you."

"I—I can't just—it's not so *easy* for a woman, Rorke! Not aboveground, anyway."

163

"Of course not…but I would think it easier now that you are free of Zweiding. Moreover, no longer beholden to the Temple." At the nervous thinning of her lips in thought, I asked, "Have I offended you?"

"No, not that! Nothing like that. It's just…it's strange to find myself here when I was by my own hand excommunicated."

"Weltyr values the soul of a hero," I assured her with confidence, "and not the obedience of a hero."

Nodding, Elishta said, "I suppose that is true."

Again, she lapsed into silence. In the gap of sound I basked in the tranquil pool of her face, closed off while her mind whirred with wild thoughts. She was right to think it a pity she had cut her hair, but her beauty was not in her hair. It was in everything about her. In her face and eyes and voice; and in her gentle, kindly nature. How a creature so fragile, so dear-hearted, could be abused by the very Temple we once served was utterly beyond me.

I was more grateful than ever that Weltyr had awoken me from my somnambulistic obedience to institutions I had not truly understood.

"We are blessed to be here in many ways," I told her, stirring her from her thoughts again. "To be Selected is beyond a great honor. It is the truest form of immortality—the only form that matters."

She nodded.

"And there are other benefits. Here together, there's more freedom to be had. What room is there for shame or guilt when our frail bodies are dead on Urd?"

That sweet coloration returned to her cheeks. Biting her lip, Elishta said, "Maybe so, but there's still—the strangeness of it."

"Of what?"

Her eyes rolled and she shyly laughed. "Of being with a man for the first time."

Though I should have known this, and I think I did on some level sense this fact about her, I was still so used to my more licentious companions that I was shocked.

"You're still a virgin?"

Elishta nodded. "Of course. Would you believe I spent all this time waiting for marriage...oh!" She made a little hiccup that sounded like a sob crossed with a laugh. Her eyes shut and she pressed the crumpled handkerchief to her brow. "It's so silly now."

"Hardly silly! I admire it. I admire you, Elishta-bet."

Enfolding her small hand in both of mine, I told her earnestly, "I always have."

The slight part of her lips accented her beauty and made me crave to kiss her—but I also knew that Elishta was not at all like the women who had aided me to this point of my journey. She was as powerful as they were; I had no more doubt of that. But her spirit was meek and chaste, and her love, which must have seemed improper to a young woman once called down the path of the nun, was buried so deeply within her that I feared harming her in its pursuit.

The Valor Hall must have known my heart, for the sounds of merriness echoing in the corridor gave me a polite excuse to relieve the pressure. Either that, or leave her to counsel her own heart and mind on the propositions somewhat ambiguously floated between us.

"It sounds like the banquet-goers begin to gather. Perhaps it would do you well to be among celebrants, rather than sitting here brooding on matters that will only upset you more."

My gentle friend slowly shook her head. "No," she said after a few seconds of thought. "No, Rorke, I don't think I'd ought to. All those people—they'll frighten me. More than I'm already frightened."

"Then be at peace here and I will check on you—when?"

"In the morning," said Elishta-bet.

I bent over her hand and kissed it.

"In the morning," I agreed, patting the back of her hand. "And in the meantime...I cannot say for certain because I have not met with her yet, but I may spend time with Valeria. Would that bother you?"

She looked at me as though surprised I would ask her. Then, blushing, she shook her head. "No, Rorke. I—I don't mean to come between you."

"Perish the thought. Once Valeria comes to know you, you won't feel between us, but alongside us. Rest easy, Elishta, and we'll talk more tomorrow."

When I left, we linked eyes for but a second. Just before the door erased my view of her face, I swore she began to smile.

13

THE QUEEN OF HEAVEN

DISORIENTING THOUGH THE eternally unfolding Hall was to mortal senses, I did not find it difficult to discern the way back to the banquet. The corridor was already populated with clusters of men who, laughing and sometimes singing battle songs in languages I did not know, streamed toward the nightly celebration that was but one of many perceived aspects of their eternal reward. Others could not be perceived: like the impossible relief that annihilated the need for faith as it was on Urd and transformed it into the great, open, factual knowingness of the hereafter.

Yet, as I watched a few men pass me with happy nods my way, never breaking their banter or songs or old war stories recited to the endless delighting of their comrades, my soul grew sick with fear.

What might happen to me if I ever did leave this place?

If I succeeded in going out of the Valor Hall, would I someday be allowed back in?

It was not for a lack of joy that I desired to leave. At every turn, my senses were delighted. A pair of Selectrices, their streaming hair vibrantly colored as a flower bed or the glorious rainbow around the Hall, flanked the doors to smilingly announce each hero in his turn, and each seemed to go with great confidence to his place at the three sprawling tables I sensed to be of the same covert infinity as the Hall. Those diners already seated called out with glee to those passing by whom they recognized, and the central table itself stretched by lengths I could not believe.

Only two men were flustered as to where to sit, and but briefly.

"Sintolt the Hegeling," called out one Selectrix, her sister shortly thereafter crying, "Wittig the Irming!"

Each man hesitated for a moment, looking dumbly around, until someone bellowed Sintolt's name from the leftmost table. The newly Selected hero cried out in recognition and said something to Wittig, who, after only a second's hesitation, followed him over.

The line moved smoothly from there. I wondered where I would sit and, growing closer, eyed the central table's distant head. There I perceived Weltyr, whose cup was filled by his smiling daughter while she chatted gaily with some hero already at his right.

For but a moment I looked with surprise on that hero, unable to make out their face from the distance as well as I could my master's. It was not the personage that surprised me, but their mortality. I had expected Anroa to fill that seat.

Instead, to my surprise, (lacking as I did any understanding of formal dining arrangements), the god-wife filled the seat at the table's foot. In this position closest to the door, all celebrants were forced to pass her on their ways to sit. Each man passing by either side paused dutifully beside her to genuflect and salute her majesty. Then, on they went.

I had just observed this custom clearly when the Selectrix to my right, her brilliant blue hair tinted with white like the ridge of the sky on the horizon, touched the back of my shoulder to welcome me in and, surprising me, called out, "Rorke the Wotsung!"

Anroa turned in her seat, fixing me with her hard stare.

Noting the empty seat to her right and wondering who was permitted to fill it, I paused. As the others had, I genuflected beside her and rested my hand on my heart for but a cursory beat or two.

"Hail Anroa, Mother of Heaven and Bride of Weltyr."

"I am pleased you know the value of respect, Wotsung," she said without really looking at me, having already settled back in her seat to raise her goblet to her lips. With a lazy gesture of her free hand as I stood and made to move on, she commanded me in the tone of suggestion, "Sit."

I nodded down at the empty chair while some other heroes passed us by. "Here?"

"You have someplace better to sit than at the arm of a god?"

"Of course not, Your Radiance" I answered her, grateful in an instant for my experiences as Valeria's servant. Knowing I was unserved by bravado in such a time, I slid the chair from the table and lowered obediently into a place of honor I could not help but suspect was either some peace offering to Weltyr, (who eyed us but briefly before re-engaging with the guests around him), or some effort to intimidate me, or both. "I'm only surprised you would invite the company of a humble man such as myself."

"If there is one thing I can tell you are not, Wotsung, it is humble...that is but a small part of your divine lineage."

With that same golden hand, Anroa caught the attention of a nearby Selectrix (Whiterose—I recognized her as Elishta's rider and exchanged a smile with her on her coming) to see my cup was filled. "How calm you seem," the goddess observed of me, drawing my attention back before I could exchange the least pleasantry with the angel that was clearly regarded by her as a servant. "Many heroes are more overwhelmed by their arrivals here."

"I am indeed overwhelmed, and by a great many things...but most of all, I am overwhelmed by love, and gratitude. And I *am*, if you would forgive my impudence in disagreeing with you, humbled to have been brought into the Valor Hall. These things outweigh whatever else I feel—any regret that might paw at me for this or that task left uncompleted."

The goddess inspected me closely, her expression unreadable.

"Have you that quickly shaken off your foolhardy craving to reject paradise? Do not deny the question was in your heart when your master took you aside."

"It was, of course. I am sure it was in the hearts of all the men who were welcomed today. But such resistance surely fades, does it not? As we gradually come to accept the death of a loved one, so, too, must we accept our own deaths."

"And what loved ones have taught you these lessons?"

"I confess I have not, in my time, lost teachers or friends to anything other than treachery…but, not knowing my parentage, I quickly thought it best to act as if both my mother and father were dead."

The goddess emitted a scoff so soft I barely heard it, though I could not tell why. She disappeared behind her goblet. "And now you have engendered another Wotsung who will never know his father. One who will be left in evil hands."

My face fell. I could not maintain the charming mask I had arranged for the goddess and settled instead on one that was firm but polite.

"It sounds as though you would wish to stir regret in me, Madame."

"Were the regret not already within your heart, my words would mean nothing. You are reckless, Wotsung, as was the progenitor of your line. Mark my advice—be satisfied with what is here. You and the three with whom you arrived may dwell forever in joy. Although your position toward matrimony reminds me for ill of my husband, I would see you and your wives blessed with more children than any hero in this Hall if you might but control your instincts to slip the bridle."

I barely heard the rest of the goddess's promises to me, (her veiled negotiations, in fact—as though, I reflected later, she was somehow frightened of what I might choose to do), distracted as I had been by her error.

"I arrived with two, not three," I reminded her. "The two you called my brides."

She looked at me steadily.

I thought for a second that she was offended by my correction.

Then—I realized.

A great wave crested up under my heart and over my mind, flooding me with mistrust of my own understanding.

"Valeria?"

"It is rare for a child born in the Valor Hall to be counted among its heroes, as yours was," she carried on as though oblivious to my racing heart, my inability to concentrate, my hope and love and excitement. "Without the world and all its time to go about in, they oft remain but cherubs—babes, or small children. A family that will forever serve to enrich a hero's joy. But perhaps your joy is to be reflected not in the flattery of a child's innocent love, but the glory of an heir's achievements?"

"Perhaps," I said softly, feigning as best I could another smile, knowing the real reason my child would grow to be counted among the Selected. "Yes, perhaps."

"I have distressed you."

"No, Madame—no, of course not. I am delighted by the news! Though, I confess…I am now even more eager to find my heart's delight among this crowd." I peered around, daring to ask, "Have you seen her pass you by?"

"She is not yet among us. But, Wotsung, there is

time to see her! Drink your wine...never fear. There's no curse on it, nor on the game."

I smiled despite myself, having been wary of just such a thing, but the Valor Hall and its holy inhabitants would not stoop to lowly tricks like those used by the fae people whom elves taught humans to beware. Therefore, trusting the goddess in spite of her prickly demeanor, I took a great swallow of wine from my cup and was at once amazed.

In my time on Urd, I have had many meads, wines, and dwarvish liquors in wide assortment to celebrate the odd holy day. Among them, none was as fine as the wine of heaven. So smooth one could not believe it a potent libation, so sweet one could not stop drinking it, yet not so sweet that one would tire of it! I took another mouthful in astonishment.

When I lowered the cup to comment, the man to my right noticed my empty plate and nudged me before hoisting up a serving platter to set it within my reach. My stomach roared with hunger as I permitted myself to admire the offerings cluttering the tables. Glistening duck, nearly sweet-smelling venison, roasted hares—any meat a man could name or long for—were arrayed before me or along the table ahead of me. Fish, too, were bountiful, and all the spaces in between were covered in bunches of fruit, bowls of colorful vegetables prepared by the loving hands of Weltyr's daughters, delicious breads to absorb the rich juices of the meal, and so much more.

Each bite I took was better than the last. What prior experience I'd had in the ways of cuisine was, you might imagine, quite limited. While the orphanage saw we were fed, it was uninspiring; and although I had visited my share of dining houses around the Temple as I trained in the ways of the Order, I had never been able to buy much on the small stipend I was awarded by taking on additional tasks with my studies. Frankly, aside from the small amount I was allowed to take from the durrow feasts I attended with Valeria, the best food I had enjoyed on Urd had been Lively's. It was made with obvious love for her guests, and the freshness of her ingredients could not be denied. Yet even that paled in comparison to the food at the Valor Hall's banquet.

I had not intended to stay overlong, now knowing the happy news that made me all the more eager to flee the Hall with Valeria and Elishta-bet—but, I should perhaps be embarrassed to admit, the food's one enchantment was that it convinced me to stay on. I could not remember the last time I had eaten, in fact, and was glad to presume one could not collapse from exhaustion in the Valor Hall, for the same could have been said of my companions (the *Battle Swan!* That was the last time…how long ago that seemed). In fact, I was wondered if I might be permitted to take a plate to Valeria, wherever she was, when the Hall knew it to be the time of our meeting.

By the time I took to wondering this, however, the tables were full end-to-end, and the speech was loud and merry, and music played even above the laughter. The men around me spoke to me with great interest, eager to know the story of how I had come to be in the Hall, and I admit I was pleased to share it. Though I limited the details to the pirate ship, the hero to my right wished to know more and had just begun to interrogate me on the women who had accompanied me when I noticed the

Selectrices were moving among the celebrants to draw them from their seats.

Looking up, pairs already danced in the broad between the heads of the tables and the vast doors of the shut kitchens. Each of the goddesses had selected a hero and, while others at the banquet tables (including Hildolfr, himself) clapped and cajoled, the pairs danced an enthusiastic round.

How free it looked! Just as I laughed at the sight, a feminine hand fell upon my shoulder.

"Come to the dance, Burningsoul," sang out Brynhildr, who smiled in that wonderful, pure-hearted way of hers while I regarded her in surprise and delight. "A hero so handsome shouldn't spend his first night watching others dance with us! May I claim your conversational companion, O Bride of my father?"

"As you will," said Anroa, dismissing me with an incline of her chin. "Remember my advice, Wotsung. Satisfaction is a choice."

Indeed, it was—and although it was tempting as the Selectrix pulled me to my feet and linked her arm in mine, I hardened my heart against that urge.

I could not be satisfied. Refused to be, however great my pleasure was to be in the Valor Hall. The goddess's attempt to persuade me had only firmed my resolve, and even Brynhildr's glittering smile upon me as we sprang together to the dance floor would not have been sufficient motivation to remain.

And, at any rate—Brynhildr, lovely as she was, was destined to be the bride of one of my sons.

Three sons! Was one of them in Gundrygia's womb? Brief wonderings of Valeria's child were quickly dashed when I reminded myself the durrow race was a female one; but that was all right. I was gladdened immensely at the thought of having a daughter, and I regarded the redheaded Selectrix with whom I swung around the floor as a noble prototype for any girl-children I might beget. Her love of her father made me hope to also be so purely loved, and perhaps it was this nature of Brynhildr's that made me so easily feel she were already a daughter-in-law.

Partway through the dance, the Selectrices switched partners, and later on did so once again. I danced with three of them before coming back around to Brynhildr, who, upon linking arms with me, danced me out of the circular formation and through the doors of the fragrant kitchen.

"Father's eye, but that was fun!" Flush-faced, beaming, the Selectrix smiled at those of her sisterhood who, among those heroes who had taken such positions in their armies, prepared more food for the long night of feasting. "I'm sorry I left you with Anroa as long as I did, Burningsoul—I know she can be very difficult."

"Thank you for getting me away from her," I said while a few eavesdropping Selectrices laughed in knowing agreement.

"I can tell your heart longs for more than banquets. Come along, cousin!"

While my heart was flattered by the appellation delivered by a goddess—and gladdened, by Weltyr, to know of any single relative that could be named for the first time in my life—Brynhildr took my hand and drew me through the busy kitchens.

"There's a way to the gardens," she explained. "To make it easy to pick herbs and other matter for the banquets."

"Could you tell that Valeria was with child when you rescued us?"

Flicking a quick glance of mingled happiness and sorrow, the Selectrix lowered her head. "Aye, I could tell—as I can tell he will one day be a hero as great as his father."

I looked twice at her in shock. "He?"

"The Wotsung bloodline has great powers," she solemnly informed me. "What is impossible for normal men of lesser, mortal clans is fated to the Wotsungs who see to Father's will, whether such is their knowledge or even intent."

His pronouncement that I was to protect and educate those of my line returned to me with new importance. I looked at her with some shock, considering the implications of this even as we navigated out a back door and into the fresh, open air of a garden colored with the long shadows of pre-twilight.

"If I, a Wotsung, beget a child, is the child not also to be a Wotsung?"

"Aye, Burningsoul, that would be the case."

"Then a single male among the dark elf race, if a hero of Weltyr's line, could change everything for their species—to say nothing, eventually, of their culture."

I was so excited by the knowledge of what just one of my three heirs might do that I barely registered the glory of the gardens until we were already surrounded by flowers. The branching path down which we walked was of the same mysterious stones that constructed the

Hall, but on all sides of all branches, the richness of Anroa's carefully maintained plants were without end. Far ahead of us lay vineyards, and farther still rose row on row of the sacred orchards which maintained the battle-immortality of the gods that ate of them. Yet, around us burst such fabulous panoplies of color and scent that I could barely keep my eyes from lowering to our feet.

"It is vital that I find some way to get us back to Urd," I told her, my voice low as my eyes in case any of the smattering of distant flower-watchers might somehow hear our words on the wind. "If this is true—if my son will have the potential to upend the entire society of the durrow people—then surely Weltyr must will for my resurrection as much as he wills the gold's return."

"Yet he is powerless to accomplish both," observed the Selectrix with a sad shake of her head. "He made merry as he could tonight, but I know my father, and he remains forlorn...ah—"

Smiling, Brynhildr stooped to pull a few carrots from a patch of earth.

"Grane loves these! They're his favorite treat—he could be talked into anything with them as his bribe. I'd better see to *his* banquet, now...he, like the other horses, is sure to be grazing along the river to the west." She gestured toward the endless sea of flowers and plants, and I memorized every word of her abruptly shifting, perfectly casual conversation. "They bed there each night, and in the morning my sisters and I will wake them up to brush their manes and take them for a ride."

"What lucky horses!"

Giggling, Brynhildr slapped me in the arm so sharply that I fought back the urge to rub the spot.

"You men and your minds! I'll leave you now, Burningsoul...carry on this direction a time, though. You'll find who you're looking for."

While Brynhildr left me to make her way to the pasture, I was rocked by excitement.

Although it is fair to say I am always eager to see Valeria, in that instant I had never been more thrilled for us to meet. I hurried along the path, my mind whirring with wonder and only the slightest hints of concern.

How would I express this to her? Should I say anything at all, in fact, or let her come to the conclusion only once we returned to Urd? I certainly had the sense that I should keep the child's sex to myself, whatever the final decision was. If I revealed that she was carrying the only male durrow, she would grow dubious. I would sound like I was spouting nonsense.

Worse—what if she believed me, and decided to return to the Nightlands along with the unborn child when we at last reclaimed the Ring of Roserpine?

Another problem...if I was to return the Deepgold on Weltyr's behalf, would I not have to return the Ring? The remains of the Lantern, as well.

And then, there was Exigence.

The weapon weighed heavily at my side while I searched, the vineyards more obvious to me when I reached the crest of a long, sloping hill and could look down at the vibrant purple carpet that produced the gods' sweet wine.

There, wandering into a row while clearly awestruck as I felt, was Valeria.

Several things struck me all at once: first, that she was dressed differently than she had been when at last I saw her; second, that she walked, her eyes unhampered, beneath the light of the sun.

Ecstatic, I called her name while hurrying down the slope. She reappeared at the row's entrance, peering up the hill at me with surprise. I sprinted down to her, taking her into my arms as she said, "I would have thought you to be with Elishta-bet."

"I did speak with her briefly, but I've been looking for you everywhere since I saw Weltyr and his bride. Ah! Valeria—you are too beautiful, by the All-Father, you are a wonder, a gift—"

Laughing as though despite herself, she said, "I expected you to be scowling still. Not so doting, by Roserpine."

"It's just the pleasure of seeing you in the sunlight," I half-lied, unable yet to tell her the news that made me giddy as a boy just to look upon her. There was a child growing in her womb, and it was ours, together! "How terrible that you need to shun it on Urd! It enriches your complexion, delivers your beauty a mystical note—but whyever would I be sore with you?"

Her brow arched while she looked at me in skepticism. "You are like a great dog sometimes, Rorke. Never dwelling on the past. Perhaps I'm the one still unhappy, then... perhaps I am sorting things in my own mind."

Ah, of course! Our quarrel, from before chaos erupted on the *Rhinemaid*.

"What does it matter now that we're here?"

She laughed at me a little, her head shaking with impatience. "You're a fool, Rorke. Surely it matters, or it will if we're to leave here. I demand that things be made clear between us."

That short temper couldn't touch me in the moment. In fact, I found myself biting back a laugh of my own.

"But, Madame, did you borrow the gown of a Selectrix?"

Valeria glanced down at herself, then back up at me, confused. "Well—no, of course not. They were in the wardrobe in the quarters I've been given. But—"

"And they didn't charge you for tailoring?"

"Roserpine knows not even I have had a gown so finely tailored in all my blessed life."

"Well, Valeria, then you must be opening your heart to the glory of Weltyr, and acknowledging his superiority above the other gods!"

The displaced Materna, who I knew would never be dissuaded from the depths of her devotion to Roserpine, scoffed and slapped me lightly upon the breastplate.

"Don't speak such nonsense."

"You haven't? Well, then…perhaps you have been Selected to consciously dwell in Weltyr's sacred Hall because your heart—and perhaps, in the future, your body—is wedded to a man counted among Weltyr's worshippers."

The rich purple-blues of Valeria's sunlit cheeks grew all the richer with her blushing. I wanted to make love to her at once, and knew I could have done it with perfect impunity. That the vineyards would enfold us in a cloak of privacy until we were ready to depart. I resisted, opting to enjoy the look of her face as she grew flustered by her whizzing mind. Unable to even begin to articulate an adequate response, she refocused on a more superficial issue.

"'Superiority above the other gods…'" She shook

her head, still stewing over my teasing. "How can you say that, having yourself seen both Weltyr and Roserpine?"

"And you, having seen only one. All worshippers would do well to fear their gods, Valeria—but it's Weltyr's love for mankinds that lets you look upon him, or speak in his presence with free heart and spirit."

"But there is nothing free about us, Rorke; we have been from the start and still continue to be pawns in their wars."

"Funny you should say that. Would you care to stroll with me, Madame, and give me your ear? We can talk about the petty things that happened on Urd later, if you would like…but for now, I think I'd ought to let you know what I've learned."

By Exigence, she was beautiful! As we walked together, her arm in mine, I was more aware of her body than I was even when I served her as her guard.

Now, of course, I was more her guard than ever; though now, as I had not been able to in the Nightlands, I could look upon her and feel her respect for me in the way I was regarded in turn. She listened astutely to every word I said, her radiant eyes fixed on my face, her ultra-pale pupils visible in the softening sunlight as they were but faintly on Urd. Here, I could examine every detail and was, as we walked together, transfixed. Her dress was more modest than what she might have worn in the Nightlands, but it still left an appreciable amount available for my eye before hiding the glamorous lengths of her very fine legs and terminating over the grass in a short train of white fabric. The slope of her collarbone, the proud column of her kissable neck, the very curve of her wrist—there was nothing of her that was not perfect to me, and that perfection made me inclined to be patient despite our quarrel. Particularly when I considered what lay within her. I spoke to her plainly of all I had heard, withholding the details of my stock only for want of understanding what it meant to me.

At last, Valeria asked, "And there is no other means of negotiation than returning the Deep-Children's gold?"

"I do not think there is—and, frankly, I am not convinced it is a matter of negotiation, as such."

Weltyr had spoken on the subject without entering into negotiation of any kind, after all. Mankind could not negotiate with godkind. My master's will could not be negotiated.

But the man who acted against his master's will also acted without negotiation, even if it was for the deeper, truer will and betterment of his master's life.

While I fought back the wave of faint nausea that came at me to imagine disobeying Weltyr's commands, no matter the purpose, Valeria had gone on speaking.

"But if the gold is to be returned in its entirety, we forfeit our most valuable tools in our quest—to say nothing of the Ring of Roserpine. It cannot be disposed of. As a sign and demonstration of power, it is necessary... to my people, and to myself"

"Yes...that has occurred to me more than once."

I had so much I wanted to say. That she wouldn't need the ring if she never returned to the Nightlands; that perhaps, if she let chaos have free rein and politics run their course, her homeland would be better off and faster to change than it would under the guidance of a Materna; that she was pregnant with my child, our child, and I didn't want her to part from me when all of this was over.

"I think," I told her instead, choosing my words with the utmost caution, "that it is too soon for us to decide how to approach that final bargaining chip. I also think it is not unreasonable that, for the meantime, I maintain possession of Exigence. Without it, we may never have a chance of finding the ring, rendering the whole point moot. Then, of course, there are the scraps of Hamsunt's lantern...I imagine they have already crashed into the sea, but we must be sure..."

"Will the Deep-Children reach it in Urd's sea? I do not think that was where we found ourselves before."

"It wasn't...but I do not think the Deep-Children's waters are restrained."

"Then we had ought to spend the rest of our lives fearing deep fountains."

I laughed at her half-jest. "It may not be a bad practice...they were frightful creatures when the tide turned."

"They were, at that."

Smiling, then releasing the expression down into a thoughtful frown, Valeria enfolded herself in her own thoughts. I stopped us in the middle of the long row through which we had strolled, catching her delicate chin in my hand.

"You are the most pensive person I have ever known. Speak, Madame. Do not bear the weight of your thoughts alone."

"I hardly know them well enough to speak them to myself, let alone you...I feel—ashamed."

"Ashamed?"

"My goddess lay in wait, within my seeing and hearing, if only I'd had courage enough to meet with her.

You say mankinds should fear their gods, and you are quite right...but I am the Materna. Her handmaiden. Am I so weak that I could not bear to look upon my mistress?"

"Perhaps you knew that if you looked upon her you might yield to the temptation to enshroud yourself with her and there spend eternity. I know that a certain base, tired part of myself longs to remain here in Weltyr's sacred home, enjoying your love and the leisure of every day until leisure was no longer enough and eternity itself cried for action."

"Yes...that could be the case. I was just so— frightened. So sick with heartache all at once."

"And are you, still?"

"...No."

While I was somewhat surprised by that answer, perhaps I ought not to have been. This was, after all, Valeria, who was as silently calculating and wise a terrestrial woman as ever I had known. She dipped into her emotions as the body into the bath, then rose back out when she had enjoyed sufficient exposure to them. Her process of self-grief was complete; in part because, as she went on to say to me, "I think I despaired until the Selectrix flew me through the stars. Until I understood what my dreams have really meant. I think, Rorke, that this was always meant to happen to us...and that we are meant to take heart, and live beyond it."

I nodded, squeezing her shoulders fondly. "I feel just that way. Your very goddess imbued me with knowledge that emboldens me to action—prophecies of my life that indicate more awaits me than what I have already lived."

Her eyes widened. Pressing close to me, her fine

body a perfect fit even against the breastplate that was my only armor from the *Rhinemaid*, Valeria asked in a tone closer to remonstration than intrigue, "Did I not counsel you to speak with caution?"

"Aye, I did...but there were things she spoke I did not ask, the conversation having been permitted to continue too long. And her features!"

"You saw her?"

"If one may see a shadow in the dark, so did I behold your fearsome goddess. I feared her, myself... but the light of Exigence gave hints of where she was, and her manner was not threatening even if I found her words disturbing."

"What did she tell you?"

I bit back my smile, my arms tightening around Valeria. "One or two things not so frightening—hints of my brides, and my heirs."

"Brides, as in many?"

"As in three," I told her, one hand sliding into the small of her back to gently stroke the length of her lovely spine. "The same as the number of my heirs."

"I am sure such information thrilled you...perhaps, had I come in with you, she might have told me the number of my slaves."

"The same as the number of your husbands, Madame—one."

Scoffing, her gaze darting askance, Valeria reminded me, "There are no husbands in the Nightlands, Rorke."

"We are not in the Nightlands; nor will be when we return to Urd."

"Not at first. But we will return eventually, of course."

"Would you really have our child raised as you

were? Belowground, in the darkness, never knowing the firmament of the gods in all its radiance?"

"Our child!" She laughed and shook her head at me. "If we were to produce a baby, she would likely be the next Materna...it would be of vital importance that we raise her in the Nightlands, accustomed to its ways."

"The question of our producing a child is not 'if,' but 'when'—and if we worry about returning you to the Nightlands right away, you will be traveling with child. Then, arriving, you will be interrogated, forced to clean up whatever mess erupted in your absence, and watch from your busy distance as the child is raised by slaves and servants."

She searched my face, demanding, "What are you trying to say?"

"Or," I continued on without explanation, "we could wrap up the matter of the ring as swiftly as possible and find Gundrygia; and perhaps, seeing you in the same state as her, she may feel some sense of womanly sympathy...if such a thing is possible for the wild witch."

"What state? What do you mean?"

"Since we will already be taking on one child, the care of another would perhaps be simpler. If she wants no part, she could forfeit the baby to us. We could raise them as twins. But, I will leave the decision to her—and to you, of course."

Now she asked no questions, but looked at me with slow-dawning comprehension.

"I do not want you to be unhappy with me," I told her gently, "but I do want you to be with me. And if my request that you forsake other men feels so unfair to you, I would fain forsake other women's arms in equal bond of trust. Yet, since women seem to be a point where our sexual interests are well-matched, I cannot help but think it would be, as I've heard it said, "burning the business to spite the tax-man," for you to close us both off to the possibility of companionship."

A shaky exhalation eased past her parted lips. Valeria's gaze darted down to herself, then at my waist. Between us, her hands slid over my belt and tugged at the buckle.

"That is a reasonable point," she admitted, staring into my face while she loosened the belt and the sword attached. "I suppose, if I fancy both sexes and you but one, a reasonable compromise can be reached without complete dissatisfaction. But, these two other brides of yours—are they to be my brides, as well?"

"Only if you find them pleasing, of course. If you would prefer to keep a—gainfully employed, unenslaved—handmaiden or two of your own around, I would only begrudge you such company if you came to prefer their time to mine."

"I would not worry...as I have said, I find men preferable. Your body is superior to any woman's caress."

With tender hands, she opened my belt, then watched me lay it and the relic attached in the tangle of vines beside us. "Will you tell me," she went on casually, "how you know? Did Roserpine, also, tell you this information?"

Knowing what she meant, I unstrapped my breastplate while explaining, "Rather, the Queen of Heaven delivered the knowledge. She hoped to persuade me to stay here in peace, but the thought has only succeeded in driving me more desperately to our liberation. Valeria!"

I had kept as calm as I could while waiting for her to understand the information that I had delivered, but now, knowing she was likewise adjusting to the news, I could no longer contain my joy. After dropping my breastplate, I collapsed to my knees and took her hands in mine. I kissed her beautiful knuckles and pressed my face to her still-taut belly through the warm fabric of her gown, sighing in ecstasy.

"I am aflame with joy, I have never felt this way—Valeria!"

"One would have thought you less excited, having already been used to fertilizing females of my race and knowing Gundrygia is with your child even now."

"But I do not yet love Gundrygia; and to your friends, I did the favor of bequeathing children I will never see. But you! Valeria—you are the joy of my heart, the delight of my eyes! I crave your companionship as I crave the companionship of no other. From the first moment of our meeting, I was struck through by you. And to imagine your body as the vessel of a child we, together, created in our passion, honors and humbles me more than dying to find myself in the Valor Hall. How I love you, Valeria; how grateful I am to you, and how much more deeply now than ever before I wish to protect you. I wish to keep you with me always. To remain beside you forever, and see to your safety in the world."

As I spoke between kisses, her fingers curled through my hair and trailed along my scalp. Every press of my lips to her stomach came with a jolt of wonder, of pride. My hands trailed up her legs, over her thighs, and she gasped as I fit my palms to the wonderful, round peach of her backside.

"Then you must truly be my slave," she told me, teasing. "Must be willing to follow me back to the Nightlands, even, if that is what I choose to do."

"If that is what you choose, then I will be forced to obey...but perhaps you will be willing to wait, at least until the child is born, to decide what you will have us do."

Upon the thin bed of grass between the rows of vines, Valeria joined me on the ground and kissed me.

14

IN THE GARDEN

WHY AM I now so reluctant to describe the passion of our lovemaking, I wonder, when before I did so without qualm? Much had to be described for the reader to make sense of Valeria's culture, her mind, our relationship. It is one thing to intellectually understand the sexual nature of the durrow, but another to experience it as I did: to see it as inseparable from the reality of living with them.

But that sweet embrace with Valeria in the vineyards of the Valor Hall was not like our previous encounters. It was the first time I had been alone with her since we had emerged from the Nightlands, I realized. That by itself made the occasion special, and something to be kept private.

More than that, though, we celebrated with our love. We basked together in delight, knowing the future life growing in her womb was her child and mine. Valeria's body knew the sun for the first time in her extensive life, and I savored the slow yielding of the proud woman who condescended to love me; to entertain the singularly aboveground fantasy of the happy family, comfortable in some remote cottage.

The kind of thing, in other words, that would have been given to us forever if we only stayed in the Valor Hall.

There was just so much to consider. What would become of our child if Valeria birthed it in the world, in Urd, and it and we all lived and grew through time together? Nothing would be perfect. People would fight; they might even be cruel, or grow apart. If our household was to include the madwoman Gundrygia, or even just her child, there would be additional perils. And then, of course, there would be the children growing up. Hurting themselves, or others; leaving the house; perhaps even living in ways I would not abide, or ways that disappointed rather than endeared me.

Was it not safer, surely, for us to remain in the Valor Hall? To create scores of lovely children who never grew up, or who grew up only to give us the pleasure of having produced well-behaved, godly heirs that obeyed my every word and did always as I told them?

In all my creations, I see nothing but myself.

No.

I did not want children who existed solely to

contribute to my prideful idea of perfect retirement in Paradise. I wanted children who could make choices of their own in confidence and power, even if those choices did not align with what I wished for them.

So it was that there, with Valeria in my arms while the shade of night closed over our bed between the vines, I understood my master's dilemma all the better.

Yet there was pain in it, too. Now comprehending how near to literal Hildolfr's fatherly regard for me had been, and sympathizing more deeply with his craving to produce a being free enough to defy him, I understood both the troubled hearts of father and son together.

Already, I had defied the Church and rescinded my bonds with the Temple, the Order—everything that had defined me. I peered into the glittering sky with eyes that were so different from the ones that had first set out on this strange journey...so they felt, anyway.

But they really were the same. The same eyes. Our bodies, the bodies we had just used to make love, were not lies. They were the same bodies as must have seemed lost at sea to our absent friends. Somehow, these eyes had managed, against all odds, to avoid being changed.

It was the beholder looking through them who had transformed. Whatever constitutes the subtle manifestation of personality, memory, being-ness in the mankinds—that was the organ that had been transfigured. The change had begun slowly, with the instant of my friends' betrayal in the Nightlands; now, I realized how much change had accumulated in me since that moment. I felt it in not just my mind, but my body. Somehow, the manner in which I perceived the very muscles of my own face had changed.

And, having changed, I had to look at the man into which I was changing with thorough scrutiny.

The man who could stand to defy the will of a god in one way, after all, could, without even meaning to, defy it in other ways.

Yet, was that perilous free will not godlike?

Was I, a Wotsung, not arush with the blood of Weltyr?

That was dangerous thinking.

I stopped myself immediately.

What mattered was not my bloodline. What mattered was my strength of will: that was what made the free man. And the free man may well have been a kind of super-man as he came into his knowledge of himself, but true self-knowledge revealed that the free man was no more or less great than any other. He was even perhaps, by virtue of the moral risks he faced in being free, inferior to those bound to live blindly in the thankless service of gods.

But he who relied on his birthright to justify his doings grew lazy and entitled to whatever prizes he managed to wrest out of life. An unearned sense of superiority would soon set in, along with bitterness. Then, inevitably, the undoing. The many myths of god-men struck down by their own arrogance, losing all they held dear—if not their very lives.

Who could be free that relied on his bloodline? Such a one was bound to a single path; to rigid thinking. The free man had to free his thinking. Had to release unilaterally the attachment to all institutions. Society, ancestry.

Even divinity.

"And you called me "pensive,"" Valeria chided, stroking my cheek. "Here you are, about to do battle with a god, and our time together is spent in your brooding silence…speak your thoughts to me, Rorke. Let me hear them from your lips."

"I am wary of the consequences of what I am about to do."

"As am I."

"Yet, I know it must be done."

"Are you so sure?"

"Even if liberating the gold will not buy our freedom, my master said aloud that the free man might somehow use that very gold to flee death. I do not know how he meant this. Only that he said it before me. Therefore, it was something he wanted me to know. Nothing idle is about him or his speech."

Her bosom heaving with her low sigh, Valeria leaned her forehead against mine.

"I'm frightened for you. What plan do you have?"

"Not having seen the lay of the land, I'm not sure what my options will be for doing battle with Dunnun. However, much as Exigence's gold remembered its mistresses and would not strike against them, I hope it will also know its present captor and doubly administer the god's quick defeat."

"Let me come with you."

"Absolutely not," I told her, adding, "and I worry that our leaving here will imperil you—that our journey will put you in danger. I do not mean to patronize you, Madame, but I hope you understand that I will be working to protect you more diligently than ever until the threats of our mission are behind us. In fact, I would like to work out some hospitable agreement with an inn in Rhineland…or, better still! Perhaps we could send you back, and Lively and Erdwud could—"

I was stopped by the warm, plush lips she pressed against mine, working so tenderly that I forgot all my fretting at once.

"You are so very dear to me, Rorke Burningsoul… for a slave, of course."

Laughing a little, then sitting up and turning away from me to fix the hair that poured down her back, Valeria said, "Well, if you will not permit me to come face Dunnun with you, we must find another solution. That Selectrix said something interesting, as I recall. We stopped at the doors to the garden but briefly while she brought Elishta and me to our chambers, and she said something about the orchard. Are the sacred fruits there that Anroa grows the very same that Dunnun lusted after before the gold sated his appetite?"

"Aye, the very same."

"Perhaps you could barter him for one."

"One! Last time, Weltyr promised him an entire tree and had to substitute all the Deepgold but Exigence and your Ring of Roserpine. Surely the entire hoard is worth far more than a single piece of fruit."

But Valeria turned wily smile over her shoulder. "Think how long he has been without it! Without even *seeing* it. Perhaps, having been so long without, his appetite for even a single apple could be so madness-inducing that he would sacrifice all his gold for a bite."

I rubbed my jaw, skeptical but intrigued. If there were a way to avoid risking myself in this matter, I was more than happy to take it. The problem, of course, was,

"What if he takes the apple and, battle-hardened, slays me against his word?"

"Is your Weltyr not the very god of contracts? If Dunnun did turn against you once the fair exchange was made, the One-Eyed God would have suitable cause to intervene."

Actually...that was a good point.

"These are all extremely clever ideas, Madame. But—how can I put this delicately..."

Clearing my throat and glancing around as I sat up, I leaned into Valeria's sensitive ear and whispered against its twitching ridge, "Anroa reminds me in some ways of you, save that she has no fondness for me. I believe she would take great pleasure in the least reason to remonstrate me. And I do not think her remonstrations would be as enjoyable as yours."

"Is it a sin to take the fruit?"

"It's reserved for the gods."

"And you are part a god already. It is not as though you will be eating it yourself, Rorke—and I saw plenty there, even from this distance away. What harm will one missing fruit do?"

"I'm sure she will know. I'm not sure I dare compound the consequences of my already complicated intentions, Valeria."

With an impatient sigh, she reached for her dress.

"Then I will take on a share of the consequences with you."

Alarmed, I caught her wrist. "What are you doing?"

She shot me a stern look and, jerking out of my grip, continued dressing. I stole a kiss of her shoulder by way of apology while she explained, "Since it is not

197

reasonable to force you to take on the burden of freeing all three of us from death, I will play my guilty part. You stay here, and I will fetch a sample of fruit from Anroa's sacred boughs."

"But if something befell you—"

"Is Anroa not the keeper of domesticity? Of matrimony, and family? Would she punish a wife working in her husband's noble will, or strike down a mother whose infant has not separated from her?"

"Well...she is cold, but perhaps we could reason with her. Even so, Valeria, if you're going to trouble yourself, I really insist—"

"That you do it, and take on all the burden anyway?" When I nodded, she rolled her eyes and bent to kiss me. "If I am to be your bride, I won't be a servile girl in need of protection at every turn. Don't think I won't die to protect you as willingly as you would me."

Quickly, before I could respond, she hid her face and walked down the row of vines.

"Wait there," she hissed back to me. "I won't be long."

The tension that settled upon me was crushing from the second she, ignoring my whispered call, disappeared. Intending to follow her, I quickly dressed and armed myself.

But, as I emerged from the long row of grapevines, a raven blacker than the night around swooped down to graze the crown of my head.

I ducked, the motion coming too late and only emphasizing the bird's flight control. Had it wished, it could have cut open my scalp with the tips of its great claws. Instead, it had barely grazed me—and flown on, in the direction opposite the orchard.

I glanced over my shoulder in hesitation, yet I could not see Valeria. The gardens, I supposed, compressed and shifted about as did the corridors of the Hall; indeed, I reflected as I stealthily pursued the enormous bird that these luxurious gardens, the forest, and everything beyond it must also have been within the structure. That, infinite as it was, it must have contained a great many things to appeal to the hearts of all the heroes who resided there.

That generous nature was reflected when a second raven, great as the first, alighted upon a hedge of roses that divided the walking paths from the entrance of the vineyards. I stopped at the bleak look its steely eye cast by the light of a nearby torch, which was the last to illuminate the flowers out of night's grip before the shadow of the grapevines dropped into place.

And the last to warn me that, arm-in-arm through the flowers, the All-Father walked with his bride.

Breathless, not wanting to risk interrogation from Anroa while Valeria raided her trees, I darted down the hedge of roses and crouched in the dark between it and the first row of vines. My heart hammered in my ears, yet above it I still discerned the sharp-edged speech of the gods whose stroll had clearly devolved into argument not long before my arrival.

"There are some things he does not need to know. You taunt him, Wife; mock him with the consequence and the motivation, both."

"He, like you, knows nothing of consequence. I spoke only to incentivize cooperation."

"You spoke to tempt him into action, for you cannot bear to look upon another of my descendants."

"Adulterous wretch!"

Their footsteps stopped near the entrance to the vineyards. I was tempted to edge farther back, but the fear of drawing their attention with errant sound seemed more pressing than the slim likelihood of being seen.

And, besides…one is better off not knowing the private business of gods, yet I cannot imagine a man who would not listen with great intrigue if given the opportunity.

"You speak of your illicit progeny so casually—with pride that goads them on to insane acts while prudence is my counsel. But if adultery pleases you so, then go on further and sanctify incest along with it."

"Such a mortal concern for one divine as yourself! The matter is more complex than that. Open your heart to what has never happened before. He is moved by her, no matter their shared root. Are your flowers not pollinated by their kin to create the stronger, purer rose?"

All the rest of night's gentle sounds silenced as I absorbed the meanings of these words.

I had thought they were talking about me—but surely, they could not be.

Could they?

"At any rate," my master went on, his firm tone catching itself to reduce to gentler timbres, "what is done in the ignorance of love is no sin; it is those loveless vows which are unholy, is that not so?"

One might have sworn Anroa's glower to be audible. At the very least, I could well imagine it without even having to see her.

"His soul is ignited by passion for her," Hildolfr surmised, his footsteps slowly resuming along with his wife's. "Bless their love, for it lies pure within the heart of whatever else is about them."

"But are these Wotsungs to be our end? They will be! I see it in your face, your being—your godliness means nothing to you, just as paradise means nothing to him! We will be destroyed: the wife whom you have endlessly betrayed will be crushed by your wild progeny!"

"Your hysterics make you blind. With one eye, I see what you cannot. There are those deeds which we gods cannot commission. Only a man free of my influence can accomplish what is forbidden by our ancient laws."

"How slyly you mislead me! At every turn, you have helped the Wotsung—you even journeyed by his side, playing the old wanderer to disguise your godly glory. What man can be free of the gods? It is your will that breathes in him, your ambition that animates him. You alone drive the Wotsung. Your sophistry falls on deaf ears, Husband. To look upon the Wotsung is to look upon you, and nothing else."

The couple passed me on the other side of the hedge. At last, I could breathe. Hildolfr's tone had meanwhile softened.

"In those moments that most mattered, it was he alone who saved himself by tenacious risks and martial prowess."

"Then do not continue to defend him to me! Fawn over him no longer. He is a hero who has been loyal to his god, and nothing more. If you will not punish him, then neither should you show him favor. Remember that before he is the apple of your eye, your ill-gotten spawn is your slave—and mine."

Now it was Hildolfr's turn to stew in silence.

I lowered my head in the dark, swimming with fright and confusion.

What had she meant by that? Incest. I had no siblings that I knew of—though, of course, neither had I realized myself to have such heavenly family.

What women had I known on my journey? No small number: but, of that number, most of them had been elvish. Branwen, Indra, Odile, Valeria. By virtue of their blood, none of them could have been my kin.

Yet there were two women for whom, as the All-Father put it, my soul was ignited by passion. Two women who were not elves: one with whom I had not yet lain, and one with whom I had.

A cold wind blew across the gardens, all the petals of the flowers on the hedge's other side ominously rustling in the night.

"Let us retire the argument for now," Hildolfr said at last, his voice fading off in a new direction while he guided his wife back toward the Hall. "I will keep my favor from the Wotsung if you agree to no longer entice him to action, hoping you may command his punishment."

"We will see how long even you can keep that consent, Husband…mind that you remember it."

The footsteps carried on, growing softer all the time.

Grim, I waited in the dark.

So much had been lain upon my shoulders. In a short time, I had answered a handful of questions about myself—yet been delivered so many others. Questions about my future; questions about my past.

Questions about what was right.

There it was again, the craving of the son: the two contrary urges. To be the pride of the loving father; to defy and surmount the father's glory. For some lucky men, they must have been the same urge—but for the godlings owing heritage to the All-Father, the notions clashed violently, blended, separated to clash again. Disobeying would move him to pride, yet he would have no choice by his own laws but to meet my actions with disappointment.

Then, again, I asked myself that haunting question.

If I left the Valor Hall and returned to Urd, would I ever be permitted back?

When the gods had left my range of hearing, I stood and made my silent way back through the vineyard rows. By then, Valeria stood with irritation at the end of the aisle where we had made love. As I distinguished her from the dark, I whistled to draw her attention without causing her to start.

"There you are," chided Valeria, meeting me halfway with something in her delicate hand. "I thought for a moment—this place seems like such a labyrinth. One always expects it to betray the inhabitant."

"That is a lifetime of durrow guile speaking in your heart. The Valor Hall is more honest and pure of intention than even the gods themselves."

"What a grim thing to say," she said, laughing softly while pressing the fruit into my hand. "There it is—a golden fruit. Which kind is it? I forget."

"An apple," I said, nudging her playfully. "Those fine eyes of yours can see its gold, but all that time in the dark has kept you from recognizing apples. Maybe a human lifetime or so of living aboveground would broaden your knowledge."

"And leave me so changed I would belong neither aboveground, nor below."

My good humor, briefly revived on seeing her, waned a little lower again.

"Well, my beloved…perhaps that is why we are meant for one another. I'm beginning to feel that way more and more, myself."

"Rorke…what have you learned? What gnaws at you so painfully? I've never seen you this way before. Earnest, yes; serious, never."

Sighing, I took her hand in my free one and marveled at how delicate, how cool, how perfect it was. I pressed her palm to my cheek while telling her, "My thoughts are so many in number—each aligned with a different axis, each poised with its own trajectory—that I could hardly begin to tell you which troubles me most…but I owe you one thought, since you carry my child."

I moved her hand away again to kiss its knuckles, then to press it to her stomach.

"The child you are destined to birth is, like his father, a godling—an illegitimate heir to the divine line of Weltyr. This is what Gundrygia called me: 'Wotsung.'"

Though my eyes were less keen in the dark than were hers, I still saw hers widen in obvious shock.

"A godling."

"I am still absorbing all this information, myself… but I would prefer it to increase the weight of my responsibility rather than add some unwanted aspect to my person. This child of ours, Valeria, will grow to be a mighty hero—but I am growing frightened of what they and my other progeny will mean to Urd, and to the gods that rule it."

My hand lifted from hers so that she alone touched her stomach: a vision that renewed my longing to escape. She, also, regarded that hand, that stomach, the early, invisible glimmers of life within it, and deeply thought.

204

"Whatever they will mean," she said, "it is better to never breathe a word of any prophecies to them, nor any intuition you may have or receive of their future. Such direction, too liberally delivered, could only lead them to whatever fates they seek to avoid."

"Yes—yes, Valeria, you are right. If we never speak these things to them, what need have we to worry? Their wills, like mine, will be free. They will not, cannot, bend to the empty words of prophecy. For instance, Exigence."

I touched the pommel, which she looked upon while I declared, "Your goddess claimed that it will someday serve as omen; that when another mortal can hold Exigence as I, my life will be winding to its end." The fright crossing her face reflected the one I tamped down in my chest. In fact, I boldly smiled to give us both comfort. "But that fate will be simple enough to evade. When we have reclaimed the ring—when this journey is over—I will return Exigence to the Deep-Children as the final piece of missing gold. In its home with Roserpine, no man will lay hand upon it, and I will be free from the goddess's prophetic warning."

But Valeria's expression remained tight with concern. She glanced down at the sword on my hip before showing her displeasure to my face.

"Be warned, Rorke—those who most cleverly seek to defy the gods are all too often the very same that are their most accursed pawns."

I could not let her see the horror that such knowledge, already one of the many thoughts troubling me, spurred in my uneasy mind. Instead, I carried on with an empty mimicry of bravado: a memory of the more carefree smile that I had produced in the confidence of unknowing so many easy times before. A smile I have never truly felt alight upon my lips since.

"Then my acts of defiance must be well worth doing. You should retire now, Valeria. Rest—if not for your own sake, then the child's sake."

Though she still did not look overly pleased, Valeria nodded and kissed me. "Be careful, Rorke," she bade me as she passed me by, her hands drawing ankle-height the hem of her gown. "I'm counting on you to return in one piece…if you don't, I will be most displeased."

15

ACROSS THE SEA

WHEN DARKNESS SWALLOWED my last glimpse of Valeria, I studied the sacred fruit in my hand and worried over our solution. Perhaps Anroa was right to say I knew nothing of consequence. Our journey into the Valor Hall seemed marked by a period of acting on instinct rather than planning, and simply absorbing or working around consequences until we were finally back to Urd. It was possible that offering to trade Dunnun one of Anroa's fruits was a gross miscalculation that would mete out greater punishment than reward.

But could I think of anything better? Valeria was

right to urge conflict avoidance with a god. Even if he had not eaten of the sacred fruits for aeons, Dunnun was still bound to be more powerful than I. Tales of his battles against giants—with the same mighty hammer that built the Valor Hall, no less—had particularly inspired the dwarvish peoples of Rhineland, who revered the hermit god above all others.

If giants meant nothing to him, how could I hope to fare?

So, it was best to attempt for negotiation before anything else; and I could not think of a more adequate tool with which to negotiate than that which he once coveted.

Still…I must confess here that the idea of taking Anroa's fruit unnerved me almost as much as the thought of riding a Selectrix's horse.

I have heard certain men, Grimalkin for instance, chastise the minds of women for insidious thinking or duplicitous aims; yet I suspect such men think as they do because they are, in the landscape of female thought, yet another of many obstacles to be navigated in a hostile world. For one reason or another, be it good looks or "good luck," as Elishta told me, I have benefited from such thinking more than I have suffered from it. This strange night was a prime example. Both Valeria and Brynhildr, each in their own method, drove me to actions I would not have brought myself to take—may not have even thought to take—if forced to act alone. Their subtle methods of solving problems added new dimensions to the choices around me; somehow managed to validate those choices more than would have Weltyr's will alone.

Yet it was Weltyr's will that drove them, I reminded myself while quietly walking through the empty garden and back to the carrots Brynhildr had pulled for her steed. It was Weltyr's will that I defy his will; Weltyr's will that I accomplish what a god could not, tightly bound as he was to the sacred laws of his rule.

Were none of that true, I would not even have been capable of entertaining these thoughts.

With the apple over my heart and a few carrots in my hand, I followed Brynhildr's sly instruction to the west. The garden seemed even longer in that direction than it did while walking toward the vineyards; yet, when I took the chance to look behind me, I found the Hall towering farther away than I would have expected it to.

And, when I looked ahead again, I detected, through the starlit dark, the western boundary of Anroa's flowers.

Each step seemed more important than the last— and more dangerous. Each step, my chances to turn around grew slimmer. Yet there was no return from death but what I could make for myself, I strove to remember as the wind brought the wild scent of horses to sting my nose. Turning around might have seemed the easier thing, might have been the safer thing; but if I did not seize my chance to experience resurrection, I would never walk on Urd again. I would be dead forever, and all my happy plans with Valeria would be dashed.

And what would happen to Urd when Gundrygia had a Wotsung child of her own?

Perhaps that was the doom foretold by the failure to return the gold, I pondered on my solemn march alone, over the long rolling hills that gradually unfurled their emerald carpet through the night. That, you see, is the awful nature of prophecy. One speculates on it endlessly, approaching from all angles, the mind reeling beneath an infinite number of scenarios that it must now strive to avoid even while knowing Fate will not be bucked. And it never stops—never.

How I now wish I had shunned Roserpine! How I wish I had taken her daughters at their words and never known all the things that burden my heart. And all those little holes Roserpine pierced through the veil had been further unraveled by Anroa.

Moreover, by my own curiosity. For as much as I long to blame these informant goddesses, my ears were open to the knowledge they offered. I took it on willingly, intrigue driving me to push the limits of what a man might safely know.

And I regret it.

How I struggled to turn my thoughts away from the fates of children who were not even born! Yet, in my heart of hearts, I knew that this child of Gundrygia's would be one of those three heirs of mine; and that knowledge became juxtaposed with all this talk of the era of the gods coming to grim collapse; and I knew I would have to do everything I could to mitigate whatever wicked yearnings the wild witch might bestow in the heart of a godling.

I had to return to Urd. It was not a matter of scorning the Valor Hall, I decided as I stood upon a ridge overlooking the crystal stream and its slumbering horses. The truth was I did very much wish to remain in such a glorious place. What man wouldn't?

But I had a responsibility that, shunned, would have haunted me like a cloak of dishonor. It was a matter of choice—of will. And if a man had the choice to leave the Valor Hall but not the will to leave it, then he did not belong there in the first place.

I had to return to Urd. And I had to trust that, when the time came, I would be welcomed back to the home of my progenitor, all my sins forgiven and forgotten.

That was the true nature of faith, which I had never before experienced as powerfully as I did while making my slow approach down to the horses.

Of course, though the Valor Hall knew my will enough to bring me to them, the horses were not as inclined to make things easy.

The grass was soft and yielding, no loose pebble or errant branch announcing my presence. It was the wind, rather than the earth, that gave me up to the beasts. Another warm, rising gust billowed gently from the south, catching my scent and delivering it into the nostrils of a slightly northward member of the herd.

Its sudden rush of movement in the dark as it clambered to its feet alerted other horses, whose flighty response in turn alerted yet more. I stepped back, cursing under my breath and looking among them for the black horse that had belonged to Brynhildr.

What if I chose the wrong horse with which to abscond? I did not want to think about what the offended Selectrices would do to me. I had permission to take from the herd one horse, and one horse only.

"Grane," I half-whispered, thinking to raise my voice only a few seconds later when I considered how long and far I had walked away from the Hall. "Grane, friend, I've a gift from your mistress…"

Alarmed by my presence, the nickering herd disguised any plausible sound of confirmation Grane might have made to hear his own name. I ran my hand over my jaw and, deciding the only thing to do was to take my time, I made my steady but slow way amid the nervous horses.

The first few I neared edged away from me—half-rearing, in some cases, their deadly hooves summoning quakes upon each thud back to the ground. Gently as a practiced groom, I clicked my tongue and murmured fond words; I softly sang hymns to Weltyr that seemed to soothe them to a place of approachability; then, with one of the carrots broken into pieces, I bribed a few example horses into showing the rest of the herd that I had only good intentions.

This was a trick I could not afford more than once without having to go back for more carrots to start the process over again, so I was glad when the sacred beasts around began to calm. A few even resumed their rest, although they continued eyeing me without intention of sleep.

"Grane," I once again called out, my tone measured. "Your mistress's cousin has been called to ride you; will you obey his will?"

The horses having calmed, I was more easily able to identify among them what seemed to be a directed snort of response. I navigated carefully toward the sound, giving the horses as wide a berth as I could; however, as I drew to the herd's center, that became less possible. A cluster of seven beasts pawed the earth at the heart of their group, one or two thrashing their tails uneasily at my arrival.

"You have no need to fear me," I cajoled on, breaking the next carrot in half and offering part of it to the most nervous horse. Its dark eyes flashed over me before it reluctantly lowered its mouth toward my palm. After its lips had swept up the carrot, I patted its nose and stroked its head and told it, "You are all such supreme examples of your species! But I seek only one; the horse bonded to Brynhildr, whom she calls 'Grane.' I, a Wotsung, will do no harm: I ask only for assistance in the service of my master, who is the master of every being, living and dead. Will my mount for the task be my peer, a hero descended from a hero? Grane!"

At that, all the horses in the heart of the group stirred. I'd heard and even seen myself the intelligence of earthly horses, but I wagered these mounts of divine stock were sapient as any man. And if that were truly the case—if they did understand what I said and what it all meant—then perhaps they, like all sapient beings, could be reasoned with.

Stepping back to give them space, I regarded among them the three black warhorses of the group. All the beasts were great, towering above me, and I could not tell them apart in the night. I therefore addressed each warhorse in its turn as I swore, "If, Grane, you make yourself known to me, I will in turn see to it all Urd knows your name: and you, above all horses save perhaps my master's, will be especially revered by the tongues of men for your service."

I extended a carrot, waiting.

"Help me, friend."

Somewhere behind me, a resting horse clambered to its hooves.

I turned around, half-startled but more embarrassed to find this holy creature had been bypassed in my search. Yet, now that Grane stood before me, the differences between him and his kin were obvious. The others of his stock were powerful, muscled beasts as capable of taking on their adversaries as their riders; Grane had the look of a horse who could best all the rest of those horses and stand alone as the victor, his long mane highlighting the muscles of a neck and back that might have borne five men aloft without strain. The gaze with which the beast fixed me was keen with understanding—and solemn with it, too.

And his bearing, as he ceased his approach halfway to genuflect a foreleg to me, was nobler than any mankind's.

"There you are, friend." Though still speaking gently as I approached the horse, I strove to free my speech from the natural humanoid condescension for animal-species. "It's good to see you again. Carrots are the least I owe you, after you and your mistress saved me."

Rising once more to four hooves, Grane bent his head to receive the carrot which was crunched up in a few thoughtful bites. I stroked his nose, saying, "I don't intend for this to take very long; your mistress said we might even be back to the Valor Hall by morning."

While the horse enjoyed my second carrot, I regarded its great height for only a second before gripping hold of its mane. Though it snorted, I suspect it was as unbothered as it would have been by a flea. Indeed, as I used this grip to scale the beast and threw an arm over its back to pull myself up the rest of the way, its tail lashed forward to beat back an offending insect.

"Sorry, friend…I'll make it up to you with more carrots when we're back."

Soon I'd gotten comfortable on the great creature, although as I found the best position by which to grip the beast without a saddle or reins, I was once again struck by what I intended to do…and, more specifically, what would be required to get there.

Was I sick for a few seconds at the thought? Yes, I'll admit I was. The idea of riding astride a flying horse was exhilarating when one had the security of reins to grip and stirrups to secure the feet. For just a second, my brain flashed with warning calculations of the ease with which I might fall from its back.

But that second of reservation passed as quickly as it had come. I would not fall; I would hold fast to Grane, a horse experienced in the art of flight, and my will would be manifest.

My will. My will, to reclaim the gold. My will, to leave the Valor Hall.

My will, which I resolved to make more powerful than the will of any man I had ever met; for, if I was to defy my god, I was determined to make the defiance worthwhile.

Digging my heels into Grane's sides, I called, "North, friend! Let us make haste."

As I said the words, my body was rocked back by the horse's jolting motion. I held fast to its mane, my breath held.

Grane kept its speed to a trot until it was some distance from its peers. Then, as we reached open field terminated along the banks of the river by which the beasts had once more settled down to rest, the powerful animal gradually increased its speed. Soon we were at a brisk cantor; before I knew it, at a gallop. Wind rushed around us and I laughed, thrilled by Grane's power. My grip of its sides tightened and I lowered toward the horse's neck, patting it in encouragement and forgetting all my hesitance.

Only when I looked down did I realize that we had, amid all this galloping, sprung above the earth and into the air.

"Hah!" I marveled at it, my hands tightening in its mane but my feet only urging it to ride on faster. "Not so bad! Onward, Grane—to the isle of Dunnun, and back again by morn!"

Amazing how naïve I was, even after all I'd been through.

Rest assured, as the distance between us and the ground grew so great that Anroa's gardens were a mere thumbprint, there were a few moments of uneasiness. Yet I held as fast to Grane as I did to my will; I had already ridden once upon this horse, after all, and I trusted it and its rider to the utmost. I also felt in my heart that, so long as I kept my intentions fixed through all doubt, I could not fail.

Beyond the garden lay the vineyards; beyond the vineyards, the orchards whence Valeria plundered the fruit waiting against my heart; beyond the orchards, the forest, of which I knew nothing other than that it must have overflowed with all manner of game for the hunt of the Valor Hall's inhabitants; and when at last, after what seemed an hour, we overtook the enormous forest whose trees had whizzed beneath us with the horse's incredible pace, the world succumbed to surly sea.

The sight of the waves affected me as I had not expected to be affected. I shuddered—not just against the memories of awakening in the hateful waves but against the memories of the Deep-Children's songs.

And then, after some time of our flying over the sea, it was not just memories that haunted me.

"Heiala Wala! Burningsoul hastens off to the island where the Deepgold dwells."

The crisp sound of their haunting melody seemed as though it had burst from my thoughts and come alive to assail me. I peered over the back of the horse and could make nothing out in the waves, in the night, save for what seemed a flashing shape darting up with the next bar of song.

"Weia! Waga! I see him flying."

"He's stolen a Selectrix's sacred warhorse!"

"He gambles all eternity on favors to us!"

"But will he forget his promises with the Deepgold's glow filling up his eyes?"

"Too true! With Dunnun gone, his island will need a master."

"And the Deepgold, a slave!"

"Ha, ha, ha, ha, ha—"

"Laugh on, you slighted maidens of the maddened seas!" I laughed at them, myself, driving their song to remonstrated silence while I went on, "Soon your songs will all be of my name, recited in gratitude to your Deepgold with the coming of each dawn."

"How happy we'd be to find you were right!" I had not been able to tell them apart during their song, but somehow Oceania's identity cried to me with her words. "And how broken our hearts will be left when you're wrong!"

Teeth grit, I urged Grane on faster than even the Deep-Children could swim.

In truth, I do not know how long Grane galloped

through the air. The horse's stamina was not something that could have been replicated by any earthly coeval. Hours passed, or their equivalent in terms of the contents of my thoughts. The darkness began to light, dashing my hopes to return to the Valor Hall before morning. My head grew heavy with the yearning for sleep, my chin nodding down to my chest until the reflexive loosening of my hands gave my body such a fright I could not have slept if I tried.

Yet while these symptoms of long hours came upon me, Grane galloped without strain. Indeed, each time I patted or praised him, the fine mount seemed all the happier. No doubt he was happy for a night to run without a bridle and second rider!

And, against all reason, I was happy, too. What I was about to do seemed impossible only for everyone else. Indeed, it might have seemed impossible to me only a few nights before. But, having come to know myself and my god all the better, I felt more anticipation for the future than I had when first setting out from the Temple to reclaim the Scepter of Weltyr. I did not struggle to imagine the details of the task ahead of me; instead, I submitted utterly to the idea of doing whatever I would need to do.

I imagined the stories I would tell my heirs when all this was over and my quest developed from the shaping of my life to the shaping of theirs. I imagined three children (more, including the unnumbered girl-children) all sitting at my feet by a comfortable hearth somewhere, eager for the details of my flight to liberate the Deepgold; one dubious, one an open-minded skeptic, one a wholehearted admirer.

Looking back, knowing them as I do now, perhaps I ought to have dreamed up three wholehearted admirers rather than just one!

Say of them what you will. These fantasies, I believe, bolstered me on my mission. They gave my sense of inevitable victory a concretized texture in the same way memory concretizes the past, keeping it stable and nearly perceptible to the senses. With this image like a fixed star ahead of me in the dimension of time, liberating the Deepgold and succeeding in my quest was a simple matter of filling in the blank space between.

The journey took a long time—and, against the advisement of the Selectrix, had taken until morning. I did feel a brief nag of fright toward its end. Had I been misled? Gone the wrong way? Missed the island somehow while the waters beneath us were still veiled? If I turned the horse around, would even its great store of energy flag when confronted by a return without rest?

But it is my experience that the moment of greatest despair is inevitably the moment of victory. Just as my anxiety had begun to mount to a certainty that something had gone wrong, I spotted it in the distance: a glimmer on the horizon, a glimmer among sun-glittering waves.

I squinted. Was it a dream? After seeing nothing but waves and sky for so long, the object was almost difficult to perceive. But the nearer we drew, the greater was its expansion until my heart hammered with the ecstasy of accomplishment.

There it was! An island alone in the lazy waves, far to the north of the Valor Hall and its fantastical lands.

Or within it, depending on how one considered the matter.

"Hahei," I cried, tugging at Grane's mane. "Hoho, Grane! Steady, now—that island's our goal! Land with all the care to which you're accustomed, friend."

Somehow, I had imagined an almost comically small island was Dunnun's home; something out of a mystery play's humble staging, perhaps, or from a child's drawing. However, as Grane slowed his stride and decreased altitude, the magnitude of the god's home became apparent. It was certainly no match for Weltyr's land, but, thinking of it carefully, I would estimate that the sandy beaches and wild woods together amounted to an area the size of Skythorn—nothing to scoff at, especially for a hermit.

All the color was overwhelming after the journey, and Grane ran swiftly amid its much slower easing down. I squinted through the rush of air against my face, searching for some sign of life: a structure, a hint of shining gold.

The smoke of a forge, trailing up into the blue sky.

"There," I said to myself as much as the horse, studying the steady emanation from someplace in the heart of the woods, a mile inland from the shore. "Let's land on that beach there, Grane—you can enjoy the sand and surf while I take care of this business, but mind that you don't journey into the water too far…I don't trust the Deep-Children."

Was it a good sign or a bad one that the horse emitted a nicker as if in place of a laugh? It was difficult to read tone in even the most articulate animal. With a shake of my head, I studied the beach on which we'd landed for an adequate hiding place for valuables.

A hollow tree. I spotted it after a few moments of

searching the tree line and, satisfied by its size, I made a gamble. It did not seem wise to either leave Exigence or take it with me, but the thought of posing any threat to the god seemed particularly ill-advised. I unstrapped the sword from my waist and rested it within the tree, hiding it and the apple beneath a few fallen fronds I collected to obscure the cache.

When I finished, Grane stood in the sand with only the barest sheen of sweat to show for a length of time that surely would have killed even the mightiest steed of Urd. I took a moment to stand by his side and appreciate the vast sea over which we'd come.

"What do you suppose is happening back at the Valor Hall?" Grane shook his head at my question even as I went on, "They must be awaking in a panic to find you missing...and soon enough, they'll find me missing, too."

With a soft whinny, Grane left my side, intent on the start of the grass that called him to graze.

"You're right," I told him as foam somewhat lazily sloshed in from the sea. "It's not for you to worry about."

Nor for me. I was not there, after all...and, although Valeria and Elishta-bet were, I knew they would not be considered guilty party to my flight.

Not until they determined Valeria had robbed Anroa's tree of fruit, anyway.

My heart thudding, I made my way into the forest to find the source of smoke.

16

THE SMITH OF THE GODS

WHEN ONE UNDERTAKES a journey such as the one I took alone to face Dunnun, one does so with acute awareness of the possibilities. The possibility of failure; worse, the possibility of retreat.

But then, there is the path of victory. Paths were more negotiable than possibilities. With the path ahead half-seen at best, one found oneself looking back at all the steps that brought one to the point of even possible failure. Seeing all these accomplishments, these moments of grace and of growth, renewed the drive and the ability to see through the task.

And so it was with me, as I made my way through the woods with exotic island birds trilling in the boughs above. I had never encountered such a noisy forest in all my life, and in a certain sense the unending chatter of the parrots formed a kind of background noise as much as the waves of the beach. I grew more lost in thought with every step nearer my destination, awash with the scraps of my childhood, the duels of my youth, the field training of my quest's first leg into the Nightlands. While my body walked, my mind replayed the victorious fights of my past with such vivid recognition that muscles in my arms or legs twitched along. I had defeated a great many adversaries over my lifetime; and I had lost to my share, as well.

A god among them.

Was I any more likely to hold my ground against Dunnun, if the fight became inevitable? Would this new self-knowledge of my heritage lend anything other than the comfort of my heart?

I would discover soon, if my negotiation skills proved poor: the trees thinned after three quarters of a mile, and not long after that they gave themselves up to a clearing within which stood a cabin made from the same wood. In the same period, the charcoal scent of smoke grew increasingly evident.

By now the birds were so much the louder I could not long retain a thought in my head. I settled for taking in the scene before me, pressing behind a thick palm that seemed to provide adequate protection even with my size. There I knelt, peering around the trunk.

Somehow, I would have expected his home to be made of the Deepgold, or at least accented in it; I had no idea how much of it he had, and could only imagine that, if it was worth a sacred tree and the goddess that tended it, then it was quite a sum.

If so, where did he keep it? I wondered about a few storehouses erected on the edge of the property, but I also knew checking them to be a fatal error. Too many stories of disrespected gods circled through my mind. There would be another way for me to find the hoard, so long as I stayed upon what my intuition declared was the victorious path.

"Are you going to crouch out there all day," grumbled the rough voice of Dunnun just as I noticed the edge of what I suspected was a forge. "Come present yourself to me before I kill you, thief; I'd know who it is I'm punishing."

So much for subtlety.

"I mean you no harm, Master Dunnun," I called without emerging from the trees. "Nor do I wish to take anything without offering fair price in trade."

"Then come out and speak to me as a man, and prove it."

Unhesitating, I rose to my feet.

"I'm unarmed. What proof do I have, in turn, that you'll not kill me before I've had a chance to explain my presence on your island?"

"Only the word of a god, if that's enough for you."

"If you would bind yourself to the same laws of contract that stay Weltyr's hand against you, I will oblige."

The air held thick with silence for a time.

"Who is it that comes to me knowing our old agreement? What are you, coming here with my past in your mouth?"

"I'm Nothing," I answered, concerned that if I gave my name the god would know me for a Wotsung and turn against me before I accomplished my task.

"Nothing! Yet you sound like Something."

"Nothing is something, of course, but Nothing's what my parents named me, so it's better if you called me that. "Sorrowing" could not be my name, for my life is full of adventure and delights; "Wandering" is closer, but that's the title for a greater being than I. "Nothing" is all that I am really called."

"Then reveal yourself, Nothing, and let the hermit god see your face."

My entire mind was tuned to Exigence, hidden a mile away along with that apple.

With my wits my only weapon, I stepped out from cover and faced the god Dunnun.

And we were both surprised.

I am not sure why I was so taken aback by his stature. I had heard it expressed that most mankinds were apt to revere the gods adhered to their own earthly likeness, and it was therefore logical that mighty Dunnun would be short as the dwarfs who revered him.

Perhaps what surprised me was that his complexion was nearer that of berich dwarves than the aboveground equivalent. The long white beard bristling down to his belly was tucked into his belt, where also hung a glittering helm of chainmail that could only be the same Deepgold as Exigence; yet the mouth and face behind that beard was stony in far more than expression. I wondered if this coloration were not some effect of losing his supply of fruit, and I let it bolster my courage while the old god spoke again.

"Nothing's taller than I expected it to be...more colorful, too. And fleshy."

"Well, mighty craftsman, as I said—Nothing, too, is something, for it was dreamed up in the eye of a man."

The smith of the gods laughed and stroked his beard in thought. The mighty hammer which he held with one hand came to rest against his shoulder, my unarmed personage striking him as unthreatening enough to pass.

"I suppose so, Nothing. But by what cause do you find yourself on my island? It's been no one but the birds and the turtles and the forge for years...which is as I enjoy it."

The arrogance of offering one of Anroa's apples for the entirety of the hoard, wherever it was, occurred to me in the second just before the statement escaped my lips. Such a barter would always be inequal...but, unbound by contract, I was not above the use of guile to get my way. Perhaps, if given a few days on the island, I would manage to find the Deepgold and liberate it as Weltyr once stole it.

"As I said, my life overflows with adventure—and on one of these many journeys, I heard the story of your great gold hoard and your renown skills at smithing it."

"So you came to stake an adventurer's claim to it? A bit lightly armed to be facing down a god, Nothing."

Smiling, spreading my hands, I assured him, "If I had my way, we would be as friends."

"Then why are you here? Speak plainly."

"I have brought a gift to barter knowledge from you—to learn the divine arts of smithing from the one that first taught mankind to imitate them."

I had hoped this idea would flatter Dunnun's ego, but his mouth contorted to an ugly sneer.

"And why might you be worthy of such a thing? Have you any knowledge of the forge?"

"Not but vaguely, from what I've gleaned in passing conversation or the pages of books."

"An airheaded knight...go on, fool, begone from here! I won't give up a single gold filing for the greed of another."

"It is not greed for gold that motivates me, divine smith, but the drive to be greater than all other men in whatever I pursue."

"Then go forth and humble yourself. Nothing's worth this sacred gold of mine."

"You're sure to teach me, then! Yes, I agree you, Nothing's worth your sacred gold...and that is why I have brought you the one thing you might trade for the materials and education I seek: a pittance of your original price, just as the small bit of gold I might use in my apprenticeship is but a forgettable part of the greater hoard."

"All the Deepgold is invaluable, and all of it belongs to me."

"Anroa's apples are likewise invaluable in their exclusivity, and yet one is upon this island with us now."

The god had been turning away, and that inattention carried on for the delay of a second: then, with understanding, he whipped back toward me.

"How could that be?"

"I brought one with me, of course, revered Dunnun. Gladly would I give it up to you for but a few ounces of your precious gold, and a few lessons of your precious understanding."

Dunnun looked me sharply up and down. "You lie."

"The man who would lie to a god is cursed; I have not lied. I am Nothing before you, and you are right to say I have come for your gold. But I also bring a gift to compensate the unworthiness of my request, and if you will deal with me, I will see to it that you are justly paid."

"Let me see it."

"I have hidden it, not wanting to provoke your temptation to strike me down and acquire the fruit by force."

The god bared his teeth in frustration.

"Then I'm to blindly trust that Nothing will be good to its word?"

"Men have faith in the gods; don't the gods, in their turn, have faith in Nothing?"

For a long, agonizing period of assessment, Dunnun stared me down. When at last he broke my unflinching gaze, it was to spit upon the earth at his feet.

"Go back the way you came, stranger. Apple or no apple, your naivety in the arts of smithing will only disgrace the gold you seek to shape."

And, saying nothing more, Dunnun made his way into the cabin with a heavy slam of the door.

Disappointment was the first, natural reaction that swept through me while I stood alone amid the steadily resuming bird-chatter.

Then, euphoria.

I had faced the god and had come through our first conversation alive, without physical conflict. True enough, Dunnun had been as disagreeable as any hermit would have been when approached with such a request; but perhaps, if I remained persistent, he would perceive my seriousness and interpret it as heartfelt dedication to learning his art.

And, at any rate, I had to admit this was a real opportunity. Most men who fight have an appreciation for the arts of the blacksmith, and it was a craft to which more than a few adventurers retired if given an early injury and an opportunity for less harrowing work. Those who became skilled at the craft could elevate it to an artform. Were I to learn the discipline, I was sure to see many benefits—and, perhaps, an occupation when the time came for me to rest in a place I called home.

So there was much genuine interest in my heart, I will say that. But Dunnun was right to turn me away, because there was other intent beneath that interest. So, accepting my fate for the night, I turned around and made the walk back to Grane without complaint.

"I am beginning to think this is going to be a longer process than I estimated," I told the horse when he greeted me with a nod from where he peacefully rested in the grass demarking our beach. "Poor Grane! Will you pine for your mistress? I wish we did not have to embroil you in this scheme."

What was going to become of all this? I sat down in the grass beside the horse for a while, the two of us together watching gulls swoop down amid the surf to snatch fish. I decided that some manner of fishing was my best supply of food before I even fully realized I was going to be camping there at least a few nights—and that was assuming the god changed his mind immediately and came to seek me out.

In fact, I sensed I was going to have to wear him down. I would be gone from the Valor Hall seven nights at least, though quite possibly more.

What would happen in that time?

Worry was useless. I had chosen my path and was too far down it to turn back. With these opportunities that no man could know but me, I had to seize them fearlessly; without regret.

After stripping from the waist up, I removed Exigence from its hiding place and set about the task of cutting the vines that would be my net. My ears tuned to the sounds of nature, I worked in silence unless it was to curse my exertion. Every errant crack of a branch was, I hoped, Dunnun coming to invite me into his trust; I would pause my work, listening, my heart high with hope.

And the birds would laugh at me.

My first net was very poor, but it did still manage to sweep up a small silver fish when I waded into the water with it as my weapon. Satisfied for now, I fixed the fish for dinner, weighted the net that it might collect for me overnight, and stared into the fire that kept us warm through the dark.

When I woke the next morning, it was in the groggy confusion of one who did not expect to have fallen asleep. Somehow, though sense implied otherwise, I had believed in my heart that Dunnun would change his mind in just that first night. With a boyish hope, I had dissociated from the reality of the situation that dawned on me with the sun.

Drained by these new certainties, I set about to use the morning well.

While Grane clambered to his hooves and resumed his peaceful grazing, I collected fallen branches for firewood and found the net had been torn by the struggles of a fish that left behind two of its brothers for me. I cut down more vines, and had by noon I satisfied myself that I would be comfortable there for another day.

I redressed, then patted Grane's nose. "Wait for me, friend; and if I never return, fly to your mistress with word of what's happened."

The horse bobbed his snout, one eye upon me as I once more made my way into the woods.

"You again," was Dunnun's unhappy greeting to me when, not long later, I once more stood on the edge of his property. The smith had been hacking wood for charcoal and waved the gleaming axe at me, saying, "I thought I told you to leave! Begone from here."

"I cannot leave until I've learned from you," I told him earnestly. "I have risked my life by taking Anroa's apple away from the Valor Hall. I will not return with it, servilely muttering apologies."

"Nor will you prove to me it exists to begin with!"

"What man would invite a god's violence with such an empty lie? The apple is here on the island with us, I swear. I will give it to you freely if you will teach me without doing me harm before I can make good my payment."

But no words could win the god to my favor, I feared.

"No!" Furious, the ancient smith threw his axe down into the chopping block. There it stuck while its master spoke to me in a snarl. "No mortal hand could ever work the Deepgold! Give it up, Nothing. Begone with you, before I see to your ejection from my island by my own two hands."

And, to signal the conversation's ending, Dunnun once more shut himself in his hut.

This time, I did not leave. I waited, my hands folded as I rested on a great stone near the edge of the property.

No movement signaled his presence within the cabin. I had the feeling he'd either taken to rest, or had set up a post by some window through which he watched me. What he could see of me, anyway, looking through the woodpile as he had to.

What a great pile of unmanaged logs! The amount of work required to cut this wood was surely hours on hours. No wonder he felt so foully toward the matter of my apprenticeship…here I came, expecting him to teach me with little more than an apple for payment. It was not just his gold I'd be using, but his labor.

An hour passed. The god did not come out.

Not wanting his hard work to be wasted, I approached the stack and took hold of the axe. With some pressure from my foot, the deeply-buried blade came loose from the wound it had made in the chopping block.

Then, after studying the abandoned log waiting to be split, I took up Dunnun's work for him.

To say the task was a simple one would be a mischaracterization. It was not long before a sheen of sweat coated my body, and not long after that when it began to drip from my brow. After what must have been at least an hour, the amazing pile seemed to have decreased precious little. Yet my muscles burned, and my body presented my mind with the temptation to simply lay down the axe and return to my camp. What was human in me told the god in me, "This is good enough."

But, knowing myself a Wotsung, how could I be

satisfied with that? How could I look at myself with the respect I requested from this hermit?

So, I drove myself on; and, truth be told, the task was so meditative that, after a time, I forgot the burning in my arms and legs entirely. In so many ways, I stopped seeing what I did or where I was. There was only the satisfaction of the work: of the task's completion drawing ever-nearer until that moment when the spell was broken by empty space where once the imposing stack had risen. My body had turned and my arm had extended, but there was no more wood to be found.

I was at once aware that I panted with exertion.

The house remained shut to me, a thin trail of smoke rising from its chimney to a sky that I was surprised to find had already softened with night's nearness.

Resting the axe upon the chopping block and mopping my brow with the tunic I slung over my shoulder, I left the clearing for my camp.

The next day, mid-morning this time, Dunnun sneered at me while stacking the cut wood in the floor of his charcoal kiln—one of many vast pieces of equipment arranged around the back of his little house.

"You think I'll have changed my mind about you just because you chopped some wood? I didn't even ask for it."

"If we are to be neighbors, Dunnun, then it is a decent thing for me to help you when I can."

"We're not neighbors! You're an interloper—this is *my* island."

"Yes; and I will leave it once I have learned what I wish to learn. Until then, whatever else I am to you, I will also be your neighbor."

"Then you're a nuisance, too…go on! Get out of my sight. I've work to do."

I pretended to leave him at his command, spreading my arms and saying, "I will be of use to you when you change your mind," before disappearing into the woods.

Really, I went loudly into the brush and then came quietly back.

From a hiding place of overgrown berry bushes and the shade of their adjacent tree, I watched Dunnun at work. Each log had to be tightly packed, based on the number he fit into the chamber of the kiln. When that was done and it all fit within, the seal was put on and the fire was brought to a rage around it.

Then, the waiting.

From my own experience, I know now that three hours' worth of observation passed me by in that time. In the moment, it seemed like an eternity. Would he see me? Would I then miss some invaluable piece of information on being truly sent away? I held my breath anytime the god's gaze turned near me, but he was busy. While he waited for the wood to pyrolyze, Dunnun set about his art.

The process of smelting gold is a different matter entirely from the art of forging, but both bear the same ritualistic quality that has a way of making their masters turn inward. So I have observed, at any rate, in myself and others. As I did while chopping wood, Dunnun went inside of himself while building the fire of his forge with charcoal he already had on-hand. While he murmured to himself—thoughts aloud I could not catch—the hermit used a stick to catch the blaze of the charcoal and light the forge's hearth.

Then, after beating the bellows for a time, he thrust an iron rod into the heart of the coals. It was not long before the rhythmic clanking of his hammer against his anvil lured me into a similar stupor. I was not drawn from it until the white vapor of wood's moisture had transformed into the lapping chemical flames that raced up from the chimney of the kiln, which was the station that was farthest from the cabin for an obvious reason. Deftly Dunnun struck, and swiftly, often returning the bar into the fire before resuming the process, sometimes appearing as though to flex off the tip with a peculiar tool. It was some time of wondering before I realized what he made. Not one thing, but many: iron arrowheads, I realized when he raised a quenched one out of the water basin into which he'd dropped them.

In the three hours that he stood there hammering away, the god must have made close to hundreds of the little things. There was no smith faster, to be sure, nor more natural in the craft for which he was revered. I was awed—and concerned.

If he fought as he forged, it was all the more vital that I earn his trust and find the gold in a subtle way.

By the time he wiped his forearm upon his ashen brow to tend the kiln and reduce the fire around it, the light signaled late afternoon. He left the inner chamber and all its charcoal sealed up, closing off the chimney and its dramatics.

Then, before even removing his work gloves, Dunnun retired to his cabin for the day.

The next morning, I made visiting my neighbor my top priority. I arrived just in time to see him sorting through the charcoal over a wire frame. Satisfied that it had all been properly rendered, he threw it into its bin alongside the cabin and dusted off his hands in satisfaction. The kiln had yielded quite a large amount, but I observed the bin was long and could not have been even a quarter full.

Yet, there were other tasks. Now he busily built a quiver full of arrows with the heads from the day prior; and, when that was done, he slung the quiver upon his shoulder, fetched a bow from within his cabin, and went off into the woods while dragging a kind of sled—through the side of the clearing opposite mine, I was relieved to see.

Having learned nothing more, I sat defeated on my haunches for a few moments before I realized that I still had one valuable piece of knowledge.

So, eager to use it, I took wood from the pile I myself had chopped and filled the inner chamber of the kiln in Dunnun's yard.

Having been built to satisfy the god's scale, the kiln filled up quickly—too quickly, I thought, given how much more wood the god had stacked within. I peered inside and, deciding I could make the fit tighter, had to empty it all out and start again.

When my second attempt was more successful, I simply mimicked the rest of what I had seen. I used flint to strike the fire, sealed the lid over the inner chamber, then returned to my hiding place to oversee it from a distance.

Mark—the temptation to search for the gold that day was immense, and the fool in me boasted that we could find and liberate it before Dunnun was back from his hunt. Yet the fool in me was but a part of me, and not the ruler of me. The Wotsung was slowly rising to control, and the wisdom of that inner nature counseled me to wait for a better time. What was the likelihood, after all, that Dunnun did not know I was near—just as he did the first time? Had he even gone hunting, I wondered, or had he taken up a post at the edge of the trees to see what I would do?

Perhaps I was becoming paranoid; but paranoia serves its purpose. Each day, I made more progress in the matter. Each day, I was closer to the gold's liberation. To ruin my chances by forever sealing myself off from Dunnun's trust would be my own ruin, too. I would be dead, I reminded myself, and forever. Then what would happen to the world? To my friends?

I resisted. Instead, I watched the kiln.

Early afternoon, Dunnun returned with a deer dragging behind him on the sled. He paused on the edge of the trees, regarding the kiln he approached with curiosity. Upon dropping the lead of the sled and unslinging both quiver and bow from his shoulder, the god went about killing the fire and shutting the chimney as he had the day before.

"You think if you make yourself useful I'll show you some favor? Don't be ridiculous…you're a meddler, Nothing. You risk your very existence by toying with me. I'll not give the Deepgold to any man. Not an ounce!"

"But would you trade it," I called back, revealing myself to the sharp head-whip and acid stare of the immortal.

"Go on," he called, hurling a stone at me from well across the clearing. Even managed to strike me in the shoulder, despite the bushes where I crouched. "Get out of here!"

And I did, of course; but I took care to come very early in the next morning, long before the hours of dawn, to sort the charcoal of the day prior and start another batch.

The same as before, I waited and watched. This time, however, Dunnun emerged with a pickaxe, the same sled as before, and a snort at the sight of the burning kiln.

Shaking his head, the god went off in the same direction he'd gone to hunt.

Was it iron ore he was after, I wondered? What a process he had to undergo to live this life of solitude! I, who had barely managed to construct a fishing net for my first night, (though they were growing better by the day), somewhat envied his self-subsistence. There was not a thing he needed from the outside world. No wonder he didn't want me around!

Intrigued, never having observed mining before, I stayed with the fire for a few long hours before it was safe to leave it be. Then, with the god showing no sign of a return, I followed the trail of his sled's tracks into the depths of the woods.

The truth was I had been so focused on Dunnun that I had seen approximately two areas of the island— his, and mine. There was a whole wilderness I might have explored if given the inclination, and a mountain that rose about a day's walk from the cabin.

But there was no time for luxury. No sweet sights or sounds could deviate me from the path the god had lain. I pursued signs of his fresh tracks for well over an hour and was rewarded by the steady clanging of his pick into the ore of a quarry.

It would seem Dunnun had picked an island that he

knew overflowed with valuable resources, though I had expected to see iron ore chipped steadily away beneath his axe. Instead, the substance was dark. Lead? I strained to tell from my vantage, high as I was upon a steep hill that overlooked the yawning mouth of the quarry.

When, at the end of another few hours of work, the sled was loaded up, Dunnun grunted with exertion. He dragged it into the woods behind him, leaving the site open for my investigation. I clambered down to the substance which I studied in curiosity. Surely, it was not lead. This substance had a way of glimmering in even the softening light.

Then, as I picked up a few brittle flakes and marked how they blackened my fingertips, it came to me: graphite.

But why?

I did not know until the next day.

On that island, all my mornings were the same. I awoke just before dawn, stirred by some internal alarm or perhaps by Grane's early mutterings. After realizing I was still there, still on that island, still empty-handed, I would get up to check the fishing net.

Necessity makes an expert of any man. I was pleased that morning, having collected such a fine selection of fish that I let a few go. Taking the best with me back to my camp, I decided that I would take a day off from watching Dunnun's life and perhaps explore the island a little, myself.

Imagine my surprise when the cracking of the underbrush overwhelmed the gentler crackle of my breakfast's cooking fire.

"Don't say anything," groused the god as he emerged from the trees, glancing at the horse without recognition and dragging his sled on past both of us. "I'd just as soon not see you, but my hands are tied."

"Then come join me for breakfast and look the other way while you do it, my friend."

"Already eaten," Dunnun grunted, adding, "not your friend."

I laughed merrily to myself, his sour attitude my most consistent source of entertainment on that isolated little island. However amusing he was, I still took pains to watch him from the corner of my eye. What was he doing, subjecting himself to my presence to get to the beach?

Clay, I determined. With a shovel that he brought with him, Dunnun harvested soft red rocks that were gathered at a towering sand dune not far from my camp. How oblivious I had been! I had barely even noticed the deposit, and when I glimpsed it wrote it off as just another stone. It was humbling to learn the smith's ways, and fascinating. When I hastily ate my breakfast and followed him back to his home that day, I watched him mix the clay with water and flaked graphite he must have broken up after getting home the night before. Then, after pouring this new black clay into sizable rectangular molds, scraping them flat, and removing the scaffolding of the mold to see the shape was retained, he left them to dry in the sun and went about other tasks.

Fascinating! What was this for, I wondered? I was so eager to learn, yet I had no teacher; I could only absorb by secondhand study. The process was so fascinating that I half-forgot about the gold and my original quest there.

In fact, I thought consciously of it only a few days later.

The graphite bricks were dry. Dunnun determined it with a knock against their surfaces and investigation of a test block he hefted in his hands. Smiling to himself, (the first time I had seen him wear such an expression, even alone), he dragged a bench out of his open workshop and into a bright patch of sunlight. Then, after collecting a few chisels of varying sizes, a small mallet, and a stool upon which he perched, the god began chipping away.

A carved mold, I realized—a mold for smelting metals.

A definite shift occurred on the island between myself and my unwilling host.

At last! I had been there already how long? One week? Two? I had lost track of time and could not seem to fully establish it; but, in that stretch, the only traces of Deepgold I had seen were the chainmail helm Dunnun always carried in his belt, and, of course, Exigence. Now, I had an opportunity to narrow the location of the precious metal's greatest hoard.

His steady chipping was as ceaseless and confident as every other task in the labors of his profession. Whatever vision he sought to replicate, Dunnun's hands were expert at the reproduction. Every now and again he did pause, but it was only to blow away a layer of graphite dust and better examine the development of his work.

Then, on the next day, he was ready.

As I had suspected he might, the god emerged from his house with a lump of gold glowing in his hand. Dawn was just breaking. While I watched, he stoked a fire in the furnace which I had not yet seen ablaze. It was like a great cauldron whose edges overflowed with flame instead of potion; I watched, awed, as he tended the furious contents, then turned with a hum on his lips to take the lump of Deepgold from the table where he'd set it. He cradled it in his hands with a tender look of love.

Then, singing soft words in a language I did not know, Dunnun slid the gold into a crucible of the same graphite as the molds. A great pair of tongs were used to grasp this container, which he lowered into the blaze.

It took about twenty minutes, to my shock. I had expected the process to go on longer than it did. What little I knew of goldsmithing at the time provided me with the vague knowledge that certain impure metals were present in Urd's gold, which required purification with chemicals before it was cast. This was a step that Dunnun skipped, and I was less surprised when I thought about it later. No physical impurity could be found within the Deepgold: its corruption was more complex.

A few times, thoughts of worse acts than the treachery I already planned crossed my mind. I eschewed them, of course, but I did occasionally consider how easily I could go back to my camp, eat of the sacred apple, and slay the god in battle before he even realized what I had done. Yet what knowledge would be lost with him! I could not accept the idea, and so I watched on as he withdrew the crucible from the fire. Still singing, the god used a different pair of tongs to pour a vibrant ribbon of molten Deepgold into the graphite mold.

Then, pleased, Dunnun admired his handiwork, killed the fire, and went off to hunt in celebration.

Alone with the cooling Deepgold, I could not help but assess the contents of the mold.

One single, perfect key.

17

BECOMING NOTHING

I AM NOT sure what I expected to find in that little graphite mold. Whatever I anticipated, a key was not high in my list.

What lock did it open? What enchantment might it hold? It was so simple—squarish in shape, and unornamented due to its mold being hand-carved rather than sculpted. Yet I sensed it was as powerful in its way as Exigence or the Lantern, and that whatever it opened could be unlocked by no other means.

How long would the god be gone? Last time, it would seem he really had been out hunting. He had been gone for some hours before returning with a buck, accomplishing the task in godly haste despite his late start. Given his early one that day, I did not wish to risk stealing the key and using it now, only for him to come upon me in some secret space of his home.

Yet, I dared not leave it behind.

While the gold cooled, I poked around the workshop and soon came upon what I sought. A block of beeswax sat amid the clutter, its soft surface marred with strikes from a chisel. I consulted the key's size before carving off a little palmful of the modeling medium, estimating the rough size of the gold lump Dunnun had carried in his hand.

Then, vigilant for the slightest sound from the trees beneath the chatter of the birds, I warmed the wax between my hands and waited on the gold.

As was the way of all life's achievements, the cooling-off was torturous. It did not take long at all—in fact, it was hardly an hour before the key could be removed without disrupting it or burning me—but, with Dunnun's return an omnipresent possibility, each second stretched into days. I hovered, my muscles tense, the beeswax alternately forgotten and massaged by my unconscious hands.

When I could stand it no longer, I tapped the metal in its mold, then rested my fingers there.

Solid, and cool.

Breath held, I turned the mold over and thumped the key into the palm of my hand; with great will and eyes that kept turned from what I did, I set it aside. The warm wax fit easily into the key's place in the graphite mold, and I waited once again for a shorter, albeit more torturous cooling process. I strained to hear above the thumping of my heart.

When the wax was stiff, I swapped them again. The gold key fit comfortably back into its mold, looking as though it had not yet been touched; I even took pains of lightly polishing its edge with a clean cloth that lay nearby for later, leaving no smudge as evidence of my subterfuge.

Eager to leave, I whisked the copy with me back to my camp.

Again, another extension of my time on that lonely little dot in the middle of the sea. I knew that I might easily have taken the key then and there; maybe even found its lock before their master came home. But the odds of something going wrong by letting the god find me in his house still seemed too great. The possibility of a trap having been lain, greater still. I did not wish to tempt Fate, although Fate was as alluring as any of the women of my acquaintance.

The wax copy of the key nestled comfortably into the hiding place with Exigence and that unflagging apple, whose golden skin showed not the least sign of wear or rot. I worried it would not last forever, but I also worried over Valeria and Elishta-bet—and, on another layer of time and space, Branwen, Indra, and Odile. I could not dwell with my worries, so I set about with my own tasks around my encampment and let the work turn my mind from them, but they were with me still, quietly, every day I spent in that serene place.

By now I had made myself something approximating a comfortable home. A lean-to of palm leaves and a few choice branches gave me a fine enough place to sleep, and the system I had developed for fishing kept me from spending precious time trying to trap rabbits or engineer a bow and arrow.

Most days that was the case, anyway. I was sorry to find after a few hours of collecting firewood and riding Grane to stretch his legs that one net had broken, and the other had gathered nothing but seaweed. My stomach rumbled at the thought of a night with no food. I replaced the nets, intent on foraging for some sort of fruit or another.

But by the time I reached the heart of my camp, my mind rotating through plausible methods of basket-weaving, the scent of a far more appealing food rose to me on the wind—much as the steps of its chef through the underbrush struck my ears.

"Hail, Nothing," the god called from the trees, making his steady way through to the boundary of the trees. "See how the respectable man awaits permission before entering his fellow's camp?"

"I am nothing if not respectable, friend," I responded with a laugh. "But the wood needed chopping, and the charcoal wanted burning, and I don't think I heard you complain to have so much fuel, in the end."

Dunnun snorted, striding from the thick of the trees and through their gradual parting. "What man would argue to find his work done for him? Especially such tedious matters as all that...I'm an artisan, an artist. Yet here, alone on this island, I've been consigned to labor on as my own assistant."

He drifted off into pondering, one hand stroking the fullness of his beard while the other settled upon his belt, thumb poised between his chainmail helm of gleaming Deepgold and the mighty hammer that rested like a sword in a sheath.

"I must admit," he said at last, "I had you fixed for some sort of thief…but I came back from hunting today, and there was my key, right where it belonged in the mold by which I cast it."

I smiled. "I am Nothing if not honest. I wish to be your apprentice for a time—only until I have an apt grasp of the mechanics of your arts."

"You could learn that from any smith what's been brought to my brother's Hall."

"But to learn such basics from a god is to learn them in a way no other man might. If I labored under you ten, twenty, thirty years in a human's Urdly time—"

"There's no such time here," Dunnun surprised me by saying. "There's only work, and what it costs to do."

"Very well. If I labored under you until complete mastery, what would my own work be? Merely an echo. A copy of a greater master's envisioning, and an unnatural one at that. I would have your eye cleaved to all I did— even once I went away from this place.

"But, Dunnun, if you might but grant me the foundation of these arts, the rules and the ways and the pleasing secrets, then I away could take that knowledge and build on it my own design. My own soul's noble fruits expressed in creativity. It might take any form, unbeholden to you—and yet in honor of you, and with respect to you, and by the ancient tradition you have imparted."

With a thoughtful smack of his lips, Dunnun turned all that over in his mind. "I'll have you working as you never have before—and before I'll let you touch my gold, there are a great many tasks you'll have to complete."

"I am Nothing if not obedient to the gods," I assured him, the double-tongued statement staying in me to ring between my ears once I had spoken it aloud.

Yet Dunnun did not read so deeply into it. In fact, he seemed satisfied. He nodded to himself.

"Very well, neighbor. Why not walk back to my cabin with me? Bring your horse along…I've a stable where you both can stay, though I'm sure you knew that much already."

Resisting my eyes' guilty strain to turn upon the friendly hollow tree not far from him, I assured him, "My encampment here suits me well, if you don't mind…but I would take you up on supper."

"Very well…let's have a conversation."

Over the venison, the terms of my apprenticeship were decided. They were rooted in the pattern to which I had already accustomed myself, I found. I would rouse early and hasten to the cabin in the middle of the woods, and there I would set about the tasks which would be needed for that day. The only difference was that now I did it with Dunnun's will aligned to mine.

What, precisely, had he meant about time and labor as applied to the island? I wasn't sure because I had never been at rest in that place, aside from when I slept at night—but sleep was its own form of labor, a duty to the body and the mind. Now, having committed to work for the god on his terms, I knew I would not have occasion to rest anytime in the foreseeable future. I could only hope that I understood him correctly, and that the island was somehow removed from the natural flow of time that even the Valor Hall seemed to obey.

There was not much time to worry or wonder, however. The god was good to his word and delivered on the promised backbreaking labor from the very first day of my apprenticeship. His first task for me was to work the bellows while he hammered out arrowhead after arrowhead, having spent his last batch on hunting and target practice at some range he'd built in the woods. It seemed it should have been an easy thing, yet the master craftsman of the gods had, as was natural, built his home and forge and kiln and furnace all to a scale that suited him.

In other words, I had to kneel to work the bellows without breaking my back. You may imagine that what relieved my arms and spine provoked a great deal of agony to my lower extremities. I was, amazingly, fatigued by the end of the first hour, and the god paused in his work to mock me.

"If this is too much for you, Nothing, you'd ought to take your horse away and give all this up now."

My body was so unexpectedly weary that I was almost tempted. Still, sweat on my brow, I compacted the leather bladder between its boards and sent another brilliant scattering of ash bursting out from the heart of the growing flame.

I had always found that, when tested, my work was the best and only reply. Seeing this, the god smirked as though to himself and thrust the rod he worked back into the blaze.

The hours were long. At the very least, the amount of work I did for him until the sun went down would have constituted a full twelve hours of labor and then some. He fed me each day, each time while explaining some valuable mechanic of forging or smelting or even the sculpting that would be required to produce casting molds; and, every sixth time the sun went down, he'd dismiss me for a day to tend to my own camp.

How Grane was not miserable with boredom and loneliness, I did not know until one of those days off. While I chopped my own firewood with an axe I had borrowed from Dunnun, the horse disappeared into the trees. Alarmed as much as curious, I followed him from a distance until a bird alighted upon his back and sang a little song. At the creature's trill, Grane wiggled his ears and moved his lips with a soft nicker.

As the bird sang back, I jested to myself that they were talking.

By the twelfth or thirteenth such exchange, I believed that they were.

Quite astonished, I reminded myself that Grane was a god in his own right. More a god than me, in truth. Not wanting to eavesdrop on even a conversation I could not understand, I returned to my business around the camp.

What a strange island! The more time I spent there, the more I observed that all things there fell into place precisely to permit a man's mind to focus on his work. Every other worry seemed to sort itself out. Food put itself in my mouth; I had no want for shelter or warmth; my horse was occupied; if I understood correctly, time on the island was a separate enterprise from time in the Valor Hall, and I might in fact still be able to return "by morning."

Day by day, all other thoughts left my mind except for ones that pertained to my tasks, my education, and my growing interest in all Dunnun's arts. I even forgot somedays that I was dead, and that only the Deepgold would free me from my state.

Then, I forgot it entirely.

It may amaze you to think these designs slipped my mind when they were the entire reason I had come to that strange island—yet, the work was of such a meditative nature that I would defy any man to remember his own name after a sufficient amount of it. Day in and out I chopped wood, burned charcoal, mined graphite, harvested clay, worked the bellows, cleaned up, crafted arrows, gutted and processed his hunts, and did so many more things that no reader would be able to withstand this already somewhat slow period of my tale (though I assure you, reader, that is soon to change). I, Nothing, dissolved as an entity. I was the work that I did, and very soon I was unsettled when my hands were idle.

Growing up, I had never taken pleasure in work. Zweiding was right to call me a priest who liked to fight. I was, in truth. I was a man made to pray—but prayer expresses itself in many forms. As a young man, my prayer was through the sword, and through works that represented expressions of Weltyr's will.

I had never much thought of what I would do as an old man, though. What would happen when, for this or that reason, my adventuring had come to its end and I still had time on Urd? Now being dead, I thought for the first time of my future, and I finally foresaw what new form prayer might take in my works. As Exigence had been shaped by my master's hand, so I learned from Dunnun how to create lesser emanations of that sacred sword and other weapons of its ilk. After many kilns of coal, many fires tended, and many pounds of graphite clay produced while I watched Dunnun work glowing metals into shape, the god turned to me.

"Well, you must by now be itching for something different."

So it was that he started me on forging. First, with arrowheads; then, knives; then swords, axes, and the like. A few of these pieces, I was permitted to keep for my own use around my camp. Many were kept for Dunnun's use, or melted back down when deemed too inferior.

And many were deemed inferior. For a very long time, or what seemed to be a very long time, it was frustrating, miserable work that went on without any feasible end. I enjoyed the flow of the task, but I felt no improvement and saw no variance in the number of pieces he rightly insulted once they were drawn from the water for examination in the light of day.

"What a clumsy little dagger! More of a bludgeon... try again."

I did. I tried again, over and over, my focus having narrowed to only the perfection of the craft. By this time, I had entirely forgotten why I had been dispatched to the island and decided to learn the secrets of the smith. I wished to perfect my skills in my apprenticeship for their own sake, and mine. There was such nobility in the act of creation—even, or perhaps especially, if the object created was a weapon by which to strike down a living creature.

In time, as my skills made their slow progression toward acceptability, Dunnun warmed to me. He invited me on hunts with him once weekly, even kindly awarding me a hunting horn when I produced my first permissible axe. My familiarity with the woods improved, as did my familiarity with bow and arrow. Together, we could corner any beast that we wished.

One night, when we had feasted on roast boar and enjoyed the inebriation of honeyed mead the old god brewed in some cellar of his, he grew drunk enough to tell me, "Song's the secret, Nothing...it's what you haven't really learned."

I had heard the god chanting or singing to himself many times while he worked at his forge, and certainly had noticed it that time I watched him cast the key; yet I had not considered it had anything to do with the process, and told him as much.

"It's not the hammering that benefits, as such. But whatever fills your mind, that's what'll come flowing out. Especially important when I finally let you work with the Deepgold. What'll you make, anyway?"

I hadn't the slightest idea and frankly laughed at the question. "I've been so occupied by the tasks you've set for me that I've not once put my mind to the question!"

"Well, you'd better consider it. I'm putting you on brass soon...I think it's about time you learned more about smelting and casting, don't you?"

"It would be an honor to learn the arts I know are dearest to you, Dunnun."

"Save it, Nothing...show your gratitude with that apple. If it's real, at any rate."

"Of course it is. As real as I am, my friend...maybe more."

Though my mouth expressed such a thing, I confess I did not feel in synch with my body at the time. Or, no—perhaps it was that I was so totally in synch with my body that I was Nothing but my body, and there was no 'I'. There was only that work that caused me to leap up excitedly.

"We'll need more charcoal," I told him. "If I fill the kiln tonight, perhaps you can show me a thing or two tomorrow."

"First you'll have to learn to sculpt…but, if you feel like loading the kiln, I won't stop you."

Somehow, of my own volition, my workload seemed to increase. There was always something else to learn, it seemed. The gulf of understanding between expert smelting and my current knowledge was a whole unknown artistic territory, and I feared I did not have the capacity…but, quickly, I was surprised to find that was not the case. With a pen and paper, I am no artist with anything save for words (or so Valeria assures me). With a three-dimensional space to work in and plenty of clay to work with, however, I found my mind adapted itself very well to the tasks of sculpting, carving, and all other steps involved in the production of molds for smelted metals.

Not that this expertise occurred overnight, either— but I think perhaps that the skills of forging had already opened my mind to work in three dimensions. With Dunnun's criticism, I learned to be thorough and particular in my sculpting. Soon it was my own dissatisfaction that drove me, with every piece of brass I cast finer than the last but never fine enough to suit me.

Would these futile skills stand up to the Deepgold? Dunnun had been right to teach me all these other arts first. It was obvious that, even with what I knew now, any effort at working it would only dishonor the sacred gold.

Soon I voluntarily broke down my own pieces, smelting old works again to be molded into a new and better form. I became so preoccupied with the perfection of the crafts that I did not notice Dunnun permitting me more and more independence. Soon I was welcome to use the workshop whenever it pleased me. I did not need to ask, so long as supplies were plentiful and he did not require whatever it was I was using at the time. It was not long before I was crafting my own arrowheads, or replacing Grane's horseshoes without hesitation.

Driven by perfection, I often worked late into the night. Dunnun was not bothered by my work and I took full advantage of the extra hours, using every second I was awake to better familiarize myself with each aspect of the craft. On this or that project I might work for hours, until the moon was high and my body, honed to an even sharper condition than it had been in when I arrived, grew worn. Only then would I return to my camp to retire for a few hours, albeit reluctantly.

And so it was that, by this search for perfection, the apprentice overheard his master addressing a third entity of which he had no knowledge.

I had just finished ensuring the kiln was shut down for the night when, unexpectedly, Dunnun's laughter rose from his house. Had an animal of some kind gotten in? I waited, ears straining, and caught the edge of another laugh; then, murmuring like speech.

A guest? On this island? I marveled at the idea that anyone else could be here at all, let alone without my knowing. It barely made sense—and it filled me with a combination of curiosity and dread. The days and nights had all been so much the same in the rhythm of my work that I might have engaged in it eternally.

Yet, here was something different. Here was a change to the season: an interruption in the pattern that had carried me away.

"That may be so," Dunnun told his guest as, intrigued, I crept to the god's house and crouched near a window that gave the best acoustics, "but don't forget, it was *you* who said he couldn't be trusted."

I strained my ears for the guest's response, but it was a murmur too soft for me to catch from outside the house. Dunnun's snort, on the other hand, was perfectly audible.

"Aye, that's just what you've told me since before he even came upon my shores. But, my friend, if the Deepgold was all that mattered to him, wouldn't he have made his move on it by now? Taken the key, at least."

The quiet guest responded in a murmur. I burned with curiosity to know who Dunnun addressed and dared inch closer to the window.

"That may be so, but I've not seen any evidence of it yet. As much respect as I have for you, cousin, I think you're wrong."

Carefully as I could, I leaned out from the facade to peer through the glass and into Dunnun's house.

While tending the fire of his hearth, Dunnun talked to himself.

18

THE MASTERPIECE

SILENT AS THE sleeping birds, I left Dunnun's camp with my mind turning the one-sided conversation over and over.

Whomever he addressed, in his mind or his cabin or some other realm unseen, they were right. I had come for the Deepgold—I had just somehow become caught up in the very deception by which I once hoped to attain it. The deception had become reality. I *had* become Dunnun's apprentice, and had gained my own love of the arts in which he educated me.

Yet, I had begun to reach the height of what I could

hope to learn from him. At least, from the standpoint of mechanics. With my work's quality growing more acceptable all the time, all that would be left soon would be artistic flair—and I would develop that with experience, regardless of whether I labored under the master smith. In other words, my time as an apprentice was swiftly reaching its end; soon, I would be a journeyman in these arts, and it would be time for me to end my acquaintance with Dunnun.

In that time, what had I done to find the Deepgold? Nothing. It had not even crossed my mind. Now knowing that he had been advised somehow of my ambitions, I was certainly sglad I had not gone looking where I was not welcome to. All the same, I felt a sudden pressure to reassess my presence on the island and everything it meant. What I hoped to accomplish by learning to smith—and whether, in smithing for its own sake, I might derive some secret that could benefit my quest.

It occurred to me the next day, though I had no idea how soon I would be benefitted.

Dunnun greeted me outside his cabin at sun-up, his arms folded. "You've certainly been hard at work, Nothing."

"The call to mastery drives me on."

"So I have seen—so you have proven. Come with me, Nothing; I've something for you."

I had expected him to take off to the workshop and was surprised when the god instead disappeared into his house. Eyeing the short door for but a moment, I soon stooped my way in just in time to see him disappear down stone stairs to a root cellar.

"Wait there, now. I won't be a moment."

At the bottom of the stairs, a second door swung open. I waited, hands folded before me even as my eyes roved wildly over every square inch of the domicile. It was compact, perhaps because he did so much of his living outside. The bed was up in a loft over my head, with a window that looked over the property. Weapons of his clearly divine craftsmanship adorned the walls, while a great cooking pot sat empty over the barren hearth.

Nowhere did I see any sign of guests, nor of gold.

Not until Dunnun came trudging back up the stairs, a small bundle of fabric about the size of an apple reverently held in his hands.

"Here it is," he announced while appearing at the top of the stairs, the slightest hint of a smile crossing his lips. "Your opportunity. The only Deepgold I'll ever give away of my own volition. The only Deepgold you may work."

My hand upon my heart, I said earnestly, "I am honored by the gesture, Dunnun."

"Don't be honored yet. It's the gold what'll decide whether or not you're worthy to shape it…and I'd be damned surprised if it allowed a mortal to do such a thing."

"Nothing is mortal," I agreed, bending to study the parcel he unwrapped with a deft hand. The handkerchief fell away.

My heart stirred even as I finished, "But he is committed to the task."

The songs of the Deep-Children at once filled my heart and my mind. I knew that they were truly singing for their gold somewhere and that I only heard it as a thought, a daydream—just as the thought of them had heralded their appearance from the sea on our journey to Dunnun, for thought and experience were one in that holy dimension. The same song swelled up against my heart, up through my chest, and made use of my voice while I fully absorbed the glittering glory of the pure little ingots of Deepgold.

"Deepgold," I sang to it in my corrupted octave, raising my hand toward Dunnun's as gently as I might if accepting a small animal, or a precious egg, "fair gold! See how you shine in the fire's soft light. As merry in smiling as an untouched maiden, all existence dances to your rhythmic delight!"

If Dunnun looked surprised to hear me singing to the gold unbidden, he bore far sharper surprise for the gold that took right away to glowing in his hand. It was astonishing how it shone, in truth—like the god held a little star swaddled in a handkerchief he, upon seeing the reaction, carefully transferred into my cupped palms.

"Girlish games once honored your eyes! Now permit me to honor your form with the gesture of my honest work, in the name of a god. Awaken, my friend, to merriment and joy! Deepgold! Deepgold! Heiajaheia! Heiajaheia! Wallalalala jahei!"

The very sun that blazed over Urd sat in my own two hands, yet its radiance did not sting my eyes. Far from it—I saw more clearly than ever I had, and I felt the weight of the absolute potential that lay within. By Weltyr! By my sacred blood.

It was pure. It could be anything. The Deepgold that I held there in Dunnun's cabin, it could become the greatest weapon ever held by man—greater than Exigence, perhaps. It could be made into the frame of an exquisite mirror that caused all men to love and agree with me, and might lead me to the height of society: to a throne, if I wished. It could become the body of a sacred compass by which all men might find their most favorable destiny. This little pile of gold in my hand could be anything, yes, anything.

A Scepter that settled matters of lineal dispute and brought peace to those monarchs who possessed it.

A Ring that read hearts and bestowed power.

"A Lantern," I said, as the light of the gold settled but, activated by my song, never wholly faded, "whose flame might turn away the unnatural, and whose form is powerful enough to contain even a god."

"What's that?"

Turning my thoughts away from ambitions of power or adventure or helping the Deep-Children, I remembered why I had come to the island—why I had died. Now, with this precious metal in my hands, I thought of nothing but helping my friends. This was it: this was an opportunity to rectify what had occurred aboard the *Rhinemaid*.

"Where I am from, there was a powerful magic lantern that I managed to break. I would like to replace it."

"Couldn't have been that powerful, could it have?"

I said nothing, studying the Deepgold in my hands, remembering with shame my critical failure to catch the lantern.

"Well," said Dunnun at last, clapping me upon the back, "rest assured, this new lantern will be so fine and so powerful that nothing but a weapon of the Deepgold itself could destroy it."

Thinly, I smiled back to Dunnun.

"Let's not go laying curses before the thing is even made, my friend!"

The god laughed, unaware how truly I meant it.

"Very well, Nothing. Whatever you choose to make, that Deepgold I've given you will prove sufficient. He that labors over the gold should dedicate himself to nothing but the gold, so I will be the assistant while you mold, smelt, hammer, and otherwise work the substance into shape."

"I promise not to work you too hard."

"You must not be satisfied easily," he urged me, ignoring my half-joke. "The gold's final properties reflect the knowledge, heart, and work of the creator. Make it perfect, and it will serve you perfectly."

And so it began—my final task on the island with Dunnun.

Lucky enough, my pursuit of perfection was genuine. That was sufficient to extend my time, but the deadline was drawing near. I now knew where he kept at least a portion of his hoard. If I could cast the key, I could get into the cellar and at the very least get a sense for what I was dealing with. Perhaps, by taking a little at a time, I could deposit the greater portion of the Deepgold into the sea before he noticed it was missing.

Now it was only a matter of making the key without him recognizing it—but how could such a thing be possible? I pondered all through the night in which I ought to have slept, as it would be my last night of full sleep before leaving the island, I was sure. The problem had to be hammered out like any metal.

The next day, still pondering it, I went to work.

If the time I spent under Dunnun's tutelage might have been measured in months expended instead of tasks accomplished, I suspect a year would have elapsed from the time Grane and I landed until at last the Deepgold weighed in my hand.

Once I had that Deepgold, the time it took me to create the Lantern would have equaled twice that, or more.

Part of the trouble was that I had skipped the journeyman's process of honing his craft and working in the world. I was dead; I had no world to work in. Mastery seemed like a treacherous cliff on the other side of a vast gulp I needed overleap.

Never one to let myself be discouraged, I did my best to jump it.

What had the original Lantern looked like? I started there in my concept sketches, although I confess I had never studied it very closely. It was a lantern, it was made of gold, it had a peculiar little switch on the side that one turned to produce the flame within—or, rather, that turned to permit the burning of Hamsunt in his prison.

And how would I whisk the god, burning all across the ship where I died, back into another prison of the type from which he had just been released?

I tried not to focus too much on the future, but it was difficult. I became plagued by the purpose of the thing, rather than the aesthetics of the thing. Therefore, once I had glass-blowing well enough in my repertoire to make my first attempt, my initial jab at producing the lantern's base was so embarrassing that I immediately halted the iteration, scrapped my plans, melted the base back down and began it all again.

And this had a way of happening, for one reason or another, over and over and over again.

If I was not focused on Hamsunt, I was concerned with how I would cast the key; if I was not focused on the key, I worried over when I might have an opportunity to explore Dunnun's cellar. Now that I had moved from apprenticeship to at least the aping of mastery, I could not enjoy as much the empty-headed bliss that had made work on the island such a breeze. I was working on the island now with the explicit goal of leaving the island; and the goal took me out of the present and into future worries.

"Where's your head with this, anyway?" Dunnun examined my third lantern—the first which had a top, bottom and handle successfully completed before I lost my taste for the design—with a curled lip and a skeptical eye. "Perhaps you'd *ought* to apprentice with me as long as I once feared you would... You could use some help with your sense of aesthetic."

"Perhaps...but, more likely, I have to refocus."

"Pressure of working with the Deepgold getting to you, eh? You're intelligent. It's a material like no other; a responsibility all its own. But don't let the pressure or responsibility draw your focus away."

"Away from what?"

"From *being* there. From the honor of it—of what no other mortal man may experience."

Yes, it was true. I started again, my fourth iteration, and wondered at the rarity of all I had endured. How many men could say they had lived through death? Had met Weltyr? Had worked the Deepgold? How many men had god-blood in their veins?

This next lantern satisfied Dunnun, who observed with enthusiasm, "That's more like it!"

I was not convinced. I knew it barely resembled the old lantern, a goal from which I increasingly strayed with every attempt. If its design was not perfect, then it was imperfect. An imperfect lantern could never hold a god.

After examining it with Dunnun for a time, I shattered its glass and knocked the pieces away while the god balked.

"What was wrong with it?"

"I'll know when I'm satisfied."

Though he shook his head as I smelted down the gold again, I could tell he was secretly pleased.

I was not. I was tired, and frustrated. I knew somehow in the bottom of my heart that I would be able to accomplish the task, but I could not imagine how. Four attempts turned to five, and five, into six. This sixth one was my finest yet, and quite close to what I remembered of the old lantern. Many men would have stopped there.

But the winged figures kneeling back-to-back at the top of the lantern looked too malformed to me, and the handle too thin, and the flare of the base was off.

When, the next day, Dunnun found me pulling out my hair over the latest charcoal sketch, the old god laughed at me.

"You're a stubborn one, Nothing."

"I refuse to settle, you mean."

"Aye, fair enough…but if you want my advice, neighbor, you'd ought to stop trying so hard."

I scoffed, putting the charcoal stick down. "What do you mean?"

"I mean, here you are day in and day out, trying to

design the Lantern you think you want. Just design the lantern the way it's meant to be, Nothing. It'll fall out of your head"—he snapped his fingers—"just like that."

I wasn't sure I knew precisely what he meant. I was frustrated, and tired. I took time off to mine iron from the hills and forge a new suit of armor, since one way or another getting the old one from the burning *Rhinemaid* would not be advisable. I began to learn more about the ecology of the island, and about its climate. The weather was beautiful every day, the sky blue and cloudless, the birds at constant song—until suddenly there would crack out a wild, tyrannical monsoon that claimed control of the island from even the birds. Grane, temporarily moved on such occasions into the stables we'd once been offered, complained endlessly during bolts of lightning and bursts of thunder, and I sympathized with him, although he did not have to work in it like I did.

After all: when I was not working the Deepgold, my liberties on the island were dependent on Dunnun's needs being met. I, too, had grown very tired of it all. I longed for Valeria's arms, Elishta-bet's tenderness—even Gundrygia's devilish mystery would have made her a welcome companion. Instead, I was there with myself, my host not truly knowing me and not even my horse actually mine.

All of this—was it a dream, some figment? A mirage of some kind?

If it was all so convincing, did it matter if it were?

I felt at times like I was going mad. I had become something like the prototype of those mad old men who hide in the hills to commune in private with Weltyr, poor or unspeaking or starving by matter of principle. Yet it was not by choice that I had spent half-dreamed years' worth of work in isolation: the Deepgold had drawn me here, and I sensed it promised me more rewards if I might fulfill its will with the vigor I showed for fulfilling Weltyr's.

Could the Deepgold have a will? Was it truly my own will, reflected in its brilliant surface? It was—and remains to me now—such a profoundly mysterious force that I dared not ponder it too long for a stretch, afraid the very thought of it would bring such pleasure I could turn inward forever. Could become like the ancient relic unearthed many centuries before my birth, a statue of a man with his jaw pressed against his propped fist while he spent eternity in thought. I had seen it in person once, when our orphanage had been sent to an historical organization in Skythorn's museum district. It felt somehow strange to look at a thing that had already been looked at by so many people so many hundreds of thousands of centuries before me, and that feeling so absorbed me that I did not really think about the piece as a work of art. About the feeling of it. The circuit of fist to head, the arcing arm from the knee to the skull: I was the skull, and the Deepgold arced up into me, bracing my own thoughts while pushing more in.

Perhaps the Deepgold really was accursed when taken from its home. It was doing things to my mind. It does things to me even as I write this; it is calling out to my heart. It asks the same insistent question I have spurned many times. The question I cannot and will not dare attempt to answer during the course of my life.

Asks the Deepgold: Am I not greater than He that coveted me even as He brought me from the Deep to pay his debts?

Was the object of desire not greater than the one that desired?

Was Weltyr imperfect in his lust of perfect gold?

If so, which of the two was the god?

Each time these questions arose, I shut them out. It will always be impossible for Weltyr to be imperfect. His actions are always in absolute accord with destiny and his own will. The slithering voice of doubt was the Deepgold, I knew, poisonous Deepgold, for oh! it was bright in the dark of my mind! Exposed to the world, untamed by a form, it tempted me to exhibit the weakness of Man.

And I decided that taming it for the sake of my friends rather than my own sake was the ultimate overcoming of that weakness.

The problem was how one tamed the gold. How could I persuade it to lend me the essence of its form? I returned to the seventh iteration of the project with the inklings of inspiration, but no real sense of direction.

"Bright was your light in the dark, cold abyss, and brightly it shines when I sing from the heart! Yet dark is your spirit, taken from its home. You seduce me to evils, turn me from my faith, yet in you there rest memories of what you were. Is the Deepgold so weak as to be so corrupted? What impurities dare defile you with their touch?"

The gold's glow was soft and mournful with the tune of the song. I studied it, feeling its pain. I understood it all too well.

I, like the Deepgold, longed to be 'good.' Behind me was an innocence, a simplicity, to which I would never in my lifetime return. Memory forbade it; knowledge, too, and duty. I prayed I would not become as jaded as the gold evidently was, but I had to admit that my view of the world had been somewhat tarnished during my journey.

My view of myself, too.

The glow settled down. I studied the blank paper, the heels of my palms resting against its smooth surface. My stick of charcoal drummed at the edge for a time.

For the first time, I designed the lantern as was true to me. Not based on what I remembered or what I thought I needed, but truly on how *I* would design it— how I would put myself into its form, along with the Deepgold.

The drawing flowed. I sang to it as I normally would have to the gold and it came to life beneath my hand, its every detail perfectly formed as though by happy accident. It felt like riding a horse for the first time. Stunned by this sudden momentum, I seemed to watch myself produce the illustration. I even realized that the switch with which one summoned the flame could easily have served a second purpose.

What was it, after all, but a key fit within its lock?

When the blueprints were finished, I knew the time had come. A certain feeling of unreality settled upon me. The Deepgold hummed within its handkerchief.

At my camp, I withdrew the wax copy of the key, broke off its blade, and took care not to deform the teeth in the process. Then, patient, I worked the bow until it was warm. First I sculpted, then carved it into the delicate, lacey structure I had drawn for the switch in my plans. A hot needle fused them back together and, satisfied, I brought the adulterated key copy with me back to Dunnun's clearing.

By this point, the god paid me next to no mind. Though we were not peers, he respected me and saw my genuine dedication to the craft as admirable. He did not bother himself with my affairs unless I had completed a project and he felt like giving his opinion of it. Dunnun barely noticed, therefore, that along with the other pieces of the lantern I had also cast a key. The nature of the switch would be hidden when it was slotted into place in the lantern. I worked with the feeling of victory assured in my bones.

And when this seventh lantern was completed, and it stood proud with its glass, handle, and switch mechanism all properly constructed, I realized with a start that, in my abandonment of the quest to reproduce the old lantern, I had replicated it perfectly.

How was such a thing possible? Perhaps, if I were to compare this lantern to the scraps of the one on the *Rhinemaid*, they would reveal some dissimilarity that memory failed to summon.

But I did not think so. For all I could tell, the object in my hands was that very lantern that had been destroyed during the conflict: from which had erupted a hidden god, all the time disguised as fire in its heart. The sacred creation glowed, delighting my eyes as I looked upon it whole for the first time after so many attempts.

"It's done," I said, half-whispering to myself. "I did it."

Never in my life had such a bliss washed over me. I actually had to sit down, and fell into a slightly taller stool I had made myself to ease the physical toll of working with benches and anvils of lower height. My hand upon my heart, I stared at it for what seemed an incalculable time.

I was almost free.

Drawn by the silence, Dunnun emerged from his cabin. He saw the lantern from a distance and produced a cry of delight to hurry over.

"Is that it?"

"That's it," I said, heaving a sigh. "That's it—seven tries, and it's done."

"Well done, Nothing! That's a brilliant piece, that is. Aren't you glad you didn't settle?'

"I'd say so…but if the next piece could come about faster, I'd be grateful."

"Common gold is easier to work than Deepgold, you'll see. This is a beauty. What's this switch here do?"

While he turned it back and forth, not thinking to pull it out, I explained, "It permits the passage out of a magical flame I left behind on Urd."

"Fine engineering…would have liked to see what went into it before you put it all together. Well, now! Are you satisfied, Nothing?"

"I think at long last I am, my friend."

"Then we should celebrate! I'll get my bow and arrow and hunt us up some venison—you bring up some fish, maybe some fruit. Bring that horse of yours, too. Looks like rain. We can have one last good night before you pay your dues and leave. Eh? What do you say?"

His tactful reminder of payment made me smile. "Of course—that sounds like a fine way to say good-bye. I admit, Dunnun—"

"Don't be saying you're sorry to be gone from here, or from me. I'll be just fine without you. Though, I will say, your company did lend a little variety to my days."

There was something in his smile that recalled the

priests and retired paladins who educated me in my youth. Colleagues of Father Fortisto, who were perhaps less gentle with their pupils but were all the same tender of heart after a certain period of acquaintance.

I regretted deeply what I had to do to him now, but I forced myself to remember that this was a man who would have taken his fellow god's wife just to have access to her sacred trees. Dunnun, perhaps like Weltyr himself, was neither wholly good nor entirely bad, but a force of nature and teacher to mankind. I was not happy to betray him…but escape from death was within my reach.

Only a madman, or one who had lived a life of complete and perfect contentment, could ignore such an opportunity.

Dunnun and I parted ways. The god went into the woods with his bow and arrow, eager to make good the hunt before the brewing monsoon could gather enough gray clouds overhead to make a storm. I, with a spear I'd made many projects before and taken to fishing with on off days, pretended to return to my camp.

In truth, I went only halfway.

I ought to have gone on and retrieved Exigence right then. I see that now, of course. But, when on a hunting trip, Dunnun seldom took fewer than three hours of work to return; and only very rarely more than five. The window with which I worked was miniscule, or so I felt it to be. Might a wheelbarrow make the entire task possible in a trip or two? It would require clapping eyes upon the hoard to make that determination…but I doubted it.

Halfway to my camp, a mist of rain already coming down, I doubled back and soon enough found myself on the edge of Dunnun's empty clearing. Keeping my fishing spear in my arm so as not to clumsily alert Dunnun by leaving it out to find on his return, I first approached the lantern that sat upon a spider silk pillow in the workshop. I had agreed to leave it there until the apple was his, but I had of course said nothing about the key, which I removed from the switch mechanism at its base and gladly kissed.

Then, heart thundering in my ears as if to foretell the developing storm, I slipped through the front door of Dunnun's house for the second time ever. The first time uninvited.

Uninvited in a god's house.

My solar plexus tightened with reticence, but there was no god but Weltyr. For all I had experienced and seen and learned, my faith in my one true master was only hardened. It was by his will, his true highest will— one of such height he could not himself achieve it—that I stood in Dunnun's house as a thief and a traitor.

This was not unlike how Weltyr himself must have felt when the time came to liberate the gold from Roserpine's dark kingdom. Could the gold be got by honest means at all? What about it filled the heart with such lust, such evil temptations? Why did the Deepgold's powers act as a weapon all too easily turned against the wielder?

I did not understand then, and I still do not understand fully now.

But, when my skillful recreation of Dunnun's key fit perfectly into the gleaming gold lock I'd known I would find at the bottom of the cellar stairs, the door swung open to reveal the hoard, and I felt for the first time the awful, staggering weight of that temptation. Indeed, I fell to my knees before it.

Coins, ingots, necklaces, crowns, scepters, boxes, figurines live-cast from small animals—a mouse, a chipmunk, a lizard, a frog—all immortalized by the fatal and agonizing process Dunnun one night described with relish and offered to teach (I politely refused), rings, armor, green plates with gold streaking through them (some form of esoteric icon? I had seen something like it in Fortisto's office once, but could not recall asking what it was), utensils, spectacles, cups, combs, anything, everything. Every object, the entire world, replicated in the Deepgold. And all of it—perfect.

The reader might think I exaggerate, but the contents of the hoard were such that I at once despaired the impossibility of sneaking it out under Dunnun's nose. Not only that, but I was overwhelmed with fantasies. A wickeder man would have abided by them, setting up some post by the door to Dunnun's cabin and fixing him with the spear as he walked through. Yes—anyone too weak to stand the sight of all this holy wealth would have succumbed, taken it for themselves. They would have used it to become a man of untouchable wealth and power, instead of returning it to the Deep-Children.

Even I struggled against these racing thoughts, these hateful urges, until I realized something very important.

The dark cellar was illuminated well enough for me to see from wall to wall, and not just by the Deepgold.

A torch had been left burning—but why?

Just as I tore my gaze away from the hoard to ponder the flame, the first notes of an evil laugh echoed through the cellar.

It was only a few seconds before I realized it came from the torch.

19

BURNINGSOUL AND THE DRAGON

I STUMBLED UP and back from Hamsunt, whose flames danced merrily upon the tip of their fodder.

<Here at last, just as I knew you would be…Rorke Burningsoul.>

It had been such an age since I had been referred to—or, in truth, thought of myself—as anything but Nothing! I was taken aback by the sound of it; far more than I'd been by the torch's hateful laugh. My identity lifted my heart, bringing with it more long-absent thoughts of all I had been through and all that still awaited me.

"As I should have known you would follow me even through Eternity, Hamsunt."

<Follow *you!* It's you who's followed me, idiot.>

I scoffed to hear such a thing. "Had I known you were here, I might have planned better for this meeting. Vengeance demands patient calculation, as I owe for what you did aboard the *Rhinemaid*."

<Remarkable how little you remember.> The flames wavered and flickered upon their wall-mounted torch, shivering with laughter. <It is not you who are owed revenge, but I. You're quite a sly one, as I warned Dunnun...but, he doesn't listen.>

"How long have you been here, attempting to obstruct my duties?"

<Oh, long before you. And I told him quite plainly, many times: "Someday, you know, a fellow's going to come and take all this gold from you, and kill you, too.">

"I do not wish to incite such grim prophecy," I said, my heart thumping with Hamsunt's remark. "I only wish to return the gold that Weltyr cannot himself."

<The sins of the father...well, Burningsoul, then you must also be planning to return that sword of yours. My prison, too.>

"The lantern has already been destroyed."

<You lie! It was just created. I oversaw its very birth, the captive midwife of its unfortunate emergence. Did you create it just to throw into the sea?>

"With you in it, perhaps. Will you come down from your torch and fight me as a man? Or will you instead, as dishonorably as aboard the *Rhinemaid*, split into many cousins and devour Dunnun's house along with me?"

<You're a fine one to talk of honor, robbing your own master.>

"I have but one master, Hamsunt, and it is by his will that I am resigned to stain my name with these deeds."

<So, you admit you act in bad faith and deception.>

"They are all I have known in these years of work, and I have been amply punished for it. Valeria, taken from me; Branwen, Indra, all my friends to even Elishta-bet, their conditions unknown until I leave this place! Even Gundrygia—she is yet another question I have neglected to answer in the name of serving my god."

<And what do you suppose will be the reward for your sacrifices, Wotsung?>

I hesitated but a second before reminding myself along with him, "The escape managed by no man before me."

<How will that work? Will he, hearing the Deepgold has been returned, throw open the doors of the Valor Hall and let all the rest of his Selected watch you walk out? Will he violate those very laws of nature to which he is eternally bound?>

Anroa, extracting his promise that he would not favor me with such a reward.

"I would not expect it of him. This sacred gold has some means by which to liberate me, I am sure."

<Aha—so you *don't* intend to return all your precious baubles when this is done! You do not work in the name of your god at all, but only in your own service.>

"Service to myself is service to him."

The torch cruelly laughed.

<All men tell themselves such tales to ease guilty doings, but surely not every man's will aligns with Weltyr's.>

"They must. There is no other will but his."

<Even wicked men?>

"Even the wickedest men, although they are duly punished for their evil ways."

The flames curved with their scoff. <Then by that admission, your own god must be wicked! What good god would permit, nay, *will* the evil of men? If he is wicked, he is no god at all, but a devil and a destroyer of life.>

"The wickeder thing would be that will which constrains all mankinds to the existence of dwarvish automata. An empty set of responses to the stimuli of life is no life at all."

My eye fell away from the torch and instead to the gold, glittering from all the shelves that lined the walls around the central pile of ingots and coins.

"But the man who is alive, who is aware of his living-ness enough to have choices in the world, gains strength by resisting temptation and defeating the evils of lesser men. It is Weltyr's will that evil men and difficult tests should exist so that his good men may excel in their subduing, and may reap rewards."

<Rewards given by whom?>

I shrugged, not knowing exactly how to answer. "By Urd, and by myself and my friends in it when I manage to return there."

<But not by Weltyr.>

"All things are by Weltyr, and it is by his will that I heard the secret powers of the Deepgold extended to death itself. Therefore, anything I give myself comes to me first by my master."

The fire heaved a sigh, its tendrils flaring in all directions before settling back down into its body.

<You are hopeless...but I suppose I had ought not to try and make a Wotsung listen to reason. After all—if Dunnun has not heeded my advice to avoid his own

demise, and Weltyr did not listen to my warnings against the poisonous nature of the Deepgold, why should I expect a mutt like you to do what gods refused?>

"There is no god but Weltyr," I reminded him. "And, save for Oppenhir in his grave, I have seen nearly all your kind with my own two eyes."

<An arrogant thing to say. There are those of us which your mind could never comprehend, on Urd or in Eternity. There are those forgotten by your races, and those among our number we have slain for going against our ways. There are those spirits which do not deign to co-exist with mankinds, and those that only do so to destroy them.>

"Like you, Hamsunt."

<I do as I please, untethered! At least, I do since escaping that wretched prison in which you captured me—and from which you freed me, you clumsy oaf.>

Though I looked at the flame in surprise, the god paid no notice of my expression and went on as though to himself. <I do recall being freed, but it's been so long since you *captured* me. Amazingly enough, I can't remember how it was done...I don't suppose you do, do you?>

I spread my hands and meekly smiled. "As you said, Hamsunt...it is remarkable how little I remember."

The roar of thunder cracked over the cabin, so loud it seemed to rattle the ceiling of the cellar and my very bones along with it. Hamsunt hummed, his flames twisting and writhing in consideration.

<Well...no matter. It won't be permitted to happen again—never again! Dunnun will see to that.>

"Dunnun is out hunting, and I aim to have much of his gold sunk in the sea before that happens."

<Then you should have thrown your back into it rather than spending time talking to me! Even now, he hurries back to catch you in the act.>

"You lie."

<I have already told him your intentions, you idiot.> The flames laughed while, teeth grit, I slammed the torch from its stand and sent it rolling across the stone floor. <I am every fire on this island. Every kiln, every forge— every tree struck by lightning along the path of Dunnun's hunt.>

Furious, I killed the flame with a well-aimed stomp and let my boot rest there. My ears then tuned to the hearth on the floor above, which sprang to life and called in a booming voice, <Here he comes! You'd better hurry... he's sure to kill you without any trouble if he finds you in the cellar. That would be very boring.>

Teeth bared, I raked one last longing look over the gold still glowing in the dark. With my spear still tight in my grip, I hurried through the enchanted door, up the stairs, and back out of Dunnun's house.

The god already stood on the clearing's edge.

Rain pelted the ground between us, the drops having increased beyond a mist and into the inklings of a deluge in the time I spent in the cellar.

"I thought I'd make it back before the rain," said the god, "but I was wrong."

I did not speak. I simply stood, red-handed, in the middle of his open doorway.

"Nothing, eh...I think perhaps 'Ambition' is a better name for you."

"'Fulfillment,' perhaps. For I am Nothing but the enactment of my master's will."

"And who's that, then?"

"The only master there could be—yours, and mine."

Dunnun narrowed his eyes.

"Then it's true what Hamsunt said. You really *are* after the gold...I almost listened to him. You had me thinking I could trust you."

"Would that it were so, Dunnun. Alas, the Deep-Children call for their treasure, and a wickedness threatens to descend upon the gods—all the gods. If you do not agree to return the gold"—I gestured with the spear as I spoke, remembering Hamsunt's slyly admitted prophecy that I would bring about the old god's death— "I will win it from you."

"In combat, you mean? Hah!" The god set down his bow and arrow and instead drew his great hammer from his belt, its weight effortlessly balanced in his hands. "I've slain giants that were bigger and smarter than you, Nothing. You'll regret your arrogance and all your filthy lies. Have at you! I'll break you in two."

The god launched across the clearing with his hammer swinging wide for the strike. I was shocked by his speed and only just managed to duck, then spring aside amid a hail of splinters from the jamb of his door. I caught a glimpse of the impact while raising my spear for a counter-blow. If it had been my skull, I surmised by the obliterated wood, I would never have an opportunity to flee my death—or even enjoy eternity.

My strike with the spear was effectively halted when Dunnun let the momentum of the hammer's next swing wheel him back around to face me. The tip of my lance glanced away and, worse, was twisted by contact with the powerful weapon.

Grimacing, I nonetheless stabbed at him while the flames within the house's hearth cried, <Go on, Dunnun! Look how pitifully his weapons compare to yours.>

"Give up while you still can," Dunnun urged, his teeth bared. "I'd hate to destroy the vessel of my knowledge when I've put so much into its making."

"And I would hate to strike down he that taught me all he knows," I assured him with a glance toward the workshop.

Hamsunt's lantern waited within. I had to keep the destructive battle far from it, if I could.

By the time motion drew my gaze, my best option was to dodge down and back through the mud. Another near miss of his hammer made me see the value in one of two things: ranged weapons, or Exigence. Only a Deepgold weapon would have the power to take down this god, I assumed. The bow and quiver I snatched up when, using the distance achieved by my dodging, I dashed to the edge of the trees, were no doubt going to manage little more than slowing Dunnun's progression.

Yet every foot counted in keeping space between us. Every tree, as I disappeared into them, was invaluable. So was my knowledge of them, accumulated from countless treks back and forth to my encampment. Dunnun, who did not know them near so well as I, snarled with annoyance each time he chose an errant path and came up against a fallen log or an unexpected bush that slowed his way. As anticipated, my arrows did almost nothing except stagger him two steps at a time each time he swung his hammer to bat them aside.

Still, with the same uncanny speed that hastened him back to his clearing, he was catching up with me.

In the trees above us, the birds chattered wildly despite the storm. I could not see them, but they screamed outrageously at the scene. Never had I heard them utter a sound when it rained.

Dunnun gained ground.

Having no other means but desperation, I called up to the trees.

"Birds! Fair inhabitants of this island we violate— there is among you a friend of the sacred horse, Grane!"

The chattering in my direct vicinity reduced to a murmur while I notched another arrow and sent it shooting off. It did precious little to slow the approach of the angry god.

"Though the storm rages, I beg you—find the one among your number who counts this horse as his friend, and have him lay in Grane's ear this urgent message: that Rorke Burningsoul will forever be Nothing without his help."

"What are you blathering about, fool?"

"Nothing that would concern you." Finding him too close for arrows now, I shouldered the bow and fixed my ruined spear on him. A bolt of lightning striking not more than a mile from us lit the island, blinding us both for a few seconds and nearly overlapping the accompanying roll of thunder.

When the flash cleared and my eyes resolved, I threw the spear.

Like the arrows, Dunnun knocked it from the air and dashed over its fallen form.

Heart sinking, I took up a fallen branch to use as a paltry club.

The god thundered on, his hammer swing too close and fast to avoid.

It caught my arm, the bone snapping through the skin and leaving me to howl with agony.

The club fell from my hand. I stumbled back, eyes averted from the limb hanging limp at my side, and raised my still functional hand between us.

Somewhere, above my pain, it occurred to me that the roll of thunder was not stopping.

"Surely you would disgrace yourself to kill me in this state."

Somehow, I managed to stumble away from the next hammer strike toward my head. The immensity of the pain was so great that, like a choir of voices forming into one, all the levels of agony merged into one single unit of numbness. To my surprise, I could still function—I might even have been a little faster than before, and I managed to hurry behind a pair of trees with such haste that Dunnun, taking the same turn, skidded under his own momentum and went toppling into the mud.

Relieved, I broke into a sprint for the source of the still-rolling thunder and raised my good hand's fingers to my lips.

My whistle pierced the storm.

"Grane," I shouted, "here, friend!"

The ground rattled as though with an earthquake, sending Dunnun back down to the mud just as he managed to pull himself up. I braced against a tree, overjoyed.

With a great snarl and snort of exertion, the tremendous black horse crashed into view.

The god resumed his approach; I dashed to meet the mount, who slowed long before he met with me to allow me to grab hold of his mane. Grane and I both screamed as I pulled myself up with one hand, all my weight dependent on a single functional limb until I could swing my leg high enough. The mild offense was quickly forgotten when the beast leaped effortlessly over Dunnun's hammer swing and, at my guidance, galloped around to return us to the beachside camp.

As Grane raced, so did my mind. What was I going to do now? My arm was shattered. Without intervention of magical nature, that condition would not improve anytime soon. If such a thing happened on Urd, with such awful severity and no miraculous servants of the unseen available, it might have been necessary to amputate. Only by reminding myself that I was not on Urd did I persevere, gripping Grane's mane with my good hand while keeping my broken arm as still as possible against my chest.

There was no time or space to make a sling. Grane was a horse faster than any, yet Dunnun's pursuit wore on. He fell behind as the horse roared away, but once we arrived at camp I would have perhaps three minutes before the uncannily quick assailant would catch up to us.

I was going to have to do something drastic.

Which of us, Dunnun or myself, broke the contract first? You could make a few arguments about it, but I still suggest that, made in bad faith as it was, it was invalid from the start. Had it not been Weltyr's will, I never would have tarnished my honor in such a way, and in a manner that went so contrary to his domain—but that is all hindsight's thinking. While I was Nothing, I agreed to behave in a manner I never would have if I had still been myself.

Yet here I was, Rorke Burningsoul, thinking Nothing like myself.

At the time, my single interest in the battle against Dunnun was in the preservation of my life and how I might come out in one piece. All matters of conscience—and wisdom, perhaps—flew away as Grane burst through the trees and paced to a halt on the edge of the beach. The thunder above us was but a trite emulation of its hooves.

"Easy, friend, easy now—this way, come."

At my nudge, the horse more calmly pranced back to the trees most familiar to us. Among them stood the one within which Exigence glinted like hope. I slid down from the mighty steed's back and drew the blade from the tree, an act I had engaged in for no reason other than to tend to its condition and clean up its edges in years. It felt at home in my hand, but without a second arm I would never manage to wield it.

Something rolled from the tree at Exigence's stir. It lay there in the roots.

Anroa's apple.

No—Valeria's apple.

"Wise woman," I said, the words a gasp as I snatched up the fruit. "Wise, and perfect! Valeria—"

I like to think myself intelligent. But, as I have said before in this narrative, the intelligence of women works differently than that of men. Here at last I saw the fruit's true purpose in her eyes—what I now saw only when necessity overcame naivety. Perhaps she had never believed that Dunnun would deal with me, but also wisely knew I would never at the time have agreed to take the fruit along for this purpose. Perhaps she always knew it would come to this, and that even a Wotsung could not claim the life of a god without extraordinary measures.

With no hesitation and no thought of consequence, I snatched up the apple and took a few hasty bites.

I say it was an 'apple,' but, even after all the many laboring days it had spent hidden away, it was more delicious an apple than any I had ever tasted. Better than any fruit! Bursting with flavor, intense and wine-like, neither overwhelmingly acrid nor sweet. I gasped, and not just at the flavor, or the heat running up and down my arm along with the glowing orange-gold of its rectifying wound.

With the fruit there came into me great comfort. The exquisite intensity of its taste, and the taste-experience in specific, somehow brought rushing with it the confident self-awareness of a divine being. Was I a god, or was I not? I felt enlightened by the sudden awareness that I was what a god was, but the difference was that a god was worshiped and while I, a servant, did the work in the name of that greater command. I was the tail of the serpent, but still the serpent; and my will was the same as that of my head.

After eating half the fruit, I offered the other half to Grane. My arm had healed and, far from stunned, I found myself invigorated. Almost eager for the fight. I needed no more of the apple; but Grane bore protecting, and ate the fruit so quickly as I rushed to put on my armor I could only assume that he knew.

A good thing that he finished it when he did, too. I had no sooner fixed Exigence's sheath to my belt than Dunnun stepped from the trees. Grane pawed the turf and shook his head with a snort.

"A sword of Deepgold!" The god balked. "When did you sneak that by me? I don't recall making that."

"You didn't. Our master did, disguising it as a Scepter during times of peace. Until his will is fulfilled, Exigence is its name—and I pity him that meets its blade."

Absorbing this with a dry chuckle, Dunnun stood unmoving beneath the heavy storm that dropped cold needles on us both.

He slid the handle of his hammer into his belt, and for half a second, I was happy.

"If that's the case," he said, "I'll take your word on it and not fight you as a man."

That chain helm of Deepgold always hanging at his belt had been there so long, with such routine, that I had forgotten its existence. I had not asked, and he had not explained.

Now, he drew it from his waist and raised it before him with a dark smile.

"I'll fight you as a beast, instead."

Thunder rolled. The god draped the helm over his face and vanished beneath its golden links, the very shape of his head transformed by this new, featureless visage. The god's skull lengthened, and as lightning struck a tree between us to set it ablaze, his body affected a similar transformation.

<The Helm,> said the snapping fire with appreciation, Hamsunt's voice effortlessly raised above the storm, <is among the strangest and most delightful of the Deepgold treasures. Don't you think, Wotsung?>

"I cannot say I have seen it in action."

<What one thinks, what is. What one wishes, one becomes. What one feels, one does.>

The god's clothing and armor grew with him but transfigured all the while, textiles and leathers splitting apart to reform as scales of a similar color scheme. I drew Exigence while Dunnun's growing snout adopted cruel fangs that, even from this distance, seemed the size of the sword.

<There is little that compares to the Helm that Dunnun designed...although I do confess, Weltyr's craftsmanship is something to behold.>

The dragon snarled while its long serpent body settled into shape. Grane paced nervously, birds scattering out of trees and toward the center of the island as Hamsunt's flames spread.

"Do not interfere in this, Hamsunt," I urged the fiery god while the dragon stretched its limbs. "This is a matter between myself and Dunnun."

<Not really Dunnun at the moment, is he?>

Its mouth opening in an earth-shaking roar, the dragon launched itself at me with such ferocity that its claws left great furrows in the earth behind. Yellow eyes fixed upon me, teeth ready for an immediate kill, the creature descended.

And it was met with Exigence.

The force with which the screaming serpent struck the blade was nothing to laugh at, but I held strong. Monstrous jaws snapped against the sword, then drew back with a yelp.

Then came the swing of its tail, which might have caught me off-guard if my entire body was not primed for the least movement from the beast. It was the fruit, I believe. I felt in the same state of flow that came upon me when I worked in Dunnun's shop: all those hypnotic hours spent building fire or hammering metal or carving molds. Flow in battle was a common occurrence for me, but seldom so quickly—and certainly not so intensely, so perfectly.

Dunnun was powerful, however. I managed to leap over his tail, but he whirled back with a sharply clawed hand. When it extended beyond my defenses and raked along my arm between two plates of armor, I expected to be left with a simulacrum of those vicious furrows in the mud.

But I looked, and there was nothing.

Amazed, I laughed, then raised my head and the sword together.

Now it was I who was on the offense. With blow on brutal blow, I beat Dunnun back toward the sea while evading his wide-swiping claws.

And then, I gained my first bit of ground.

The sword, which had but nicked the beast to this point, slashed so deeply into its paw that a pair of digits were lopped clean off.

Minorly disarmed, the serpent howled and snarled. Its head raised to the sky, one blazing eye falling hatefully upon me before lifting again. I drew Exigence back, ready to make a killing blow.

Great wings burst from Dunnun's transformed shoulder blades. The god sprang into the sky, roaring while he flew off toward the island's solitary mountaintop.

At my whistle, Grane galloped up to take me on his back.

<Sometimes we gods cannot help but interfere,> Hamsunt's trembling flames warned us while we overleaped them to soar betwixt storm and trees.

"But they need not be so overjoyed by it," I told the troublesome entity in a shout.

The serpent disappearing into the clouds told the tale of how large the island and its mountain truly were. Grane pursued the beast up through the storm, effortlessly conquering lightning and thunder and the rippling atmosphere of mad static to meet our target. I raised Exigence as the gap narrowed.

Dunnun's great serpent-mouth opened to receive a bolt of lightning that crackled from the clouds.

Turning in the sky, my opponent flew backwards while gaping wide its hateful jaws.

Before I might turn the horse, the spark dancing on the back of the serpent's tongue grew to a fierce flame that blazed forth like a column of evil breath. Grane, immune to injury until his half of the apple wore off, shook his mane and whinnied. I was able to at least raise Exigence before me, its enchanted blade splitting the flames. As the horse ducked down, I sheathed my sword in favor of a simpler weapon.

The bow and arrow were still slung upon my shoulder. While Grane committed himself to keeping up with the dragon and dodging its fiery breath, I notched an arrow.

When the horse swept up to avoid the next column of flame, I shot down into it, through it, and sent a newly flaming arrow into the underside of the beast's spiked tail.

Dunnun howled. The god sprang at us through the air, aiming for the horse beneath me, but I shot another pair of arrows into the membrane of the beast's wing in a hole torn wider by a reflexive twitch. The dragon flagged, its healthy wing working faster even while its altitude suffered.

Another flaming breath, this one weaker than the last. My heart grew with the possibility of the impossible task completed—of so many impossible tasks, proven possible. Urging Grane on, I drew Exigence again. At the glint of the blade, Dunnun dove back into the clouds and out of sight.

"On, Grane! We nearly have him—hurry now, hurry!"

The horse thrashed his head with his neighing and whinnying, galloping all the faster at my urging. I did not want to give Dunnun time to transform again—nor to heal himself in any way. What I wanted was Urd. I wanted to be alive in my home again.

As we emerged from the clouds, I caught sight of the beast diving down into the clearing that was its home. Grane stormed after, undaunted by the arrows I shot ahead of our flight. Only one struck the quick-moving dragon, but I knew it was true from the scream that echoed across the island.

When it landed with a great thud, I tossed away the bow and quiver entirely. Exigence was all I needed.

In the wet grass outside the cabin, Dunnun thrashed and panted and bled in the rain.

Seeing me, he raised his head to produce another long burst of fire. Grane avoided it easily and the breath instead caught the trees, the charcoal kiln—anything but us.

The storm had reduced to a steady if somewhat impressive downpour. I hardly saw it anymore. My boots hit the ground and I raised Exigence.

"If you yield me the Deepgold, Mighty Dunnun, I will gladly leave you alive."

The serpent snarled, teeth bared and breath sparking.

It leapt forward, its remaining claws poised to rend my flesh.

I sliced Exigence through the air and cut one of the creature's paws cleanly off.

While Dunnun howled and screamed, rolling in the mud, I looked for a way to remove the Helm but could not find one. There was only a dragon before me. Could Dunnun take it off if he wanted to? Was he in any condition to know what he was doing?

I did not have long to question. Raging, its thorny tail striking out against my skull like a cudgel, the beast got in a blow that would have easily killed me in a lesser condition. Even in this one, my head rang with the impact and I found myself staggered back, nauseous for but a second.

Just as quickly as it occurred, though, it cleared, and I overcame it by charging the beast with Exigence held high.

Dunnun roared.

I swung the sword beneath the dragon's muzzle, the resistance with which I was met almost meaningless against the enchanted weapon.

While Dunnun's true body fell before me, his Helm-shrouded head flew aside. It gradually rolled to a stop before Grane.

Snorting, the horse stepped back.

The moment was so strange I expected to awaken from a dream. What had just happened? What had I just done? I looked down at the blood on my sword; the body at my feet.

<Just as I remembered,> Hamsunt commented from the burning trees with a low chuckle. While I fought through my incredulity enough to clean Exigence on my tunic, the god continued. <He really should have listened to me…now, Rorke Burningsoul is Master of the Island—and the Deepgold.>

Above my head, the storm had further reduced to a patter. The clouds looked gentler.

If only returning the Deepgold would prove as simple as slaying its master.

20

DEEPGOLD

ONE OBSTACLE STILL remained between myself and freedom from Dunnun's island. Hamsunt's fires burned everywhere. With the storm receding, it felt like a grim recreation of my final moments aboard the *Rhinemaid*.

First, knowing the power of the Helm and also requiring some proof of the deed I had done, I went straightaway to snatch the object before the growing flames took hold of it themselves.

<Here it begins,> said the fire, chuckling to itself as I slid the Helm into my belt. <The greed, the ambition. It

all flows from you, Wotsung. Burningsoul. Have you ever wondered why that name?>

"It's a common name given by the Church when young orphans in its care reach a certain age. For women, it's names like Larksong and Pureheart. For men, titles such as Burningsoul or Stridentkind are more common."

<But why that one? Why not the other, or any of the many others? Do not condescend to a god when you do not even understand his speech, mortal…for mortal you remain. Anroa's fruit shall lose its luster eventually; when it does, my flames will claim you.>

"Say I complete my task and leave you here on the island before its charms evaporate?"

<If you can do so with the house collapsed upon you,> Hamsunt ominously replied, <then I would urge you to try.>

The raising crackle of fires all around us drew my attention to my right. Dunnun's cabin had at some point caught the blaze, its thatched roof quickly on the verge of collapse as the fire ate chunks from it.

What could I do? I had learned upon the ship that fighting the god with sword was futile. The rain had died down for the meantime, so water was not likely to be on my side, and at any rate I was not convinced it would help me do battle with the enchanted flames.

I had, then, the only weapon I'd had all along: my mind.

"I find it strange that men and godkind alike confer such prestigious titles to you, Hamsunt."

<What mean you?>

"Only that you are a cruel being; cruel without mercy or reprieve. The times were gods rewarded their worshippers, as you have rightly observed to me. Yet those who respect you, I've heard it said, are often more twisted up in the threads of unfriendly fate than are their enemies."

<Fool! Half-breed. What god finds itself under obligation to reward? To deal with kindness or honesty>

The angry flames leapt down from the trees, consuming a shrub not far from where I stood. I held my ground against this show of power, my hand resting upon Exigence's pommel.

"I do not make my observations out of disrespect, but disappointment—perhaps even confusion. Your powers are great, yes. But godlike? I should say not."

<"Not!"> Enraged, the flames spread further. Grane reared back, newly seeing the circle of fires in which we and the clearing were surrounded. He regarded me with a look that seemed the equine equivalent of an arched brow. While his ear twitched, the fires went on in bitterness.

<After all I have given to mankinds, that one of their number should deny me is unfathomable! I taught men to cook and craft tools! Without me, Dunnun's forge never would have come into existence. If I did not burn far and wide as I do, humanity, the progenitor of all mankinds, never would have left their caves!>

"Yet, in all the times I've met with you, you have demonstrated no compassion to any mankinds. Your powers are not godly at all. They are base, and typical."

<"Base!" "Typical!">

Windows burst in the house. Neighing, Grane galloped to the clearing's other side. There he paced into the air and back down to the earth as he waited for our business to finish. To avoid more breaking glass, I backed away from the house with its raging fires and toward the more fireproofed workshop behind it.

"Is destruction," I asked the fires upon which I never turned my back, "not typical, not base? It is a simple matter! Gods may destroy, yes—but to be true gods, they must also create. They must heal, or otherwise reverse those forces of chaos that steadily unweave the tapestry of existence. But you, Hamsunt, have done only violence: an expression of being so unremarkable even the smallest of mankinds' children can accomplish it."

Literally sputtering, the flames of the wicked god danced up and down and quivered into themselves.

<Have I not just recounted the list of great gifts I have given your sort in the past?>

"Too far in the past to matter now. The times are not as they were, mighty Hamsunt. Those gifts which you have given mankind are gifts which Weltyr might have given on his own; I say again, you have done nothing remarkable to justify the title 'god' as applied to your existence."

The man in the flames appeared briefly, his sneering face flickering out of the kiln whose flames angrily flared around its inner chamber.

<How pitifully wrong you are! I'll prove my powers to you, Wotsung, if that is what you wish…but I expect you to bend the knee to me, humbled by my glory, when the demonstration has been made.>

I spread my hands, suggesting, "When I am suitably impressed by you, Hamsunt, I will gladly pay you the respect I show all Weltyr's courtly friends and relatives."

The fire scoffed at that, but from within all the flames upon the island bellowed the word <Behold!>

By now, Grane looked like he was very seriously considering leaving me behind and saving himself by riding up over the trees; yet, as his head next thrashed nervously my way, his pawing and pacing stopped short. The horse's head bobbed, his body turned, and very soon I realized what it observed with such obvious incredulity.

The fires upon Dunnun's house, on all the trees and shrubs and the grass, began steadily shrinking, or so it seemed. Looking closely, I realized with an uncanny start that they were burning it reverse. Smoke trailed back into the fire and debris, while the roof's collapsed pieces leapt back up into place. Shrubs regained their leaves; trees were left clean and bright and good as new when the flames drew back from them. I felt as though I dreamed, struggling to contain my amazement at the sight.

‹Here is the reversal you demanded; more evidence of my nature. Only a god is capable of such a feat as the instantaneous and perfect repair of this entropy! Wouldn't you agree?›

Studying the effects of the reducing fires, I stroked the beard that had come in while on the island and suggested, "This is an extraordinary effect, to be certain, but I have seen mankinds accomplish such things with relics or brews. I was healed by such a potion, as it happens, likely created in conjunction with the strange dimension from which magicians draw their powers— or perhaps even blessed by Roserpine, whose might, I suspect, surpasses yours."

Nearly spitting, the fire that was now relegated to the kiln alone said, ‹That invalid! Roserpine is a goddess nearly dead as Oppenhir—he that men call a god in spite of his destructive nature, I remind you.›

"Yet Oppenhir is also a creator. If Death did not exist, my master would not have called upon Dunnun to construct the Valor Hall. Death must exist so the mystery of Eternity may be enjoyed by those who are Selected for it."

<But if Death's ways are not evil, how could mine be?>

"Death is something with which all creatures must live, in one way or another. Trickery is what men do to get their way when they are weak, or cowardly, or when there is no alternative."

<And did you not yourself trick Dunnun most foully from the moment you landed on this island? All the more reason you should pay homage to me.>

"I did, and I regret it. Now a mighty god lays dead: a craftsman, well-regarded for his work, defeated there. Yet is this island not the very same as that Valor Hall which contains it? Do the warriors of the Valor Hall not merrily fight one another to the death time and again, healed the next day by Weltyr's will? Another way in which my master is greater than you! I doubt you could accomplish such a feat as resurrection, even if only within Eternity."

<See here,> the flame said with an angry gasp, the fires of the island having completely disappeared and its tone therefore coming off as far more impotent than before, <my powers are twice those of Weltyr's! To breathe life into a man—even another god who has been killed in Eternity—is nothing if I wish it! Watch, Wotsung, and marvel!>

With this command, a spark flew from the kiln and danced toward Dunnun's headless body. This light of life entered the dead form and, somewhat disturbingly, seemed to somehow attract the head. With the slow, steady pace of a wounded animal closing in on its burrow, the god's head replayed its rolling-away, its flight through the air, its detachment from its owner's body. The corpse moved with it, raising to its feet just as Dunnun's dragon form had stood when I sliced its head off.

As my arm had glowed with the healing of its bone, so did the god's neck glow with the reattachment. Then, abruptly, the fused body collapsed to the ground.

I hurried over to check his pulse. Relief unwound my shocked nerves. The god lived!

"How grateful I am that you managed such a thing for my former mentor! It felt awful enough to play the traitor; to play the killer would have been too much for me."

<Do you now admit that I am at least as much a god as that smith at your feet?>

"I'm just not sure." Once again stroking my jaw, I returned to the edge of the workshop and contemplated the kiln whose contents murmured incredulously. "After all, I have heard it said there are those dark magicians who reject Death and Eternity both. They instead cling to material reality on Urd through dark incantations and depraved, unholy means. By their hands, skeletons, ghouls, and all manner of other hateful undead may rise; in fact, it happens that a captain of my recent acquaintance, the very same your flames consumed at the time of my death, has proven undead. Tampering with death is not a power exclusive to gods alone."

<Then what would satisfy you!> Spitting with rage, sparks flying up from the kiln and dashing across my face, the outraged fire demanded, <It would seem to me that you are not willing to accept any measure of power. For

every demonstration of godhood, I have pitiful mortal echoes thrown back in my face. What will it take to prove the truth to you? What will make you kneel before me?>

It came to me then. I seized my opportunity, my eye searching the flames for that fleeting face.

"Only he that is greater than the Deepgold," I said to Hamsunt, "may be called a god."

The fires scoffed. <By that measure, perhaps not even Weltyr would be called such.>

"My master is greater than all things—even the Deepgold. Anroa, I would even say, is greater than it, for it took the entirety of the sacred hoard to equal the worth of her and but a single tree. Dunnun is greater than the Deepgold, for his furnace melts it. And though your fires may burn in that furnace, Hamsunt, it is only by Dunnun's will, by the smith's will, that the metals are tamed. Metal means nothing to a fire without the smith. Are you greater than the Deepgold, then? I cannot rightly say…after all…"

With a patronizing chuckle, I set a hand atop the lantern still waiting patiently on its pillow.

"You spent an aeon trapped in this lantern before. It would seem to me the Deepgold is far mightier than you—and, if so, you are not a god at all."

At my words, the fire raged up out of the kiln as though liable to restart the immolation of the house, if not the island.

<"Not a god,"> mocked Hamsunt. <The Deepgold, mightier than me! How foolishly your tongue flies, Wotsung. There is nothing I despise like an arrogant mortal. The Deepgold is less than a rock beside my power!>

To my astonishment—and, I confess, no small measure of uncanny horror—the fires took hold of the edges of the kiln as though they made up mortal hands. Forming together into a slender body, they pulled themselves over the edge of the kiln and complained all the while.

<When you trapped me in that Lantern, I was younger and far more ignorant than I am now. Weaker, too. You'll see, whelp—and when I've freed myself with ease, I'll claim your life as recompense for this little show.>

While the man of fire strode toward me with hate in his burning face, I understood something very strange.

I looked down at the lantern, identical to the old one. The Lantern of Hamsunt, just created.

Strange flights of impossible fancy—an understanding of something I could not fully articulate, could not prove, but knew by the comprehension of faith's heart alone—eased my confidence before him.

I inclined my chin, staring back at the god.

"When you free yourself from the Deepgold, Hamsunt, my life is yours to claim."

Hamsunt, laughing, collapsed his body into a single point. One spark. It burst and crackled like a star in the air before me.

<You'll regret those words.>

"I think," I said as the god freely passed into the glass of the lantern in the form of this ball of light particles, "that I already do, my friend."

<I am no friend of yours,> Hamsunt declared, his sneer audible even though, as light, he had no form. <Now, Burningsoul: Are you satisfied I am inside the vessel?>

I nodded, patting the top. "So it would seem."

<Then watch.>

I watched. The light cluster burst into a great flame that pounded up and around against the insides of the glass.

Nothing happened.

The fire once again reduced to a small spark.

<What? That's not possible. That's—wait a minute... no! Oh, no!>

Again, the fire exploded against the glass of the Deepgold lantern, which did not even move. As the blaze lowered again, Hamsunt's voice echoed in the timbre of a pained moan.

<No, no—let me out! Let me out of here, Wotsung!>

I raised my eyebrows at the raging spark. "You mean to say you cannot free yourself?"

<I suppose you feel very *clever* now, don't you? Let me go, damn you!>

"Not greater than the Deepgold, after all," I observed, withdrawing the removable portion of the key mechanism from the pocket of my tunic. "Why, Hamsunt—it would seem to me you're less a god than Brynhildr's horse over there."

<Laugh on, Wotsung!> The spark raised to an angry, barely controlled blaze in the center of the Lantern as I slid the key into the switch mechanism. <Laugh now. I'll have the pleasure of laughing at you for the rest of your life. Now, I remember not just how I am captured: now I remember how I love to watch you age and suffer. Yes! I remember. I remember how I love to see the fear in your eyes on the day your son picks up that blasted sword.>

My entire body froze. Roserpine's terrible whispers enfolded me like a death shroud.

Jaw set, I snapped off the flame in the lantern and stood alone in the empty workshop.

In the silence, with Hamsunt controlled and Dunnun recovering from being vanquished, I stood in the silent wonder of it all.

The Deepgold was mine. Fairly I had won it, after a time of unfair dealing. The gold, the island: I was the master of the property. If I wished, I could do anything I saw fit.

Grane, having approached on hearing his mistress's name, pawed the ground behind me and produced a few soft snorts.

My breath came unsteadily. I set a hand upon the stallion, studying its dark eye.

"Strengthen my resolve, my friend. There are temptations too great for some to bear; pray I'll be among the rest."

The horse lowered his head in an affectionate gesture I returned. What a pity it would be to surrender the kindly steed to its mistress once again! I patted its nose, then looked around the clearing and decided what to do.

One load at a time, I hefted the Deepgold to the top of the cellar stairs, loaded it in the wheelbarrow, and carted it off through the woods. The clouds that had lingered after the storm were beginning to evaporate by the time I reached the beach, their very darkness having faded to a dull but pleasant gray. A soft wind caught up the sweet smell of ocean, the salt so fresh and rich in my nose it reminded me of my boyhood.

One piece at a time, I unloaded the Deepgold I had brought to the shore. A great sadness settled upon me to see it piled along the stone bluff overlooking the sea. Such fine craftsmanship! So many hours of work. Such power and possibility. And all of it, unused. Created to be thrown away, back into the sea.

"Deepgold! Deepgold! Deepgold!"

I peered into the waves at the familiar cries, knowing what I would see amid their rising foam.

"Your poisoned mind can now be cleaned by baptism in your home! Come back to us, sink in our arms, we'll kiss away your taint! Polished like new, gleaming and true, we'll play like the old days."

My thumb worked over the exquisite detailing of a diadem that had ended up at the far end of the row. I glanced down at the beautiful work of art, then into the water and the maidens who serenaded the glowing assortment of gold.

I drew back my arm and hurled the diadem as far as I could into the sea.

While the Deep-Children sang, I threw. With each piece of Deepgold I threw away, the process seemed somehow easier. The attachment lessened. Away went the jewelry I might have plundered to decorate my lovers; off went the tools that could have made any man an expert in any art he wished. I threw away weapons, statuettes. Everything. Anything.

And when the process was over, I started it again.

I do not know how many wheelbarrows it took me to empty Dunnun's house of the Deepgold (down, I should say, to the lock on his enchanted cellar door). It was not long before I was awash in a kind of dream-state, drunk on the repetition of pushing the wheelbarrow back and forth, back and forth, back and forth. Feeling the beauty of the gold, the possibility of the gold. Letting go of the gold. Over and over and over again. The singing of the maidens. "Heiaha! Heiaha! Deepgold! Deepgold!"

The clouds, stubbornly obscuring the sky despite their hints at relief, blotting out any sense of time the sun might have afforded.

It seemed the task was endless. Dunnun slept the entire time; Grane grazed as though it were nothing to him. I felt it took an eternity, yet to them it might have seemed a few hours, or maybe even minutes. Time on that island was a strange matter, and I do not pretend to have perfect comprehension of it to any extent.

Yet, the Deepgold hoard in Dunnun's house was finite. There came a point when my meditation was disrupted by the realization that no more gold lined the cellar walls; not so much as a coin had been left on the floor.

Overcome with a strange admixture of relief and mourning, I made my way to the main floor of Dunnun's cabin and tossed the last few pieces into the wheelbarrow outside.

"Oh…my head…"

Outside, the god sat up and rubbed his brow with a miserable look. "Hey," he said groggily, struggling to get to his feet and quickly giving it up, "where are you going with that?"

"I won it from you, Dunnun, by slaying you in battle. The gold is mine; the island and the cabin, you may keep along with your life. I have no use for anything but what I came here for."

"What a sorry deceit this has been. How am I to be the greatest craftsman, the mightiest smith, if I cannot demonstrate my powers in the mightiest material?"

"You are a craftsman so mighty, my friend, that you do not need the Deepgold to prove it. Perhaps you could even create your own Deepgold! If there is one art you have not yet conquered, it may still be alchemy."

"Huh...not a bad idea. Finally leaving then, are you?"

I whistled for Grane, who ambled over to walk with me for the final delivery to the shore.

"Yes, my friend, I am. And I hope you know—though my deception had its purposes, the knowledge you imparted to me and the companionship you provided as a mentor will stay in my heart for all time."

With a slight scoff and a shake of his head, Dunnun said, "You're an odd man, Nothing."

"My name," I told him, "is Rorke. Rorke the Wotsung. And if I seem odd, it is only because I must do those things in the name of Weltyr's will that go against my mortal will. But, that is the nature of faith."

Together, Grane and I made our way into the woods.

My previous treks had beaten a path in the grass. We followed it for the last time, my heart heavy, Exigence bobbing at my side.

This would be difficult.

"Deepgold! Deepgold! Deepgold!"

The maidens sang again while, with Grane waiting patiently down the slope behind me, I eyed the final arrangement of Deepgold upon the bluff and began to dispose of it. I sang with them, somehow knowing what they were about to sing even though every word was new.

"Back to your home, where darkness shows your light all the better! How long you've pined, how far away, how lost and sick you've been. Now smile again, my gleaming friend, your journey's at its end!"

Oceania waved and smiled with approval, catching a bracelet upon her wrist straight out of the air through which I tossed it. She blew me a kiss while her sisters caught more, weeping with joy to cradle Deepgold once again.

Then, I reached the end of the row. The Lantern of Hamsunt sat at my feet, its gold glimmering with the gradual emergence of the long-overdue sun.

"Just a few more," Oceania called on, "and we can take you back to the place where your death was ill-met! The rest of the Deepgold, Burningsoul—hurry!"

I hesitated. My hand rested upon Exigence; my eye, upon the Lantern.

"I cannot return these to you yet," I said, also touching the chainmail helmet hanging in my belt. Their faces fell at once, even as I continued, "If we are to retrieve the last piece of Deepgold, Roserpine's Ring—"

"Burningsoul is a liar! Treacherous Wotsung! You swore you would return the gold to our Deep! Its corruption seduces and sways you!"

My hand tightened into a fist of frustration. I had known this decision would not go well, but I had no other choice.

"I swear to you, Deep-Children, when my quest is complete, I will sacrifice these last pieces of Deepgold to you! Exigence, the Lantern, the Ring, and the Helm"—I found myself wondering why it had not been counted among the four sacred objects named by Gundrygia, but quickly pushed the thoughts away—"all of them will be back in your arms when they are all in mine."

"Liar! Liar! The Wotsung is spoiled, the Wotsung is

cursed! All into whose hands the tainted gold passes will fall in its shadow, disgraced!"

Were they right? Would it be safer to throw everything away and continue my quest without Exigence?

"I can't," I said, remembering in perfect clarity the strange moment I realized the Scepter of Weltyr had, in a miraculous sign, been transformed into this sacred sword. "By my master's will, this sword was put into my hands in my hour of greatest need. I must keep it until the task he has set for me is completed—until all the women carrying the progeny of the Wotsungs are safe under my protection. Valeria will not be satisfied until her ring is secured; and to subdue Gundrygia, I will require this Lantern, this sword, maybe even this helmet if Weltyr does not take it from me when I prove my quest complete."

"Traitor! Traitor! Burningsoul is a man without honor! Distrust the Wotsung! He has the lust for the gold in his heart! We have been deceived, as was our poor mother before us."

"I will return it all to you," I promised them, a cold wind biting at my limbs. The sky may have cleared, but, at long last, night was close at-hand.

"I'm sorry I can't see the entire hoard home now." Grane, sensing my need of him, approached with a snort. I took the Lantern and clambered upon the steed's back, one hand resting on its neck. "But when all this is over, Deep-Children, I swear it—the gold will be yours again."

"Deepgold! Heaven's gold—how gaily we basked and played in its shine! How supple and bright our waters grew when the morning light first kissed its cheeks! Merry gold, grieved gold! That sacred pendulum, waking and sleeping again—stolen from our ecstasy, by guile misused and abused!"

Shaking my head, realizing they could not be reasoned with, I looked out over the vast waters to the south. Over our heads, the blue of the firmament fast faded to black.

I dug my heels into Grane's sides and sent the horse rushing forward, off, and up into the sky while the Deep-Children cursed us from the cradling waves.

What a strange feeling it was to be flying back! The return journey had become such an abstraction that I had forgotten to even dream of it in my last stretch with Dunnun. Now, the ocean crashing beneath us and the stars twinkling above us, I found myself laughing in amazement.

I had done it. The Deepgold was free—and what remained of it was in good hands. I turned the switch of Hamsunt's lantern and enjoyed the dance of his flame within, his hateful speech having lapsed into the same surly silence I had known from him before the glass broke.

The only voice was the one of the ocean, and the song of my heart as Grane thundered eternal home.

There was something bittersweet about that flight to the Valor Hall, however. For a substantial time, I sat without speaking my thoughts aloud to Grane. I was too buried in them: utterly suffocated by the terrible notions of not just what I was about to do, but of what would happen eventually.

I wished to un-hear Hamsunt's words more than I wished to reverse Roserpine's! Her prophecy had been awful enough; framed enough in gloom and dread that I was frankly eager to rid myself of Exigence when all this was over, though it would be difficult to do so.

Adding Hamsunt's cruelly delivered knowledge that the harbinger of my death would be one of my own unborn sons, I felt sick with the future. Yet turning my face to the past yielded nothing but shame and heartbreak. I saw myself as I had been before the Valor Hall with cold clarity: a gleaming youth. A young man, still half a child, who had clung to his innocent views of himself and his simple understanding of his god until the last possible moment. Until I realized that, like virtue, sin is the property of my master. It is Weltyr's unique privilege to act with wrath, or greed, or to speak slyly in dealings with others, and there were those times when such experiences were necessary to the enactment of his true will. What I had done in deceiving Dunnun was also in line with that will, but I was human before I was any kind of godling. Therefore, the human man had to come to terms with the nature of himself as imperfect, and not in keeping with what he envisioned for himself as a boy.

Yet, what mortal was? As a child, I had been convinced that to be a paladin was to be a beacon, shining and pure, protecting the faith and the faithful while doing good deeds and holy wars in the name of Weltyr. Yet paladins were but men; Zweiding was but a man. He that put his identity in anything outside of that humbling condition doomed himself to forever fail the measure of each self-assessment. To be a paladin, a hero, a godling, a Wotsung, before I was a man—I would never be satisfied with myself. I would never be honorable yet humble, powerful yet kind, in a manner that mattered enough to me.

It were as though, in the time spent on the island, I really had become Nothing. My identity was stripped away and I saw now every vice, every wasted scrap of time or opportunity, in absolute clarity. Perhaps my body was as young as it had been when I left for the island, but my mind was so much older I could not articulate the change. It were as though I had been subject to a kind of initiation. Into what, I was not fully sure.

As we had the first time, Grane flew us all through the night and straight to our destination. No storms buffeted us, nor did the wind freeze us unfavorably; and, as color marked the edge of the ocean where in darkness it blurred into night, the waves ahead broke for land that made me cry aloud. Grane, too, gave a satisfied snort and hastened his pace.

As the sun rose, its golden rays warming the dark sky with hints of floral pink, we arrived at the Valor Hall. The land was covered in trees, and the trees grew into woods, and the woods soon enough yielded to manicured orchards, and then into the gardens over which we swept, craning around and flying on, on, past the Hall and down into the creekside meadow where Grane's family slept. The horse landed at a run some distance from the herd, slowing his pace and resisting his momentum while the sleepers stirred. Soon we came to a stop beside them; a few lifted their heads to see Grane.

Rather than acting as if it had been years since they'd seen him, they set their heads back down and resumed their last few moments of rest before the sun rose too high.

A good sign, I decided.

"Grane, my friend—" I hugged the horse around

the broad neck once I dismounted, patting him fondly and saying with a look into his eyes, "Thank you. Truly, I cannot express the measure of my gratitude."

As though saying I shouldn't, the horse softly shook his head back and forth, then ambled back to his place and settled down to rest.

Beaming, I admired the reunited herd before climbing the long slope back through the fields around the Hall. It was only then I realized how exhausted I was from my battle with Dunnun—and, of course, the long task of hauling the Deepgold up the stairs and to the sea. I needed some rest of my own…and I knew where to get it.

Within the Valor Hall, I found myself before a familiar door and rapped lightly on its surface. There was a short delay before it cracked open. Elishta-bet's fine white face filled it.

"Who—Rorke?"

Her eyes widened as she saw past my beard and to the face beneath. I would have laughed, but I was so awed by the sight of her (the first woman I had seen in what felt to be more than three years, by Weltyr's eye!) that all I could do was let her curving throat, her radiant body, her soft fragrance serve as a balm to my weary mind. She made me dizzy; I reached up and caught myself on the doorjamb, listing forward. Elishta cried out and jerked toward me, catching me at the waist and chest with both her hands. She blushed to feel my body beneath my tunic.

"What on Urd happened to you, Rorke?"

"How long has it been since we last spoke, Elishta?"

"Only since last night. Where did this beard come from? Poor Rorke! You look so dazed—come in, dear friend, dearest, oh, come in—"

With those gentle, loving hands, Elishta drew me into her room and let me shut the door behind us.

When it was closed, I bent my head and kissed her.

Shocked, Elishta-bet froze against me for only a few heartbeats. Quicker than I'd expected, though, her lips melted shyly apart, and her gasping breath pulled at mine, and I drew her back toward the bed she had left to answer me.

"Wait here," I bade her. "I'll make haste, but suffice it to say you deserve somewhat better than my present state."

In the blue light of that enchanted morning, Elishta-bet intended to yield to me in the Valor Hall as she had never yielded to any man. I decided I would have her yield to Rorke, rather than Nothing. She trembled wildly as I left her to set down my equipment, the Deepgold I had brought with me, and went to wash myself in the strange, pleasantly humid room adjacent. Even Valeria's palace in the Nightlands had lacked baths attached directly to her chambers; the opulence of the mighty hall was an experience differing so vastly from what I had gotten used to on my journey—in my life!—that the thought of leaving it stung my eyes with tears.

Still—how sweet it would be to walk on Urd again!

So exhausted I operated in a dreamlike state, I made quick work of bathing and shaving, although I made no attempt to trim my hair. When I returned to the darkened chamber where Elishta lay with the blanket pulled to her chin, as nervous as a bride on her wedding night, her eye fell upon me and her lips turned up in a small smile.

"There you are, Rorke! You had such a wild look about you with that beard!"

I sat upon the edge of the bed. Blushing, she sat up to speak with me. Her smile faltered as she looked into my eyes.

"Yet there's still a wildness to your eyes, my beloved friend...oh, Rorke! What's happened to you tonight?"

Lowering my eyes from hers, I took her hand from where it had come to rest upon my chest and drew it to my lips. Tenderly, I kissed her fingers, her knuckles, her palm. Then I lifted my head and delivered another kiss upon her mouth. She gasped tenderly, each press of her lips to mine experimental and eager. When we drew apart again, her smile was as radiant as the dawn.

"There will be time to tell you everything soon enough. For now, Elishta-bet...will you let me lie here with you and listen to the birds wake up?"

Her lip bitten, her face so red I could perceive it even in the bluish dark of her curtained room, Elishta nodded. She drew aside the covers and let me in.

21

JUDGMENT DAY

I WENT TO Elishta-bet rather than Valeria not just because of our prearranged agreement. I went to her first because I knew that Elishta would accept "not now" for an answer to her many questions. Had I awoken Valeria to be comforted, I would have been acting in error. She would have demanded every last scrap of information, allowing nothing to stay held back, and would then at once launch into determining the wisest course of action in response to what she learned. She was a calculating woman, used to problem-solving by virtue of her rank. Elishta-bet was simpler than that.

Glowing in my arms, Elishta raised a hand and stroked my cheek with the look of a more informed and eager woman than she had been before.

"I suddenly find myself in much less hurry to leave," she whispered, laughing, then shyly resting her face in my chest.

"I feel much the same at times," I told her, hand resting upon the back of her soft neck to glide down the length of her spine. "Yet I worry too much for my other friends, and for Urd, and...well, for very much." Just having made love to her for the first time, I thought it unwise to bring up Gundrygia and instead changed the subject. "I have liberated the Deepgold—as much of it as I can."

"Rorke! did you really?"

I nodded, basking in her smile even if I did not feel victory in my heart as I might have before. It was the Deepgold, perhaps. The Deepgold changed everything for me; in me. Never having owned Deepgold, praise Weltyr, Elishta was shielded from its influence, and she closed her eyes to rest her smiling face over my heart.

"How proud I am to love you! The Deep-Children must be thrilled."

"They would have been, but there were those pieces I needed to keep for our journey—a Helm, for instance, brought back to prove to Weltyr what has transpired."

By then the sun glowed fully over the landscape, creeping around the edges of the curtains and illuminating her face well enough for me to see she lost her color.

"He hasn't been told yet?"

I shook my head. "I'm not sure when to address him, or how, frankly...but I suspect it will be clear to me soon."

I fit my hands to Elishta's slim arms and looked into her face.

"I need you to do something for me—rouse Valeria. See that she is dressed and ready to leave this place at a moment's notice."

"But…how will we do that?"

"If bargaining with God fails us, then—I am willing to consider desperate measures."

"Like what?"

A knock at the door, soft and cheerful, interrupted our conversation. Elishta looked at me with fright but got up all the same. She took the night dress from the foot of the bed and drew it around her as she moved. I sat up, blanket over my lap, somehow certain who it was even before Elishta relaxed and Brynhildr called merrily to her, "Hail, Elishta-bet Highwind! Has the Valor Hall kept you well this last night?"

"Oh, yes, very well, thank you. Um"—bashful, she glanced over her shoulder at me—"were you looking for Rorke?"

"I hate to impose upon my friends, but—"

"No, no," said Elishta quickly, while I called, "I'll be dressed and out in but a moment, cousin."

"Let's meet in the gardens," the Selectrix said, her voice a little lower than was normal for her. Then, her smile audible, she told Elishta-bet, "Your wardrobe overflows here, doesn't it! You may even find some things to fit him."

A shadow crossed Elishta's face from the Selectrix's movement out of the doorway. My friend smiled slightly and shut the door, shaking her head to herself.

"It is a rather strange thing that my chambers are as

well-equipped to match your needs as a they are mine…
that bed is so big, and those baths—well, I can see you
must have found the razor in there. Oh—"

I had uncovered myself and gotten to my feet, and
Elishta's eyes dipped away from my face to something
else entirely. Bright red at once, she covered her eyes with
both hands and said in a girlish, almost quivering lilt
behind her palms, "Oh, uh—uhm, I can give you some
privacy, Rorke, I'll—"

She had tried to step blindly toward the bath
chamber, but I caught her around the waist with one
arm and drew her body against mine. Gasping, Elishta
lowered her hands only as I said, "It's all right to look at
me, Elishta…I don't mind it. In fact, I prefer it."

With a nervous laugh, Elishta-bet waited for me
to laugh along and bit her lip when I didn't. Her eyes
trailed down my throat and over my chest, and soon
down between our bodies.

"I'm still so giddy over everything that I can barely
look at you straight…and, anyway, that thing of yours—
it's awfully frightening."

"Don't be frightened." I chuckled, caressing her
cheek and marveling at the way holding her delicate
body eased my heart to rest. "It lives as I do, Elishta-
bet—to please you."

She gasped as I kissed her, the sweetness of her
mouth so irresistible to me I could have enjoyed it forever
had not one delicate hand trailed shyly over my thigh.
We separated, and I caught her eye before her gaze could
dart away.

"You probably don't have time," she suggested,
eliciting a laugh. My laugh turned into a sigh very

quickly, though. Her tender hand was so uncertain, yet so cool and soft in its bold caress that it was almost teasing.

"I always have time for the women I love," I assured her, drawing her back down upon the bed. "You're comfortable after last time?"

She nodded, her throat speckling as I gently drew open her robes and sighed at the moonlight of her nakedness beneath. "Yes, oh—it didn't hurt nearly like I'd always been afraid it would. A little, at first, but—oh, it's amazing something so large can fit there, let alone feel so good, oh Rorke—ah!"

She flinched as my hand caressed her soft breast, still so unaccustomed to matters of lovemaking that they clearly frightened her. I let her grow used to my touch and kept it consistent, drawing my fingers down her ribs and stomach while my mouth folded around one soft pink nipple. Gasping, Elishta parted her thighs and let me explore. Soon her sighs were like yelps of incredulous pleasure, whimpers of bliss trembling up from her lips while I caressed her wet center.

"Oh, Rorke! Rorke—that's all they ever talk about, the pain to expect, oh...they never say how *good* it feels! It feels so good, Rorke—you make me feel so good—"

"I love you, Elishta-bet," I told her softly, her features entrancing.

"I love you," she yelped, almost shouted, the words bursting up from her unready lips along with a quavering moan. "Oh, Rorke! I've always loved you—Rorke, oh—"

I kissed her, her body tight in my arms and tighter still around me. I did my best to satisfy the new-awakened desires, though I knew they would not be lain to rest anytime soon. Lacking all education in these matters,

Elishta relied on me utterly and begged me to use her as I thought would teach her best. Sooner than I expected, she quaked with bolts of pleasure; then again, and once more before I reached the peak of my own pleasure. With the furrowed brow of a woman near to tears and a mouth that strained not to scream too loudly, Elishta slid her legs around my hips and arched her pelvis up toward mine.

"Rorke," she gasped, "oh, Rorke—please, yes, just like that—"

"It's not too hard?"

"No, no, I want it—I want you, oh, Rorke! I think I like it deep—yes, please, go on, don't stop—"

"I'll have to soon, you're driving me to dire straits…"

"Oh! Then—oh, then give my body all yours promises! Your seed, Rorke—oh, Rorke, if you would find me worthy of your child, bury your seed deep inside me and let me nurture it to life!"

I pulsed with pleasure at her request, catching her beautiful face in my hands. "Are you sure, Elishta-bet?"

"Yes, Rorke! Yes, my heroic friend, please. I love you, oh! I want your baby. Even if—"

"I want you to be my wife," I blurted, drawing a delighted cry and a look of near astonishment from her. "Be counted among my brides, Elishta-bet, and come with me wherever I go."

"Oh! Yes!" The tears which had for some time glossed her delighted eyes spilled over now. With a look of almost frantic ecstasy, Elishta drew me to her mouth to exchange a kiss. "Yes, Rorke—let me be that joy to you. Bring me joy as my husband! Rorke, oh, Rorke! My greatest friend—my only love—"

While Elishta melted into her final rising action for the morning, I kissed her one more time and caught the focus of those beautiful hazel eyes.

"Let our child be conceived in heaven," I murmured, folding her hands in mine in prayer. "Let us beget here a son as virtuous as his mother, as heroic as his father—a child who one day will be a man with great deeds known across the land."

Nodding, joyful, Elishta gasped, "Yes, Rorke, yes.'

Yet those tears of hers continued silently rolling; and I knew she felt the same weight, the same trepidation, that I did.

While she rested, I dressed from the selection of clothes left for me along with hers. There were all number of pieces fit to noblemen, a plethora of artfully dyed textiles in red and gold and purple that invited my interest. But, in the end, it was a simple white tunic I removed from the wardrobe.

"I think it would be best if you take the Lantern of Hamsunt with you," I said with a gesture before picking up Exigence and the Helm. "As to where we should meet…perhaps it would be best were I to send Brynhildr with that information. Find her in the garden, or wait for her there if she's not around."

"All right. Rorke—"

I had bent to kiss her brow and already turned away, but she stayed me with a hand upon my forearm.

"Please, please stay safe, Rorke," she begged me with another twinkling teardrop in her eye. "I don't want to lose you now that I finally have you."

"I feel just the same…please tell Valeria I'm eager to see her."

Without waiting for Elishta's response, I exited her chambers and made my way to the gardens.

It was strange to think that, after all my dealings with women, this was the first time I had ever consciously hoped to engender an heir. The breeding purpose to which the durrow put me had only been their desire, after all. Valeria now carried my child as a matter of consequence rather than intent, and Gundrygia stole one from my loins with her seductive magics. Only Elishta-bet had invited me into her body as a partner in creation—and for this reason above any other, my heart burned with delight at the thought of someday calling her my wife.

My will could not falter. I had to return to Urd with my brides to fulfill my private vows to them. However low my honor had fallen on Dunnun's island, these women offered me an opportunity to restore it.

If only all women were always so kindly disposed toward me!

In the gardens, Brynhildr idled nervously through rose of flowers, her hands folded behind her back. Her eyes bounced between the ground and the rear of the Hall at least twice before she saw me. Brightening, the fully armored Selectrix waved as if I might have missed her and waited for me to make it to her side. A few others, mostly Selected and their wives, strolled through the garden in other areas, but there were such wide swaths of space between pairs that we did not hesitate to speak openly. At once, she threw her arms around my neck to hug me, then released me just as fast.

"Hail, Burningsoul! How was your journey? Grane looks tired!"

"Your valiant steed deserves his rest. Well he's

served me this last night. 'Last night!'" I laughed, and the Selectrix grinned in that knowing way of hers before I went on, "I say that, but it feels like it's been so much longer."

"The Hall exists on another axis from the ones supporting time and space...but it went well?"

I nodded. "As well as could be supposed." I told her about the gold, the apprenticeship, Dunnun and the rest. She listened with deep interest, asking many questions that had ways of sidetracking us far from the heart of whatever point I was making at a given time. Yet that quality of hers was delightful. Her interest was genuine, and her enthusiasm so refreshing it was almost childlike in its honesty. Which son of mine would she marry, I wondered! He had better be fleet of mind as well as foot if he was to keep her happy.

Yet I could see even then that something was behind her mirth. By the time I finished my tale, she still smiled, and it still crinkled her eyes and dimpled her cheeks; but a little of the light had gone out of the entire affect. She spoke to me as the adult speaks to the innocent babe of carefree matters when the world weighs on their aged mind.

"How pleased I am for you, Rorke the Wotsung!" Jostling my shoulder, Brynhildr enthused, "Well would I have liked to behold that battle—or fight it myself."

She laughed at her own joke. As her laughter faded, she appeared intensely sad.

"What's the matter, Brynhildr? You're not quite the same cheerful Selectrix I remember from—yesterday."

"Oh, is that so? Perhaps I'm just tired. Thinking of you and Grane all night kept me awake too long."

That wasn't it, but I didn't want to press her. I nodded and settled for saying, "Then only give me a little advice and I will leave you to have your rest. How should I approach your father to tell him the deed is done?"

"Would I could rest! But I will help you speak to him today, exchanging words in his masterly court. Though you have faced more than one god alone, none of them compare to my father in his rage…and if he were to take you for a horsethief, he might misjudge the situation before his temper is soothed."

I had heard more reassuring things in my life, but I had no better petitioner than the Selectrix who ranked highest in Weltyr's paternal esteem. "Thank you for helping me, my friend," I told her.

She shook her head.

"It is not you I help. I but enact my father's will—no matter what it means for me."

I wished to ask her what she meant by that, but she did not hesitate to launch into motion.

"Come, Rorke. We will speak to him now."

There was much I wanted to ask or tell her. For instance, I still did not know how the Deepgold would lead to my liberation from death; and I had promised to send Brynhildr to speak to Valeria and Elishta-bet, but I had not had a chance to communicate the plan. Yet, as we entered the Valor Hall, opportunities to speak freely were limited. The corridors bustled with activity, with glad-hearted work and cherubic children rushing off to play games. There were so many people occupying my eye that it seemed all too soon we had whirled by the entirety of the Hall and come to a stop on the other side of Brynhildr's preferred entrance to the great hall.

One of her sisters watched the door while Hildolfr stood in the center of the room, arms folded and head occasionally nodding as he dispensed advice to some petitioner in semi-private. Left behind in her throne, Anroa wore a look that was, as ever, fatally unimpressed. Brynhildr took advantage of her sister's nearness to whisper in her ear, and only then did Anroa stir.

While Brynhildr's sister went off to catch their father's attention, a dizziness passed over me. I rubbed my brow, an unpleasant thought passing over and through me along with the vertigo.

If this did not work—

"Of course! No need to stand on ceremony, daughter; King Atli and I are finished here, at any rate. A glorious day to you, Monarch."

The bowing man thanked him, kissed his sacred hand, and went off, smiling. As I recovered from my surprise to discover the petitioner had been a king, (though what did such terrestrial titles mean here, I asked myself), Hildolfr strode over to embrace his favored child.

"I must act with formality, for I am not the one asking your audience. The Wotsung"—she gestured behind her and I stepped through the doorway, hanging by it with little more than a bow—"has requested your time."

Before her husband could speak up, Anroa said without looking at me, "Tell the Wotsung that if he has come to bargain over his death once again, he does so in error. We will not have the day tied up in malformed arguments."

"He bears news for the benefit of your divine husband," my Selectrix responded to her stepmother, either far more patient or far more accustomed to her ways than I was. "Perhaps, if you cannot condescend to entertain him, Her Holiness would prefer a stroll through the flowers? The morning is divine."

Returning Brynhildr's thin smile with an even thinner one, Anroa smoothed her dark gown over her knees and rejoined her husband's child, "We have already enjoyed our morning constitutional, girl, thank you for the fine suggestion…no, no. After yesterday, we think it best that whatever our husband hears, we hear. At least, when it comes to present company."

"The rest, though," Hildolfr said, raising a hand, "need not concern themselves. Wait without the chamber, my Selectrices! You will be called when we are through."

When Brynhildr's sisters filed out, one or two of them glancing at me with intrigue for whatever gossip I represented, I was led by my Selectrix deeper into the chamber. Brynhildr and I soon stood where I had the day before—which, now that I had spent time in the Valor Hall, began in mysterious ways to truly feel like the day before. Indeed, my time with Dunnun felt like some dream. But I had evidence the dream was more than a dream, and brushed my hand across the Helm while genuflecting before the throne into which my god sank.

"Now, then! What news could be brought to me that was not recorded by my ravens—not seen by that old eye of mine, lost in the world?"

As I spoke, it occurred to me that I had never been so nervous in all my life. My gums vibrated with a strange kind of heat that spread to my tongue, as if the energy of the words I was about to speak required special preparation. I lowered my gaze, studying the luxurious carpet leading up the short set of stairs.

"The Deepgold has been returned, Master," I found myself saying before I was prepared to, the words somehow circumventing my brain altogether and instead leaping from somewhere unknown. As the gods inhaled, I went on without pause; without looking. "Under cover of night, I traveled across the ocean to the island where the hermit god, Dunnun, fled with the gold that paid for your Hall. There I learned his crafts so well that, with that very Deepgold, I cast a key permitting me to find the remainder of the hoard; but the wicked god, Hamsunt, was on the island also, and alerted the smith to my designs. We did battle, Dunnun and I, and although he was vanquished, he walks again. The Deepgold, forfeit to me, was returned to the sea and once more gladdens the hearts of Roserpine's daughters. The only pieces not returned are those upon which my duties hinge, and this"—I drew the Helm from my belt and stood to hold it high, discovering as I did that Hildolfr had leaned forward—"a helm of Dunnun's artistry, retained as proof of the deed done."

"Your fears may be lain to rest," extolled Brynhildr, joyful as Hildolfr strode down the stairs to take the Helm from my hand and study its chains. "Let the sun forever shine high above the rule of the gods! When the Wotsung's quest is over, he has sworn to return the balance of the gold. The curse will be lifted. A new aeon has been secured."

"This is indeed a creation of my brother's hands... and Deepgold, beyond all doubt." Hildolfr ran his hands over the chain links, turning the Helm this way and that to appreciate it and its gleam from various angles.

"How is it," asked Anroa, her eyes glittering less like

the gold and more like a serpent's, "that you, a mortal, managed to overcome a god?"

The image of her golden fruit flashed through my mind before I settled on a darker figure, thinking it better to admit a lesser sin for now.

"The mighty Selectrix that brought me to this place offered me her horse. Grane's spirit is like that of no steed I've met! He was an invaluable ally in the battle with Dunnun, particularly when the god donned this Helm and changed his form to a far more hideous guise."

Smiling with pride, Hildolfr passed the Helm back to me and ignored the slowly growing fury of his wife. "A worthy challenge for a Wotsung—a noble feat for a hero near to my heart."

Still on the attack, Anroa interrogated on. "Yet why not relinquish all the gold at once? Your quest was ended, Wotsung, when the Selectrix plucked you from the clutches of death. What use have you for any trinkets of Deepgold at all?"

I lowered my head, then dared into Anroa's face.

"Is my accomplishment worth no reward? Is the security of your reign not enough to merit the resurrection of three mortals?"

"Four," corrected Anroa haughtily, then pausing with the look of someone listening to something very distant. "No—*five*!"

Balking, her mouth open and her eyes wide, the goddess said, "You have conceived a child in the Valor Hall, and still you have the temerity to expect resurrection!"

I said nothing. Hildolfr, who had smiled to hear of another Wotsung child, erased his expression when his eyes met with his wife's.

But Brynhildr remained defiant on my behalf. "Such accomplishments are not wholly impossible to Nature! Does the Deepgold not exist within its system? And did you, Father, not say yesterday that the Deepgold might grant the free man the power to liberate himself from death? What Burningsoul asks is not all that unreasonable, then, you surely must admit."

"*You* must refrain from telling the Queen of Heaven what she "must" do," Anroa snapped. "Particularly as you are culpable in what my husband regards with admiration, but what I call a crime."

"A crime!"

At Brynhildr's shock and Hildolfr's sharp look, Anroa bared her teeth.

"Yes, a crime. A mortal, deceiving and killing a god?"

"Only in the name of the god-king's will!"

"Is it true, husband?"

Her piercing gaze now upon Hildolfr, who stared back without flinching, Anroa leaned forward in her throne.

"Is it by your will that this deicide was accomplished?"

"I only expressed in private those wishes of my heart which I cannot myself commit. I did not invite the deed, nor command it."

"Then you must agree that the crime merits punishment."

I could not help my scoff. Hildolfr glanced at me only briefly before shaking his head.

"If Dunnun consented to the battle, no crime was committed."

"Yet the question remains." Anroa looked coldly upon me, her face a perfect but cruel mask. "Even with—

especially with—Dunnun consenting to the duel, how was a mortal capable of overcoming the Giant-Killer?"

I gritted my teeth, pressed again for the whole truth. Brynhildr spoke up on my behalf, saying with pride, "He is a Wotsung, of course! The greatest of warriors, only mortal in part!"

"I have fought alongside him," agreed Hildolfr, "and against him, and I can attest to his excellence in battle. It is no surprise to me that he could strike a blow that would fell a god."

"Oh, that I do not doubt." Regarding me, sly Anroa said, "Yet Dunnun is no shirk in matters of combat, as I have *myself* beheld. The Wotsung may be an equal fighter, but a single blow from the smith's hammer is sufficient to cripple the strongest of mortal bodies. Did he evade every blow? Withstand without effort all beastly claws and monstrous teeth? How? How has this mortal proven equal to a god in battle, I must ask once again?"

The breath went raggedly from me.

Brynhildr, her eyes shining, opened her mouth to form the first syllable, "He—"

I extended an arm before her, stopping her on the breathy sound. My hand rested upon her shoulder.

"Thank you, my holy friend! You have helped me in so many ways—more ways than I dare suppose I could even know. Pray for me, and think of me often."

Brynhildr looked at me with shock, confusion, darkness: in that order. Her expression grew utterly withdrawn.

She stepped back from me, her hands folded behind her in the fashion of a soldier.

"I cannot maintain this deception," I said, "no

more than I would ask the Selectrix to indict herself by my defense. I took an apple from your sacred orchard, Madame, hoping to bargain with Dunnun; but when he caught me at my true intent, I ate of the fruit to escape certain death."

Brynhildr stared at her feet, her shoulders and expression taut with pain. I could see her reflected in the shining metals that adorned my master's throne, his armor, the otherwise dark patch over his missing eye. With great force I shifted my focus to Hildolfr, who absorbed this information far more stoically than did his wife.

Anroa had slowly risen from her throne as I spoke, her lips parted with astonishment.

"A mortal has disgraced my sacred orchard?"

So far as I was concerned, Valeria had nothing to do with it. She had presented the idea, but I had gone along with it; and, of course, it was an idea she never would have had were it not for me. A place she never would have been—an eternity she never would have truly known—without me.

In my heart, everything we had done was justified. I would not be dissuaded of the fact.

"It was not an act in which I took pleasure," I assured her. "Neither the theft nor the eating of the apple bring me anything but shame when I think on them; yet, how else could the gold be liberated from Dunnun? What other champion do you have, Your Holiness, who is foolhardy enough to buck the laws of the gods in the name of doing their will?"

A small smile, I swore, dashed across Hildolfr's lips, but it quickly hardened as his wife stormed down to his side.

"You heard him," she hissed, one hand upon his shoulder and the other gesturing toward me. "As plainly as he spoke to me, so he just spoke to you as well. Move your tongue! Is it not a crime, what has happened? The criminal himself calls it such!"

His eye closing, Hildolfr said as though with great effort, "Anroa's apples are not for the pleasure of mortals, Wotsung."

"You will have to punish him," insisted the goddess. "At the very least, such a crime must be met with a period of exile from this holy place."

"Yet it would seem that, this very night, he endured a self-made purgatory, and would be resistant to such measures. Besides—if I must punish Rorke, I will also be forced to punish the Selectrix that aided him in his undertaking."

"No!"

Anroa looked sharply at my protest; Hildolfr, upon opening his eye, had never looked away from me. Brynhildr remained, still and silent, nobly awaiting the judgment I fought for us both.

"These deeds I committed were all my own design. The Selectrix acted in the best interest of her father. Her only crime was showing me the preferred carrots of her steed."

"And disgracing this sacred place with an arrogant fool. Speak, Selectrix!" Anroa turned her petulant look upon Brynhildr, who stared back in a kind of stern tranquility. "Did or did not your father command you to favor the Wotsung as a crafty informant, meaning to deliberately defy my will that neither of you show undue favor to this whelp?"

"I exist to serve my father's will," the Selectrix replied solemnly, addressing her stepmother but studying her father. "And I was raised into the duty of fighting for him against his enemies. In that moment that you counseled him to work against his will, Father became his own enemy. I have acted in accordance with that judgment."

"Yet must I not avenge treason against the gods," asked Hildolfr, his attention having been drawn from me by the voice of his daughter. "Is Anroa not immaculate in speech in matters such as these? I must punish conscious defiance of the law."

"So this is all that will come of my sacrifice?"

Perhaps the question had a hint of wounded self-righteousness about it, but, as the gravity of this conversation settled upon me, I grew more appalled by the second. The gods turned their gazes back to me.

Now ignoring Anroa's hateful looks altogether, I pleaded directly with my only master.

"Is my achievement in the name of your highest will to be met with only punishment? Will the liberty I have bought you with the Deepgold—*my* Deepgold"—I was surprised to hear myself adding—"—mean nothing to the gods?"

Anroa sneered in my periphery. "You still expect reward, even having revealed your unholy theft!"

"For holy purposes! But—no."

Rubbing my hand across my face in exasperation, trying to remain calm and composed before my god and his wife, I stared into my palm as though in search of some truth.

"I won't continue on with excuses, with bargaining.

Not on my own behalf. But I beg—if my deed requires punishment, let that reward that is due to me instead go to the women and innocent children who have accompanied me to this place."

Hildolfr's eye shut again, sadly.

"Women and children die every day, Rorke," he told me when he looked upon me again. "Many valiant mothers have been Selected from the childbed. Valeria and Elishta-bet are no more unique than you are for their presence here."

"But it isn't just," I protested. "We were murdered by a god, a bitter god with reason enough to despise me. Can the master of all divine arts not restore what an inferior god destroyed?"

"Do not think you may put me to the test as you did Hamsunt," said Hildolfr simply, earning a spark of ire as I had never felt against Weltyr or even his manifestation.

"I *knew* you were with me, your sacred eye following me on that island." The master said nothing while his aggrieved slave went on. "Never would I demand a test of you, nor special privilege—but it was you yourself that set me upon the quest that calls me back to Urd! By your own lips, I was commanded to protect the women with my children—and Gundrygia, wild and mad, is somewhere in the world with a Wotsung in her womb. Am I to leave it wholly under her influence? Am I to scorn Valeria's missing ring and leave my task undone, the gods' rule plunged into darkness? Who will do these things, if not I?

"When I negotiate for resurrection," I said, bringing my echoing volume down with my next words, "I do not do so for pleasure. The pleasure would be in staying here. Never thinking again of death, never suffering, aging, hating, worrying. I ask for resurrection so as to endure yet more burdens on the behalf of my god—my *only* god, whose honor commands him he must respect his wife even when she acts out of wounded pride."

"How dare he speak to me that way." Anroa's words were a hiss as she grabbed her husband's arm. To everyone's surprise, Hildolfr tore from her grip and left her standing there with her hands empty.

"The Wotsung must be punished," he declared, his eye as pained as the teeth that seemed bared between his words. "Along with the Selectrix who helped him. That is my final judgment. There will be no further negotiation."

All meaning collapsed away in an instant. Brynhildr hid her face when I looked back at her in shock.

Hildolfr turned away, intent on his throne.

No recourse remained. There was no point in half-measures. If was to be dead forever, I was willing to do anything.

But, because I lived, what happened next fills me with shame I will never escape.

It is, in this life, my only and greatest regret. It is the memory that rises up in me when, sweating alone in a hot bed at night and anxious to avoid disturbing the woman beside me, I rise in the dark and wander the rooms of my citadel all alone. I touch the objects in my life, pat my sleeping children on the head, sit by the window and watch the stars while I remind myself that none of this would exist if I did not do what I did in that moment.

But with all those wonderful gifts have come a lifetime of regret, and horror, and sorrow that makes me wish I could hide my face from myself as I have from the world.

Hildolfr's words flowed through me from the past.

Never challenge me again.

Such a hero would be a man so free that one might think us at profound odds!

Where is there a man who, liberated, makes himself closest to me by defiance?

There, in the Valor Hall, I took a step back from the gods.

And I drew Exigence.

22

THE FREE MAN

ANROA LEAPT BACK, an arm swinging high before herself even as Hildolfr stepped between us. Brynhildr, also, leapt to attention, crying out while her father snatched up the sacred spear that glowed with power.

"Run, Brynhildr! Get the women from the gardens and flee this place—hurry!"

Unhesitating, I raised Exigence and launched myself at Hildolfr. He raised the staff of his spear and glanced the blade away, meeting my next strike, and the next. The Selectrix looked between us, wide-eyed, then at the cohort of her sisters rushing in to the sound of the fight. While one whisked Anroa back, the others tried to interfere with my battle: I diverted my god's spear-tip, side-stepping it and raising Exigence from the glance to meet a Selectrix's halberd. Muscles braced, I pushed her back in time to see a sword swinging down on me from the left.

It did not fall.

Before Hildolfr's next set of blows required response, I caught a glimpse of Brynhildr between me and her sister. her hands had caught the flats of the fast-moving blade. With a hard kick in the stomach that sent her sister flying away like a doll, my Selectrix claimed her weapon and tossed it in the air above her head. By the time she had caught its grip, she had dodged the blows of two more sisters and was ready to face off with the third.

"Let our father deal with the Wotsung," called their captain as, splitting off from the group, Brynhildr darted from the great hall and into the adjoining corridor. "Catch the traitor!"

Crying out that she would have to come to her senses and accept her punishment, the guards chased Brynhildr amid the crashing of weapon on weapon.

This was by no means my first occasion fighting Hildolfr, but it was the first time since learning his identity. Every blow with which I beset him filled me with remorse. My creator, my master, my friend—like a fool I now turned myself against him, but I could see no other way.

If I was to be punished, let me be punished. If my existence was to be annihilated after all, then so be it. So long as the Selectrix might make good her escape from the Valor Hall and take the women with her, the gods could still be saved. Urd, still preserved.

I met the spear with a blow whose force appeared to surprise my god.

"I see you have the hunger for fighting immortals," he supposed of me, turning his spear over and using it instead as a staff by which to catch my sword and quickly strike me. "I suggest you sate it with the victory you already have."

"This battle is one that gives me no joy." I wheezed as I took a crack in the ribs that might have been enough to break something under normal circumstances. The fruit still affected me, I knew then. I fought on, a small light of hope discovered in the darkness. "I would rather fall upon my knees in worship of you and all you have created—but if worship of you requires defiance of you, then I would fain be considered the holiest traitor."

Another strike, this at my knee, was stopped by my sword. Hildolfr's spear rang in his hand. Once more he turned it around, now to stab straight at me. I dodged its blows more cleanly than I would have known it possible.

"Disobedience to the laws of the gods can never be considered holy, Rorke."

"Then I practice sacrilege out of love for you!"

I struck out at him, forcing him back toward the throne from which our fight had taken us and behind which Anroa crouched with her guard. Hildolfr regarded me with more surprise by the strike. Though the god met my blows, he did not always seem fully prepared from them. Instead, he appeared to act only at the belated prompting of self-preservation.

"Already have I been turned away from the bosom of that church that raised and loved me. Now, I find that the accomplishment of your will requires I incriminate myself—tarnish my image beyond all recognition. So be it."

Hildolfr's spear met an overhead blow from Exigence with a noise like a whine. I barely heard it even as Hildolfr turned his eyes, wide with shock, in pursuit of its source.

"If my soul must be annihilated in service to you—if I must be turned away from this sacred Hall forever, never to return—then I will accept whatever fate I must in the name of preserving you."

Once again, I raised Exigence, that very blade that Weltyr granted me as a sign of his favor.

Once again, the blade hammered down into the sacred spear of my god.

This time, the sacred weapon gave way.

A vicious snap filled the air. A distant groan followed it.

Anroa and the Selectrix cried out. Hildolfr sucked in a sharp breath.

The famous spear fell to the floor, splintered in pieces.

Stunned, I lowered my sword. Anroa's scream rose to a wail. She collapsed on the spot, her hands hiding her tears as the Valor Hall rattled around us.

That very relic carved from the Tree of Life—that very spear that preserved the laws of Nature over which Weltyr ruled—was broken. Fully broken, like a toy.

I looked helplessly up at Hildolfr, not understanding, yet somehow knowing in an instant the full gravity of what I had done.

As his wife was wracked with piteous sobs, Hildolfr looked me in the eyes.

Just as I realized he was smiling at me, his lips formed a single, silent word.

"Hurry."

In my daze, I did not understand what he meant. Hurry? Hurry and do what?

The Valor Hall rattled once again. A terrible groaning filled the chamber and I thought for a few flashing seconds it was Anroa; then, realizing the direction of the noise, I looked behind me and was shocked.

The doors of the Valor Hall groaned steadily open, its façade spreading out like the petals of a flower.

Heart rising in my throat, my master's last word to me revolving in my head the entire time, I did not look back. I did not pause.

I dashed away from Weltyr's avatar with my sword still in my hand.

All thought in any complete sense of the word flew out of me: I knew only one thing, and that was that the doors of the Valor Hall had been opened by the breaking of the laws of Nature, and I did not know how long they would remain accessible to me.

As fast as I could, I ran. Selectrices outside the palace poured in to apprehend me. Others rushed in behind me. No man has ever been as desperate as I was: sliding my sword away, I sprinted the length of the hall while ducking arrows and dodging blades.

There it was, there it was right there.

And, from high above the fortress I escaped, over the clamor of other, far more outraged shouts and the wild snorts of horses, there rang a sound happier than even the opening of the Hall:

"Hojotoho! Hojotoho! Heiaha! Heiaha!"

Ecstasy imbued my limbs with a vigor befitting my heritage. I burst through the open portcullis and sprinted down the wide mouth of the landing platform, craning my neck skyward for only a few seconds.

Just long enough to see all three of them on Grane's powerful back. Their cries of my name rose in unison, arcing with them around the infinite building and its miasma of pulsing colors.

The Selectrices behind me carried on their pursuit.

Farther still, Weltyr watched me with a smile that even his wife, visibly remonstrating him, could not erase.

I resumed my sprint, dashing on and on until there were no more stones on which to run.

My stomach lurched; my body dropped.

Two pairs of hands caught hold of me, dragging me onto the back of the enormous horse that went flying past.

"Rorke!"

Valeria leaned around Elishta-bet to touch my face with a gasp of delight. For her part, Elishta bore this so well I had the feeling she might embrace her fellow brides better than I'd expected. She simply twisted at the waist to hug me, begging to know, "Are you all right?"

I did not know how to answer the question without frightening her, so I didn't. Instead, I looked past her, at Brynhildr. The Selectrix drove her horse into a frenzy, leaning forward with her head low along Grane's neck as she spurred him into the fluctuating sea of colors.

"Can Grane bear so much weight at once?"

"And more. Fly, friend! Give haste new meaning, fly on!"

Foaming at the mouth, the steed did as it was told,

though I could tell even it strained with exhaustion. Still—tired though Grane was, when I looked behind us to check our pursuers, I was shocked to find them and the Valor Hall already so far behind that I could detect no individual features, see no horses—find no one standing in the mouth of the Valor Hall, watching me go.

My heart grew immensely heavy.

"It's so small," I said, producing a noise like a laugh and a sob all at once.

"Oh, Rorke," said Elishta softly. Still twisted, she forgot her own comfort and folded her arms around my shoulders.

Weeping, I lowered my head to her bosom and pressed my cheek there. Valeria's hand sliding back into mine without her turning somehow only deepened my grief, my questions, my endless self-flagellation.

"What happened, Rorke?"

As I had been unable to answer Elishta's question, neither could I answer Valeria's. Instead, forcing myself to endure my sorrow without gross overexpression before a noble warrior like Brynhildr, I gasped my emotion into submission and sat up.

"Brynhildr—will we ever be able to return?"

Her head turned back just so, though I could not divine any hint of expression on her cheek from the helmet she wore.

As Grane plunged into the storm of colors bridging the Valor Hall to other dimensions, Brynhildr admitted with frightening solemnity, "I don't know."

Though I knew she could not see it, I nodded.

When I covered my face with my hand to brace my mind while I thought, the women left me alone.

Really, I could not think. My consciousness sank into such black pits of despair that I thought only of a worry that had never been a part of my life before, ever. Before, in even my most frail moments of human doubt, I never flagged in my belief that someday my life would be perpetuated without end in the Valor Hall. It would be true as long as I lived righteously and served Weltyr, and I had never doubted that.

Now, in serving Weltyr, I had scorned the Valor Hall. Not just that, but I had sinned against the gods, *challenged* the gods, and escaped punishment. I had broken the very laws of Nature always present in Weltyr's hands. Indeed, the Deepgold *had* liberated me from Death, I realized— but at what cost?

I cursed the sword at my hip, but I loathed the ring, missing somewhere in the blue and green world that spun out of the deepest, darkest void left before us when at last the vibrant tunnel spat us out. Valeria cried out in almost girlish delight while Elishta gasped in wonder; I simply blinked away more tears, unspeaking, unable to imagine myself living another day of my life without being humbled by fear and uncertainty.

I had meant what I said. The true punishment was leaving the Valor Hall—my true exile.

Brynhildr understood that well.

"I am not sure where to go," she said abruptly, the one to break the silence into which we fell as the horse, slowing its pace, approached Urd and caught its breath. "In rejecting my father's judgement, I have erred all the more. He will pursue me."

"And me?"

She shook her head at my question. "If you are not

in the Valor Hall now, it is no sin for you to walk on Urd. You won your freedom by making good your escape. But I—I have sworn oaths to serve him, to never go against him. The minute I helped you, I broke that. Never more will I be his favored daughter—"

Her voice broke. Her head lowered. I felt her pain as deeply as my own but knew that comforting her would only insult her, so I waited until she raised her head and continued.

"I do not believe he will seek you out," she summarized, "and do not think he will punish you if your paths cross."

I felt like telling her of the broken spear to see if she still felt that way, but refrained at the fleeting memory of Weltyr's prideful smile.

"If that's the case," I told her, "then journey with us." Her head turned toward me, her shoulders twisting and then correcting when she decided there were too many people to see past. "We still have some ways to go, and a warrior of your power would be well appreciated."

"If you would have my company, I would go with you…but, if my father comes to meet me, Burningsoul, you must swear not to stand between us."

"I won't."

"Your instinct will be to try, because you are a noble man who values women. But you must resist your instincts. Permit me to take the burden of my father's wrath, and I am certain any offenses of yours will be by him forgotten."

I did not argue, not wanting to relive the events rapidly cycling through my mind. Instead, drained, I rested my mouth against the back of Elishta's neck. She jumped a little, sighed, then relaxed and let me lay my cheek upon the back of her shoulder.

Slowly, the horse descended to the world.

For a few moments, sorrow left me in exchange for wonder. I recognized the continent nearest us as we descended and felt as happy as a schoolboy who was about to ace a test. Clouds drifting over the benign sea of Urd took us into their embrace and I let myself thrill at the memory of battling Dunnun; then we passed down and through them, and amid the crashing waves far beneath us I looked for the Deep-Children.

What a strange and wonderful journey we had endured! It was not all sorrow, no. It was just that the sorrows were far-reaching, expanding through all time, while the joys would be part of a memory.

Yet one memory was still incomplete.

A glow on the distant waters caught my eye and inspired a glance down at the lantern Valeria gripped. It was off. I looked again, straining, then recognized with a start the source of the far-off glow.

In the distance, the *Rhinemaid* was wreathed in flames.

23

UNFINISHED BUSINESS

IT IS AMAZING how fast grief and exhaustion both fled when I clapped eyes upon the ship. All three of us recognized it at once, crying aloud at the sight of the familiar blaze. Brynhildr leaned up and peered ahead.

"Aye, those are Hamsunt's tendrils if ever I've seen them at the feast. What's the plan, cousin?"

"I rarely have one," I confessed, eliciting an annoyed glance of Valeria's that made me smile, and laugh, and just barely refrain from kissing her. The horse soared in a wide arc over the water, always drawing closer to the ship that struggled to maintain altitude. I kept my eye fixed upon it, searching for our bodies in the waves.

"Let me handle Hamsunt, whatever the case," I told them all. "As for you three, try and help the Captain, if you can. She's below deck, immolated by the god's flames."

"The only way to put them out will be by the loss of Hamsunt's influence," Brynhildr informed me grimly.

"All the more reason for me to make short work of him. Here we are, Grane! Almost time for you to finally have more than a moment's rest...although, if any of the pirate wenches try something foolish, I'm sure you know what to do."

The horse snorted in response.

Valeria laughed.

"You speak to this animal as if you've known it for years."

"I'll have to tell you all about my strange night when we get a chance," I said, leaning up from the horse's back as we at last were within landing range. The horse had slowed, and the ship was close, and I extended my hand to Valeria. "For now—may I have that lantern?"

She set it in my hand, and I leaned past Elishta to kiss Valeria's cheek. "Thank you," I said, adding one to Elishta's cheek, "Be careful."

Then, the instant Grane's hooves crashed down upon the *Rhinemaid's* deck, I leapt from his back and rushed toward the captain's quarters.

"What are we going to do," cried Indra, real terror highlighting her shriek.

The familiarity of the voice was so relieving that I did not register the terror in it until I saw she and Odile were pressed to the edge of the ship, peering to the waters beneath. Odile looked wild-eyed, truly as I had never seen her, and began stripping off her light armor.

"We have to save her, obviously. Oh, Roserpine's eight eyes—"

"I think she had more than that, actually," I called to them from the center of the deck, gaining a pair of fast-whipping heads and some deeply shocked looks.

"Rorke?"

"Valeria is back there," I said, pointing toward the horse. "Hurry! Watch over her, one of you. The other, help the captain!"

I did not tarry to enjoy their incredulous expressions, though when I summon them up again in my mind they bring me endless delight. Lantern in-hand, I simply hurried on to where more female cries alerted me. The captain's quarters pulsed with noises, like jets from a great fountain blasting against stone and accompanied by short incantations—or broken up by occasional cries of pain.

Branwen, fighting Hamsunt alone! It was that noble bravery of heart that made me love her so. I rushed to the open doorway with its splintered remains of the sofa and door. Sure enough, Branwen had been backed treacherously near to that same widening pit that had been my demise.

I called out to her, but the steadily encroaching man of fire responded first.

Hamsunt whipped toward me with a great flare of not just his form, but the tongues of all the fires around.

<Impossible!>

"Nothing is impossible to the free man," I told him, raising high his perpetual prison.

"Rorke!"

"Cover your eyes, Branwen."

As she threw her forearm over her face, I twisted

the mechanism of the lantern to let its light blaze forth. Within the confines of his glass prison, the future Hamsunt I had brought back from Eternity burned as hatefully bright as he could.

<How can this be!>

Crying out with a horror more intense than any wild monster had shown in the sacred light, Hamsunt stumbled back. Another, more wretched scream rose from him as I raised it high, stepping into the flames that meant nothing in those last precious moments of the fruit's protection.

"You were right to call me a slave, Hamsunt, for I have been my whole life. But I will always free myself. You will forever be the instrument of your own incarceration."

Howling protests, the god erupted in a greater burst of flames. Branwen cried out, but bore it with the remainder of a magickal shield that absorbed the blow and at last spent itself in a vivid green glow.

Anything humanoid of Hamsunt's body having disappeared into this great explosion of flames, he arced up toward the ceiling of the captain's quarters and tried to get at the doorway behind me. I raised the lantern once again: away he flew, a demon more than a god, down through the great hole his fires had made in the structure. I pursued, standing at the edge of the floorboards to watch the flames skip across the thrashing waters like a stone: leaping, arcing, springing into the darkness while Hamsunt's eerie screams echoed through the night.

Breathless, dizzy, I stood there and wondered if I might collapse right down again. Only Branwen's hand on my arm brought me back to reality, drawing my attention to her and her happy cries of my name.

"How did you manage to survive that fall? Where are the others?"

I said nothing. I simply hugged her, one hand upon the back of her golden head, my chest heaving with a great sigh of relief.

"I am so happy to see you, Branwen—so happy, so grateful. I love you!"

"I—love you," she returned, obviously baffled by my affection and even more confused when I darted away. "H—hey! What's up, where are you going?"

"Come on, hurry! If we can save the captain, we can save the ship."

Both were in dire need of help, to say the very least. When my friend and I had run along the burning bridge, we discovered the Selectrix was finished clearing out the ruins of structural collapse enough to allow rescuers below deck. Elishta cried out, waving us rapidly over.

"We're almost through! She's down here, right?"

"That's right—can you see her, Brynhildr?"

"She's on the other side of this debris," the Selectrix answered from the bottom of the stairs with a cough, turning her face away from billows of smoke. "But she doesn't look well."

"Here, let me—"

The Selectrix stood aside and let me hurry down to ram against the flaming boards. At first contact, more of the ceiling treacherously groaned. Ignoring the dangerous sound, I shoved past a pile of burning detritus and into the heart of the fire.

The flames stung fiercely and the heat was next to unbearable, but with the fruit it was only as unpleasant as the times Dunnun's forge had licked the eyebrows from my face. I endured it for the sake of drawing the captain's apparently lifeless form into my arms, beating out the flames emanating from within her as best I could.

Water's hiss deadened the fires behind me and drew my attention: Elishta supported me, her magic flowing from her fingers in the form of liquid bolts.

The burning captain in my arms, I clambered to my feet and carried her back to the base of the stairs. The Selectrix had removed her cloak and used it to suffocate the flames that still raged in the woman's clothes. Without Hamsunt there to maintain the enchantment, the undead captain soon only smoldered between us.

Just so, her mouth moved.

I exhaled a breath I hadn't meant to hold.

"Support her for me," I asked the Selectrix, shifting the captain into her embrace and yielding something like a hoarse cry from the hurt woman.

Now was the true test of far more than one crucial detail. I studied the wounds on the dead woman and found that, though they were severe, they were in the purview of the healing prayers I knew.

But would they be enough to also heal the ship?

Better still—would they be answered?

I could not question. It was not for me to ask such things, nor to care. I spoke truthfully to Hamsunt. I liberated myself.

And, having liberated myself, my faith in Weltyr—my understanding and love of him—was deeper than it had ever been before.

As I had for her comrade aboard the *Battle Swan*, I laid hands upon the captain, and I prayed.

After the expected delay of a handful of seconds

that nonetheless seemed to me an eternity, the blue-white light linked to the phenomenon glowed between our bodies. The healing began.

I laughed with delight, exchanging a look of relief with smiling Brynhildr. And smile, she did—though a brief tumult played out across her lips when she thought my gaze had fully returned to the captain.

"What's going on…"

The captain peered down at herself with a look of groggy confusion, fighting through the effects of oxygen deprivation—if such things mattered to an undead woman. Her mottled flesh gradually recovered its superficial beauty, though some of her worse burns looked like they would only be so healed. Would they recover on their own, I wondered?

"Just hold still," I urged her. "Just a moment more…"

"It's working, Rorke!"

Elishta-bet called out to me from behind us, directing my attention in a glimpse that showed me the fire receded steadily down the hallway. Just as it had upon Dunnun's island, it appeared to burn in reverse: flame by flame, the destructive teeth of nature shrank away from us, from the ship, from the air, and then were nothing.

The glow of my hands faded, and the captain slumped against the Selectrix with a groan.

"Would you be willing to bring us north of Rhineland," I asked her, earning a distant laugh from Valeria as she listened abovedeck.

Her eyelids contorting open, then squinting through the lingering pain as she found her ship no longer actively aflame, the captain coughed and shrugged off the Selectrix's support.

"Maybe we can work somethin' out after all," she said, one hand upon the wall as she limped her way up the stairs. "But swear ta me I'll never clap me sorry eyes on yehs again."

24

ON TO RHINELAND

WITH THE FIRES out, the stunned crew gathered on the upper deck to piece together what happened, what needed doing, and what would happen next. Though we were nearby I did not listen to any of it, instead taking that time to introduce Brynhildr to the three companions who had not been acquainted. By the time we had finished giving the barest footnotes, (not that we had died and undergone so much, but that the Selectrix had saved us), one of the wenches in the *Rhinemaid's* crew asked, "What about them?"

We turned to find the entire crew looking at us— and, of course, at the tired horse that had settled down for a well-deserved rest not far from where we softly spoke.

Annoyed, the captain leaned back against the rail where she stood. She sighed, fixed her hat, sighed again, and shut her eyes to speak.

"Much as I hate ta say't, Burnin'soul here saved us all tonight. Even if he was only tryinter save himself, we'd oughter do the decent thing and drop him off in Rhineland…only a short diversion, at any rate."

I beamed as a few of the wenches rolled their remaining eyes or shook their cracked skulls.

"I think it's right," said Dinah, who nodded at me in approval while the captain scoffed.

"Ain't nobody asked you what's right, or would care ta know what you think's so. Now come on, ladies! There's a lotta repair for us ta do, and we've lost time."

"But there's plenty more." Dinah sniffed at the air, her head lifting like a dog's. "Smell that? A storm's on the way."

While a few of the pirates made excited noises, I asked, "Isn't that bad for flying?"

"Not for us! A fine enough storm system and we can fly all day, just as long as we keep up with it. Worst that happens is it fades away and we go below deck awhiles… bully for you, you'll get to where you're headed all the faster."

In truth, I was in no hurry. After all I had been through, all the energy spent by my body and my emotions, I wanted nothing more than as long a period of unbroken rest as I could acquire. Oblivious to the sounds of sawed wood and hammered nails ringing out all around the dark of the ship, I made my way along the deck in search of a place to sleep—

And found Grimalkin, collapsed beneath a fallen door.

"Friend!"

I'm embarrassed to say that I had forgotten about him, as focused as I had been on my closest companions and as altered as I was by my time on Dunnun's island. I rushed to his side, pushing the heavy door away with a grunt that told me the apple was nearly or entirely spent. The equivalent of twenty-four hours of immortality had taught me much, but by far its most valuable lesson was how important it was to defend life in oneself and others. I shook him awake, wondering if I would be able to call upon Weltyr's good will so soon after the last demonstration.

Luckily, Grimalkin stirred without divine intercession.

"Ugh, hell...what a headache..."

"I'm glad to see you alive! What happened, friend?"

"I was fighting off oneathem pirate lasses and next thing I know you're wakin' me up...you tell me."

"Well, I'm glad to see you in one piece. They've agreed to take us to Rhineland—you can get real medical attention there."

"How in Dunnun's beard did you manage that?"

"Oh, I have my ways with women." While he scoffed at my teasing and dragged himself to his feet, rubbing the back of his head with one hand, I handed him his axe and suggested, "The Selectrix may have some prayer with which to heal you more effectively than I."

"The what?"

"That woman there, in the armor." I gestured, earning a second look from Grimalkin.

"Say—that *is* a woman, isn't it! Where'd she come from? Well, well...awful tall, isn't she?"

"You're sounding better already," I joked, disappearing down toward the galley with confidence I wouldn't be found by the undead inhabitants aboard.

Deep, rich, black sleep. I rested my head upon a bag of flour, my arms folded over my chest, my body folding beneath the pressure of gravity. It was the kind of sleep that catches hold of the mind in a near-conscious way, where one can feel the sweetness of sleep as it drapes over the soul. Perfect, immense, blank sleep!

Like a woman's lips against the eyelids, the brow.

The ear.

"I knew you were not dead," Gundrygia whispered in my ear, her sweet breath curling out against my nerves in a pleased chuckle. "Come to me, Burningsoul."

I jolted awake, frightened to find the witch with me. No one was there.

Twelve hours had passed in the blink of an eye. There I lay, alone upon a sack of flour with the ache of a man who had not moved enough in his sleep. The room was full of the wild scent of Gundrygia; I knew she had been there, truly been there, driving me mad in her seduction of my senses. My heart sped.

It didn't matter. Not really. It just felt so good to awaken, so crisp and cool—so fine to know I was on Urd! Another day spent alive. Not even the painful memories of the shattered spear could dull the joy. I was here; I was among the living.

Rubbing my face, I emerged and relieved myself over the side of the ship only when I saw the deck immediately around to be empty. The sky was gray with consistent rain, but the clouds hinted at sunshine. I supposed the crew had left the ship to drift down its course for now.

Finished, I made my way along the bridge in pursuit of distant voices. My soul warmed with delight at what I found not far from the remains of the captain's quarters. There they were, all my friends.

Grane lifted his head on my approach. Brynhildr had removed her helmet and set down her polearm: she sat in a square with Indra, Odile and Elishta-bet, her face arranged in a serious expression as she attempted to absorb the rules of their preferred card game. To the side, Branwen and Grimalkin laughed and joshed about previous adventures.

Only Valeria stood alone, her white hair flowing in the wind as she gazed across the sea.

"Isn't it beautiful," I asked her, sliding my arm around her waist. "We must nearly be to land by now— but, I will never tire of flying over the ocean."

"Elishta told me a little of what you experienced going to Dunnun. You defeated him?"

I nodded, gesturing to the helm at my waist. "I took this from him as proof for Weltyr—now, of course, it is just another responsibility. Another relic to return to the Deep-Children when all of this is done."

Valeria studied me, her pale eyes as detailed under the filtered light of the clouds as they were in the Valor Hall. "Will you really return them all? Even Exigence?"

My mouth set itself firmly; I gazed out over the ocean, on the cusp of answering.

But I heard it—them—before I could.

"Deepgold! Deepgold! Deepgold!"

Valeria and I looked sharply at one another. Together, we leaned over the edge of the ship to search for the unseen singers. We looked in vain, but their song carried up to us all the same.

"For Burningsoul's innocence all beings weep! Relinquish our purity, give us its shine! How sweet and clear its light once was in our Deep."

"You'll have it back when it's time," I called down to them. "I swear—the Deepgold is destined to return to your hands."

Yet, all the same, on they sang.

"Deepgold! Pure gold! Shining and bright! Gay was the smile you showed in the night! Freshly you greeted the sun every morn. Now, upon land, the gods' glory you scorn!"

Valeria and I exchanged another look. I wished to reason with them further, my instinct being always, (somewhat foolishly), that sense can be talked into anything. I needed the pieces I had in order to retrieve the piece that was missing: and when we had the ring, everything would be returned to the Deep-Children. It made sense; it was right.

But there was no opportunity to explain. Elishta called, "Oh! Look!" and I thought for a moment she had seen the maidens swimming in the sea beneath us. I whipped around and hurried to the card-players, Valeria close behind me.

Instead, as we skidded to a stop before them, we saw what had so delighted her.

A rainbow, pure and brilliant against the backdrop of its clouds, arced across the sky through which we sailed.

Breathless, I slid my arm around Valeria's shoulders. We admired it side-by-side, captivated by its new meaning.

The *Rhinemaid* sailed into the storm, and the colors intensified until cloud gave way to light.

ABOUT THE AUTHOR

Regina Watts is the penname of M. F. Sullivan, founder and flagship author of Painted Blind Publishing. From her cozy home a few universes away from this one, Watts transmits stories to Sullivan that are then transcribed and published. Her available titles range from transgressive erotica to psychedelic fiction to horror to romance. Be sure to check out her website and sign up for her mailing list at hrhdegenetrix.com!

ABOUT THE PUBLISHER

Painted Blind Publishing and its erotic imprint, Painted Blue Publishing, are the brainchild of author and devoted editor to Regina Watts, M. F. Sullivan. Founded in 2015 while Sullivan resided in Tucson, PBP is a house dedicated to bringing readers the finest in consciousness-expanding fiction. Be sure to check out the wide variety of essays available for free at paintedblindpublishing.com to learn more about the company, Watts, and Sullivan.

OTHER PAPERBACK WORKS
FROM PAINTED BLIND PUBLISHING

REGINA WATTS

INDUSTRIAL DIVINITY (2020)

WILD GIRL RUNNING (2020)

DOTTIE FOR YOU SEASON 1 (2021)

SEDUCED BY SABINE (2021)

I WAS AN OP DEMON LORD (2021-2022)

BE MY BULLY (2021)

MAYHEM AT THE MUSEUM (2021)

IDOL (2022)

M. F. SULLIVAN

DELILAH, MY WOMAN (2015)

THE LIGHTNING STENOGRAPHY DEVICE (2017)

THE DISGRACED MARTYR TRILOGY (2019-2020)